RAMSEY CAMPBELL

SERIES PREFACE

Gothic Authors: Critical Revisions is dedicated to publishing innovative introductory guides to writers of the Gothic. The series explores how new critical approaches and perspectives can help us to recontextualize an author's work in a way that is both accessible and informative. The series publishes work that is of interest to students of all levels and teachers of the literary Gothic and cultural history.

SERIES EDITORS

Andrew Smith, University of Sheffield
Benjamin Fisher, University of Mississippi

EDITORIAL BOARD

Kent Ljungquist, Worcester Polytechnic Institute, Massachusetts
Richard Fusco, St Joseph's University, Philadelphia
David Punter, University of Bristol
Angela Wright, University of Sheffield
Jerrold E. Hogle, University of Arizona

GOTHIC AUTHORS: CRITICAL REVISIONS

Ramsey Campbell

Keith M. C. O'Sullivan

UNIVERSITY OF WALES PRESS
2023

© Keith M. C. O'Sullivan, 2023

All rights reserved. No part of this book may be reproduced in any material form (including photocopying or storing it in any medium by electronic means and whether or not transiently or incidentally to some other use of this publication) without the written permission of the copyright owner. Applications for the copyright owner's written permission to reproduce any part of this publication should be addressed to the University of Wales Press, University Registry, King Edward VII Avenue, Cardiff CF10 3NS.

www.uwp.co.uk

British Library CIP Data

A catalogue record for this book is available from the British Library

ISBN   978-1-78683-985-5
eISBN   978-1-78683-986-2

The right of Keith M. C. O'Sullivan to be identified as author of this work has been asserted in accordance with sections 77 and 79 of the Copyright, Designs and Patents Act 1988.

Typeset by Chris Bell, cbdesign
Printed by the University of Wales Press

*To Denise, who gave this Wanderer a home,
and in loving memory of my father,
Robert Michael O'Sullivan*

Contents

Acknowledgements	ix
Introduction: A Neglected 'Poet': Campbell and Gothic Tradition	1
1 Impractical Magic: Campbell's Agnostic Gothic	21
2 Of Bonds and Beings: Campbell's Gothic Sociopaths	57
3 Writing with Intensity: Campbell's Gothic Novellas	95
4 'Ghosts' from the Machine: Campbell's Gothic Techno-Fictions	131
Conclusion: 'Something to Believe in': Repositioning Campbell in the Gothic – and Beyond	171
Notes	187
Select Bibliography	225
Index	241

Acknowledgements

My thanks go to Ramsey Campbell himself, who in correspondence has been as amenable, approachable and friendly as all sources attest.

My deepest gratitude to the following members or former members of the English department at Manchester Metropolitan University: Xavier Aldana Reyes, Sorcha Ní Fhlainn, Linnie Blake, Dale Townshend, Paul Wake, David Wilkinson, Rachel Lichtenstein and Rachid M'Rabty. Above all to Xavi, for his diligent and thorough reading of the various drafts of chapters during my initial doctoral project, and for his tactful suggestions which helped it take shape. Matt Foley at Manchester Metropolitan and Kevin Corstorphine at the University of Hull, my examiners, are also owed a huge debt for their careful scrutiny and constructive input.

My thanks and appreciation go to Neil Curtis, Head of Museums and Special Collections, and to other colleagues at the University of Aberdeen, particularly Jane Pirie, Michelle Gait and Dan Wall, for their encouragement and support.

Staff at the University of Liverpool's Special Collections department, especially Robyn Orr, were most helpful in answering queries about the Ramsey Campbell archive.

Finally, thanks to my family: my mother Helena and my brother Stuart, but especially to my wife, Denise, for her support and boundless patience living with the variety of monsters in my head over the last four years.

Introduction: A Neglected 'Poet': Campbell and Gothic Tradition

☙❦

'I write horror', Ramsey Campbell declares boldly on his own website.[1] Although Campbell himself is clearly content with such a label, he and his work present a number of challenges and contradictions, both within and beyond the Gothic. From one perspective, Campbell is difficult to ignore. Born in Merseyside in 1946, he has been described as 'Britain's most respected living writer' of horror fiction by the *Oxford Companion to English Literature*.[2] Campbell was a precocious author: what was to become his first published tale, 'The Church in High Street', was accepted by August Derleth at Arkham House in 1962, and his first collection of short stories, originally entitled *The Inhabitant of the Lake and Less Welcome Tenants* (1964) by 'J. Ramsey Campbell', followed from the same publisher, when the author was just eighteen.[3] In an ensuing career now spanning over half a century, Campbell has also been extremely prolific. His output to date has included around three hundred short stories, the form for which he remains best known, and, beginning with *The Doll Who Ate His Mother* (1976), over forty original novels and novellas.[4] Campbell was recognised at an early stage by Stephen King, his almost exact contemporary, for both a 'lucid' prose style and a keenly delineated 'sense of place'.[5] In addition, Campbell has been an active professional commentator and a meticulous scholar in his own right. He served as a film and later

DVD critic for BBC Merseyside radio for nearly forty years, from 1969 until 2007, and has been an assiduous editor and anthologist. In the latter capacity, he has promoted the work of both established authors such as M. R. James, and emergent or forgotten ones like Thomas Ligotti or Adrian Ross, whose 1914 novel, *The Hole of the Pit*, was reprinted for the first time in Campbell's anthology *Uncanny Banquet* (1992).[6] A frequent and candid interviewee, Campbell has also produced a trove of other paratextual material in the form of stand-alone reflective essays, introductions and afterwords. Finally, Campbell has been the recipient of numerous honours, from the British Fantasy Society, the Horror Writers' Association and the International Horror Guild amongst others. Recognition seemed to reach a new zenith when, in 2015, Campbell was awarded both the World Fantasy Award for Lifetime Achievement and an Honorary Fellowship from Liverpool John Moores University for an outstanding contribution to literature.

However, despite this level of productivity and acclaim, one is struck by the contrasting reception accorded to Campbell compared with King, unquestionably the world's most famous contemporary writer of Gothic horror, or indeed with Clive Barker, Campbell's fellow Liverpudlian. The discrepancy is glaring in two respects. One is obviously commercial: Campbell's name recognition outside the field of horror fiction and sales are simply not on the same scale as King's, while Barker, since a spectacular debut with the *Books of Blood* collections (1984–5), has both relocated successfully to the United States and diversified widely into other forms of media and genre.[7] In stark contrast, despite being a full-time professional writer with more than thirty published books and over a dozen awards to his credit, Campbell could still be found working in a bookstore as late as 2003. In terms of prominence in popular culture, adaptations of Campbell's work to other media have not been undertaken on anything comparable to the industrial scale that King's have been, and there is no equivalent to the *Hellraiser* or *Candyman* franchises in his oeuvre.[8] 'John Horridge', the antagonist in Campbell's novel *The Face That Must Die* (first published in 1979, revised in 1983) has enjoyed nothing like the iconic status of Thomas Harris's 'Hannibal

Introduction: Campbell and Gothic Tradition

Lecter'. This is despite Campbell's novel having anticipated the enduring proliferation and popularity of serial killer-related literature since the late 1980s by almost a decade. His embrace of being a 'horror' writer notwithstanding, a certain protean nonconformity has contributed to this curious and paradoxical lack of recognition. Campbell's output, as well as being substantial, has varied widely in subject matter. As exemplied in the shift within one year from a social realist suspense thriller, *The One Safe Place* (1995), to a haunted-house narrative, *The House on Nazareth Hill* (1996), the writer has alternated between supernatural and non-supernatural content. He has also frequently revisited themes and even characters. While comparable range (and often great individual length), have not impeded King either commercially or, latterly, critically, Campbell's apparent heterogeneity and hence resistance to categorisation partly accounts for this British author so far experiencing the same combination of an artist's respect but minority, niche appeal that H. P. Lovecraft, Campbell's early and enduring influence, experienced during his lifetime.

The second disparity relates to academic scholarship. Both King and Barker have now received substantial attention from critics.[9] In contrast, any major project on Campbell can make claim to what has been comparatively neglected territory. His fictions have been simultaneously both lauded and, at least thus far, comparatively overlooked and marginalised. In brief, to date, the academy has not known quite where to place Campbell. This is not to deny that, as with Lovecraft before him, there has been much laudatory and critical attention given to the author, both in print and online, from amateur enthusiasts and critics in the form of book reviews and web blogs.[10] As well as having his own website, Campbell himself is a regular on the conference circuit and, with S. T. Joshi and Stefan Dziemianowicz, even produced a bibliography and reader's guide to his own collected works as early as 1995.[11] However, it remains the case that, after two brief introductory studies by Michael Ashley and Gary Crawford, his work had generated only one full-length monograph prior to the writing and subsequent editing of the present volume: Joshi's *Ramsey Campbell and Modern Horror Fiction* (2001), from Liverpool

University Press.[12] Joshi usefully groups together the varied content of Campbell's output to that date, with chapters devoted to the fictions most obviously inspired by Lovecraft; his oneiric narratives and treatments of urban horror, paranoia, the child and other Gothic motifs such as the haunted house. In this and his other studies, the critic places Campbell squarely in the tradition of the weird tale as an heir to figures such as Algernon Blackwood and Arthur Machen, and, alongside Shirley Jackson, as one of the 'two leading writers' of the weird since Lovecraft.[13] However, the breadth of Joshi's enterprise in *Ramsey Campbell and Modern Horror Fiction* is not equalled by depth. Inevitably, by virtue of its publication date, that particular book could not cover Campbell's sizeable twenty-first-century corpus. This aside, for the benefit of readers unfamiliar with Campbell's works, most space is also accorded to plot exposition for the various narratives. While this is understandable, there is limited room for critical analysis and an eschewal of any theoretical perspective – an omission which the present volume seeks to redress. Aside from Joshi's valuable studies, various chapters in books surveying the Gothic have addressed Campbell's fictions, but these essays have tended to focus on his earliest works, especially the short stories or individual novels.[14] As of 2020, there had also been two *festschriften* dedicated to the author.[15] Yet, for such a garlanded writer, there remains a dearth of attention from leading Gothic specialists. Campbell's fiction is notably absent, for example, from Catherine Spooner's survey, *Contemporary Gothic* (2006), or later study of the mode's comedic tendency, *Postmillennial Gothic: Comedy, Romance and the Rise of Happy Gothic* (2017). This is despite, as this book will also illustrate, a frequently darkly humorous tone within the writer's work. Elsewhere, David Punter, in the second edition of his seminal survey, *The Literature of Terror* (1996), gives Campbell painfully short shrift, according the author scarsely a paragraph. For Punter, who defines the Gothic by its 'general opposition to realist aesthetics', Campbell's work lacks intellectual depth in comparison with 'more complex assertions' about the nature of fiction made by other twentieth-century writers such as J. G. Ballard or John Hawkes.[16] He cites only a single Campbell text, the novel, *The Long Lost* (1993). This transposition of the Celtic sin-eating tradition to a contemporary setting is denigrated for what Punter deems its 'cardboard cutout' characterisations, lack of suspense, and 'remarkably incoherent' ending, in which the opaque enigmatism of the sin-eater is ascribed to confusion on the writer's part.[17] 'We do not know *exactly* what Gwen is', Punter asserts, regarding this mysterious figure, before adding, witheringly, 'but, to be honest, it's not clear that Campbell does either'.[18]

Ramsey Campbell aims to rehabilitate Campbell and redress the undeserved critical neglect and misrepresentation into which the author has fallen. For a perceptive group of fellow horror writers and critics within the Gothic, the author's careful craftmanship, economy of style and bleak imagery have long earned Campbell admiring sobriquets such as 'the poet of urban squalor and decay'.[19] This 'poetic' quality is exemplified by the description of a dystopian Liverpudlian street as 'a desert of waste ground' in 'Concussion' (1973), one of his early short stories. Of this bleak landscape, Campbell writes:

> that image was clearest of all: the humps of spewed earth, the ruts and folds of bulldozer treads like the gums of a toothless mouth, a dog urinating brightly in the sunlight against the noticeboard which claimed the wasteland; the abandonment, the disorientation.[20]

Campbell's speciality throughout his career, denoted by evocative prose style and acute visual sensibility, has been the elicitation of horror amidst the urban, the contemporary, the quotidian, even the drably mundane: council estates, modern offices, shopping centres, railway stations and underpasses. Arguably, few writers could combine, as here, metaphors of vomit ('spewed' earth), similes of ageing and mortality ('like the gums of a toothless mouth') and depictions of prosaic canine bodily function with such crispness and elegance. In contrast to his more commercially successful peers, Joshi places Campbell among contemporary horror's 'literati' alongside Ligotti and T. E. D. Klein, and, for Xavier Aldana Reyes, he is a member of a group of contemporary '*auteurs*', artists operating on their own terms, who are 'foundational to the growing cachet of horror as literary, resourceful and polymorphic'.[21] By his own acknowledgement, Campbell's work appeals to the connoisseur, a mature and 'fairly literate' audience.[22]

To this end, Campbell's Gothic writing is markedly 'literate' and subtle. Both the sources and the representations of horror in much of his work are interiorised as opposed to externalised and physical in nature. As Joshi notes, perceptively, 'the weird' is most frequently deployed by Campbell 'as a vehicle for the examination of a wide array of psychological states and the probing of an individual's relationship with others or with his or her own environment'.[23] In a 2012 interview, Campbell notes his own creative development away from imitating Lovecraft 'to a more contemporary style of psychological horror'.[24] His *magnum opus* shows a progressive concern with challenges to autopoiesis, the system by which the subject can independently maintain itself.[25] For these evocations of interior enervation, Campbell has drawn repeatedly upon his own traumatic childhood and adolescence. The writer's formative years were marked by parental estrangement, in which Campbell's father, a psychologically abusive police officer, continued to share the family's household as an unseen, but frequently heard, presence upstairs, and his mother descended into paranoid schizophrenia. Despite this undoubtedly harrowing experience and his endorsement of horror fiction's role as 'the branch of literature most often concerned with going too far', and of its being 'in the business of breaking taboos', Campbell has rejected what he sees as a 'more recent teeming of writers bent on outdoing each other in disgustingness'.[26] He strongly opposes what he views as 'pornographic' and 'misogynistic' exploitation fiction that 'drags horror into the gutter', and has been vociferously critical of popular authors like Shaun Hutson, whom he describes as 'cynical'.[27] Campbell is also clearly not aligned with the less 'cynical' but still explicit splatterpunk tendency, nor with the latter body horror, *avant* pulp, surgical horror or slaughterhouse movements. Aldana Reyes reads these various trends as 'a contemporary update of the Gothic genre for a generation that has largely left the spiritual world behind and prioritised the material reality of the body'.[28] Indeed, as with Andrew Minihin, the self-admitted writer of 'crap' adored by teenage gore fans in his novel *Ancient Images* (1989), Campbell's work occasionally parodies the generic shift towards what the writer views as a visceral excess obsessed with corporeality.[29] What is notable in such parody is the declamatory self-reflexivity on Campbell's part – that is, of a 'horror' writer who appears to reject the strong physiological affectivity associated with horror literature.

Rather, Campbell's works incline towards the covert, reflecting an acute awareness of, and haunting by, the past. These are traits more associated with classic Gothic predecessors. In one interview, the author alludes to what he deems 'knowing your tradition', so that a writer 'can see what there is to work with and then take a subject and do new things'.[30] Moreover, Campbell's works ally with an onus to disturb the reader's equilibrium with discretion, with 'showing just enough', rather than explication, and to generate fear, rather than revulsion.[31] In part, this reticence reflects clearly the influence of M. R. James, and a shared aversion to what the latter deemed a 'charnel house' tendency towards what is seen as an excess of explicitness in the representation of viscera in modern writing.[32] Campbell, though, is more philosophically engaged with respect to his chosen field than his learned but notoriously laconic predecessor. 'Despite its name', Campbell has argued, horror 'is most often concerned to produce awe and terror in its audience, but it is not unusual for a horror story to encompass a wide emotional range'.[33] The reference to 'awe and terror' recalls Edmund Burke's definition of the sublime, ruled and sourced by a principle of 'terror', to produce 'the strongest emotion which the mind is capable of feeling'.[34] As pointedly, it echoes Ann Radcliffe's defining preference given in her posthumously published essay 'On the Supernatural in Poetry' (1826), for the subliminal potentiality of 'terror' over 'horror', the former 'expand[ing] the soul and awaken[ing] the faculties to a higher degree of life'.[35] Campbell's qualifier regarding 'emotional' breadth also infers a sophistication in narrative practice. So, it follows logically that, for Campbell, 'horror' writing should be both informed by an awareness of Gothic precedent in its conception and marked by conscientious attention to nuance in its execution.

As the description of post-Blitz 'desolation' in 'Concussion' illustrates, Campbell's Gothic is also distinctly British. Initially imitative of Lovecraft, Campbell quickly followed the advice of Derleth, his first editor and early mentor, in replacing a highly derivative Lovecraftian New England setting with the postwar Merseyside and Severn Valley locations with which Campbell himself was more familiar: 'my personal Gothic landscape', as he has described it.[36] This imagined terrain was developed to maturity in *Demons by Daylight* (1973), Campbell's second collection of short stories, in which 'Concussion' appears. The 'personal Gothic landscape' is one which the writer has largely, although not exclusively, remained in ever since. Campbell's narratives have, for the most part, recognisable urban settings, often Liverpool or Manchester, or fictitious rural ones. These latter locations, isolated and beset by literal or metaphysical darkness, allow the author to evoke a rich tradition of folklore. As Stacey McDowell describes, folklore has been of significance 'in constructing a sense of national identity', and Campbell's works, up until at least his novel *The Wise Friend* (2020), repeatedly draw upon the same well of inspiration as BBC television screenplays of the 1970s such as John Bowen's *Robin Redbreast* (1970) and David Rudkin's *Penda's Fen* (1974).[37] However, although his landscapes are recognisably British, Campbell does not specifically identify himself as a writer devoted to and working exclusively within folk horror in the way, for example, that Andrew Michael Hurley, at least up to *Starve Acre* (2019), may be described.[38] Instead, as this book demonstrates, Campbell's preoccupations are wider and transnational. While he has praised Terry Lamsley for example as an 'inheritor of all the qualities of classic English supernatural fiction' and R. R. Ryan as 'one of the earliest British novelists to specialise in the horrific', Campbell has been equally enthusiastic about American writers like King, Ligotti and Poppy Z. Brite.[39] Campbell is concerned with exploring the liminal boundaries of the genre, for which he fulfils nothing less than the dual function of historian and ambassador.

Within his chosen field, Campbell is also strongly engaged with the aesthetics of authenticity in 'doing new things'. Repeatedly, the author has emphasised the importance of personal satisfaction with

Introduction: Campbell and Gothic Tradition

'sound[ing] like myself'.[40] Informed by consciousness of precedence and tradition, and drawing upon equally keenly felt autobiography, Campbell's works appear to exemplify what Spooner describes as the 'new self-consciousness' of the contemporary Gothic.[41] Such metatextuality has been a consistent feature of his writing from the beginning. Campbell was a prolific writer of short stories before turning to the novel form with *The Doll Who Ate His Mother* in the mid-1970s. Two key short stories in the *Demons by Daylight* collection encapsulate this quality of self-inflection. These tales are both worth some attention here, as they form a thematic template for the later, and, this book will show, even richer longer fictions which were to follow.

Firstly, the story 'Concussion' itself demonstrates Campbell's early and enduring preoccupation with the liminal space between dream and reality, a recurrent theme of the Gothic. In this complex narrative, which shifts between time frames in a series of reveries, an elderly man, Kirk Morris, remembers a former lover from his youth. Believing that he sees her as a young woman again in the present, he tries to precipitate a reunion through engineering a fatal traffic accident. In one such memory, the girl, Anne, who may herself be a dream of Kirk's, ruminates on the true nature of 'ghosts' after sharing a ghost train ride with Morris at a fairground. She argues:

> But ghosts aren't really like that . . . I think they'd be just like people, and you wouldn't know what they were like until afterward. Those things in there are straight out of a Gothic novel. Mind you, I don't mind Gothic novels. Being carried away by a horseman in a black cloak over the mountains under the moon to a castle! – No, I'm only joking, I'd rather be with you. (pp. 141–2)

Allusions to 'Gothic' novels and settings and to mysterious cloaked figures obviously betoken authorial consciousness of tradition. Here, Campbell's tale, one within a collection of tales self-defined and marketed as 'demonic' and thus macabre, playfully ironises its own perceived mode. 'Concussion', thematically, is an extraordinarily multilayered text. Displaying an awareness of different forms of media, its oblique narrative also presents a series of elisions. The story is at once a self-conscious 'journey into nostalgia' (p. 134); an exploration of both the tensions between past and present and between 'a lovely dream' (p. 148) and a yearned for reality, and an attempt to express the sensation of being or of not-being. However, the past and dreaming are presented as being as threatening as they are benovolent. Kirk at one point senses his body 'fighting to correlate the illusion of movement with the conviction of stasis, as if he was in a Cinerama film' (p. 157) – feeling as if one is in a 'film' being a recurrent metaphor in this tale for displacement and alienation. Underlying the protagonist's quest narrative is a fear of ontological negation, or of 'fall[ing] through his memories' of his past love into a 'void' of non-existence: 'sometimes', Campbell narrates, Kirk 'felt that he'd dreamed Anne, and sometimes, on the rim of the void, that she'd dreamed him' (pp. 157–8). Through such passages, in which the boundary between reality and dream is presented as liminal, both opaque and unstable, Campbell's story becomes an exploration of spatial and temporal otherness. Equally deliberately, the narrative leaves unresolved the question as to whether its protagonist is psychologically delusional or whether his experiences of time travel have actually been real. Kirk's near-victim feels finally as if 'she'd met him' and finally, like a mourning lover, 'begins to weep' (pp. 160–1). This angsty ambivalence or porousness of the boundary between reality and the supernatural was to be repeated and explored in later works.

Demons by Daylight marked Campbell's emergence as a distinctive new voice, and another narrative in the same collection, 'The Franklyn Paragraphs', constitutes as significant a forerunner of what was to come. The story, related in the form of epistolary collage purporting to reconstruct the circumstances surrounding the disappearance of a writer, is a transposition and update of Lovecraft's familiar *faux* documentary 'warning' regarding the invisible and malign forces besieging the material world. It is not just rich in intertextual allusion – the wallpaper of the ill-fated Errol Undercliffe's apartment has 'a Charlotte Perkins Gilman look' (p. 41) – but is even more explicitly metatextual than 'Concussion'. Anticipating works like Brett Easton Ellis's *Lunar Park* (2005) by decades, the author interpolates himself into the narrative in the persona of 'JRC', a recipient of critical letters from Undercliffe. Yet Undercliffe is not just a fellow writer or surrogate for Derleth. He is a doomed, Lovecraftian seeker after forbidden knowledge, in this case researching, unwisely, into the mysterious fate of a cult leader. Campbell sets the contemporary intellectual and artistic scene drily early on, with a reference to Roland Barthes and bourgeois dinner party gossip: 'All bow ties and "God, Bernard, surely you realize the novel is absolutely *dead*"' (p. 41, emphasis in original). 'The Franklyn Paragraphs' is, in short, a deeply refracted text. It is as much concerned with the act of writing; with the status of its practitioners and the relationship of creativity with reality, as it is with the supernatural themes of the occult, reincarnation and predatory entities. 'The peril of the writer', Undercliffe's final, hysterical letter to 'JRC' rambles, is that 'he can't stop thinking. He may survive by writing, but he doesn't really survive' (p. 60). Similarly to 'Concussion', 'The Franklyn Paragraphs' constitutes an interrogation of philosophical and formal norms: 'no longer', Undercliffe laments, 'could I trust the surface of the world' (p. 60). Thematically and artistically, both texts anticipate and demonstrate the major preoccupations, the fevered delving beneath a conventionally accepted 'surface', that was to characterise Campbell's fictions throughout his ensuing career. Aware of diverse and proliferating media, his vision of the Gothic increasingly centres on the author as protagonist and the individual psyche of professional or amateur wordsmiths, be they writers, editors, booksellers, literary agents or librarians; with their relationships with readers and reality, and with the processes and the consequences of creativity.

Nevertheless, since the early 1980s, an important element of Campbell's quest for authenticity has been a shift away from such short stories and an increasing reliance on longer fictional forms – novels and novellas. This development has been much to the chagrin of critics like Joshi, who has described the author as being 'only indifferently successful' in the novel format.[42] Underlying such consensus is a fidelity to the formalist tradition exemplified by

M. R. James's short stories: that of a belief in the inherent superiority of the shorter narrative's depiction of a single macabre incident and an undistilled concentration of psychological terror, either in terms of representation or of evoked, physiological response. For Joshi, historian and advocate of James and the Lovecraftian weird tale tradition, Campbell's novels are, narrowly, 'compelling only when told from some twisted perspective', or when 'they suggest that human beings are symbols for vaster phenomena'.[43] However, this volume quite deliberately focuses on Campbell's hitherto neglected longer fictions as vital to understanding the author's unique contribution to Gothic studies. His writing is intuitive, as opposed to ideologically-driven, and there is, accordingly, a sense of exploration, experimentation and self-discovery in his longer works. For example, of the long early novel, *Incarnate* (1983), Campbell has admitted that

> this was being written in the period of the last year of my mother's life, that terrible nightmare period. And here I was writing this immensely elaborate book, pretty well on instinct. And I can only assume the book was somewhere I had to go in order to let go in a way, and that was how the structure came about, composed itself.[44]

Strikingly, a cathartic value in the process of novel writing is here linked to an imputation of autonomy and near sentience to the form itself. Far from its being '*dead*', Campbell has spoken repeatedly and approvingly of the inspirational and dynamic nature of the novel, as the form 'acquires some impetus and actually goes off into places you never would have thought of'.[45] Campbell has also hightlighted 'growing at ease' with the novel as his greatest satisfaction as a writer, its larger scope 'generat[ing] the most energy and inventiveness'.[46] For the Gothic scholar then, rather than regret, a response that can only truncate full understanding through a dismissal or marginalisation of much of Campbell's output, there is an alternative approach. This route takes the writer's preference for the longer fictional form on its own terms, and opens the possibility of exploring the meaning and significance of those 'places never thought of'. In presenting a broader and richer canvass to explore ideas than that afforded by the short story form, novels and novellas allow Campbell, always an instinctive artist, scope to develop his ideas.

Campbell's candour as interviewee, the choice of the language of imperative such as 'had to go', and the aforementioned wealth of paratextual writing, all suggest a confessional tendency. This trait may reflect the author's personal history as a lapsed Catholic. The 'confessional' narrative is, obviously, an established Gothic trope, familiar from such seminal works as James Hogg's *The Private Memoirs and Confessions of a Justified Sinner* (1824). Asked in a 2016 interview about the simultaneous presence of a humanist perspective and the cosmic or numinous in his own work, Campbell has admitted that 'my only excuse is agnosticism, however timidly or vaguely I define mine'.[47] In contrast to Lovecraft's atheism or the pessimism and antenatalism articulated in Ligotti's treatise, *The Conspiracy Against the Human Race* (2010), this book proposes that Campbell's fictions present what is, in essence, a more liberal vision of haunted agnosticism. The attribution by Campbell of a level of autonomy to his own work also affords to the reader licence to interpret texts on multiple levels and derive and ascribe meanings unencumbered by authorial didacticism. Indeed, Campbell himself has championed more broadly the 'right to question'.[48] Accordingly, he expounds the virtue of ambiguity, in, for instance, acknowledging the influence of Robert Aickman, the subtle creator of oblique short stories, upon his work.[49] Aickman, writing of the ghost story, had extolled the merit of its 'offer[ing] neither logic nor moral'.[50] On the contrary, according to him, and of great relevance to Campbell, a successful narrative 'must open a door, preferably where no-one had previously noticed a door to exist; and, at the end, leave it open, or, possibly, ajar'.[51] Campbell's admiration for the *auteur* Alain Resnais's mystery film, *L'Année dernière à Marienbad* (*Last Year at Marienbad*, 1959), which 'convinced' Campbell 'that an enigma could be more satisfying than any solution', is also revealing.[52] In the context of such influences, this book contends that the often ambivalent endings of Campbell's fictions, denoted by a resistance to formal closure, should be interpreted not as being symptomatic of creative weakness or of muddled thought, but as signifying a deliberate and exploratory strategy. Rather, ambiguity provides Campbell's fictions with much of their fascination and richness. Far from lacking intellectual cogency or complexity, the apparent irresolution decried by Punter in Campbell's work demonstrates constant interrogative engagement with contemporary social, political, aesthetic and wider philosophical concerns.

Ramsey Campbell also attempts to apply some modern and post-millennial theoretical discourses to analysis of Campbell's fictions. It is certainly the case that irresolution, authorial self-consciousness and metatextuality are recognised traits of postmodernist literature. Within Gothic studies, Allan Lloyd Smith's comparison of the affinities between postmodernism and the Gothic affords useful reference points for interpreting stylistic features and themes within Campbell's work: for example, a common pastiche and self-reflexivity, as demonstrated above; the featuring of taboo and criminality; the use of the comedic; resistance to formal closure, and a sense of paranoia with respect to science and technology.[53] The 'web of independent semiotic systems' that so animated Patricia Waugh and other premillennial critics has since grown, wildly, into the World Wide Web and other manifestations of a 'virtual reality' on a scale even then not foreseen.[54] As relevant is the increased tendency towards an ontological rather than epistemological dominance in the themes of contemporary literary discourse noted by Brian McHale, an ascendancy leading to a focus upon the 'self' and the subject's integrity, or otherwise, in a 'reality' which has itself become a contested site.[55] Punter notes that the Gothic may indeed be considered a forerunner of post-modernism in its manifestation of self-awareness and, in some cases, 'a certain playfulness that resists being drawn into the fold of seriousness'.[56]

Despite such affinities, critics and theorists have taken divergent views on the aesthetic value of the relationship between the Gothic and postmodernism. The emphasis on veneer and surface in postmodernism famously led Fredric Jameson to dismiss the Gothic as 'a boring and exhausted paradigm', dependent on representations of 'the emptiest form of sheer Otherness [evil]'.[57] Nevertheless, as Alex Link argues, there remains between the Gothic and postmodernism a shared sense of 'terror' and 'threat' experienced by the subject.[58] This perception of oppression, applied to Campbell's fictions, together with the author's iconoclastic flexibility and cultivation of the power of suggestion and the imaginative sublime instead of visceral horror, suggests a logical affinity with Maria Beville's densely argued attempt to marry postmodernism to the Gothic in *Gothic-postmodernism* (2009). Beville's concept of a distinct literary mode within postmodernist literature is based specifically upon the terror implicit in the subject's experience of postmodernity. According to Beville, this mode 'merely hints at the evil and grotesque and opens up a space for fundamental human curiosity and ontological enquiry'.[59] She defines postmodernist works in themselves as 'experimental, radical and often metafictional literature which problematises the relationship between reality and fiction, reader and text'.[60] Beville omits Campbell from her survey of canonical postmodernist texts like *Lunar Park*. However, his fictions also increasingly centre upon what Beville, drawing from Burke's concept of the sublime, aptly describes as the very 'lingering emotion of terror as it relates to loss of reality and self'.[61] Campbell adopts the depiction and evocation of terror as creative stratagem. In contrast to Beville's examples, this book shows how Campbell's work is characterised by the presence of postmodernist tenets within what remains, for the most part, although not exclusively, a realist narrative paradigm. Campbell's fictions align with postmodernism in their mistrust of explanatory metanarratives such as belief in organised religion. Shared characteristics include the presence of supernaturalism; the portrayal of paranoia as the default psychological response to a world perceived as encroached upon by surveillance; the self-conscious use of humour and parody, denoted by a mixing of registers and tonal dissonance, and the perceived ontological threat to both the integrity of the subject and the stability of the 'reality' that it inhabits. Such tenets are reflected in recurrent and distinctive elements of Campbell's imaginary Gothic landscape: cults, magic and religious belief; psychopathology, both social and individuated; writers, audiences and texts as artefacts; and the proliferation of multimedia and information technology in a digital age. These four themes are the foci of the chapters which follow.

Close textual readings of some eleven of Campbell's key or representative longer fictions are central to this book. My selections cover what is demonstrated to be both a significant and representative thirty-five-year period of Campbell's career, from 1981 to 2016. As mentioned, one of the ways in which this publication differs from Joshi's substantial work is with reference to application of theoretical paradigms and other contemporary discourses. Specifically, *Ramsey Campbell* examines Campbell's longer fictions in the context of the experience of postmodernity and, latterly, posthumanism, a school of thought emergent in the late twentieth century that, in challenging anthropocentrism, also interrogates the ontological status of the subject and its relation to reality. The book employs a critical materialist approach, insofar as its analysis starts from the premise that literary works reflect, mediate, reinforce, interject in or affect the various debates and mores of the culture from which they emanate. Its approach within a cultural studies framework is thematic rather than chronological, although, with Campbell's evolution and response to his environment as a writer in view, in each chapter earlier texts are discussed first prior to later ones. In preference to a reading of the author from any one perspective, the monograph cites the works of a range of theorists, mainly but by no means exclusively associated with postmodernism and posthumanist studies. With respect to postmodernism, it draws eclectically from major writings by Jameson, Jean Baudrillard and Jean-François Lyotard. For posthumanism, use is made of works by leading theorists N. Katherine Hayles, Stefan Herbrechter, Pramod K. Nayar and Anya Heise-von der Lippe. There may seem to be a philosophical contradiction in deploying some inherently aesthetic paradigms, particularly from postmodernism, to evaluation of works infused by an agnostic and humanist, if sceptical and secular, worldview. Nevertheless, such analyses, disclosing a complex and reflexive relationship between Campbell's fictions and both the postmodern and posthuman, is invaluable in elucidating his unique contribution to the Gothic. Where appropriate, the monograph widens references beyond these theorists to include, for example, the idea of the numinous explicated by Rudolf Otto, the existential psychiatry of R. D. Laing, research conducted by science fiction author A. E. van Vogt, Stephen King's own fictional and non-fictional meditations on authorship, Michel Foucault's concept of the heterotopia and Marshall McLuhan's pioneering work on mass media. Lastly, use is also made of the extensive body of paratexts – interviews, essays and other non-fictional writings – in which Campbell himself discusses his methodology and views on the genre. Ranging from theories to interviews, such discourses, diverse as they are, provide the foundations of a language with which to articulate Campbell's highly personal vision of the Gothic, and posit this worldview as being one of peculiar relevance in our postmillennial times.

The first two chapters of *Ramsey Campbell* examine how Campbell's texts mediate, provide metaphors for and critique a secularised culture of postmodernity denoted by crises of faith, both religious and sociopolitical. Religious and sociopolitical belief systems are examples of what Lyotard terms a 'grand narrative', a totalising metadiscourse that serves to provide ideological legitimacy and ensure cultural cohesion.[62] Over half of Campbell's novelistic output to 2022 features cults or black magic. Chapter 1 shows how three of Campbell's major early works from the 1980s, his first full decade as a practising novelist, set the template in reflecting epistemological and ethical challenges posed by their markedly polarised social and political context, and articulating his agnostic and sceptical vision. After discussion of Lovecraft's lasting influence on Campbell with respect to development of a decidedly secular perspective, the chapter offers a reading of *The Nameless* (1981) as a noviciate work of urban and female Gothic defined finally by its inner ideological irresolution. It then analyses *The Hungry Moon* (1986), for three decades Campbell's richest and most overt but most conflicted transposition of Lovecraftian cosmicism. In contrast with the panoramic sweep of this text, Campbell was already beginning to focus on interior psychology, and the 'fake' occult thriller *Obsession* (1985), with its eventual focus on a tragic villain, is shown to introduce a central theme: autonomy and integrity of the subject, complicated by a tension between a foregrounded secularism and the numinous.

Chapter 2 focuses explicitly on Campbell's presentation of aberrant psychology as an expression of distrust of secular, sociopolitical metanarratives. This critique has its apotheosis in the Gothic 'serial killer' trope. The depiction of antisocial mental dysfunction, especially obsession and paranoid persecution complexes, is pervasive in postmodernist fictions and has been recurrent in Campbell's works, assuming centrality in his second, groundbreaking novel, *The Face That Must Die*, and being reiterated and transmuted in succeeding decades, notably in *The One Safe Place* (1995) and *Secret Story* (2005). The chapter contextualises Campbell's work alongside now iconic texts by Harris (*The Silence of the Lambs*, 1988) and Ellis (*American Psycho*, 1991). It is suggested that antisocial behaviour, respectively individual and societal, in the first two novels considered, *The Face That Must Die* and *The One Safe Place*, has cultural origins rooted in late capitalism, simulacra and consumerism. There is obvious affinity here with Jameson's discourses on spatial and social confusion, the erosion of idealism, and despair. The chapter demonstrate how Campbell's distinctive transmutation of Gothic develops from a complex sociopolitical critique. It is then shown how *Secret Story*, with its self-inflecting structure and murderous author as protagonist, displays a destabilisation of ethical and aesthetic boundaries, including the relationship between authors and readers – redolent features of postmodernism. It is demonstrated how Campbell's critique of prevailing secular metanarratives within capitalist society, articulated as psychological horror, both anatomises causes of violence, and satirises the Gothic horror fiction industry and the relationship within that industry between author and audience.

The third chapter explores the extent to which the figure of the author in Campbell's Gothic vision functions as a surrogate for the contemporary subject. Campbell's singularly intense poioumenomic novellas (that is, texts concerned explicitly with the process of creation) are shown to combine an acute sense of paranoia as predictive response with a simultaneous degree of scepticism towards associated postmodernist notions of debilitating 'simulacra' and the perceived helplessness of the subject. For the first time, Campbell's portrayal of the author-as-protagonist is contrasted with that offered by King in the latter's far more familiar writings. Comparison serves to demonstrate the distinctively paranoic, self-haunting quality of the British writer's fictions, in what amounts to a challenge to a teleological concept of history and narrative being viewed as being, as Lyotard terms it, 'the quintessential form of customary knowledge'.[63] Campbell's deliberate use of the novella form is discussed, and two key examples are analysed: the semi-autobiographical *Needing Ghosts* (1991), in style still his most overtly postmodernist long fiction to date, and a late work, *The Booking* (2016). Both novellas are seen to address and crystallise Campbell's evolving engagement with aesthetic and philosophical questions regarding the nature of creativity, selfhood, and autonomy – concerns that betoken engagement with the posthumanist sphere of enquiry.

Chapter 4, the final chapter, focuses on Campbell's contribution to the emergent field of the posthuman Gothic. It explicates the writer's representation of the implications of digital technology for the subject through analysis of three major metaleptic postmillennial narratives: *The Grin of the Dark* (2007), *Think Yourself Lucky* (2014), and *The Seven Days of Cain* (2010). In all three, digital technology is both source of fear, what Baudrillard describes as 'the deep-seated virtualization of human beings', and of life.[64] The chapter develops arguments proposed by Herbrechter on a linkage between postmodernism and posthumanism, and by Heise-von der Lippe on a commonality between the latter and Gothic, in particular anxieties around the subject's subsummation and transformation by and into the 'other'. The coulrophobic *The Grin of the Dark*, with its plethora of media forms and malevolent electronic mail presence channelling an ancient malevolent force, is shown to be a harbinger of what was to follow in Campbell's work. Since that text, the personal computer has become, for Campbell, both a creative tool and a recurring theme. It is, therefore, also a Gothic motif for the postmillennial era, an updated synthesis of the found manuscript and the haunted house or 'Bad Place' archetype.[65] The chapter then examines the 'virtual reality' constituted by web blogs and websites in the two later novels. Both ostensibly revisitations of the familiar Gothic serial killer theme, they explicate the nature of virtual lives, respectively malign and benevolent, created by the

Internet. While *Think Yourself Lucky* shows fidelity to Gothic tradition in reviving the *doppelgänger* trope and evoking monstrous alterity, it also draws out the isolation, loneliness and vulnerability of this 'other'. *The Seven Days of Cain* is shown to develop this preoccupation with interdependencies in its rewriting of Mary Shelley's novel *Frankenstein* (1818). It foregrounds science fiction elements, in particular the consequences wrought by an ensemble of artificial, posthuman characters' consciousness of their own fictionality. It is shown that these later fictions thus combine representation of incursion of alterity conferred with sentience upon the subject with simultaneous precipitation of debate as to the ontological status and 'rights' of these transformed or new posthuman lives.

Ramsey Campbell thus articulates Campbell's distinctive and unique contribution to and mediation of the Gothic. It draws attention to the author's style, which combines a highly personal 'poetics', to appropriate Joshi's term, with a markedly intense evocation of paranoia and psychosis. Campbell's long fictions offer unsettling portrayals of psychological disturbance and social dissonance. As horror texts, they are shown to display pronounced consciousness of form, liminality and generic hybridity, ranging from Lovecraftian cosmicism to social realism, comedy and science fiction. In critiquing the maxims of contemporary Western culture, they reflect the concerns of a perspective that is religiously agnostic, politically liberal and ethically humanist. Further, Campbell's long fictions are shown to satirise the author's own publishing industry, and to trace the challenges posed to the subject, author, and author as subject, by mass media and information technology. Perhaps most profoundly, they illustrate the possibility of literary works simultaneously displaying strong alignment with some implicitly aesthetic and apolitical postmodernist and posthumanist paradigms without abandonment of liberal humanist stance or ethical commitment. The very possibility and practice of applying such paradigms illustrates that Campbell's work, in being *both* generic 'pulp' and serious literature informed by a consciousness of tradition, can be instrumental in precipitating and contributing to debates on canons – a discussion that is returned to in the conclusion of this book.

1

Impractical Magic: Campbell's 'Agnostic' Gothic

※⊙≪

'How We Live Now': The Insecurities of Postmodernity

> Ritual and dogma are merely the framework of organised religion. They do not touch on religious experience itself, which is the experience of mystery, of the indescribably enigmatic.
>
> Lesley Hazleton, *Agnostic: A Spirited Manifesto* (2016).[1]

A degree of agnostic scepticism towards 'ritual and dogma' has remained with Campbell throughout his career. The writer describes himself as 'a sceptic who mostly writes about the supernatural'.[2] In his 1991 interview with Stefan Dziemianowicz, the author admits to being 'deeply worried that so many people are going to find some kind of total system of belief which will set [*sic*] away all of their fears, as long as they give up the right to question'.[3] At that time, Campbell was expressing a sense of anxiety about the then approaching millennium. However, the writer's views have remained remarkably consistent. In interviews given a quarter of a century later, Campbell was still lamenting what he perceived as a widespread propensity for succumbing to authoritarianism, with its accompanying suppression of intellectual freedom. In one such exchange,

Campbell neatly pathologises aspects of contemporary Western societal praxis, commenting that

> I don't think I'm likely to stop looking in my work at how we live now ... Themes keep recurring: gullibility, the human eagerness to find scapegoats, the willingness to embrace belief systems that purport to give you all the answers as long as you give up the right to question; the vulnerability of children, the increasing unwillingness of people to intervene when they see or suspect wrongdoing.[4]

The manifestation of scepticism in Campbell's literary texts is an equally consistent iconoclasticism. As a writer of Gothic fictions, Campbell practises what Hazleton describes as 'the agnostic's faith: not in answers, but in possibilities' and in 'inquiry'.[5] The principal targets of his nonconformist approach are these metanarratives, or what he describes as 'belief systems'. This chapter focuses upon Campbell's representation of religious belief systems, whether those sets of principles are marginalised in the form of cults; polytheistic and pre-Christian survivals; entirely orthodox and centred upon conventional church-based worship, or modelled on more general and less sectarian lines of enquiry addressing issues of magic, spirituality and supernaturalism. For clarity, my study accepts the commonly understood meaning of 'occult', derived from the Latin word *occultus*, that is, the clandestine, hidden or secret.[6] 'Magic' is broadly interpreted as referring to both the associated use of ritual to harness what are perceived to be supernatural forces, and the result or consequences of such ritual upon the phenomenological and experiential world.

Whatever definition is accepted, the recurrence of secretive, self-marginalised groups and their leaders in Campbell's *oeuvre* is striking. A preoccupation with cults, magic and questions of religious faith and doubt was well established by the end of Campbell's first decade as a novelist. Specifically, the 'magic' invoked is almost invariably of the 'black' variety, that is, malevolent and associated with diabolism or evil spirits.[8] The figure of the cult leader is, similarly, always flawed or villainous. Campbell, creating his own mythos, occasionally reuses these characters. For example, Peter Grace, the antagonist from Campbell's early novel *The Parasite* (1980), is referenced almost three decades later in *Thieving Fear* (2008), and even Roland Franklyn, from the early short tale 'The Franklyn Paragraphs', reappears in the much later novel, *The Kind Folk* (2012). The template was established early on. I will examine the representation and critique of heterodox and orthodox belief structures in three of Campbell's longer fictions from a specific and, as will be seen, pivotal decade, the 1980s: *The Nameless* (1981), *The Hungry Moon* (1986) and the complex, transitional and reflective work, *Obsession* (1985). Through showing the early points of influence upon Campbell exercised by H. P. Lovecraft, and analysis of the affinity of Campbell's work with postmodernist and other paradigms, it becomes possible to trace the emerging development of a distinctive, agnostic vision.

The philosophical, sociohistorical and literary contexts for Campbell's engagement with occultism are multifaceted. Nevertheless, outlining their contours is straightforward enough. Campbell's emergence and development as a professional writer in the 1960s and 1970s coincided with profound and sometimes traumatic paradigmatic shifts within Anglo-American and European culture and discourse. As Jean-François Lyotard maintains, this was a period in which the totalising 'grand narrative' appeared to have 'lost its credibility'.[9] In the religious sphere, this insecurity was symbolised by the iconic 'Is God Dead?' issue of *Time Magazine* (8 April 1966).[10] In contrast to Enlightenment values, there were no longer guarantees of epistemological or ontological certitudes – that is, the encompassing metanarratives such as human emancipation, Freudianism or Marxism – or orthodox forms of religious beliefs, with their hierarchical structures and doctrines. Naturally, such crises of meaning and of identity stimulate a quest for amelioration and solutions by way of response. For Lyotard, this entails the replacement of a universal, totalising metalanguage by what he terms as 'a plurality of formal and axiomatic systems capable of arguing the truth of denotative statements', a plurality 'described by a system which is universal but not consistent'.[11] In the context of the 1960s, such enactment can be seen in the reframing by a popular or so-called 'counter-culture' of pre-existing belief systems within manifestations of the then emerging social liberalism. These substitutes included various *avant-garde* ideologies, sexual liberation and recreational drug use. For example, writing of the United States in the 1960s, Hugh McLeod notes a growth in alternative religious movements, especially amongst highly educated demographic groups, devoted to 'new ways of thinking and behaving'.[12] Both there and in Britain, such a 'quest culture' for something to invest belief in, has continued, and indeed proliferated, to the present day.[13] The British scholar Christopher Partridge takes a positive view of such new religious movements, seeing them as evidence of a benign cultural shift which has been 'both helping people to think through theological and metaphysical issues', and 'also providing resources for the construction of alternative religious world views [sic]'.[14] However, where Partridge sees empowerment, it is clear, and demonstrable, that the more sceptical Campbell has seen malign contradiction, control and abjection.

Campbell's work both reflects its sociohistorical context and mediates its literary antecedents. In their sweeping survey, *A Short History of Fantasy* (2009), Farah Mendleson and Edward Jones describe his fictions as symptomatic of a growing 'conspiracy element' affecting British and American culture in the 1970s.[15] For Mendleson and Jones, Campbell's narratives, to an even greater degree than Stephen King's, focus upon the 'nature of evil', and upon 'exploiting the cracks in the moral order that was emerging as organised religion was losing its hold and New Age religions were increasingly visible'.[16] Fleeting though its reference to Campbell is, *A Short History of Fantasy* raises important elements to consider regarding the writer's inheritance, influences, interpretation of the concept of 'evil' and emergent value system. From the post-Manson trials 'cult controversy' of the 1970s which drew upon fears of abduction and brainwashing onwards, the *zeitgeist* that Campbell 'exploited' as a writer was certainly rich in a paranoid 'conspiracy element'. To appropriate Hayden White's argument regarding the fictional quality of factual representation, the 1970s and 1980s were a period in which history itself could be interpreted as 'no less a form of fiction than the novel is a form of historical representation', and, accordingly, the notion of 'value neutrality' in discourse was 'an illusion'.[17] The boundary between reality and fiction became opaque. For example, the journalist Kenneth Wooden's purportedly documentary account, *Children of Jonestown*, appeared alongside anonymously written memoirs of abuse such as *Michelle Remembers* (both 1981) and reports, subsequently discredited, of a secretive but vast 'Satanic' network operating in pre-schools and day centres in the United Kingdom and United States.[18] There was thus a concurrent matrix which both created and reinforced a prevailing narrative of social disaffection and unease. Whatever one's view on the veracity or morality of these discourses, such a climate of *ennui* and paranoia would have been creatively fertile for a writer to use, particularly one as sensitive to prevailing mores and as well read in the Gothic horror genre as Campbell.

Campbell drew heavily upon literary forebears in negotiating his own pathway in his chosen field. The most glaringly obvious influence in representations of supernaturalism and the occult is, of course, Lovecraft. Campbell's own admitted 'timid' agnosticism contrasts markedly with the earlier American writer's assertive and consistent atheism. 'In theory I am an agnostic', Lovecraft avowed in a famous letter, 'but pending the appearance of rational evidence I must be classed, practically and provisionally, as an atheist.'[19] As S. T. Joshi has described in two important studies, Lovecraft's philosophy is a form of non-teleological 'mechanistic materialism', and, if not pessimism, an evolving 'cosmic indifferentism'.[20] In Lovecraft's schemata, humanity is insignificant in the cosmos: there is no God or gods, soul or afterlife, and religion is dismissed as 'an opiate dream', and 'a pompous formalisation of fantastic art'.[21] Such uncompromising views seem to preclude any accommodation with an agnostic perspective. The latter, in the philosopher Robin Le Poidevin's opinion for one, affords a positive quality for 'uncertainty', in that it promotes 'creativity, theoretical progress, [and] social tolerance'.[22] However, this book proposes that Campbell's fictions in essence reinterpret Lovecraft's materialist philosophy, which was itself partly a reaction against modernism, for a postmodern era.

Campbell's portrayal of cults and those he sees as their victims draws upon various Anglo-American discourses. The historian Philip Jenkins, in his critical account of the so-called 'Satanic panic' of the 1980s, suggests that Herbert S. Gorman's novel *The Place Called Dagon* (1927) influenced Lovecraft and other authors for the pulp magazine *Weird Tales*.[23] It is not hard to see why, with the novel's supposition of the survival of devil worship through the practice of going 'underground in the modern world'; nor is it difficult to perceive an indirect effect upon Campbell. The writer has certainly acknowledged the influence of his fellow British writer Dennis Wheatley, specifically *The Devil Rides Out* (1934) and its successors dealing with witchcraft and diabolism.[24] Virtually all Campbell's work, like Wheatley's 'black magic' narratives, employs a contemporary rather than period setting. It is reasonable to ascribe some pragmatic as well as artistic reasons behind this. The commercial success of King's novels, Ira Levin's *Rosemary's Baby* (1967) and William Peter Blatty's *The Exorcist* (1971) and their lucrative cinematic adaptations, together with later imitators such as David Seltzer's *The Omen* (film and novel, 1976), all texts anchored firmly in the present day, had an undeniable bearing on authorial strategy. In an interview given in 1991, Campbell admitted to a commercial drive dictating the writing of one early novel: 'I tried to do what appeared to be the perceived model of the contemporary horror story, which is characters in an ordinary environment and something *out there* which is attempting to get them for whatever reason.'[25]

Yet commercial considerations aside, of greater relevance are common themes indicating a loss of consolatory metanarratives. These themes are the deconstruction of the family unit represented by lost, demonic or possessed children, and degenerate and threatening forces at large within what had been 'an ordinary environment' of safe, domestic space. As far as the alterity, the 'something' which threatens or encroaches upon the protagonist, is concerned, Campbell draws no distinction between the inhuman, the demonic, and human agents. The externalisation, as being 'out there', is also crucial. The term 'cults', as opposed to the more benign-sounding 'New Religious Movements', has negative connotations, being described by Douglas E. Cowan and David G. Bromley, for instance, as seeming to represent 'all that is evil and dangerous and deviant in the compass of religious belief and practice'.[26] Campbell's stance as a writer towards these groups aligns with the pejorative. In the course of his exploration of 'evil', the function of the supernatural generally has been as much internal, as 'an excuse we invent for things we do or want to do ourselves', as external.[27] He has sought to define 'evil' in relation to society, so that it may be better understood as being socially constructed rather than as non-human and metaphysical in origin.[28] For Campbell, the 'cult' represents the abject: an abnegation of independent thought, and thus freedom, an abandonment and surrender which is oppressive and invidious. In this hostility, Campbell is obviously following, but also expanding upon, a view held by Lovecraft, for whom cults also represent a consolatory pseudo-mythology and, as Joshi describes, 'emotion, brainwashing'.[29] Repeatedly in Campbell's fictions, as in the short story 'The Depths' (1978), the writer returns to what he calls 'the central metaphor of giving up your name and with it your responsibility for your actions and your right to choose'.[30] The quintessential example of Campbell's negative portrayal of the sect phenomenon as almost morally unspeakable is the deliberately titled *The Nameless*, to which 'The Depths' is described by Campbell as 'a companion piece'.[31] This early long fiction, a complex example of the urban and female Gothic presented as an occult suspense thriller, also represents an important dialogue with, and departure from, Lovecraft.

Home to Mother: The Nameless *and Unquiet Domesticity*

Campbell's 1981 novel is set in contemporary London and Glasgow. The third-person narrative relates the desperate attempts of the guilt-ridden protagonist, literary agent Barbara Waugh, to trace her missing daughter. Angela Waugh had been abducted years previously, Barbara discovers, by the eponymous cult, an elusive and shadowy group responsible for numerous disappearances since the 1940s. *The Nameless* thus obviously articulates its author's concern regarding the 'vulnerability of children'.[32] Not only a familiar generic staple, as exemplified by Henry James's *The Turn of the Screw* (1898), anxiety for and about the child was to be a recurrent preoccupation for Campbell, as other novels from that decade, *The Claw* (1984) and *The Influence* (1988), would exemplify. In an afterword to *The Nameless*, Campbell, then a new father of an infant daughter himself, is aware and wary of autobiographical influence and its attendant 'pitfalls' of exhaustion and self-indulgence.[33] This notwithstanding, the group of child abductors in this novel are the quintessence of parental nightmare. Dedicated to torture, sadism and murder, the Nameless symbolise monstrous alterity: the external, secretive and clandestine presented as a wholly malevolent force. In a deliberate conflation of paganism, satanic ritual and antisocial practices, there is no attempt at nuances of character for this collective. Campbell's sect are practitioners of undifferentiated 'very bad things – black magic and torture and that sort of stuff' (p. 215). As such, the depiction of the cult phenomenon echoes Lovecraft's in, for example, the story, 'The Call of Cthulhu' (1927). However, Lovecraft's lurid descriptions of this 'voodoo' cult's activities, 'free and wild and beyond good and evil, with laws and morals thrown aside and men shouting and killing and revelling in joy', convey a neo-Nietzschean hedonism.[34] For the American author, cults represent what he was to describe as a misguided but understandable attempt by a vulnerable and fearful social unit to pursue a consolatory credo against an indifferent universe: 'a principle of freedom or irregularity or adventurous opportunity against the eternal and maddening rigidity of cosmic law'.[35] Campbell, however, goes further in presenting the cult as not just delusional, but as oppressive. Indeed it represents a destructive, anti-natal perversion of the life cycle.

A typically Lovecraftian concern with verisimilitude is established in the novel's prologue, set in San Quentin prison, California, in 1940. This introduces Kaspar Ganz, the enigmatic cult leader, who is posing as a psychiatrist to visit an inmate on Death Row. Although dead, Ganz serves as the novel's principal antagonist via his malign posthumous influence. As such, he is another in the mould of Campbell's charismatic occultist Roland Franklyn who 'haunt' the author's long fictions, after the similarly deceased John Strong in *The Doll Who Ate His Mother* and Peter Grace in *The Parasite* (1980). Likened to 'a praying mantis', Ganz refrains some of the classic 'aristocratic' vampire traits popularised by John Polidori and Bram Stoker in the nineteenth century, being described as tall, dressed in black, gleaming-eyed, and possessed of a 'sharp ageless face' and effortlessly aloof manner (p. 10).[36] The prison guard thinks that Ganz should be incarcerated himself, and, indeed, another character later confirms that such prejudice and trepidation are well founded, for the cult leader has long held a 'morbid fascination with sadism and mutilation' (p. 220). Although Ganz's credentials as a doctor and psychiatrist are clearly entirely bogus, the connotations for health and 'caring' professions are obviously negative. A critical portrayal of medics and social workers in fact typifies Campbell's work.[37] In this sense, Campbell's interpretation of the contemporary Gothic aligns with David Punter's description of the 'obsessed' attempts by a 'therapeutic culture' to both obtain resolutions for its problems of 'sociopsychological abuse' and, simultaneously, to find 'ways of invalidating them'.[38] The text thereafter alludes to, and so invokes memories of, the 'Moors Murders' trial (1966); the Scientologists suing the Olympia Press over publication of the journalist Robert Kaufman's critical exposé, *Inside Scientology: How I Joined Scientology and Became Superhuman* (1972), and the Tate and La Bianca murders carried out by Charles Manson's 'family' (1969). In accordance with this documentary approach, one character even announces that 'I did some research', before confiding to Barbara:

> You remember the Manson trial obviously. One of his women said something to the effect that maybe people thought the Family was bad, but there was a group that made them look like Disneyland. They were people with no names who were into things even Manson wouldn't touch. (p. 113)

Campbell is here imitating Lovecraft's familiar *faux* documentary style, where the wholly imaginary is validated through juxtaposition with the real, in the process blurring the barrier between them.

Overt comparison of the Manson trial with 'rumours' (p. 112) and reports of the activities of the Nameless from London and Manchester in the 1940s and 1970s, in which 'kids were lured away by other kids who said they had no names, to see their parents who didn't have names either' (p. 113), are intended to confer authenticity upon the latter, to create, in effect, the texture of a new urban myth.

Like Gorman's modern-day worshippers of Dagon, Ganz's group of followers operates 'underground'. Through its London and Glaswegian settings, *The Nameless* thus accords strongly with conventions of urban Gothic. As described by Emily Alder, for example, the urban metropolis evokes the uncanny, that is, 'a sense of the buried past that shapes experience of the city and re-emerges as repressed secrets, desires and histories marginalised by a culture formed by capitalist dynamics'.[39] Campbell's text signposts a number of overt references to Gothic forebears other than Lovecraft, as in the deliberate evocation of Arthur Machen's story 'The Inmost Light' (1894) in use of the title, the 'Undying Light', for a meeting for seekers of 'someone better than the Spiritualists' (p. 163). In this revealing scene, Campbell portrays vividly the social malaise, enervation and moral vacuum in which an extremist group may gain purchase amidst an audience seeking a consolatory 'grand narrative'. Barbara observes that the crowd of attendees at the 'Undying Light' gathering,

> looked like people who worked in dingy offices or in shops in half-derelict streets if they worked at all, people who grew old looking after their parents and who would die unmarried and almost alone in their parents' senile houses. They were here tonight because they were starved for faith, for anything that would explain their lives. (p. 167)

Campbell's novel combines the presentation of personal isolation and social alienation, and the desperate desire to ameliorate both. As such, this preoccupation symptomatises what Hazleton describes as the social drive for the 'illusion of knowing' which underlies theism.[40] Through deploying familiar Gothic tropes, Campbell's text critiques such an imperative, suggesting that societal atomisation and the entailed surrender of self have invidious consequences. Various anxieties are evoked regarding the family unit; violence against women, especially in the context of maternity; the above-mentioned simultaneous vulnerability of and danger posed *by* children, and the threat to ideation of the nuclear family posed by strangers, manifestations of alterity and 'otherness'.

As a group, the Nameless themselves incarnate social abjection. Members of this cult have not only given up their 'right to question': they have also forsaken individual identity altogether. Ganz's disciples are in pursuit of 'the ultimate atrocity', a state of antisocial and depersonalised alterity on behalf of 'something outside themselves' (p. 216). This 'something' is a force or entity which is never identified or defined. Nevertheless, it is a force which the reader is encouraged to assume is 'evil', being destructive and life-negating. Amongst numerous criticisms of the novel, Joshi argues that the significance of 'namelessness' itself is never even addressed, appearing to be 'merely a device for the cult to evade detection'.[41] However, to this reader, Joshi's comment somewhat downplays Campbell's intention with this 'central metaphor', ignoring the text's disclosure that the 'Nameless' have deliberately given up their names in order for group members 'to show that they were only the tools of what they were doing' (p. 224). Rather, Campbell has clearly taken some inspiration here from Aleister Crowley's *Magick in Theory and Practice* (1913). For the successful practice of 'magick', Crowley prescribes 'first and foremost the destruction of the individuality' posed by the ego, for 'each of our ideas must be made to give up the self to the Beloved'.[42] In Campbell's sceptical reconfiguration the abnegation of self takes a markedly negative and destructive turn, rather than a joyous, life-enhancing or enlightening one. By interpreting the 'replacement of physical life and death by an evil dream' as the 'keynote of the Gothic', Simon MacCulloch, for example, has equated occultism in Campbell's works to a rejection of fertility and Darwinian evolution, a 'collectively imagined' equivalent of seizing and finally 'perverting' the imagination.[43] The eponymous cult's abduction of children in *The Nameless* represents a 'perverted' alternative to the traditional family unit and notions of reproduction. As such, it reproduces, in a contemporary postmodern context, what Gerry Carlin and Nicola Allen describe as a characteristic of modernism as depicted in Lovecraft's fictions. These portrayed the simultaneous 'horror and allure of primitivism, otherness and historical annihilation' – a dichotomy that, paradoxically, allows a 'rebirth'.[44]

To apply a postmodernist paradigm, the nomadic 'Nameless' in Campbell's novel represent an overarching anxiety and tension over the moral implications implied by their lack of definition through anchorage or alignment with referents. The sense of ethical and spiritual crisis expressed in this text is symptomatic of a culture experiencing an acute collapse of viable metanarratives. That culture is characterised by a loss of confidence in the existence of what Jean Baudrillard describes as 'truth, reference and objective causes'.[45] Such truth, referents and causality have been replaced by a 'current procession of simulacra'.[46] Simulacra are non-hierarchical and non-dialectical, so there is, thus, no moral hierarchy or promise or assurance of progress. In Baudrillard's schemata, such nullification of the real and attendant notions of structure and of progress results in 'evil'. It is not desire which is inescapable, Baudrillard maintains, but 'the ironic presence of the object, its indifference and indifferent interconnections, its challenge, its seduction, its violation of the symbolic order', in short 'the principle of evil'.[47] The proximity of this 'seductive' chaos, the fear that moral and social norms and widely held assumptions are somehow in the unmaking, both energises and haunts *The Nameless* and Campbell's other Gothic narratives. Yet at the same time such traps constitute an invidious situation against which his work seeks to posit, however tentatively, a humane alternative.

The apotheosis of chaos and 'principle of evil' is (un)naturally represented in *The Nameless* by the titular cult. This antagonistic and malign force acts as an existential threat to any conventional guarantors of social cohesion, but principally to conventions of natalism and parenthood. The text endeavours to articulate a defence for these credos as a reassertion against the cult's negation of the life cycle. It does so in a self-reflexive and inconclusive manner which aligns the novel with the postmodern – thematically if not stylistically. *The Nameless* is an early example of the complex hybridity achieved by Campbell's long fictions. The novel clearly qualifies as, as discussed, an instance of urban Gothic. However, it can also be described as an example of the female Gothic, in the sense described for example by Diana Wallace; that is, as a male writer's appropriation of key elements associated with the mode.[48] Foremost amongst these characteristics is a female lead character and representation of the experience, especially the trauma, incurred by motherhood. Campbell has admitted that a working title for this novel, alongside *The Loud Houses*, was *Home to Mother*.[49] Indeed, the worst fates that are depicted in any detail in the narrative are reserved for women who embody or assume maternal roles. Margery Turner, the mother of another abductee, is apparently consumed in a derelict house by an entity which is 'hardly formed, a foetus covered with cobwebs and dust or composed of them' (p. 87). This explicit association of the foetus with mysophobia recalls Julia Kristeva's identification of the abject with unclean waste matter, as something which 'disturbs identity, system, order'.[50] Similarly, Gerry Martin, an undercover journalist, is later lured to torture and death in the cellar of another property, the darkness and dinginess of which consciously evoke the Gothic. For good measure she meets her gruesome fate while an unnatural 'something the size of a child' (p. 146), possibly the same paranormal entity, traverses across the ceiling overhead.[51] Amongst the text's many discourses is a half-'formed' meditation on foetal development. Barbara, the grieving mother, is described as having a dream, in which she is climbing an escalator and perceives her lost daughter 'waiting against a darkness that looked impatient to take shape', but, on second glance, 'a snake with a frozen head, pink and moist as a foetus, was waiting' (p. 155). The connotations here are not only foetal, but, with the references to 'snake' with a head being both 'pink' and 'moist', phallic and sexual. Even the independent-minded and androgynously named 'Gerry' is given a sudden protective, maternal instinct – 'she knew only that she had to save the child' (p. 145). Gerry is being used to articulate her creator's view, given in the novel's Afterword, that the 'strongest fear is parental' (p. 278). Yet, as with Carrie White in King's novel *Carrie* (1974), parental 'fear' is both for and *of* the child. Angela Waugh, the daughter, like Carrie, transpires to be a powerful psychic, becoming both victim and villain.[52] Names in Campbell's fictions often have some symbolic resonance. Here, the name 'Angela', like 'Gerry', is no exception. It conveys the ambiguity of the angel, a supernatural being whose message or motives may be either benign or destructive. Barbara's daughter, coveted, mourned, recovered and finally feared, is incorporated into the novel's overall suggestive matrix of meanings. The text seems balanced between an ideological validation of the maternal instinct and the equation of maternity with danger and death.

The contradictions within this positioning become apparent at the novel's conclusion. This is a densely packed and apparently rushed denouement in which protagonist, child and what appears to be the entire Nameless sect are united on a ship. Typifying a recurring feature of Campbell's earlier longer fictions, the ending seems to attempt to resolve issues quickly, and, in doing so, raises more intellectual problems and reveals more than it resolves. A literal manifestation of the many textual 'loose ends' in Campbell's fiction is the undefined supernatural entity, the cobweb creature, described in the novel's finale as having 'an unstable head' and 'flapping' skin (p. 259). The entity is a jarringly overt element of supernaturalism in what is otherwise a predominantly realistic narrative of psychological suspense. Beyond drawing upon a long Gothic tradition of arachnophobia and associated repulsive corporeality to evoke fear, the creature's exact relationship to Ganz or to the living members of the Nameless, as Joshi points out, is unclear.[53] Whether it is intended to be a spectral manifestation of Ganz, or an expression of the collective subconscious of the Nameless, the entity certainly appears to be a somewhat randomised and unintegrated element. Perhaps most apparently credibility-straining is what amounts to be, by Campbell's own admission, a final *deus ex machina* on the boat.[54] In this dramatic climax, Barbara's dead husband appears – again symbolically named, this time as 'Arthur', as if he has materialised out of myth to save the day. In quick succession, both Ted, Barbara's current consort, and Angela, her daughter, also undergo an entirely sudden, and in Joshi's view for one, 'highly implausible', psychological conversion.[55] Campbell himself has also been candid about what he sees as the novel's conflicted aesthetics throughout its diegesis, but most apparent in this ending. 'The book comes dangerously close', he has reflected, 'to expressing attitudes I have little time for', specifically 'the notion of evil as an external force – "nothing to do with us" – and the idea that independent women are suspect'.[56] In the novel's Afterword, Campbell admits to finding the final appearance of the spectral Arthur to save the day as 'one ghost too many', and to some unease 'with the [Dennis] Wheatley-ish notion of evil at large' (pp. 278–9).

However, there is an alternative perspective to such vexed and baldly qualitative artistic judgements. The somewhat irresolute climax of *The Nameless* enacts Lyotard's maxim that 'consensus is only a particular state of discussion, not its end'.[57] Angela's pivotal reversal may be unprecedented, but it serves to convey a grimly determined optimism. It is a *volte-face* which combines elements of Christian and humanist belief. Her infliction of torture upon the cultists becomes, it is narrated, 'a child's exaggerated show of repentance, an acting out of her self-disgust, proof that she repudiated to regain everything the cult stood for, perhaps in order to regain her father's love' (p. 269). Rendered ambivalent though this reversal is by the qualifier 'perhaps', Angela's granting herself 'another chance' (p. 272) suggests a counterbalance to the preceding narrative, which has given no indication that the psychically powerful Angela grieves or feels empathy for her dead father, or indeed for anyone else.[58] Her reversal reasserts a concern with social structures, particularly the integrity of the family unit. Like its almost token 'monster', therefore, although the novel may seem ill defined, 'baggy' and unfinished, the sense of incompletion also extends to the ethical issues raised, which, here, centre on notions of maternity and generation. Campbell's narrative articulates abjection of the mother, in the forms of the Nameless; the fates of Margery and Gerry as their victims, and the character of Angela. The cult presents one form of familial structure, if a repressive and destructive one. Yet, through Angela's final 'repentance', and the unstable, shifting position occupied by the child in the narrative, the text also presents a humane alternative. It enacts a desire for an embrace of the maternal, in opposition to a fundamentalist alterity which is both inhuman and inhumane, expressed through struggle. Thus, both artistically and philosophically, Campbell's text, typically for those inflected by postmodernity, articulates the search for a consolatory credo beyond the 'grand narrative' of religious dogmatism, but, simultaneously, demonstrates the difficulty of and struggle involved in attaining one.

Folk Wisdom? Theological Conflicts in The Hungry Moon

While *The Nameless* anatomises the phenomenon of the secretive 'cult' with its perverse substitute for the family unit, Campbell's later novel *The Hungry Moon* critiques more orthodox religious forms, both pagan and Christian. Lyotard maintains that the purpose of narrative is to confer and transmit knowledge, 'to recount experiences, positive or negative, allowing society to define its competence'.[59] To achieve this, Lyotard privileges language games, mini-narratives (*petits récits*), which derive from the difference, diversity and incompatibility between sender and referent as 'the quintessential form of imaginative invention'.[60] In turning to Campbell's 1986 novel, one of his most panoramic and certainly most overtly Lovecraftian longer fictions of the 1980s, one sees a veritable *smorgasbord* of such 'mini-narratives': it is a text that is brimful of ideas. Ideological anatomisation, however, is never completed by 'consensus', much less resolution. Fidelity to a Lovecraftian view of the insignificance of humanity in the cosmos and scepticism towards forms of worship coexist, uneasily, with a fragile liberal humanism. Instead, Campbell's text seems to dramatise and exemplify, even if it does not finally endorse, what Baudrillard describes as the 'radical antagonism' of the universe, non-dialectical in nature and moving 'towards the extremes', rather than towards a state of equilibrium, reconciliation or synthesis.[61]

Unlike *The Nameless*, *Hungry Moon* is an ensemble piece.[62] Set in the fictional Peak District town of Moonwell, its plot, updating and transposing Lovecraft's ascription of an extraterrestrial origin for supernatural, 'god'-like beings, concerns the infection of an isolated community by an ancient lunar entity imprisoned upon the earth. The creature is unwittingly unleashed by the actions of Godwin Mann, the leader of a sect of evangelical Christians. Joel Lane observes that Campbell's novel 'successfully creates its own mythic and symbolic territory'.[63] However, as in all Campbell's Gothic fictions, this 'territory' is richly imprinted with literary antecedents. Campbell admitted that his book began as 'a riff' on James Herbert's earlier novel, *The Dark* (1980), in seeking to 'portray the human psyche's simultaneous attraction to and repulsion towards and condemnation of a monstrous other'.[64] Joshi also sees William Hope Hodgson's apocalyptic work *The Night Land* (1912) as an influence.[65] To these may be added Nigel Kneale's television screenplays, *Quatermass and the Pit* (1958) and *Quatermass* (1979), in the central theme of the manipulation of a contemporary human settlement by an older, extraterrestrial intelligence. Yet the novel's interpretation of myth embraces much wider temporal and spatial referents. These extend historically to classical literature, exemplified by the sudden appearance of ferocious dogs, which are clearly meant to evoke memories of the hounds of the ancient Greek goddess Hecate, and the climactic Oedipal blinding of most of the town's inhabitants.[66] The text also draws upon a more recent and, at least until the 2010s, specifically British trend which has been loosely identified as 'folk horror', exemplified by Michael Reeves's film, *Witchfinder General* (1968), Piers Haggard's *The Blood on Satan's Claw* (1970) and Robin Hardy's *The Wicker Man* (1973).[67] Although his own analysis focuses on cinema and television, Adam Scovell usefully describes folk horror as 'a type of social media that tracks the unconscious ley lines between a huge range of different forms of media in the twentieth century and earlier'.[68] Further, in terms of its plot, Campbell's novel replicates the pattern of what Scovell defines as a 'folk horror chain': landscape, isolation, 'skewered' belief systems, and a supernatural or pseudo-supernatural 'happening/summoning'.[69]

In such texts, pagan or neo-pagan practices are presented as being identified with, integral to and a confirmation of a community's historical identity as much as they are a 'threat'. With Campbell's novel, this is especially noteworthy in the early establishment of locale, a synthesis of elements of Christianity and paganism:

> Throughout the peaks, towns decorated wells with pictures made of flowers and vegetation, a tradition that combined paganism and Christianity in thanksgiving for the waters that had stayed fresh during the Plague and the Black Death. Watching the townsfolk carrying floral panels big as doors up to Moonwell to fit together at the cave last Midsummer Eve, Diana had felt as if she'd stepped back in time, into a calm that the world was losing.[70]

Into this setting, Campbell introduces a mixture of recognisable topical and generic elements. At the beginning of the novel, the narrative follows Nick Reid, a journalist covering the relocation of a missile base. The employee of a plutocratic newspaper proprietor, he is resigned to having only 'the token left-wing observation of his slip through into print', as the best that could be expected 'when the newspapers were owned by fewer and fewer proprietors and were becoming mouthpieces for bigger and bigger mouths' (p. 46). Given the historical context of the vilification of British anti-nuclear campaigners by national newspapers during this period, the reader's expectations of a critique of the said media and of nuclear power are raised.[71] However, Reid becomes a subordinate if not background character, and, although there is a brief speculation that one of the subsequent ectoplasmic apparitions is a nuclear mutation, the missile base becomes of peripheral importance in the narrative. Similarly, the blonde-haired children brought to Moonwell by Mann's group, clearly recalling the alien brood in John Wyndham's novel, *The Midwich Cuckoos* (1957). disappear half-way through the text. Campbell's preoccupation with *Hungry Moon* lies elsewhere. The novel presents an intense theological conflict, in which widely divergent belief structures and ethical systems are deconstructed and, moreover, shown to be equally destructive.

From one perspective, Campbell's narrative creates a Lovecraftian mythic texture in the manner of the earlier writer's classic story, 'The Dunwich Horror' (1928). It too uses a finely delineated location to attempt to encompass aeons, from the birth of the universe to the present day, as in Lovecraft's tale, the appearance of the monstrous 'other' is deferred and prepared for through the testament of hearsay: 'what's down there is older than Satan' (p. 166), one fearful commentator remarks. As Joshi observes, the figure of Nathaniel Needham, village sage and local historian, clearly recalls and serves the same expository function as the nonagenarian narrator Zadok Allen in 'The Shadow Over Innsmouth', and, like Nahum Gardner's unfortunate wife in Lovecraft's 'The Colour Out of Space' (1927), another character also mutates into a glowing monster.[72] As some critics have argued in relation to Lovecraft's narratives, the proscribed 'other' here is represented as a manifestation of aspects of the subconscious, demonstrated in an early, jocular and self-conscious allusion to the 'whole idea of a deep, dark, evil well' sounding 'pretty Freudian', and one town inhabitant's later reflection on being 'shown a part of himself he didn't recognise' in common with 'virtually the whole of Moonwell' (pp. 111, 231).[73] These manifestations of 'parts' take familiar, often animalistic forms, drawing upon popular herpetophobia and entomophobia as well as, again (and centrally), arachnophobia, the lunar creature being repeatedly compared to a monstrous fusion of human and spider. As in *The Nameless*, alterity is portrayed as abject and loathsome, and physical contact with it as unendurable. What was 'formless' in the earlier novel is now, initially, a desiccated, possessed and ambient human corpse. Its corporeal invasion and merging with the body of the evangelist Godwin Mann in the cave is a literal enactment of Kristeva's notion of utmost abjection, 'death infecting life'.[74] The grotesquely parodic affinity drawn between the procreative act and the negative, repellent and monstrous accords with MacCulloch's description of the moon entity as representing 'the predatory morbid imagination', sterile and hostile to life.[75] Such a misanthropic portrayal is lent further weight elsewhere when a mother throws herself and her new-born deformed baby down a lift shaft, and an ectoplasmic being briefly imitates a couple's miscarried son before mockingly degenerating into a 'beast on all fours' and 'scuttling' away (p. 373). Like *The Nameless*, this text thus portrays its monstrous 'other' in terms of parody, delineating negative and destructive implications for birthing and the next generation. However, alterity as presented in *Hungry Moon* is even more overtly anti-natal: parenting, childbirth and children themselves, as either representation or as experience, are prey for the abject and material for trauma.

There is, though, more than one incarnation of monstrous alterity at work. Godwin Mann's human evangelical group, through fostering bigotry, intolerance and suppression, are presented as being as malevolent as the hybrid compendium of traditional generic images which denote the text's supernatural antagonist. The cult's portrayal is in keeping with what Campbell views as the intellectual suffocation incurred in surrendering unquestioningly to ideology. Mann's sect is enabled to do what it does because Moonwell is, as one inhabitant describes, approvingly – and thus, to the reader, ironically – 'so cut off, safe from outside influences' (p. 85). The implication is that, far from making it 'safe', isolation renders a community vulnerable to insularity, isolationism and predatory extremism. Lane rightly describes the 'infiltration' of the small English town by Mann's group as carrying 'disturbing echoes of right-wing popular movements: Nazism, McCarthyism, Thatcherism'.[76] In himself, Mann, the group's American leader, embodies a reverse colonialism akin to Bram Stoker's Dracula, but his name also evokes an ironic divinity, both in and of humanity, together with an echo of the anarchist and utilitarian philosopher William Godwin.[77] In a long set-piece sermon, Mann articulates the need for a consolatory 'grand narrative', preaching that 'people still need to believe' (p. 50). However, his solution is, obviously, an uncompromising dogmatism. The harmonious accommodation of Christianity and pre-Christian practices in 'thanksgiving' seen at the beginning of the novel is dismissed: 'paganism', Mann declares, 'was always Christ's enemy' (p. 54). Mann's anti-intellectual version of Christianity on the basis that 'you can't think your way to God' (p. 51) offers the exact opposite of free thought, liberation and tolerance. Abnegation of the right to 'think' is also, in its purest form, a surrender of the 'right to question', and represents prostration before a totalising 'belief system'.

Such fundamentalist doctrine finds a ready audience in a community in which scapegoating, ostracism and victimisation of minorities has already been established. Campbell skilfully portrays a social microcosm beset by paranoia, one in which crime has been attributed to 'strangers moving in' and 'hippies squatting in the holiday cottages', anonymised and dehumanised as 'filthy creatures' (p. 24). Like health professionals, teachers in Campbell's fictions, influenced by his own educational experiences, are usually portrayed negatively.[78] Here the headmaster's wife is an embodiment of fascist populism, declaring that children 'aren't here to think, they're here to learn' (p. 91). Even prior to Mann's arrival in the town, Mrs Scraggs launches a petition against the use of a deconsecrated chapel as a bookshop. Mann's subsequent book burning, in which such diverse discourses as *The Joy of Sex*, *A Handbook of Witchcraft*, *Life on Earth* and *A Child's Book of English Folklore* are immolated, demonstrates the invidious collaboration of evangelical Christianity and local politics in the destruction of knowledge, and underlines the anti-intellectual, anti-Enlightenment nature of religious fundamentalism. It is Mann's (and, by symbolic implication, *man's* as shorthand for humankind's) folly which releases the moon entity and its literal and metaphysical darkness. Once the evangelist leader is possessed by the creature, Mann's preaching rhetoric is largely abandoned, the cynicism terse, as in his proclamation on emerging from the cave that 'it's done at last. Praise God as much as you like' (p. 177). Afterwards, the equation of fundamentalism with malignancy is intensified, represented by Scraggs's increasingly hysterical, McCarthyite behaviour and accusatory, almost archaic language. Diana Kramer, who emerges from the novel's ensemble as its eventual heroine, is successively condemned as permissive and irreligious, accused of consorting with the devil and threatened with execution as a witch. Scraggs's vindictiveness echoes Matthew Hopkins in Reeves's *Witchfinder General*, as described by Scovell, in that the character also personifies 'theology used as an excuse to hide the greater sense of sadism under a black veil of piousness'.[79] There is even a final suggestion of communal degeneration into cannibalism. A child being served meat described as tasting like pork is instructed not to 'start getting finnicky over your food' (p. 364). The text does not elaborate further on this theme, but it is possible to infer reference to the subterranean Morlocks in H. G. Wells's *The Time Machine* (1895) and a similar fear of the dark precipitating an inverse evolution, which will 'turn us into cavemen' (p. 166). The clear impression is also of a parody of the Christian sacrament of communion. Such representation of a final atavistic degeneration and perversion may reflect Campbell's own rejection of the Catholicism in which he was raised.

There is certainly interrogative scepticism towards even orthodox religious belief systems. Diana, for example, struggles to find theological certitudes sufficient to explain, much less justify, her own parents' deaths in a plane crash:

> She wondered how Mann would have dealt with that – not so much that God had failed to respond to her prayers, but that if he'd wanted to take her parents he'd taken dozens of others just to do so. Or didn't the individual lives matter to God, just the number of lives, the statistic? All that could justify that sort of behaviour by a god would be life after death. (pp. 60–1)

Later, similarly, the child whose father has been monstrously transformed through contact with the moon entity, finds his confidence that God would not permit 'evil things' to come into the house wilting when he contemplates 'some of the things God let happen in the world, things that were nobody's fault except God's' (p. 242). Reflecting its author's agnosticism, the novel refuses to accord privilege to any one discourse – even where, as in the case of Christian evangelism with its deceptively 'easy' answers, that credo is overtly bogus and demonstrably dangerous. Mann's argument that 'druidic rites' have helped 'evil' establish itself in the world (p. 58) is, in fact, subsequently validated both by Needham's narration and by Diana's vision of Celtic rituals which were intended to appease the moon entity on earth. The apparent absence of God and the advent of evil is a conundrum for which orthodox Christianity appears to have no answers. Father O'Connell, the novel's representative of established churches and belief, is on the one hand portrayed as a reasoning and sympathetic figure. In his statement that 'the notion that you mustn't think your way to faith is obviously not far from the intolerance that leads to burning books' (p. 108), an event literalised later in the novel, the priest expresses a rationalist view which is diametrically opposed to Mann's. This may reasonably be surmised as articulating Campbell's own liberal viewpoint, for the author has professed to 'loathing' totalitarian tendencies in religion and politics, a 'stultification that seems to be designed to take away the creative urge'.[80] Father O'Connell seems to offer some philosophical bulwark against the evangelical insurgency as a transient 'bit of childishness' (p. 35). This confidence is not, though, sufficient to save him from later being savagely killed. Nor does it prevent the priest's body then being mockingly reanimated by supernatural forces in a grotesque parody of a religious service, Diana and others wondering, as his semi-decapitated corpse throws objects about, as 'if it was trying to say mass' (p. 379).

It is Diana, like Mann another American immigrant, who provides the only effective opposition to evil and who, as Gothic heroine, ultimately saves the day. Named after the Roman goddess of the moon and of hunting, she finally becomes the text's representative of 'mother nature'. Joshi describes Diana's 'vision', a chapter-long episode of exposition concerning the emergence and history of the moon entity, as 'an awkward contrivance' on Campbell's part.[81] Yet, while it may be clumsily out of sync with the rest of the novel as a narrative device, imaginatively it is still an extraordinary interpolation of the universal into the quotidian, and Campbell's earliest and, until the *Three Births of Daoloth* trilogy (2016–18), his most sustained attempt to replicate Lovecraft's 'literature of cosmic fear' at novel length. For, clearly, the aim is to convey the sublime: Diana's is an epic journey of 'awesomeness', from the birth of the cosmos through time and space, in which only her 'awe and terror' differentiate her from 'the churning gaseous matter she was part of, spreading across infinity' (p. 313). Campbell even imitates Lovecraft's language in referencing the imprisoned moon entity's ability to influence 'minds in which racial memories of the old worship lingered' (p. 318). This echoes a similar power attributed by the American writer to his 'Old Ones'.[81] Moreover, Diana's experience of the vision demonstrates a prominent duality of theme in Campbell's fictions, namely the struggle to retain a sense of ontological as much as epistemological certainty. Before embarking upon her psychic journey, Diana 'couldn't help holding back, trying to cling to her sense of herself' (p. 312). Other Gothic novels by Campbell in the 1980s, such as *The Parasite* or *The Influence*, address themes of metempsychosis and a disassociation of mind from corporeality. However, it is *Hungry Moon*, in its juxtaposition of the universal and the intimate, the cosmic and the human in scale, which most suggests the vulnerability and, more pointedly, the smallness of the latter. This is in keeping with the materialist quality of cosmic horror that Campbell inherits from Lovecraft, in which the cosmos is vast and humanity is insignificant, but in which the latter must pursue a self-validating path, be it in the form of creation and adherence to tradition or some other form of consolation. From his atheist perspective informed by studies in anthropology, Lovecraft argues that the 'mystic and teleological personification of natural forces' as 'gods' is essential to the 'peasant or workman' to comprehend the cosmos: 'take away his Christian god and saints, and he will worship something else.'[83] The applicability to cults and their appeal in Campbell's as well as Lovecraft's own fictions is obvious here. However, Campbell's agnosticism signifies the development of a specifically secular and humanist perspective. A beleaguered humanism underpins Diana's final, successful, defence against the creature through song, 'a cry for healing', which is described as 'lonely and desperate as the first human voice might have been on the first night of humanity' (pp. 416, 418).

As with *The Nameless*, the conclusion of *Hungry Moon* is sudden and seems rushed. Although Joshi is satisfied that 'the simplicity, poignancy and reaffirmation of humanity' of its ending is 'more effective than any blood and thunder climax could have been', it is still logically problematic.[84] No explanation, after all, is given for Diana's sudden insight or outburst. Further, given the inequity of power between predator and prey detailed in the preceding narrative, the ending can be interpreted as sentimental and unconvincing: it is not clear what exactly needs to be 'healed', nor how the 'lonely and desperate' human voice, precisely because it is so isolated and vulnerable, can overcome the strength and awesome scale, of the alien 'other'. Campbell himself has judged that the novel, with its large ensemble of characters and ideas, consists of 'too many books'.[85] Its plethora of 'mini-narratives' certainly concludes in irresolution and compromise, with, as MacCulloch describes, the curtailment of human evolution only 'narrowly averted' at the finale.[86] However, the ending also clearly suggests the notion of the circularity of history. Needham's earlier speculation that 'the thing down there wiped out all memory of the place until it was ready to come back' (p. 137), after its imprisonment by the Romans, prefigures the creature's climactic reconfinement and the blindness and amnesia, both literal and metaphorical, suffered by Moonwell's population. This refrains another distinctly Lovecraftian idea, that of the 'awesome grandeur of the cosmic cycle', larger than and impervious to the human.[87] The implications are also pessimistic and attain the tenor of warning: populations forget and learn nothing, and history, unless its pattern can be recognised and changed, repeats itself with the reappearance of old dogmas in 'seductive' new forms.

At the Crossroads: Obsession *and After*

Despite the debate that may be had regarding the artistic effectiveness or otherwise of *Hungry Moon*'s climax, its heroine's vision and endeavour to retain a sense of identity and reality accords with Maria Beville's description of Gothic-postmodernism. In Beville's prototype, Gothic-postmodernism features both the subject's experience of 'sublime terror' and their 'struggle for self-knowledge, definition and access to the real', 'reality' being defined in terms of epistemological and ontological certainties.[88] Moreover, as in *The Nameless*, the dramatic climax of *Hungry Moon* contains an element of transcendence. That is, it implies the elevation of a liberal and humane perspective to the status of some essential, possibly even metaphysical 'truth'. Again, this aligns with 'the possibility of supernatural or transcendental existence' which Beville identifies as an intrinsic feature in both the Gothic imagination and postmodernism.[89] This transcendence can be examined in a Gothic text which, differing from these two others, appears to largely eschew overt supernaturalism in its consideration of magic, faith and belief systems, Campbell's 1985 novel, *Obsession*.

Although *Obsession* is another ensemble piece, it is set on an altogether smaller and more domestic scale than *Hungry Moon*, which appeared the following year. Indeed, on the surface, *Obsession* seems to have only slight affinity with the Gothic in terms of plot, and even less in terms of tone. The latter displays more fidelity to a realist, even naturalistic aesthetic, as exemplified in one character's sour realisation, late in the narrative, of spousal infidelity: '[s]o this was how marriages end … messily, absurdly, overbalanced by just a few words' (p. 192). The novel's story line, concerning how a pact made in adolescence by four childhood friends in a small Norfolk coastal town affects them in later life, is, as Joshi notes, a conscious variant on W. W. Jacobs's classic macabre tale of the repercussions of wishes, 'The Monkey's Paw' (1902).[90] Like the other two novels, *Obsession* can immediately be seen to address at least two familiar Gothic concerns: the hidden and covenants. However, in a prime instance of the novel's metatextual flirtatiousness, the actual supernatural content of *Obsession* appears to be minimal. Instead, it consciously prioritises the 'mess' and 'absurdity' of individual psychology. Unlike *The Nameless* or *Hungry Moon*, there is no actual 'monster' here, although another character in its ensemble belatedly and self-consciously dons a skull-face disguise to frighten children and thus becomes a stock horror figure wearing a mask. *Obsession* marks Campbell's first major shift into the foregrounding of the psychological realist aesthetic after the non-supernatural novel, *The Face That Must Die*. Yet it is, as mooted, coquettish: a conflicted and ambiguous text, caught between privileging discourses of rationality and an elevation of the very inheritance of myth and folklore that at one level it eschews. To appropriate Baudrillard's terminology, this is symptomatic of a struggle in postmodernity for aesthetic determinism and self-definition on the part of both the writer and the fictional characters that they create in narratives, amidst – and against – what has become 'a single hyper-real nebula' of simulacra.[91] Ultimate 'truth' is indecipherable and unattainable. There is, therefore, a preference for discourses of 'crisis' and of 'desire' which have an affirmatory value, to 'counter the mortal blows of simulation'.[92] The mini-narratives within *Obsession* illustrate both such endeavours and the vexed ethical compromises which these strivings entail.

Obsession is a curious hybrid of mixed registers, combining subtle psychological realism and sometimes overt social critique. As usual with Campbell, the setting is a distinctly British landscape, this time without an American lead, as in *Hungry Moon*, or even an overseas interlude like *The Nameless*. Campbell's portraiture of the lives of ordinary working- and middle-class people typifies a naturalistic, localised and again rather British sense of understatement. On this observational quality, Lane has described Campbell's novels of the 1980s as having value as cultural indices. He argues that they 'explore the condition of modern life', and 'their historical perspective has the purpose of uncovering [in Foucault's phrase] a history of the present'.[93] Yet whilst this is certainly a redolent quality of these texts, their significance extends beyond the merely reflective to attain a symptomatic status of self-reflexivity. Lane also oversimplifies in claiming that these narratives address what 'appeared to be a right-wing consensus' in British politics, for such homogeneous 'consensus' did not exist. Although Britain was governed by ideologically driven Conservative administrations throughout the 1980s, the period was marked by escalating polarisation between rich and poor; the political right benefited from a divided opposition, and such events as riots across several English cities (1981) and the national miners' strike (1984–5) attest to political fragmentation and acute social conflict during the period.[94] It is more accurate to assert that the texts reflect and mediate such bitter and irreconcilable tensions.

In *Obsession*, on the one hand, mistrust of metanarratives is manifested in a negative portrayal of law enforcement.[95] With the exception of a main character, Jimmy Waters, the state's agents of 'law and order' are unsympathetic creations. The police officers

Dexter and Deedes, the name of the first another instance of Campbell's word play through its derivation from the name of Inspector Morse-creator Colin Dexter, are uncharacterised ciphers. Their pronouncements, like the bigoted Mrs Scraggs's in *Hungry Moon*, are stereotypical, exemplifying the repressive 'stultification' which Campbell rejects, as in Deedes's disagreement with Waters on the 'kind of world' that the latter wants to raise his children in:

> 'I hope', Jimmy said mildly, 'not a world where the innocent are treated like hardened criminals.'
> 'None of us are innocent, Inspector, although too many of us think we are. If fear is taking the place of religion, so be it. Something worthwhile has to.' (pp. 86–7)

Yet, conversely, and to a greater degree than the other novels discussed in this chapter, *Obsession* also foregrounds a strongly autobiographical mode. Campbell's own experiences of dealing with his mother's schizophrenia and death are portrayed in the split, dual form of both Robin Laurel's tensions with her increasingly neurotic parent and the vexed encounters of Peter Priest with his grandmother.[96] In adulthood, both Robin and Peter have taken roles in 'caring' professions, she as a doctor and he as a social worker. The latter has done so as an act of conscious atonement: 'his job was helping people not to grow as desperate as he had been when he'd made the wish' (p. 80). It is these two characters, the guilt-ridden, who articulate belief in supernatural agency. The exact nature and motives of this force are unfocused and mysterious, but are perceived as malevolent. Peter can sense that some external power is feeding on his anxiety, 'though he had no idea of its form or where it was' (p. 202). Robin admits to her mother her involvement in

> I suppose you'd call it magic. I only wanted to help you. Four of us wrote a wish, only there was more to it than just wishing. Some power was invoked, I'm sure of that now, something that took advantage of us, God knows why. The point is, everyone's wish came through in some way. (p. 145)

Such perceptions are akin to 'the lingering emotion of terror' produced by an encounter with the sublime, the undefined, 'unrepresentable' force discussed by Beville. [97]

The novel also seems to endorse a wry critique of both the prevalent materialism of the 1980s and any such expressed sense of a transcendent spirituality or of the numinous being at work. Steve Innes, the childhood communist, grows up to be an estate agent. Both his own family business and eventually Jimmy's wife Tanya are victims of the dilapidation of a theatre which is unsold and being left to rot. As Lane argues, Tanya's eventually fatal accident at the Grand conveys 'the idea that negligence can do as much harm as conscious violence'.[98] Yet, through the state of the theatre being the result of a stalemate between the wishes of the owner and a local council preservation order, it can also be interpreted as an indictment of the government bureaucracy and political machinations symptomatic of late capitalism. The character of Steve also articulates most explicitly the author's own recorded scepticism regarding supernaturalism. Having, in childhood, dismissed their pact as harmless 'fun' (p. 43), in adulthood Steve again tries to pacify Peter through rationalising that 'the supernatural is just something people invent as an excuse for what they want to do themselves' (p. 125), a direct refrain of the author's own view which I alluded to earlier. As with the fate of the priest in *Hungry Moon*, orthodox Christianity appears to be no guarantee of protection against misfortune. Scepticism towards any kind of consolatory religious faith is, if anything, more overt. It is exemplified, above all, at Tanya Waters's funeral, when the bereaved Jimmy savagely if silently equates her mother's attempt to comfort their children with belief in children's fantasies:

> Jimmy stared at the worn stone floor as Tanya's mother told them she was sure Tanya was in heaven because at the last she must have remembered what she'd been brought up to know was the truth. He could feel the children relaxing. If they needed to believe that, he wasn't going to argue. Maybe if they believed hard enough, it would come true, maybe if you clapped your hands to show you believed in fairies, the fairy wouldn't die. He took a breath that stung his nostrils, to keep back the tears. (pp. 150–1).[99]

Such dismissal appears to suggest and underline a prevailing realist pattern. In this respect, *Obsession* looks forward to later narratives like *The Long Lost* (1993) which combine a supernatural element with a prevalent realism, even naturalism, in the portrayal of domestic lives and tragedy. According to Lane, for example, *Obsession* 'deliberately avoids becoming a horror novel; its darkest moments arise through the realistic portrayal of human misery.'[100] It is certainly the case that all four main characters in the narrative undergo psychological anguish, the attribution of which extends beyond guilt. In one image of temporal suspension, Jimmy Waters himself serves to suggest the intense quality of the emotion of grief, embracing his children in a tableau which he wishes 'could go on for ever', for 'at least then, nothing worse could happen' (p. 131). In his role as detective, Jimmy also finally discovers that the address from which the original letter was sent is non-existent. Further, it emerges that the abhorred teacher whom Steve had wished to be removed had suffered a stroke *before* the quartet of friends had committed their wishes in writing. These 'logical' explanations allow a rationalist perspective to concur with Jimmy's viewpoint, and to conclude that there is nothing supernatural in these events – and that, therefore, there is 'nobody and nothing to confront' (p. 278). Naturally, this materialist perspective implicates the belief that there have been paranormal forces at work as being irrational. Peter Priest, as an advocate of such belief, who has by this time emerged from the ensemble to become the novel's antagonist as both a killer and a child-kidnapper, is accordingly portrayed as mentally unstable. This is enough for the critic Gary Crawford to interpret the novel as being partly a study of internalised delusion, in which the character of Peter has 'created a religion at the heart of which there is a mystery', a 'delusory inner light' which finally destroys him.[101] Crawford's argument, drawing upon and drawing out a symbolic quality for the name 'Peter Priest' in a comparison with the biblical figure of Saint Peter, is a compelling one. However, like Lane's reading, this offers an incomplete interpretation of the text.

For while *Obsession* may not be easily classified as 'horror' in terms of presentation of explicit violence, it is still very much a novel infused by consciousness of Gothic tradition. There is, for example, a sense of a spell being cast, of a fateful and irrevocable covenant, in the 'sudden gust of wind' that snatches the pages on which the four friends have written their wishes, and which suddenly loses momentum, plunging the sheets of paper 'together into the dark sea' (p. 44). Obviously, the plot mimics Jacobs's classic cautionary narrative on the 'three wishes' theme, but there are other flirtatious referents at work here. In his analysis of the text, Crawford mentions that the Latin word for wind or breeze is *spiritus*, but curiously omits an overt echo of another familiar work, M. R. James's ghost story, '"Oh Whistle, And I'll Come To You, My Lad"' (1904).[102] In that narrative, of course, a repeated 'gust of wind' against the hapless Parkins's casement serves as an omen for the professor's misfortune after he has, twice, blown the fateful whistle.[103] As in James's story, in which Parkins's colleague suggests that he accompany him on holiday just to 'keep the ghosts off', there is a playful ironising in Jimmy's scolding of Peter Priest that 'you'll be seeing ghosts next if you aren't careful' (p. 40).[104] For a text which seems to prioritise adherence to a realist aesthetic, *Obsession* preserves a persistent fidelity to the tenets of the ghost story. This is demonstrated most obviously in the presentation of the adult Peter's deceased grandmother. The rationalist psychological explanation for her appearances after death is that she is a manifestation of Peter's guilt. This interpretation renders her as purely imaginary and as perceived only by him. However, at various points the text does not preclude a supernatural explanation, implying repeatedly that the spectre is a real, physical presence. For example, the apparition leans into and spatters Peter's face with food. 'This close, and in daylight', the narrative insists, 'there was no doubting that she was real' (pp. 80–1). The grandmother is also seen by other people: a hostile client of Peter's, and by Steve, who thinks that he sees an old lady looking in through the glass at her grandson in hospital. Nor, as Joshi points out, is she the only 'ghost' in the text.[105] In another deployment of the 'demonic child' trope, Jimmy's wife Tanya is lured to her fatal accident in the Grand by what she thinks is a child's voice. It is left ambiguous as to whether her last words, 'up the ladder' (p. 117), allude to a memory of the traumatic fall or something that she had perceived which induced trauma. Tanya and Jimmy's son, Russell, is almost lured into jumping overboard from a boat by what he perceives is a drowning baby calling his name. Hilda, the sister of Roger whom Peter has killed, comes to believe that he has been telephoning her in a disguised voice. Again, it is open to conjecture whether this is in fact Peter masquerading as Roger, but, in the context of other unexplained or ambiguous events, a supernatural interpretation also becomes plausible. Finally, and most crucially, there is a multilayered representation of Peter Priest himself. Crawford astutely connects the description of the sky as 'black glass that white fire kept cracking' (p. 33) in Campbell's novel to the 'sea of glass' in the biblical *Book of Revelation*.[106] However, the text also invites a more explicitly generic comparison. For Peter's shout of 'something, he didn't know what – a plea or a curse – into the storm that was sweeping towards him' (p. 33), echoes Charles Maturin's Gothic novel, *Melmoth the Wanderer* (1820). The attendees at the doomed Melmoth's final hours also cannot distinguish whether they hear 'the shrieks of supplication, or the yell of blasphemy'.[107] As with Maturin's tragic villain, the last scene of Peter's earthly life involves a dramatic, and ambivalent, juxtaposition of land and sea. At the novel's climax, it is stated that Jimmy, the rationalist, is left 'not knowing what Peter had met on the night of the storm, when he finally stopped running' (p. 279). Contrary to Crawford's argument, there is thus a 'mystery' here which is more than a 'delusional religion', and it is one which resists formal closure.

To a greater degree than Campbell's other long fictions of the 1980s, *Obsession* reflects a tension between secular humanist and quasi-religious belief systems. The text appears to align with Beville's concept of the Gothic-postmodernist novel, in functioning 'to resurrect both the real and the fictional in that sublime moment when binary ideologies are destabilised and we are confronted with the unrepresentable'.[108] The novel ends not just on a note of moral transcendence, as the various 'victories' of Angela and Barbara in *The Nameless* and Diana in *Hungry Moon* over the abject 'other' suggest, but on one, via a flashback, of literal transfiguration or rapture. Peter 'never felt himself hit the rocks', the last sentence runs, 'for it seemed to him that the lightning reached for him and lifted him up, towards the light beyond the storm' (p. 280). Peter's psychological journey to this rapturous moment is prefigured in an earlier storm scene, in which there is ambiguity as to whether he is struck by lightning. The rational explication for what Peter undergoes in this primal scene, that is, that he experiences symptoms induced by an earlier head injury which had been inflicted by his grandmother's attackers, coexists with portentous tenets of folklore and mythology. The episode happens at a crossroads, an archetypal liminal space between the natural and supernatural realms. Peter also senses, with dread, 'as if he'd called something that was rushing towards him, at his back, now in his brain' (p. 33). The language of powerlessness and invasion, in which 'the light seemed to be in him as well as outside him' (p. 34), recalls the theologian Rudolph Otto's description of 'the speechless humility' of a human subject, at the moment when it is 'submerged and overwhelmed' by its encounter with the numinous, or 'that which is a mystery inexpressible and above all creatures'.[109] As with Otto, the 'mystery' is simultaneously, and paradoxically, both frightening and fascinating, an experience of 'dread' and 'awe' which brings the subject into proximity with the sublime.[110] Peter feels both helpless and as if he has been granted the gift of insight and clarity by the experience:

> Everything had the sudden glassy clarity of a slide snapped into the holder of his eyes, and he couldn't close them, for the light was behind them too. It was lasting too long for lightning, but he didn't care what it was; he welcomed it in a breathless, terrified way – he could do nothing else. (p. 34)

Otto describes the 'magical' as 'nothing but a suppressed or dimmed form of the numinous, a crude form of which great art purifies and ennobles'.[111] The theologian's description can serve to articulate the struggle undergone by characters in *Obsession* to explain their lives and relationships to forces perceived as being outside themselves. These forces are but dimly comprehended – and thus described as 'magic' – but are keenly felt as being more powerful than the experiencing subject. The personal and humanist thus coexist with a sense of the cosmic and numinous. *Obsession* displays to the full Campbell's 'timid' insecurities about the perception and experience of universals, and about the sense of self, within a secular culture. Like Peter Priest, its tragic victim-villain, *Obsession*, both realist and non-realistic, is a text at the 'crossroads'. It incarnates in fictional form what Hazleton describes as 'the creative value of doubt' and of 'mystery'.[112]

In his application of Otto's account of the 'non-rational' to define the purpose of, and ascribe an ontological structure to, a range of Gothic fictions, the critic S. L. Varnado cites Campbell as amongst the modern writers who have successfully emulated Lovecraft in displaying a 'sophisticated employment of techniques and themes developed by earlier masters of the genre'.[113] Arguably, as Campbell has admitted, this 'sophistication', especially of technique, has not always applied to his endings. The swift, almost abrupt conclusion of *Obsession*, as with *The Nameless* in particular, may appear from one perspective to be artistically problematic, demonstrative of an authorial preoccupation with a formal convention of closure which is actually at variance with the issues of irresolution and 'mess' addressed in the text. For example, like Angela's moral *volte-face* in *The Nameless*, Peter's rapid progression from child kidnapper to a potential child murderer who then equally suddenly repents – on the grounds that 'as soon as he'd seen the light come back into their eyes, he'd known that he wouldn't be capable of harming them' (p. 268) – arguably stretches psychological plausibility. From another perspective though, such a paradox is fully consistent and logical, given the context of the strain of besieged but persistent liberal humanism which permeates Campbell's works. His fictions display an acute sensitivity towards, and mediate, their vexed social and historical contexts. The ill-fated leader of Enoch's Army, a 'New Age' movement in Campbell's novel written at the end of the 1980s, the aforementioned *Ancient Images*, articulates a markedly jaundiced, Baudrillardian perspective on the efficacy of artistic representation. On the subject of violence, Enoch complains that he and his followers have been scapegoated, 'made into fictions', and dismisses all fictional works as 'an act of violence' and 'revenge on the world by people who don't like it but haven't the strength to change it' p. (113). However, Campbell's own fictions continuously exhibit engagement with profound formal and ethical challenges and contradictions. His works display a mistrust of metanarratives, and especially, as shown here, forms of religious dogma and the perils of following leadership blindly, which resonates fully with Campbell's agnostic and secular vision. It is timely to consider in more detail Campbell's complex and unique anatomisation of societal conventions and the relationships between atomised, struggling subjects. Accordingly, the next chapter focuses upon Campbell's representations of the antisocial phenomenon of violence itself, especially that perpetrated by the generic figure of the 'killer'.

2

Of Bonds and Beings: Campbell's Gothic Sociopaths

ಖಡ

A 'Therapeutic Culture' and Its Discontents

This chapter focuses on purely secular metanarratives as represented in three of Campbell's key non-supernatural novels appearing over three decades: *The Face That Must Die* (1983), *The One Safe Place* (1995) and *Secret Story* (2005). *Face* and its successors are all tales about violence. They signify another expression of the Gothic in that they feature killers who operate, in contrast with Peter Priest in *Obsession*, under unambiguously non-paranormal influence. Specifically, these texts reflect and transmute a prominent historical manifestation of the contemporary Gothic: the serial killer. The Gothic has functioned, as Philip L. Simpson describes, as the 'earliest breeding ground' for the 'moral leprosy' of the repeat murderer narrative. It is a trend that has attained an enduring popularity and relevance in Anglophone fiction, film and television.[1] Further, however, they represent a deconstruction of certain sociopolitical norms. According to Jean-François Lyotard, in addition to its totemic religious beliefs, society has also defined and maintained its 'competence' by a shared consensual narrative surrounding certain civic maxims, involving history, tradition, community and family.[2] In Campbell's iconoclastic vision, such cosy consensual understandings are undermined.

Campbell's notably melancholic anatomisation of society and of the psyche of the individuals who constitute it has a corollary in the analysis of a 'devitalised existence' given in Julia Kristeva's *Black Sun* (1989), although, as a psychoanalyst, Kristeva resists a cultural interpretation or contextualisation for mental illness.[3] Kristeva writes of the experience of depression:

> Absent from other people's meaning, alien, accidental with respect to naïve happiness, I owe a supreme metaphysical lucidity to my depression. On the frontiers of life and death, occasionally, I have the arrogant feeling of being witness to the meaningless of Being, of revealing the absurdity of bonds and beings.[4]

The reference to 'Being' is clearly Sartrean: Kristeva's depressive persona experiences a 'loss of being – and of Being' itself – and becomes 'a radical, sullen atheist'.[5] Such professed 'alienation' does more, though, than suggest psychological displacement of the individual. Lyotard maintains that 'no self is an island', even within the complex and potentially isolating 'fabric of relativism' that characterises postmodernity, while the American psychologist Kenneth J. Gergen goes further, deeming postmodernism to be the product of 'an array of technologies' that has 'saturated us with the voices of others' and 'immersed us in an array of relationships' to an unprecedented degree.[6] Over the last half century there has been a spiralling increase in the forms and sophistication of communication, and a commensurate expansion in diagnostic health services in the West, including psychiatry. All these developments are symptomatic of what Robert M. Collins calls 'a therapeutic culture of self-regard'.[7]

Yet, while accepting that our capitalistic culture is characterised by introversion and self-diagnostics, Kristeva's description implicitly suggests an estrangement from such 'voices of others' and 'relationships', the vital guarantors of social cohesion. It conveys liminality and detachment from society, even a rejection of engagement that borders on, if not narcissism, then a belief in individual exceptionalism. Such conscious self-separation and self-elevation, where the subject is simultaneously beyond and somehow *above* the 'absurdity' of social bonding with, and thus social obligation to, 'other people', can be interpreted as a form of antisocial behaviour that is, at best, passive-aggressive, and at worst destructive. As Jean Baudrillard observes in *The Consumer Society* (1970), there is an insidious double bind in social relationships. The negative emotional experiences of 'fatigue, depression, neurosis', he maintains, are 'always convertible into violence and vice versa'.[8] With respect to 'violence', I broadly accept the definition given by Oxford Living Dictionaries as denoting individual or collective behaviours involving physical force that are intended to harm or kill living beings, although the facticity of mental as well as physical agency and suffering is a vital qualifier.[9] Whatever definition is employed, it is inescapable that predatory violence, both individual and social, is a central theme in Campbell's work.

In particular, the figure of 'the killer' recurs in Campbell's longer fictions from his first novel, *The Doll Who Ate His Mother*, to, at least, *Think Yourself Lucky* (2014). As expected, a sense of threat to the subject's physical and psychological wellbeing, to the point of the infliction of death, permeates his supernatural writings. The perceived or actual capacity of paranormal forces or creatures, or of beings under their influence, human or otherwise, to cause harm are integral to the conception, design and effectiveness of these narratives in the representation or evocation of fear – just as they had been to M. R. James, H. P. Lovecraft and other Gothic forebears whose influence Campbell has openly acknowledged. This said, whether or not the tenets of supernaturalism are deployed, most of the texts discussed in this book focus upon the deliberate terrorisation and even murder, or contemplation of murder, visited by humans upon other humans. Aside from the lauding of his short stories and the evocation of an urban milieu alluded to in my Introduction, it is the understanding and portrayal of such abnormal psychology that has earned Campbell most critical recognition. S. T. Joshi, for example, notes how the author's numerous crime fictions 'probe diseased minds and mental illness with uncomfortable intensity'.[10] Commenting on contemporary trends in the mid-1980s, Campbell himself has declared an abiding interest in the link between crime and horror, 'terror and insanity', in 'psychological horror novels'.[11]

According to Campbell, the subgenre of 'psychological horror' intends to disturb. It shows an audience 'what it would otherwise find hard to bear', and to this purpose the writer admits to finding early inspiration in the 'recurring urban nightmare' presented in texts such as Jim Thompson's *The Killer Inside Me* (1952).[12] It is highly indicative that the central character and antagonist in Thompson's novel is a multiple murderer, or *serial* killer.

Campbell's own fictions are distinguished by a consciousness of violence, and, repeatedly, the potency of the criminal 'other' that is the serial killer. There are conflicting opinions as to both the historical origin of this term and its precise definition. For convenience, this book accepts the United States' Federal Bureau of Investigation's revised definition (1996) of serial killing as 'a series of two or more murders committed as separate events, usually but not always by one offender acting alone'.[13] What is beyond dispute is the impact of the serial killer upon the *zeitgeist* of western culture over the last four decades, as manifested in both news media coverage of real-life events and in popular forms of entertainment. Factually, despite the murderous activities of many pre-twentieth-century historical figures such as Liu Pengli and Gilles De Rais, the serial killer has become, as Anthony King describes, a 'dominant cultural representation' since the late 1960s, in the wake of such criminological landmarks as the 'Moors Murderers' and Manson 'family' trials.[14] Amongst the substantial corpus of works that coincided with Campbell's emergence and establishment as a novelist, Colin Wilson and David Seaman's *The Serial Killers: A Study in the Psychology of Violence* (1991) typifies non-fictional discourses. Although tracing serial murder back to the nineteenth-century H. H. Holmes and 'Jack the Ripper' cases, Wilson and Seaman's study portrays the serial killer as a relatively recent and 'alarming' post-war phenomenon.[15] Noting a record number of 23,000 murders in the United States in 1980, Wilson and Seaman describe that country as a 'fortress society'.[16] The authors label the 1970s as 'positively a vintage decade for serial killers', and warn that the exterior 'civilized world' is 'only just waking up to 'the threat' that they pose.[17] Aside from the morally problematic comparison of murderers like Ted Bundy and John

Wayne Gacy to the pleasures of viticulture, Wilson and Seaman offer some serious analysis. However, their book exemplifies and encapsulates an enduring dichotomy of simultaneous condemnation and fascination with what is proscribed. This is revealed more recently in the market for 'murderabilia' exemplified by the *Serial Killer Calendar: Murder, Madness and Merchandise* website; the burgeoning 'true crime' publications industry and the continuing stream of television programmes such as the British documentary television series, *Born to Kill?* (TwoFour Productions, 2005–12).[18] The commodification, fascination and familiarity associated with the serial killer have caused this socially aberrant individual to become what David Schmid describes as 'the exemplary modern celebrity'.[19]

With respect to fictional representations, the serial killer has also been ambiguously respected by Campbell's peers. These include Joyce Carol Oates, whose own serial killer novel *Zombie* appeared in 1995 and who has described the repeat murderer as an 'icon of popular culture'.[20] Wilful aesthetic transgression within a culture that is already prone to paranoia finds a natural channel of artistic expression in the Gothic, the mode of writing that Fred Botting defines pithily as 'a literature of excess'.[21] Conflation of the act of repeat killing with the figure of the lone 'psychopath', broadly defined as 'a mentally-ill or unstable' person, especially one 'affected with anti-social personality disorder', affords a transmutation of the traditional, and usually male, Gothic villain into a figure of myth: a demonised 'other' or 'monster'.[22] Despite conscientious medical distinction, from a literary perspective there has been little attempt to differentiate between manifestations of mental illness, whether they take the forms of psychosis, schizophrenia or paranoia, in the transmedia narratives of fear that have permeated Western culture. For example, Dr Chilton casually describes Hannibal Lecter as 'a monster, a pure psychopath' in Ted Tally's screenplay for *The Silence of the Lambs* (1991), Jonathan Demme's film adaptation of Thomas Harris's 1988 novel.[23] *The Silence of the Lambs*, in both its literary and cinematic forms, is one of many now familiar texts alongside its prequel and sequels, Brett Easton Ellis's *cause célèbre* novel *American Psycho* (1991; filmed in 2000 by Mary Harron) and Jeff Lindsay's *Dexter* series (2004–15; adapted for television, 2006–13). Schmid notes a 'cult' around Lecter in particular that betokens an abiding 'fascination and admiration'.[24] In fact it is more accurate to describe Harris's cultured and savage creation as a veritable cultural industry, with, to date, four novels, five cinematic adaptations and an NBC television series (*Hannibal*, 2013–15).

Amidst the many cultural manifestations, two tendencies are prominent and of relevance to an evaluation of Campbell's contribution to this burgeoning field. One, as demonstrated by the 'Lecter' narratives, is an obvious generic hybridity, a trend towards what Catherine Spooner describes as crime fictions becoming increasingly 'Gothicised' in the 1980s and 1990s.[25] This can be discerned not only in Harris's marriage of Gothic tropes and the epistemological police procedural, but in writings such as Patricia Cornwell's 'Kay Scarpetta' (1990–present) and John Connolly's 'Charlie Parker' (1999–present) series, the latter of which fuses neo-noir construction of the detective protagonist, complete with 'hard-boiled' dialogue, and supernatural elements, exemplified by *The Black Angel* (2005). The other, in both the primary and secondary literature, is an overwhelming geographic bias: the serial killer, in terms of creative outputs and critical analysis, has hitherto been predominantly a phenomenon of the *United States*. For example, the Irish writer Connolly makes Parker a former New York policeman, whose adventures take him across North America, the author variously adapting New England idioms and Southern Gothic motifs as appropriate. Accordingly, the voluminous scholarship on the serial killer has shown a largely US-centric bias. Academic analyses by Simpson, Schmid, Mark Seltzer and Richard Tithecott variously assume that serial murder has become defined as 'a particularly American crime', descant upon the serial killer's relationship to 'America's wound culture', or, more bluntly, and simplistically, deem this figure 'an American problem'.[26]

Whatever kind of 'problem' the serial killer is, popular culture has certainly aestheticised this antisocial character. Lecter as aberrant psychiatrist, for example, is an inspired choice of villain for a so-called 'therapeutic culture'. 'I know he's a monster', the FBI director tells Clarice Starling in Harris's novel *The Silence of the Lambs*, but 'beyond that, nobody can say for sure'.[27] Literary scholar Peter J. M. Connelly and criminologists Sarah Hodgkinson, Hershel Prims and Joshua Stuart Bennett have noted the obscurantist and 'reductionist' consequences of such mythologising.[28] For Connelly, whose own research ranges across fictional and non-fictional examples of the phenomenon, from Thomas De Quincy's account of the Ratcliffe highway murders (1811) through Shelley's *Frankenstein* to writings by real-life murderers Carl Panzram, Donald Gaskin and Ian Brady, portraying the serial killer aesthetically euphemises consequentiality – that is, the brutal reality of the act of killing and the victim's suffering involved in murder.[29] In his discussion of Lecter, Connelly differentiates between 'psychopathy', which is indicative of innate biological or genetic causality, and 'sociopathy', suggestive of environmental influences.[30] The two descriptors are often employed interchangeably, but the division is extremely pertinent in discussion of Campbell, whose fictional antagonists are explicitly *sociopaths*: human 'monsters' produced by and reflecting their environments which have manifested dysfunctionality in the form of societal and familial abuse. For Hodgkinson, Prins and Stuart-Bennett, mystification by the media, placing the serial killer outside 'our moral universe', also serves, regrettably, to 'dehumanise' the perpetrator as 'evil', and distracts from the increased understanding of such behaviours that could be yielded by a sociocultural approach.[31] Such sociological ideas as Hodgkinson and her colleagues list – on inequality, the anonymity rendered by increased urbanisation, the growth of mass media, rise of celebrity culture and a self-justifying means/end rationality – are, again, highly relevant in the placement and evaluation of Campbell's long fictions with respect to sociopolitical metanarratives.[32]

The writings of Campbell that are discussed in this chapter arise from and are informed by this cultural context. This notwithstanding, both singly and cumulatively they constitute a radical departure from the dominant ideologies and artistic practices delineated here. To begin with, they retain mostly British settings, and they thus inherently reflect and transmute national as well as local political and social mores. Further, the milieu of these texts is deliberately deglamourised and prosaic, with socially unelevated characters. While maintaining a connection to Gothic tradition, especially to that of the urban Gothic, these fictions develop a progressively more overt alignment with literary postmodernism. As indicated, when it comes to primary sources, there is no shortage of choice, given that this writer has returned to the subject of killing repeatedly in fittingly 'serial' fashion. However, *Face*, *One Safe Place* and *Secret Story* are stylistically varied and innovative to a marked degree, as well as being, as this book demonstrates, seminal texts within Campbell's *oeuvre*. Each illuminates a different aspect of a singular vision. The first, Campbell's short sophomore novel, *Face*, establishes its author's prosaic, starkly anti-romantic tonality in its depiction of warped psychology. The killer here is the opposite of the aristocratic and charismatic anti-hero, while the narrative parodies conventions of detective fictions. With *One Safe Place*, perhaps Campbell's most atypical and ambitious novel, the scope is broadened to critique the origins of violence across Anglo-American culture; the culpability of mass media within it; and the genesis and construction of a young killer. Finally, having deglamourised what had become, as discussed, an aestheticised figure, Campbell simultaneously *re*constructs the serial killer, this time as author, and *de*constructs the repeat murderer narrative in the satirical Gothic novel *Secret Story*. A metatextual tendency that was present in *One Safe Place*, despite it being a quite different kind of narrative, comes to the fore. This harbingers an increasing preoccupation with creative aesthetics and philosophical issues concerning the subject and boundaries between fiction and reality. These texts are examined with reference to two well-known novels, *The Silence of the Lambs* and *American Psycho*. It is an incidental benefit that such study implies that Campbell's less familiar fictions stand artistic comparison to these two now iconic works. The primary intention is to demonstrate Campbell's critique of secular grand narratives, to explore his alignment to a postmodern position and vision, and to explicate his reframing of the parameters of the Gothic.

An Encounter with 'Medusa': The Face That Must Die

It is no coincidence that the dark flowering of Campbell's imagination as a writer of substantive fictions about violence and its perpetrators coincides with the abandonment of post-war Keynesian consensual politics embodied in the extended period of right-wing Conservative governments (1979–97) in Britain, led primarily by Margaret Thatcher. Although as a conservative politician, it must be caveated that Thatcher would probably not recognise the comparison, her argument that 'there is no such thing as society' has a certain affinity with postmodernism in its explicit social atomisation, and thus dissolution of what had served as a prevailing metanarrative.[33] In the political sphere, the principles undermined by monetarism and other ideologies embraced and embodied by the Thatcher governments included certain hitherto widely accepted assumptions and expectations. These included aspirations for full employment; amelioration to extreme disparities of wealth; sufficient care for the socially and economically vulnerable, and even any concern for civic cohesion expressed in exercise of mutual respect between individuals and groups. According to Colin Hutchinson, much British fiction of the 1980s articulated a causal connection between the advent of Thatcherism and 'growing levels of [civic] hostility', but suggested that the values fostered were 'essentially alien imports', the 'alien' source of this usurpation being the United States.[34] Campbell's post-1979 novels reflect and engage with the fracturing, decay and radical reorientation of belief structures, but suggest that such tensions were transcultural, and, in a British context, indigenous and already present.

Face is Campbell's first non-supernatural novel. Set in Liverpool, this stark, spare narrative recounts how John Horridge, a paranoid schizophrenic living on invalidity benefit, conceives a delusional belief that an innocent man, Roy Craig, a homosexual, is responsible for several local murders of young men. The deluded Horridge, assuming a mission he imagines himself 'meant' to undertake, becomes an urban vigilante and a serial killer himself.[35] During the course of events, Horridge murders Craig and one of Roy's neighbours to cover his tracks. He also crosses paths with and finally terrorises a young couple, Cathy and Peter Gardner, two other neighbours of Craig's, who he thinks can implicate him. After a climactic struggle in a quarry, an ambiguous coda implies that Horridge has survived and pursued the Gardners to their new home.

As in *Obsession*, there is plainly some refracted autobiographical influence at work here. Cathy, the heroine, works in a public library, while her husband Peter, a mature hippy-ish student who experiments with drugs and researches in conspiracy theory and paranoia, is also clearly intended to represent the author. Beyond the obvious metatextuality, it is Campbell's barbed commentary on generic and social conventions that is striking. Although the novel is a third-person narrative, the opening of *Face* immediately assumes the embittered and obsessive perspective of Horridge. Like *The Killer Inside Me*, the narrative's protagonist is simultaneously its antagonist. 'Why should he deny himself?' Horridge asserts, seeking to prolong the pleasure of savouring boiled sweets on a bus, for 'he hadn't had much in his life' (p. 5). These terse sentences also establish much that distinguishes Campbell's vision, not just in this narrative but its successors: the allusion to past abuse and to implication of low social status (indicated here by reliance upon public transport); the quotidian urban setting and solace in modest pleasures taken by the economically compromised and socially isolated; and, above all, the notably bitter tone. Campbell presents a literature of *resentment*. Notions of civic responsibility and social bonding have broken down or are entirely absent. The urban landscape across which Horridge limps is similarly bleak, conveying historical indifference to liberal, nostalgic sensitivities. Description of the loss of his childhood playground develops the distinctively sour and bleak imagery of the short story 'Concussion' a decade earlier. Horridge wonders despairingly:

> What had they done to the end of the street? Beyond the crossroads there had been a similar terrace; he'd used to imagine he was gazing into a mirror. Now there was nothing but mud ... Where four streets had stood, there was an enormous square of desolation, surrounded by derelict houses that looked shrunken by the waste ... Smoke wandered over the mud, where puddles shone in ruts left by bulldozers. (p. 65)

It is, at once, an anaemic vista of urban post-Blitz malaise, drudgery, conformity and the new destruction of nostalgic sensibility wrought by forces – the impersonal, philistine and insensitive 'they' – of modern mechanisation. The blighted landscape and sense of despair seems to reflect in literal form what Fredric Jameson describes as the 'waning' of a 'sense of history' and 'resistance to globalist or totalising concepts, like that of the mode of production itself', that are inherent in postmodernism and the advent of late capitalism.[36]

The autobiographical aspect of *Face* has been well delineated, not least by Campbell himself, who has admitted that Horridge is based partly upon his mother and his memories of her mental illness. Of more significance is the date of the narrative's conception and its publishing history. First appearing in an abridged form in 1979, Campbell's text pre-dates the 'boom' in the literature of serial killing by almost a decade. Harris may be, as Simpson claims, the acclaimed 'creator of the serial killer formula' with the first Lecter narrative, *Red Dragon* (1981), but it is arguable that Campbell quietly owns the patent – that is, he might have done, if his long fictions were at all 'formulaic'.[37] Moreover, it is revealing that Campbell's novel was rejected by several publishers because of its 'grim' subject matter.[38] It is suspected that this is not primarily because of the descriptions of violence, which, unlike, for example, *American Psycho*, a text which also had a complex publication history, are brief and elliptical. The convoluted journey of *Face* rather stems from Campbell's lack of compromise: the novel's firmly parochial location, eschewing charm or glamour; the lack of a convincing romantic interest (Peter Gardner, for example, is hardly a heroic presence), and, above all, its sheer intensity of description. Writing decades later, Joshi described *Face* as still Campbell's 'most chilling treatment of paranoia' and 'the supreme epitome of urban horror'.[39] The novel's central character has been forced into liminal status, both physically and mentally. At one point, Horridge's mind is described as 'clenched', vice-like: 'it squeezed his thoughts into a small hard impregnable mass that felt as though it might explode and sear his head with pain' (p. 168). In the tradition of peculiarly claustrophobic urban Gothic familiar from cinematic texts like Roman Polanski's 'Apartment Trilogy' (1965–76) or David Lynch's *Eraserhead* (1978), the protagonist experiences a sense of persecution in which everything appears to be addressing him, and is haunted by hallucinations like 'the voice of the plumbing' (p. 29) in which the explicable, the natural and the imaginary are combined.[40] Horridge's persecution complex and sense of enclosure exemplify a feature of the subject's lack of 'ontological autonomy' described by the psychiatrist R. D. Laing in his observations of schizophrenic patients.[41] According to Laing's existentialist paradigm, 'to the schizoid individual every pair of eyes is a Medusa's head which he [*sic*] feels has power to actually kill or deaden something precariously vital in him.'[42] Indeed, this novel seems to dramatise vividly what Linda Hutcheon describes as a paranoid 'terror' within postmodernity, that it is really someone else, an external other, who is 'plotting, ordering, [and] controlling our life for us'.[43] Horridge's personality and behaviour are aberrant, antisocial, hellish – but he is also, in his psychotic delusions, experiencing a form of hell.

Such a depiction of psychological disturbance, with its potential to disturb the reader, partly accounts for the novel's comparative lack of popular acclaim. The content, denoted by a villainous lead, is far from what David Punter describes as the final 'deliberate refutation of the psychotic' typified, for example, in Harris's fusion of the Gothic and crime narratives.[44] On the contrary, *Face* and its successors align with Simpson's observation that that while there is an ideology of conservatism underlying the challenge to epistemological limits posed in such texts, 'it is impossible to suppress a text's own internal resistance to a unified authorial voice'.[45] In one scene midway through *Face*, Horridge, a frequent patron at the library where Cathy works, scans the shelves and observes balefully:

> Fiction, fiction, fiction. Adventure and horror were mixed on the shelves, as though one might be a consequence of the other. Detective stories displayed fingerprints on their spines. He grunted low with mirth. That was the one way the police might have caught him.
> (p. 115)

In this passage, Campbell slyly encapsulates the novel's entire plot. In typically protean, nonconformist fashion, *Face* parodies and inverts the conventions of detective fiction. As in *Obsession*, the metanarrative of law is compromised, not this time through the stereotypical representation of its agents as ciphers, but through metatextual misrecognition and reappropriation. The ominously named Fanny Adams, who is to become Horridge's second victim, mistakes him for a private investigator, with a sweet tooth 'like one of the idiosyncrasies novelists gave their detectives' (p. 82).[46] Cathy, her professional life spent working in an environment of 'fictions', not only misrecognises Horridge as a policeman and incorporates him into a Holmesian-sounding fictional mystery of her own, 'the incident of the limping man' (p. 34), but assumes the role of trailing detective herself, enjoying the slow pursuit which she likens to 'a parody of a car chase' (p. 173). Ironically, her self-conscious investigation brings Cathy to the killer's attention and increases her and her husband's endangerment. This is an atomised, compartmentalised environment in which individual lives are shown as isolated and vulnerable to predation. After Craig's murder, Cathy muses of homosexuals that 'sometimes their emotions must be too much for them. It's a different world' (p. 108). At the novel's conclusion, Fanny, the couple's other ill-fated neighbour, is remembered purely for the legacy of paintings she bequeathes, which 'might be an investment' (p. 230). The 'world' depicted by Campbell is one where the value of lives is interpreted reductively, in this case in terms of financial commodification.

Functionally, the greatest paradox is, of course, that Horridge, the villain of this narrative, also perceives himself as, and enacts the role of, detective. His psychology and behaviour as an adult continue in violent forms the persecution complex he has held against society for being questioned about cat burglaries as a child. The thought patterns of Horridge's investigative 'research', characterised by wild displays of cognitive dissonance – for example, he concludes that Craig must be guilty because his name 'sounded too masculine, too strong, that betrayed it – that and the fact that "Roy" was a little like "gay"' (pp. 37–8) – reveal the depth of his mental aberration.

Face is the first novel to feature what was to become a recognisable staple in Campbell's writing: the unreliable narrator. All exterior events, no matter how disparate and disconnected, are internalised and transformed to have a relevance to Horridge's own life. In one of the few references to then recent external political events (the 'Watergate' scandal, 1972–4), Horridge, conflating public and private realms of experience, asserts:

> he knew about conspiracies; the world was full of them. Even presidents could be involved in them, which showed that anyone might be. Sometimes the plotters were careless enough to be found out, but what of those who weren't? What about those homosexuals and their dupes, conspiring against him? (pp. 177–8)

The character's paranoia aligns with the conventions of urban Gothic as seen in *The Nameless*. All Campbell's narratives about killing refrain Gothic familiar tropes such as the vulnerability and abuse of children and of women; abduction and threat; confinement; terrorisation and the haunted site or what Stephen King calls the 'Bad Place' archetype, transmuted to a contemporary setting. In contrast though to, for example, Lecter's physical alterity, denoted by characteristics like the character's polydactyly and vampire-like 'maroon eyes' behind which lies 'endless night', Campbell's villain is a study in bland anonymity.[47] Horridge is plain, 'fortyish, bland and scrubbed' (p. 78), and a man about whose appearance Cathy and Peter cannot agree a single feature at the novel's end. The killer's home, a council estate named Cantril Farm, is similarly closed and homogenised, looking 'like its purpose, to make everyone the same' (p. 41).

Horridge's lack of physical distinction, his sheer *un*remarkableness, is consistent with the attribution of a non-metaphysical origin for negative and destructive forces defined as 'evil'. Prior to *Hannibal* (2000), which by delineating a history for Lecter pathologises the character, Harris's criminal psychiatrist rejects behaviourism and insists on his own 'evil' as causality. In *The Silence of the Lambs*, Lecter declares that '[n]othing happened to me, Officer Starling. I happened. You can't reduce me to a set of influences.'[48] However, Campbell's interpretation of the phenomenon of wickedness aligns with the philosopher Alan Morton's view that 'a large proportion of evil in the world is the result of actions of people well within the range of normal activities of social life'.[49] Similarly, Wilson and Seaman's ascription of a sexual motivation for their antisocial behaviour, a point developed by Connelly in his discussion of a 'sex/crime meme', is patently not a motivation for Horridge or Campbell's other killers.[50] Instead, their actions are determined by a perceived need to recover and exert power. Moreover, they originate in the primal trauma of physical and emotional abuse at the hands of other, socialised beings. These are crimes generated by environment, by nurture rather than nature. Horridge's abused childhood, with memories of being dragged off a ladder for nocturnal enuresis and masturbation and of being blamed for his mother's early death by his drunken father, is alluded to repeatedly. His own violent actions can be interpreted as a partial retaliation for the memory of stripping of identity signified by his father's taunt: '[s]ometimes I wonder if he's my son. Maybe they gave us someone else's by mistake' (p. 66). Above all, as in Horridge's questioning of his own masculinity for not telephoning the police about the crimes that he imagines that Craig has committed, the character fears being emasculated and feminised. It is a fear that propels his pathological homophobia. Rather than endorsing the dominant culture's assumptions of some metaphysical or innate genetic cause for crime, then, the facticity of the killer's sociopathy and transgression to murder in Campbell's fictions serve to indict aspects of the host society's implicitly violent and regressive prevailing ideological system.

The portrayal of killers and the society they inhabit in *Face* and subsequent narratives represents what Jameson and any other left-wing or liberal commentator might lament as 'the utter eradication of what used to be called idealism'.[51] Horridge is portrayed as obsessively homophobic and, variously, anti-feminist, anti-Semitic, xenophobic and racist. From the jaundiced observation regarding 'students tripping on their drugs – sooner or later they'd trip themselves up' (p. 8) onwards, the expression of reactionary prejudices throughout are both explicit and relentless. Almost every thought presented, as when homosexuals are deemed 'a cancer on the human race, perhaps even its source . . . as closed as Jews, protecting one another from normal people' (p. 47), conveys an acid and acrid malevolence. Depiction of civic hostility, as seen with the malevolent headmaster's wife in *The Hungry Moon*, is a recurrent feature in Campbell's fictions. Such a harsh social landscape aligns with the portrayal of 'a decay of the public realm' described by Hutchinson as typifying Anglo-American fictions under the prevailing neoliberalism of the late twentieth century.[52] It is a trend, indeed, still ascendant in the twenty-first, albeit under the guise of right-wing 'populism'. Horridge, rigidly puritanical and thus the antithesis of the random sex killer, is described as hating people who 'corrupted' the young. The character incarnates an endlessly misanthropic reaction against the liberal social reforms regarding homosexuality, race relations, drug culture and feminism represented by the 1960s. For example, on hearing about the mugging of a pensioner by a gang of girls, he concludes that this is the inevitable consequence of 'women's liberation' (pp. 23–4). Against such 'corruption', Horridge sees himself as nothing less than a crusader, charged with making the world 'cleaner' (p. 180). As, thus, a *counter*-'counter-culture' figure, Horridge aligns with what Hutchinson describes as the political right's re-evaluation and condemnation of that earlier decade, the 1960s, as being 'to blame for the damage done to social cohesion and to family values', even though, politically, it is 'they', the political right, as proponents and agents of free market capitalism and consumerism, who have actually been driving the 'bulldozers' that have threatened and indeed demolished such ideals.[53] The deliberate irony with respect to the extreme moral relativism dramatised in *Face* is that the 'traditional' moral and social values system which Horridge, the supreme 'Thatcherite', proceeds to promote with such messianic zeal, is undermined by its advocate's equally extreme antisocial personality and destructive behaviour.

Although rooted in its time, *Face* addresses a strain of illiberal politics that is instantly recognizable and which has retained its currency. Campbell acknowledges the lasting resilience of such belief systems through careful portrayal of a psyche as self-validating as it is warped and fragile. Aside from his ambiguous fate, to the end, Horridge maintains a belief that his actions are 'right and necessary' (p. 88), and that through committing his murders he has 'conquered evil' (p. 165) and cleansed or 'exorcised' (p. 139) his world. In a trait shared with both real and other fictional serial killers, and which is developed in the later *Secret Story*, Horridge simultaneously both avidly consumes the press coverage of acts that he has perpetrated and deplores seeing 'his exploit served up as entertainment to the mob' (p. 112).[54] Significantly, in a public house, he defends the activities of an apprehended murderer reported on television with a tub-thumping claim that 'I'd call him a guardian of the law. . . . Someone who stands up for what he knows is right' (p. 180). The role of the media is addressed in more detail later in this chapter, but Campbell's setting here is wryly deliberate: the British urban pub is the kind of environment traditionally identified as both working-class and self-consciously masculine, in which such uncompromisingly retributive positions on vigilantism and 'law and order' issues might be imagined as finding favour.[55] As Connelly says of the real-life killer Donald Gaskin, Horridge is an example of a lone actor, 'behaving as if he is the member of a group and appealing to the values which [he imagines] are held by the majority of members of society'.[56] In his analysis of the serial killer's construction of a self-justifying narrative, Connelly refers to A. E. van Vogt's American study, *A Report on the Violent Male* (1956). Van Vogt's research on the violent or so-called 'Right Man' is not based upon marginalised, psychotic and fantasising subjects, although the descriptions of the absent, emotionally detached or disciplinarian father 'who tried to enforce manliness on the boy beyond his ability'; the pathological 'need to be right'; and the symptom of 'feeling as if he is the person who has been put upon past all endurance', are all certainly applicable to Horridge.[57] A critique of male adversarialism, in which almost any of the case studies included in van Vogt's report would not look incongruous, is one aspect of the anatomisation of society given in Campbell's later novel, *One Safe Place*. The social structure portrayed within this text, which manages to combine 'mainstream' realism and the explicitly Gothic, also aggressively asserts its functionality, but in fact is shown to be deeply conflicted and dysfunctional.

The Breaking of 'Bonds': The One Safe Place

'Positioning the serial killer as gothic monster', Schmid asserts, 'represents our attempt to salvage and locate a (national) community by defining what stands outside that community.'[58] *Face* is an intense and claustrophobic chamber piece. The idea of a broader canvas of a vulnerable 'national' community against which the proscribed, alien outsider is contrasted attains significance with *One Safe Place*. At one point in the narrative, we are duly introduced to a police composite picture of a 'cartoon face for everyone to hate on sight', looking 'like an outlaw trapped by a wanted poster in an Italian western'.[59] Yet, superficially, this book, one of the longest of his fictions, presents a stark thematic anomaly within Campbell's corpus. As a crime thriller, it is not obviously reconcilable to discussion of the novelist as a Gothic writer. Unlike with *Face*, there is also no single warped, machinating Gothic villain or 'monster' at work here. *One Safe Place* does not even feature an initially recognisable serial killer, as that term has been defined. Nor, as what has been described as a 'mainstream novel', does it seem to be a text aligned with the postmodern.[60]

Certainly, *One Safe Place* eschews supernatural elements. Set in Manchester, it is a linear, third-person narrative, although the focus and perspective alternate between characters. The novel's plot takes the form of a secular neo-Hegelian tragedy. An American family, the Travises, relocate from Florida for a new beginning in Britain. Although foreign, familiarly for Campbell, they are both literate and literary: Susanne Travis has secured a lecturing post in film at a Manchester college; her husband, Don, works as a second-hand and antiquarian bookseller, while their son Marshall is a bookish, sensitive and imaginative adolescent. Through a chance 'road rage' traffic encounter that Don experiences with Phil Fancy, a member of an ironically named extended clan of local petty criminals, both families are drawn into a descending spiral of verbal and judicial conflict and violence, resulting in four deaths. The second half of the novel focuses on the relationship between Marshall and Darren Fancy, Phil's vengeful teenage son, who has, unbeknown to Marshall, drugged him in a shopping mall café and abducted him.

The Gothic qualities of *One Safe Place* are subtle and not immediately apparent. The book is, in the broad sense defined by Dominic Head, a 'social novel' in that it is a work that explicitly addresses contemporary social and political concerns.[61] It is set in a city with a prominent gangland and drug culture; a metropolis whose chief police officer the decade before, the evangelical Christian James Anderton, had ordered raids against vendors holding so-called 'video nasties' in the presage to the Video Recordings Act (1984). The novel also evokes memories of the then recent abduction and murder of toddler James Bulger by two other young boys in 1993, although that tragedy occurred in Merseyside. In addition, *One Safe Place* fully realises the tendency, noted in *Obsession*, towards not just social realism but a stark anti-romantic naturalism in both observation of the phenomenological world and its depiction of interpersonal relations. The misanthropic tone of civic dissonance and hostility, familiar from *Face*, is present throughout: even before the initial, fateful confrontation with Phil, Don is asked whether he is 'a Jew as well as a Yank' (p. 45) by an aggressive prospective client. Writing from a Gothic scholar's perspective, Joshi argues that Campbell's novel offers 'a magnificent etching of the troubled relationship between the middle and lower classes in England and its potential for hideous violence'.[62] I agree to the extent that the social 'bonds' represented by class, family, heteronormative relationships and community, and their dissolution, treated with varying degrees of obliqueness in *Face*, assume centrality here. Equally aptly, Joshi describes *One Safe Place* as examining the culture of a perpetual 'cycle of violence engendered by domestic abuse'.[63] Conversely, Joshi rather understates the international, *émigré* element. For the novel's range is also more panoramic. It critiques perceptions of nationhood as well as social class, particularly aspects of

Anglo-American culture. Simultaneously, the narrative of *One Safe Place* also tightens its focus to become a case study of 'corruption of the young' and the construction of a potential serial killer. It is thus a far more significant conduit of Campbell's vision than Joshi's evaluation of the novel as a straightforward if idiosyncratic suspense thriller would suggest.

Campbell himself has stated that *One Safe Place* 'becomes' a horror narrative.[64] It retains a fidelity to the 'mainstream' of realism while displaying the dialectic between literary modes that typifies a genuine hybrid text. An element of metatextuality pervades all Campbell's narratives in that characters are literate and media aware. As with Cathy in *Face*, the educated Travis family represent this analytical consciousness. Nevertheless, this knowledge does not help them. Indeed, the betrayal of the expectation of a Holmesian *denouement* is even more overt than in the earlier novel. Don catches sight of himself holding a magnifying glass in a rear-view window and muses that it makes him 'resemble some eccentric sleuth in an English detective story' (p. 40). However, he immediately encounters Phil, and is quickly made to realise that they are 'in a different kind of movie now' (p. 50). Don's later death at the hands of Phil's relatives reiterates the scepticism towards the metanarrative of 'law and order' expressed in the epistemological form of detective fiction. It is also a shocking narrative development, in the manner of Robert Bloch's *Psycho* (1959): the apparent lead character is eliminated, and the text thereafter is transformed into something else. Given Campbell's self-description as a writer associated with 'horror', it is unsurprising that what critical attention *One Safe Place* has received has sought to interpret the novel according to, and accommodate it within, its parameters. As a scholar of weird fiction, Joshi claims that it is a 'mainstream' fiction, 'pure and simple' and that only the passages involving Marshall's drug-induced hallucinations and abduction by Darren include 'an element of fantasy' or are 'remotely *outre*'.[65] These scenes, exemplified by Marshall's visions of the vagrant disintegrating into grey dust, or of his own reflection in a telephone booth, his head substituted by that of a doll are certainly macabre and vivid. Yet aside from abduction and imprisonment being in themselves key tenets of the Gothic, Joshi surprisingly omits or does not elaborate on other Gothicised elements in the text. For example, in a prophetic dream before Don's death, Marshall brushes his father's scalp, 'only to notice that each movement of his brush enlarged a red stain that was pulsing through his father's hair' (p. 133). Moreover, the presentation of the Fancys and their environment repeatedly employs Gothic imagery. Like Cantril Farm in *Face*, the housing estate on which this family lives is portrayed as a dispiritingly homogeneous but threatening mass of uniformity. Marshall's acid trip renders what is, to him, an unfamiliar neighbourhood, as uncanny, the lair of non-human predators. The houses themselves assume an arachnid quality:

> When it leapt out of its crouch, glaring at him, he knew that any house he approached would do so. They were lying in wait for him – they were controlled by whatever lived at the centre of the overhead web, the thing which grew more aware of him each time he triggered a house. He saw the lines trembling, and knew it was coming for him. (pp. 350–1)

This language prefigures, in Gothicised form, his mother's negative impression of the 'ghetto architecture' and houses 'designed for secrecy or for caging their occupants' (p. 434). The Fancys' dwelling itself, with its dirty carpet 'grey with spilled ash and decorated with trampled cigarette-ends', and 'wallpaper blotched with blurred handprints, the smell of trapped, stale sweat and worse' (p. 437), incarnates the claustrophobic 'haunted house': this is, again, King's archetypal 'Bad Place'. With respect to the house's inhabitants, Joshi does not include Campbell's explicit presentation of the grandfather as a grotesque, monstrous presence. The lengthy descriptions of this bedridden but lecherous old man, a figure likened more than once to rotten 'perished whitish rubber' (p. 22), is intended to function purely as a source of horror, in the sense of evoking physiological revulsion. It is implied that he has been responsible for past familial sexual abuse, but in his withered dissolution the grandfather is finally 'just one more object' in this decayed, haunted environment (p. 401). Of greater centrality to the narrative, Darren, a boy of similar age to Marshall, with his prematurely aged thin and pale face, serves as the other youth's Gothic double. He even consciously assumes the mantle of Gothic villain, feeling, in his pursuit of the other boy, 'like a camera that was being the eyes of a maniac stalking his prey' (p. 308).[66] Darren's eventual death releases him from a state analogous to a vampire's curse, and he assumes 'a little boy's face, slack as though asleep, the lips slightly parted' (p. 496). Yet prior to this, like a vampiric 'other', he also partly prefigures the 'monster' that Marshall will become.

Middle-class anxiety about the working class and comparison of the latter and its environment to a threatening alterity can be interpreted as potentially problematic for liberal humanism. After all, this is a perspective that, itself, typically hails from the educated, urban bourgeoisie. This uneasy dialectic continued over the next two decades in so-called 'Broken Britain' narratives like James Watkins's film, *Eden Lake* (2008).[67] Such narratives have attracted criticism for perceived negative representation of the urban proletariat as a primitive, feral force.[68] Certainly, the Fancys and their associates live by and dispense verbal and physical violence without hesitation. The adult males of the family are undifferentiated vehicles of menace, as when Marshall, in court for Phil's trial, sees the doors burst open and 'the identikit face' apparently split into three as three of his relatives advance on him 'blaz[ing] with sunlight' (p. 99), like a vision of some unholy trinity. Whether turning to robbery or other crimes or, in the case of Darren's mother, prostitution, this patriarchal and homophobic group share a brutal social Darwinist philosophy combining aggression – they intimidate neighbours on their estate by the ready threat and delivery of violence – and a besieged, self-pitying sense of grievance, summarised in their associate Barry's assertion that 'the world's not fucking fair. That's why anyone like us has to even it up for ourselves' (p. 455). This aggression naturally correlates with van Vogt's concept of the 'Right Man'. Darren's physiological display and mental internalisation of this belief system, 'growing hot with the promise of violence' (p. 160), and later repressing how much his mother is psychologically hurting him 'until he could pass it to someone else' (p. 425), directly echoes van Vogt's finding that 'if the person could project destruction or inflict pain on another, it relieved him, as if some feverish feeling was abated, temporarily'.[69] An inherited perception of victimisation, of being at a disadvantage due to acutely perceived class difference, propels Darren's hostility towards and taunting of Marshall. Yet despite the family being apparently too financially poor to own a working telephone, Darren's room is furnished with new commodities: a computer, hi-fi system, television, video recorder and game console. This plenitude of goods amidst poverty echoes Baudrillard's baleful vision of rampant consumerism, in which 'there is no such thing as an affluent society'. According to the philosopher, there is instead 'structural excess and structural penury', a state of spiritual impoverishment 'in which growth itself is a form of inequality': the more society's members possess, the more they are aggrieved and seek more.[70] Even if it is stylistically not consciously postmodernist, Campbell's humanist vision of sociopolitical life, as articulated in *One Safe Place*, amounts to something more complex than endorsement of one social class over another.

Campbell's multilayered text interrogates the metanarratives, specifically the defence mechanisms, that Anglo-American culture has deployed in its struggle to explain the phenomenon of societal violence, a phenomenon for which this culture is itself at least partly responsible. The consumption of goods is equalled by saturation with the forms of mass media. In *One Safe Place*, this serves to bombard the subject, and reader, with reportage of a cacophony of atrocities for undifferentiated consumption. In subtle contrast to *Face*, the media, as portrayed in this novel, serve not as an intensifier of the antagonist's self-justifying psychosis, blurring the public and private realms, but as social chorus, a background device, to delineate, in the manner of a paintbrush, a pathologised culture. The accretion of detail of crimes from newspaper, television and radio headlines is deliberately lurid and overwhelming, as in the newsreader listing reports of a nine-year old Asian boy set on fire by three of his white schoolmates, and a policeman beaten up by the drivers of both cars involved in a traffic accident, and a gang who's gouged out a jeweller's eye to make him tell the combination of his safe, and a teenager who'd tried to drown his girlfriend's baby in a toilet. (p. 297)

The cumulative effect of this catalogue of atrocities is anaesthetising, the gravity and reality of each appalling crime losing its power to shock and engage. The undifferentiated description accords with Baudrillard's paradigm of a media-dominated world that neutralises the possibility of uniqueness through 'a multiple universe of mutually reinforcing and self-referential media which becomes so that events become each other's reciprocal contents', this constituting 'the totalitarian message of the consumer society'.[71] In Hutchinson's words, such a jaundiced view may be 'playful nihilism' on the part of Baudrillard.[72] However, as presented in Campbell's fictions, authorial intent is not so much what Hutchinson describes as 'conciliation' motivated by nostalgia, or 'a desire for recuperation and for the association of value in the context of mutuality and social being', but rather a critical dissection.[73] The power of mass media in *One Safe Place* is shown to deprive the subject of differentiation between representation and reality. This is exemplified when Darren, on seeing a rabbit hit by a car, is 'less disturbed by the mess that had spilled out of it than by the colour of the innards, a duller red than they ever were in videos' (p. 18).

Still more invidiously, the lack of ethical hierarchies induced by consumerism and media domination facilitates cognitive, and thus moral, dissonance. This is displayed in the consistently contradictory behaviour of the Fancy family and their associates. These are people who hoard mostly stolen material goods but simultaneously blame television for 'making kids want the earth' (p. 215), and who condemn homosexuality as an animalistic perversion whilst keeping bestiality videos in the house. It is also on display in the television debate on causes of violence that Susanne participates in, and the commentary offered by authority figures. The former, overtly satirical, scene parodies the likes of the American *Jerry Springer Show*

(1991–2018), an instance of what Schmid describes as the 'tabloidization' of newspapers and television.[74] *One Safe Place* portrays the media as reducing complex issues to glib soundbites for a mass audience, its confrontational style also, as one of Susanne's students observes, serving only to encourage anger and antagonism between people as a precursor to violence. In the form of a student's mother who threatens to split Susanne from 'gob to navel' unless she returns to America with the violence that has 'infected' her daughter (p. 36), Campbell delivers a vivid character sketch of simultaneous righteous indignation, self-contradiction and complete lack of self-knowledge. Nor does the author, predictably, accord greater insight to representatives of the 'educated' establishment. The manslaughter trial judge's assumption of the influence wrought by 'films and television' consciously evokes the conclusions expressed in the Bulger case about violent videos and tabloid newspapers.[75] 'His Honour' is, however, presented as an emotionless cipher, a droning recorder of a list of right-wing clichés such as 'the duty to rebuild the wall of law against the tide of violence . . .' (p. 240). Still more patently worthy of ridicule is the incongruous equivalence between Marshall's vandalism as being 'as unlawful' (p. 268) as the killing of his father drawn by the pompous headmaster, Harbottle. Far from being inspirational, schoolteachers in Campbell's Gothic fictions accord with Laing's tart observation that society 'educates children to lose themselves and to become absurd, and thus to be normal'.[76]

This notwithstanding, it is obviously another educational figure, Susanne Travis, who articulates Campbell's own, pragmatic, views on 'causes of violence'; the culpability of pornography and media as contributors to it, and the flaws with censorship as a means of combating it. As Susanne argues to her head of department, people 'consume' violence 'even if they think they don't and it's our job as educators to equip people to analyse' (p. 82). In an otherwise positive appraisal of *One Safe Place*, Joshi regrets an apparent narrative evasion on Campbell's part with respect to the disappearance from the plot of the police and university censure of Susanne for use of certain then banned films.[77] The text's inconclusive treatment of censorship aligns with the tendency of some literary postmodernist works to resist the very notion of final closure. However, there is, I think, a degree of commitment on the part of the author that is both subtle and pragmatic. Campbell himself has maintained a liberal position on these issues, arguing not only that fiction 'expresses the emotions of its chosen audience rather than corrupting them', but that censorship functions as 'a method used by a culture to deny what it has itself produced'.[78] In this context, the novel's apparent irresolution becomes explicable as deliberate strategy. Here it is the avoidance of 'easy' answers, whilst concurrently critiquing the adversarialism represented by judiciary and media, with their over-simplified Manichaean oppositions between guilt and innocence and good and evil, as being the true source of harm.

Campbell's concern in *One Safe Place* is with the tragedy presented by 'the contagion of violence' and with tracing the corruption of the individual that it entails.[79] The overtly Gothic 'doubling' of the novel's two juvenile leads is prefigured in the juxtaposition of violence in Florida and Manchester that opens the narrative. From the menacing opened beer can that hisses 'like a snake' and a bully's railing against liberal 'campus bitches' who 'think the army shouldn't have a say in things no more' (pp. 3–4), it is apparent that violence is not the prerogative of Mancunian housing estates, or some alien import, but is indigenous to both cultures: there is *no* 'safe ground' (p. 11). The reference to armed forces and Marshall's own name harbingers the text's analysis and indictment of gun culture. The firearm in *One Safe Place* is the symbol of violence and, indirectly, and finally directly, the cause of three deaths. It is Don Travis's friend's fateful advice to procure a weapon, ironically for safety, which triggers his family's catastrophe and the novel's chilling denouement concerning Marshall. The boy is initially content with the power of verbal retort. Nonetheless, he is disturbed when imagining punching another child, at the degree of 'ease with which he could be driven to pointless violence' (p. 126). Although they are induced through a hallucinogenic drug, Marshall's repeated and intense dream visions of stamping his own father's head to pieces imply a developing 'infection' by his environment. The prognosis is a fatal one, because in the epilogue Marshall is finally shown to have been transformed into both a consumer of 'true crime' literature and a committed gun advocate. His defiant challenge to anyone 'to try to fuck with him' (p. 501) reproduces the profanity-laden language of the Fancys. As such, it exemplifies and appears to enact Baudillard's despairing conclusion regarding the amorality and destructiveness of contemporary culture, that 'there is no longer such a thing as a strategy of Good against Evil ... only the pitting of Evil against Evil – a strategy of last resort'.[80] At this point, Marshall is already the unrepentant killer of two people. The implications are that he will account for many more, and that Susanne, having already lost her husband, has now 'lost' her son: the last familial 'bond' has finally been broken.

Ethically, this is undoubtedly a bleak conclusion. In one respect, the corruption of Marshall Travis also represents an aesthetic diminution. As with the brutal killing of his literary father, a bibliophile enthused by spotting a rare first edition of a Lovecraft short story collection, Marshall's aspirations to be both a university librarian and a best-selling author have also been kicked or bludgeoned to death. He ends the novel aspiring to be a police officer – never, in Campbell's imaginative universe, an unqualified positive. Nonetheless, the death of the artist depicted in *One Safe Place* coexists with an almost playful consideration of the creative mechanics of murder, notably in the scene in which Darren's mother taunts her son as to what he will do with his captive. Marie Fancy asks:

> 'Kill him, you reckon? Or torture him first? Cut him open like in one of them videos and make him watch his guts fall out?'
> Darren felt apprehensive and queasily excited. 'Ooh God, mam ...
> His mother stood up to drag her chair away from the door.
> 'Here you go, get a spoon from the kitchen.'
> 'What for?'
> 'So you can poke one of his eyes out and feed it to him and he'll have to watch. Sound good?' (p. 361)

The passage is visceral, but it is also strikingly metatextual, presenting authorial critique of a 'horror' audience or readership's sensationalist appetites. As such, despite a dominant style inclined to social naturalism as well as realism, this text anticipates a concern with the aesthetics of creativity in relation to the Gothic. It is an interest brought to fruition in the following decade with the much more overtly postmodern longer fiction, *Secret Story*.

The Mask and the Mirror: Secret Story

Returning to a Merseyside setting, Campbell's later novel is his most comprehensive and subversive portrait of an adult serial killer. *The Count of Eleven* (1991), fourteen years earlier, had represented an innovation in detailing its central character's relationship with the forces of capitalism through introducing a serio-comic turn. However, that novel had retained a fidelity to conventions of both social realism and dramatic structure, especially in its tragic conclusion. By contrast, *Secret Story* presents what Jeremy Dyson describes in his Introduction as 'a vitriolic satire on the creative process itself'.[81] Dyson's assessment is entirely accurate as far as it goes, but an incomplete assessment of this complex work and its significance within Campbell's overall treatment of postmodernism and vision of the Gothic.

Secret Story is an acutely metadiscursive text. Its narrative is concerned with both fictions and the people who create them. The novel presents psychological horror not through depiction of inner-city social marginalisation, as with Horridge in *Face*, or conflict in a council house, as in *One Safe Place*, but this time in the lower middle-class setting of a sunny suburban lounge. The central character, Dudley Smith, like Horridge, Marshall and Darren, and like Campbell himself, is an only child. A civil servant working in a job centre, Smith writes unpublished short stories in his spare time concerning the exploits of a serial killer, and lives with his overprotective mother, Kathy. Kathy, a civil servant and aspiring author herself, who has sublimated her own creativity in over-devotion to her son, is divorced. Smith is also estranged from his father, Monty, an insensitive, boorish poet and self-proclaimed 'Scouser that's proud of being Scouse' (p. 202), who abandoned the family when Dudley was thirteen. 'Your writing's never more important than your audience', Monty lectures his son, to which Dudley counters, 'perhaps we'll have to disagree about that' (p. 286). The novel's dramatic action is triggered by Smith winning a short story competition run by a local magazine to which Kathy has submitted one of his efforts without Dudley's knowledge. Smith's macabre tale of a young woman being pushed onto a railway line by a serial murderer that he christens 'Mr Killogram' attracts the attention of a local filmmaker, Vincent Davis. Smith, while relishing the recognition, feels pressured by the magazine and by Davis for more stories, and begins to feel the need to seek inspiration. He eventually fixates on a young female journalist from the magazine, Patricia Martingale, to aid in what he euphemistically describes as his 'research'. It emerges that not only do all his stories feature the same killer, but they are based on each occasion upon real-life unsolved crimes, of which he is himself the perpetrator: Smith has written each narrative after the event. Unlike Horridge, he is already a serial killer. As with Carl Panzram, although unwittingly, Smith's stories posthumously become his 'journal' or testament of murder.

Campbell's novel adheres to some degree of convention and antecedence within the Gothic with respect to portrayal of the serial killers; their behaviourism and the familial and societal abuse that have played a role as factors in their formation. Smith is not psychotic in the sense of being delusional, as Horridge in *Face* clearly is. Nor does this text present a process of corruption of innocence, a moral descent that lends a degree of sympathy to Marshall Travis and, arguably, also to Darren Fancy, as the other juvenile lead in *One Safe Place*. Instead, Smith is an organised, sadistic and, to the end, unrepentant murderer. Laconic and calculating, almost every utterance he makes is a sly *double entendre*. 'I've got plenty of sense,' he tells an unsuspecting Patricia, menacingly: 'there's quite a few people who've found out how much. Maybe you ought to meet them' (p. 145). In contrast to Horridge, whose misanthropy against all forms of post-1960s Keynesian liberalism crystallises around homophobia, arising from what has been suggested is a fear of feminisation, Smith is a classic misogynist, railing and defining himself against women. He refrains the violent misogyny of the serial murderer noted by Simpson amongst others, a 'tradition' of deliberate, vicious verbal abuse (Smith repeatedly refers to women as 'bitches'), abduction and terrorisation. These female victims all suffer because, in Smith's view, they deserve to, or invite their own fates. The trait of victimisation of women is familiar. It has been shared by countless antagonists such as Harris's Jame Gumb in *The Silence of the Lambs* or Ellis's Patrick Bateman from *American Psycho*, and *Secret Story* deliberately evokes both these earlier texts. Like Gumb, for whom the imprisoned women are merely 'material' for his project, the abducted and bound Patricia becomes a dehumanised 'package' who does not even 'sound like a person' (p. 281).[82] A previous victim whom Smith had flung to her death had become a broken 'insect' crawling on the road (p. 233). Bateman's isolation of his human prey in *American Psycho*, the dismissal that 'no-one' cares or will help, is echoed in Smith's various taunts that Kathy has never asked about Patricia's wellbeing; that he has texted her parents, lying that she has moved away to London, and that 'nobody's going to hear you but me, however much noise you make' (p. 263).[83] Smith is, then, a cruel and meticulous murderer.

The influences governing Smith's violent sociopathy are carefully delineated. Firstly, Smith's disorder is accorded historical contextualisation through reference to formative time spent with his cousin, and, in a gesture of acknowledgement to conventions of classic Gothic villainy, his Catholic uncle, a hare beater under whose influence the serial killer's familiar tendency to torture animals was nurtured. Smith's childhood friend Eamonn Moore also recalls the pair of them watching banned videos from his parents' film library, a pursuit in which young Dudley most enjoyed scenes of torture. In oblique reference to the censorship issue raised in *One Safe Place*, Eamonn remarks that 'twenty years later the law says these films are all right for people to see after all' (p. 117), although it will be seen that Campbell's text does not ascribe causality for antisocial behaviours to the availability of violent material. Secondly, Smith as an adult has clearly been suppressed and infantilised by his mother. When they are not insinuating, Smith's utterances are laconic, bland, immature and petulant, as in his protest that 'it isn't fair. I won' (p. 133) on learning that his story has been pulled from the magazine to placate the family of a young woman the anniversary of whose death is imminent. Kathy has preserved her son, as in aspic, in one of her own amateur narratives, as an angelic being with 'a cherub's golden curls that were heavenly in their untidiness' and 'a face that would disown its innocent chubbiness too soon' (p. 217). Smith's reaction is a terse, worsening hostility and a projection of his resentment against his mother into undifferentiated misogyny. 'Nobody tells Mr Killogram what to do', he rails, 'especially not women' (p. 364), and his rage finally culminates in the accusation that Kathy has not protected anything but has in fact 'destroyed' everything that he ever was (p. 372). Most powerfully, and perhaps most subtly, the text conveys what Joshi describes as 'the slow-burning hell' of white-collar working life, with the hierarchy, boredom, loss of personal autonomy and abuse of being perceived as 'nothing but an office worker' (p. 75) that it entails.[84] Despite the advent of ostensibly more centrist and liberal 'New Labour' administrations (1997–2010), social relations at the level of normal day-to-day experience are shown to be as discordant as in earlier texts. The malign incivility represented in *One Safe Place* has not diminished: 'I wouldn't feel superior to anyone if I were you', Dudley is rebuked by a client at one point, 'not with your job' (p. 20). Both Smith and his mother are shown as subordinate to the formal petty tyranny and timekeeping of their respective managers. After a physical assault by a client's brother, widely witnessed, but in which no bystander has come to his aid, Smith, like Darren in *One Safe Place*, experiences 'an ache that felt as if it mightn't be assuaged until he transferred it to someone else' (p. 57). Environmental factors, not least this rigid social stratification and callous indifference, are shown to be psychologically and physically harmful, and, in Smith's desire for 'transference', generative of violence.

Dudley's frustration, naturally, generates psychological withdrawal into a compensatory fantasy existence, or what Wilson and Seaman describe with reference to serial killers as 'a dream of transcendence'.[85] 'Away from the office', it is narrated, 'he was himself' (p. 23).

Smith's alternative life is, in both contemplation and execution, retaliatory. The behaviour exhibited by Dudley accords with the 'alienation' noted by Wilson and Seaman as being experienced by the working and lower middle classes in a competitive and hierarchical culture under capitalism; his self-ascribed status as an author expresses those classes' desperate 'longing to be important'.[86] Hodgkinson and her colleagues, writing nearly three decades later, reaffirm how serial murder is viewed by perpetrators as one method of 'transference', and of 'cheating the system' that has rendered them as underachievers.[87] Smith's proclivity for murder also places him as an actor in a cultural context in which, as Simpson argues, 'high art' and the notion of the elite artist have combined with romantic notions of self-assertion.[88] Smith constructs an alternate, highly egocentric reality, in which his mind 'seemed to own everything around him', his drab suburban environment confirms there is 'much more to him', and the world might have been 'a show' staged for his benefit (pp. 23–4). In the workplace, this narcissistic mental canvas enables Smith to indulge in contemplation of violently attacking and killing his manager, the overbearing Wimborne. Eventually, in a key scene, his superiority complex allows Dudley to stage a grandstanding departure in which he denounces Wimborne, asserting that she is

> Dull. Unimaginative. Not just you, the whole boring lot of you. If you knew half of what I am, none of you would dare to talk to me the way you do. You ought to be proud if you're associated with me. People might even think that you were interesting. (p. 164)

The irony with Smith's egotistical allusion to 'half of what I am' is that *Secret Story* is Campbell's most detailed character study of a *non*-character. To a greater degree even than Horridge in *Face*, the adult Smith is physically anonymous. He is barely ascribed any features, except as 'a figure in a grey suit, a visitor so non-descript as to be invisible' (p. 182). This is not just deliberate self-mystification in which Campbell's protagonist draws vicarious pleasure from the fact that 'nobody ever finds out' who his nameless killer alter ego is, 'or anything about him' (p. 62). In common with his literary forebears as serial killers, Dudley is also psychologically an incomplete person, striving for transformation and facing an existential crisis. Like Harris's Jame Gumb, who is described as 'not anything really, just a sort of total lack that he wants to fill, and so angry', Smith, and his similar 'baffled rage' (p. 39) are anatomised.[89] In this case, the agent of a particularly ruthless dissection is the separatist and confrontational comedienne, Shell Garridge, herself a victim of parental abuse. Shell's withering critique of Smith's fictional alter ego also summarises, all too accurately, Smith's real psychological history and present domestic life:

> I told you he'd be like they all are. Tortured animals as a kid. Scared of women. Hasn't got a girlfriend. Likely brought up by a single mum. I'm not dissing them, but she'd have kept telling him he was better than everyone else, treating him like every time he farted somebody should bottle it and sell it. Only deep down he'll know he's nothing and hate her for not stopping him knowing. (p. 66)

Her assessment is validated in Smith's complete identification with his own fictions and final protest that he has nothing to live for after Kathy destroys them.

However, Garridge, fatally for her, does not recognise how dangerous Smith is until it is too late. The kind of cognitive failure manifested by Shell is endemic in *Secret Story*: this is a culture in which insight coexists with ignorance. Kathy believes that she and her son are 'two of the healthiest people she knew' (p. 195), and she stubbornly preserves, as the evidence of her son's criminality becomes inescapable, a 'sense of domesticity' (p. 368) in attention to minor detail, to the bitter end. The killer's insensitive father, who wrongly attributes the deaths of Dudley and his mother to murder-suicide by the latter, also blames Kathy for not leaving Smith alone so that he could have got some help, and the magazine for not trying 'to get him to write something healthy' (pp. 378–9). Monty is incapable of accepting his own failures as a parent. Deception and misrecognition are, of course, key sources of irony and generators of suspense in Gothic serial killer narratives. As Ellis's first-person narrator asks pointedly in *American Psycho*, 'I mean, does anyone really see anyone? Does anyone really *see* anyone else? Did you see *me*? See?'[90] For the damaged sociopaths in Campbell's fictions, being observed – 'seen' – is a vital means of assurance, of both conferring and confirming their own identity. Just as Bateman pauses to note 'my reflection in a mirror hung on a wall – and smiling at how good I look', so Horridge in *Face* shares a grin with himself in a disfigured mirror, Darren assumes a cinematic killer's point of view in *One Safe Place*, and Smith, assuming a persona to inveigle his way into Eamonn's house in an abortive attempt to murder his wife, is 'beguiled' by glimpsing his 'decisive progress' (p. 185) in a mirror.[91] He realises that he is 'acting out' a character created for him by the film director. This consciousness of how one may be perceived by others suggests affinity with what Slavoj Žižek describes as the function of the Other's 'gaze' as 'a kind of ontological guarantee' of the subject's own being.[92] Smith's awareness of film also reflects his, and his creator's, consciousness of visual media, especially – in this instance, and both *One Safe Place* and *Secret Story* as texts – the cinematic. In a cultural context, as opposed to a psychoanalytical one, Baudrillard argues that the present 'simulacrum of violence', the distinguishing terror within postmodernity, has emerged 'less from passion than from the screen: a violence in the nature of the image'.[93] Žižek's specific argument refers to web-camera sites, but my juxtaposition of discourses by both philosophers intends to highlight just how important cognition and the role and forms of media are in Campbell's own Gothic 'vision'.

In an address to younger writers of horror, Campbell has cautioned against a repetitive endorsement of pre-existing metanarratives under the guise of 'tradition'. On the continued tendency to include representation of violence against women in fiction, he observes, 'I think it's time for some in the field to acknowledge that, when we come face to face with the monster we may find ourselves looking at not a mask but a mirror.'[94] Campbell is alluding, highly critically, to male authors whom he perceives as either struggling with aspects of reality that they cannot cope with, thus typically indulging in misogyny, or with the problem of explaining the phenomenon of evil (and hence taking recourse to simplistic explanation or excesses of representation). *Secret Story*, with its protagonist who protests that 'they're stories. I write stories' (p. 127), echoing the introductory line of Campbell's own website, articulates this critique as narrative.[95] The novel satirises both the contemporary horror fiction industry and the appetites of a society that consumes such narratives in a non-discriminatory manner, analogous to serial killers' use and consumption of their victims as depersonalised commodities. In what can be construed as a sly commentary on his less talented peers by Campbell, Smith's dubious writing talent is undercut by his former teacher's scathing dismissal of him as being 'wholly devoid of imagination' (p. 125), confirmed by the ease with which Patricia guesses the password to his computer files.

Campbell occasionally takes recourse to comic symbolism, exemplified by the brief encounter in a hotel between Kathy and Jim Cunningham, the sexually submissive role player whose job happens to involve the disposal of unsold, remaindered books. However, mostly the stratagem is one of irony or dark satire, as when the *Mersey Mouth* photographer poses Smith with a carving knife to make him 'look dangerous' (p. 47), or Dudley's murder of Garridge, which although partly an act of vengeance also provides the killer with renewed creative inspiration. In Smith's discussion on a ferry with a then unsuspecting Patricia on how to render Shell's seemingly accidental death by drowning 'more spectacular', Campbell, as he does in *One Safe Place*, clearly parodies the perceived excesses of the genre. Patricia, retracing Marie's interview with Darren in the earlier novel, teasingly asks Dudley:

> 'What kind of spectacle are you thinking of? A girl's body being shredded under there? Her bones being ground up and splintered and broken? All her blood?'
> 'That sounds good'.
> Her attempt to shock him had merely succeeded in making Patricia feel uneasy about her own depths. (p. 243)

The effect here is both darkly comic, and, in its allusion to 'depths' and connotations of potential for violence to condition and influence, disquieting. Like Darren's comprehension of the death of the rabbit in *One Safe Place*, spectatorship anaesthetises the brute reality of death through distancing and the invocation of comparisons to a more vivid, more 'real', form of media representation as substitute. The pursuit of a more satisfying 'real' becomes paramount. As Dudley fantasises about slashing or mangling the throat of Eamonn's wife, he is sure that 'the real thing would be different and worth witnessing – worth at least a photograph, maybe more' (p. 183).

Desensitisation, and the sensation of dissatisfaction and quest for satisfaction through consumption, in this case through staging the 'perfect murder', are symptomatic of the levelling of forms of representation into a monotonous landscape that characterises postmodernism. As Mark Currie argues, the cultural context of postmodernity is not one divided neatly between fictional texts and critical readings of these narratives, but 'a monistic world of representations' in which 'boundaries between art and life, language and metalanguage and fiction and criticism are under a philosophical attack'.[96] *Secret Story* tests several such 'boundaries'. The novel continues Campbell's critique of the moral relativism denoted by respective media representation and cultural reception of violence and serial killers. Smith and his crimes are finally both proscribed and lauded. 'I can't believe you want to be mixed up with a film about killing women for pleasure', the actor portraying Smith's Mr Killogram indicts the film crew, who protest that they 'need the work' (p. 306). However, in the chapter set in a restaurant with which the novel concludes, the reader learns that Smith has become the subject of a website, T-shirt and another proposed film, this time a documentary. His death, although unintentional, enacts literally Jean-Paul Sartre's key argument, that 'if nothing compels me to save my life, nothing prevents me from precipitating myself into the abyss', and is an event which confers, in appearance, a degree of tragic grandeur to the narrative, however unwarranted.[97] Smith is described as a 'cultural icon' (p. 377), and a book tie-in is even proposed to Patricia, 'while he's hot' (p. 380), refraining, and thus validating, Smith's earlier self-description as 'the hottest thing around' (p. 75). In death, Smith achieves the elevated social status he has craved, and, as the 'Scouse Slayer' (p. 377), has ascended to become an urban legend like the 'Yorkshire Ripper'.[98]

Most profoundly, *Secret Story*, through enactment, audits the division between reality and its representation. In the final scene, Vincent Davis, now an enthusiastic would-be maker of a documentary on Smith, calls for investigating 'other things as well, like how fiction and reality depend on each other' (p. 378). To a greater degree than the earlier serial killer texts, *Secret Story* represents an authorial self-consciousness as a notably self-consumptive narrative. The novel opens almost immediately with Smith's prize-winning, but here untitled, short story 'Night Trains Don't Take You Home'. In its inclusion of a self-referential allusion to its female victim 'reading the latest prizewinning best-seller by Dudley Smith' (p. 6), 'Night Trains' represents a compound instance of a metatextual text within a text. Smith's exploits are reconstructed in Davis's original film, the abortive making of which is depicted in the ensuing narrative. During the project, Smith subsumes his own identity into the depicted character of 'Mr Killogram' and elides 'Killogram' with Colin Holmes, the actor portraying him. 'As long as Mr Killogram was on his side', Smith thinks, 'Dudley wouldn't care, and whose part could his other self take except his?' (p. 302). The idea for a murder on a ship that had been formulated through his earlier real-life conversation with Patricia aboard the ferry is actualised. However, this scene of reconstruction becomes *de*construction when Smith's 'other self', Holmes, a collaborator with the friends of Smith's victim, Angela Manning, turns on him. Like his fictional namesake, Sherlock Holmes, the deliberately named Holmes, in yet another reference to detective narratives, has proved a master of disguise. Finally, virtually the last image in the novel is of a menacing youth wearing a 'Bring Back Mr Killogram' T-shirt on a train planting his heels on the seat opposite, a refrain of the doomed Greta's encounter with the gang which opens 'Night Trains'. Patricia glimpses 'someone all too reminiscent of Dudley Smith spying from deep in his eyes' (p. 382). The text thus ends, like *One Safe Place*, with an implication of the circularity and perpetuation of violence.

Campbell's serial killers are, in totality, a study in the banality of evil. In his survey of the representation of repeat murderers, which cites Campbell as an authority on the literature but does not analyse his work, Connelly concludes that a 'pessimistic culture' that draws upon negative depictions of society 'will tend to produce misanthropic and life-devaluating narratives'.[99] In common with texts like *American Psycho*, Campbell's fictions depict misanthropy to an intense, although unlike Ellis's text, not viscerally explicit, degree. However, they maintain a grimly determined liberal humanist perspective, in which the forces of violence that 'devalue' life are seen to have social rather than biological, genetic or metaphysical causality, and are thus amenable to analysis and, in theory, and however difficult, capable of future redress.

This chapter has focused on Campbell's analysis of a consumer culture's responsibility for violence, and the inadequacy of grand narratives of sociopolitical maxims to either account for or ameliorate it. It has also addressed the transmutations which take place within his fictions of the Gothic, particularly the figure of the serial killer. Above all, I have sought to highlight an increasing tendency towards the self-reflective and metatextual, propensities which, although present in Campbell's writing from the beginning, were now assuming an increasing level of sophistication and alignment with the postmodern. The resistance to formal narrative closure signalled in the three texts discussed in this chapter, with John Horridge left possibly still alive, Marshall Travis transformed into a killer; and Dudley Smith's poisonous, posthumous cultural 'legacy', both exemplify the theme of paranoia within Campbell's fiction and attest to the author's iconoclasticism. Patricia's insistence at the conclusion of *Secret Story* that 'this is our story now' (p. 382) expresses a desire to take control of the 'narrative' of her own life after her victimisation by Smith. Yet it also simultaneously both represents an address to the reader regarding choice of ethical codes and summarises an aesthetic challenge to authorship. It is Campbell's representation of authorship, the challenges to its creativity, and the control (or lack of it) wielded over 'reality', that will be addressed in the following chapter.

3

Writing with Intensity: Campbell's Gothic Novellas

ಐತ

Constant Writers: Campbell and King

From its first appearance in the 1960s, Campbell's work has been infused with a marked self-consciousness around notions of authorship, the craft involved in writing and the relationship between writers, their readers and environment. The notions of the novel as being 'absolutely *dead*', or the writer who 'can't stop thinking' in the early short tale 'The Franklyn Paragraphs', discussed in the Introduction of this book, are echoed in much later and more expansive works, like *Secret Story*. 'You don't stop being a writer', Kathy Smith tries to assure her doomed son at the dramatic climax of that novel (p. 378). After Dudley's death, his near-victim Patricia Martingale dismisses the suggestion from her magazine's proprietor that she might author any reconstruction of the serial killer's crimes: 'I don't want to write', Patricia insists, 'I want to survive.' However, her interlocutor, the enthusiastic but insensitive Walter, is undeterred, asking, 'can't you do both? Mightn't one help the other?' (p. 380). This is an indicative and revealing exchange. For, in Campbell's Gothic universe, the act of writing and 'survival' are entwined. Writing attains the status of an ethical imperative. Self-expression becomes an intense activity carried out under compulsion, and over which the subject has no choice. It defines one's existence or 'survival'.

This chapter focuses on Campbell's vision of the self-conscious author, a metatextual figure described as postmodernist literature's 'stock character' by Aleid Fokkema, the texts or 'artefacts' created by the writer, and the 'survival' of both.[1] I suggest that the author functions as a surrogate for the contemporary subject, and that the writer's 'text' is a metaphor for the subject's endeavours to ascribe or create, mediate and control a valedictory reality and 'meaning' in relation to their own existence. I begin with a brief comparison and contrast between Campbell's portrayal of the author-protagonist and that offered by his contemporary, Stephen King, for whom the theme of authorship has been equally important, and certainly more comprehensively and intensively studied. The chapter then discusses Campbell's deliberate use of the novella, the highly specialised prose form in which he has explored ideas of authorship and textual self-inflection most thoroughly, before analysing two highly germane examples of this disciplined form of long fiction from his *oeuvre*. Published over a quarter of a century apart, the semi-autobiographical, if surreal, *Needing Ghosts* (1990), and the late meditation on bibliophilia, *The Booking* (2016), are multifaceted and complex works. They respectively foreground distinctive interpretations of the author and of literature. Moreover, taken together these texts can be interpreted as reflecting a nuanced and developing interpretation of and response to central tenets of postmodernism: metatextuality, stylistic or narrative experimentation, the questioning of notions of authorial authority, literary canons, moral absolutes and 'truth', and a tendency towards final open-ended irresolution rather than resolution.

As this book has already implied, despite significant differences, theorists and critics associated with postmodernism have identified and congregated around several traits. The area of convergence is an interrogation of previously accepted maxims or 'grand narratives', such as a teleological interpretation of history, and a concomitant challenge to the interpretation of narrative as being, to appropriate Jean-François Lyotard, 'quintessential' as a form of 'customary knowledge'.[2] Aesthetically, such a perspective critiques the worldview that had traditionally conferred authority upon the author as creator, or which preserved hierarchical differentiation between so-called high and low cultural forms. Philosophically, postmodernism undercuts the traditional status of literary fictions as affording what Patricia Waugh describes as 'a useful model for learning about the construction of reality itself' by virtue of a supposed affinity between the subject's mediation of reality through language and the presentation in fictional texts of 'worlds constructed entirely of language'.[3] Instead of clearly delineated hierarchies, boundaries and assurances relating to the subject's integrity and the reality that it inhabits, the postmodernist paradigm typically substitutes fluidity and insecurity. A society characterised by mass consumerism represents, according to Jean Baudrillard, 'an age of radical alienation'.[4] Fredric Jameson, equally pessimistic about the process of cultural transformation, goes further in arguing that 'the alienation of the subject is displaced by the latter's fragmentation'.[5] The implications of such splintering are far-reaching. Thus, for example, postmodernist literary works frequently exhibit metatextuality, as Waugh describes, 'an extreme self-consciousness about language, literary forms and the art of writing fictions', and an inflective tendency in which 'the 'conventions of realism' are 'laid bare'.[6] In respect to the traditional authority of authorship prescribed by realism, the omniscient narrator conflicts with and is supplanted by the unstable and unreliable narrator. This reflects the dual and paradoxical existence of the human subject under postmodernity. The subject becomes what Linda Hutcheon deems both 'a coherent, unified whole and a contradictory dispersed multiplicity'.[7] Moral objectivity or 'truth' amid this fragmentation becomes opaque and elusive. Instead, as Hutcheon puts it, the subject and, by extension, the reader, face 'a questioning of what is real, and how one can know it'.[8] Nor do postmodernist texts end neatly with the panacea of formal resolution of the ideological and other contradictions featured within. Instead, such narratives are, as Laura E. Savu describes, 'suspicious of closure, unity and absolutes'.[9] It is in articulating and displaying such ambiguity and irresolution that Campbell's nuanced Gothic fictions align as directly with postmodern paradigms as the works of King. They do so, however, with a less informal or populist and a more unmistakably paranoid voice.

As noted, the academy has had a burgeoning if belated interest in King in comparison to Campbell. This scholarship extended to the application of postmodernist concepts as early as Jesse Norman's 1997 reading of King's *Pet Sematary* (1983).[10] More recently, Clotilde Landais, for example, analyses a metatextual reflection on the artistic identity of the writer and of writing in two of King's other Gothic fictions, *The Dark Half* (1989) and the novella *Secret Window, Secret Garden* (1990), in her own interpretation of King as a postmodernist writer.[11] On Campbell's part, his detailed historical knowledge of the horror genre, especially in its American incarnations from Edgar Allan Poe to Thomas Ligotti, makes consciousness of and engagement with the most commercially successful peer in his own field inevitable. Even Campbell's *The One Safe Place*, stylistically a naturalistic work, and one, as discussed, seemingly on first appearance at some distance from the Gothic, let alone 'high' postmodernism, contains a playful reference to Marshall Travis 'reading a book which Stephen King had been unable to put down' (p. 87). Some comparison of Campbell with King is, therefore, both overdue and rewarding. For the outputs of both writers present a wealth of material on authorship and audience in both fictional and paratextual form.

The recurrence of the author as protagonist or as significant character in King's literary corpus, from *'Salem's Lot* (1975) to, at least, the crime novel *Finders Keepers* (2015), the plot of which features the murder of a reclusive writer, has been studied extensively.[12] Moreover, an identifiable subsequence of his texts, including *Misery* (1987), *The Dark Half*, *Secret Window* and *Lisey's Story* (2006) are more overtly autobiographical,. They engage explicitly with various aspects of the literary profession, including anxiety over plagiarism and authorial legacy. While Campbell, as noted, is a prolific commentator and essay writer, King has also produced at least two substantial non-fictional disquisitions: *Danse Macabre*, on the history and conventions of the horror genre, and the later practical 'tool kit' manifesto, *On Writing: A Memoir of the Craft* (2001).[13] Therefore the practice of writing, as John Sears notes, is not just King's vocation but a central theme in that author's own imaginative vision.[14] In totality, King's output has been even more prodigious than Campbell's, so spatial constraints must inevitably dictate a similarly selective citation of examples.[15] I have, therefore, largely restricted discussion here to these two substantive non-fictions and to the novel *Misery*. This 1987 novel is still probably King's most notably self-referential literary work. The text constitutes, as Punter describes, 'a Gothic labyrinth of writers and readers', and it is one which has the vexed minotaur figure of the author at its nexus.[16]

Even a cursory comparison of Campbell with King discloses obvious similarities on the theme of authorship. This affinity can itself be interpreted as a response to, and even a degree of self-assertion against, the disappearance of the 'Great Writer' under postmodernity once described by Jameson.[17] For example, both King and Campbell endorse implicitly the Romantic concept of artistic inspiration and the autonomy of creativity. King maintains a 'basic belief' regarding the composition of stories that 'they pretty much make themselves'.[18] Paul Sheldon, the protagonist who serves as King's alter ego in *Misery*, maintains that 'when I start a book I always *think* I know how things will turn out, but I never actually end one that way'.[19] Such faith in the mystery of the creative impulse is echoed frequently in Campbell's discussion of his own working practices. Always intuitive and instinctive, he prefers to 'let them [fictions] develop their own energy and direction'.[20] Thus, for instance, the short story 'Concussion' was, he has said, 'more important to write than to understand', and the novel, *The Nameless*, 'pretty well composed itself'.[21] With respect to *Needing Ghosts*, Campbell disclosed in a contemporary interview that the experience of authoring this text was 'more like dreaming itself onto the page than anything I'd ever written', and his decision was to simply 'carry on letting it be strange and see where it went'.[22] The writer's view of this particular work has remained notably consistent over the decades: he admitted to the present author in 2019 that the story was dictated to him by his 'subconscious'.[23] In keeping with the notion of professional and authorial integrity, both King and Campbell also espouse fidelity to 'truth'. King, in *On Writing*, alludes to 'the unspoken contract that exists between writer and reader – you promise to express the truth of how people act and talk through the medium of a made-up story'.[24] Campbell has similarly asserted: 'I persist in committing myself to the principle that the purpose of writing is to tell the truth.'[25] At root, both writers are seeking to validate what they do, creating fictions, and to defend the value of those creations – especially generic fictions – against their perceived detractors. As Undercliffe in Campbell's 'The Franklyn Paragraphs' remarks wearily of one such, 'I could tell he looked upon all fiction as the poor relation of non-fiction, like all academic librarians – so much for our writing' (p. 50).

However, there remain important artistic and philosophical differences between King and Campbell. Firstly, there is divergence on the matter of identification with and unqualified support for 'our writing'. For example, although in its self-referential complexity King's novel *Misery* may appear to propose and constitute an elevation of literary status for horror fictions, its diegesis, as suggested in Sheldon's vexations over the 'degenerate' art of popular fiction, is more ambiguous and revealing.[26] Clearly, both here and in *The Dark Half*, the plot of which (in a poignant instance of art anticipating life by two decades) involves a former National Book Award nominee, the text is also articulating authorial concern with status, and thus with attaining the respect of mainstream critics.[27] The accusation of being 'degenerate' obviously rankles with an authorial consciousness focused upon, if not obsessed with, the divide between genre and literary fiction. This is no more vividly demonstrated than when Sheldon admits that dismissal of his work as 'popular' 'hurt him quite badly', in that it 'didn't jibe with his self-image as a serious writer who was only churning out these shitty romances in order to subsidise his (flourish of trumpets please!) REAL WORK'.[28] There is an obvious critique of a perceived cultural elitism at work here. However, this critique is itself undercut by the self-contradictory inflection of creative self-loathing, not least in the context that this, the novel within the novel that Sheldon is being forced to write, and *Misery* itself are themselves by implication 'shitty' horror fictions. In her innovative analysis of King as a writer of popular fiction outside the familiar umbrella of Gothic studies, Amy J. Palko, employing the concept of *habitus* drawn from Pierre Bourdieu, seeks to 'release' the writer from 'the confines of the horror genre', portraying him instead as engaged with 'exploring and questioning the cultural forces and processes that give rise to such designations as "popular" or "literary" writing in the first place'.[29] The contrast with Campbell's self-positioning as a horror writer could hardly be more marked. Valuable as Palko's thesis is, the implication of imprisonment given by her references to confinement and release seems at odds with such comfortable self-description. Nor, it can be contended, does Campbell's overt embrace of categorisation preclude his work from being of relevance in the kind of debates raised by Palko. For his part, Campbell repeatedly and vigorously propounds the value of imaginative literature in his own narratives. As a video shop proprietor in *Needing Ghosts* asserts, albeit defensively, there is 'nothing in here to be ashamed of. Stories, that's all they are.'[30] Further, while placing himself squarely within the 'confines' of and defending horror fiction – 'our writing' – Campbell has expressed the desire to expand its parameters. He professes to stand 'for broadening the genre, not narrowing it'.[31] The sheer diversity of Campbell's own output, while never abandoning the generic label of 'horror', testifies to this ambition.

The second area of difference between Campbell and King arises from this very desire for, and spirit of, experimentation. In *Danse Macabre*, the American author elevates the primacy of the 'made-up story' above all else. King argues that

> My own belief about fiction, long and deeply held, is that story *must* be paramount over all other considerations in fiction; that story *defines* fiction, and that all other considerations – theme, mood, tone, symbol, style, even characterisation – are expendable.[32]

On Writing refrains this mantra, with the insistence that 'good' writing 'always begins with story and progresses to theme'.[33] Annie Wilkes, the antagonist and, among several guises, the reader-surrogate in *Misery*, expresses distaste for narratives which are 'hard to follow' and keep the reader 'yo-yoing back and forth in time', and her creator's strong opposition to the experimental *in medias res* technique is also expressed in paratextual writings.[34] In contrast, Campbell's aforementioned formative admiration for the cinematic auteur Alain Resnais has led King's British contemporary to follow a less formally conservative and more innovative pathway. It is a minor irony in comparing the two, given the disparity in the number of adaptations into other media of the writers' works, that Campbell in his fictions displays a filmic sensibility which equals King's. In a 1994 article, 'Horror Fiction and the Mainstream', Campbell discloses that

> the film-maker whose influence most shaped my prose was Alain Resnais, with *Hiroshima Mon Amour* and especially *Last Year in Marienbad* . . . I found the instant flashbacks and other narrative dislocations of these films profoundly disturbing and exciting . . . I've been trying to achieve similar effects in prose for as long as I've sounded like myself.[35]

This influence is manifested in the prominence within Campbell's fictions of those 'characteristics' or 'effects' which King would deem to be of secondary importance, such as mood or style, and, above all, with the ambiguity signified by this 'dislocation' including irresolution at the closure of the narrative. With Campbell, and this is as applicable to his long fictions as to his short stories, it is often the protagonists' situation and the experience of their journey, rather than the 'story' and the final destination, which attain greater significance.

Moreover, it is ambivalence, especially moral relativism, and the absence of a simple Manichaean opposition between good and evil, that characterises the most profound contrast between the two writers. Despite an evident desire for critical recognition, King has also described himself as a producer of 'plain fiction for plain folks'.[36] The self-deprecation belies an acute and commercially canny awareness of readership. King's writing is governed by perceived needs for both accessibility and for giving this envisaged readership what it wants. Implicit in this self-description is thus a belief in a final unambivalence with respect to fundamental moral clarity – the reader may be 'challenged', but not so much as to invalidate a text's marketability – and formal closure: King is, fundamentally, a populist *par excellence*. For example, the novel *Misery*, King has argued, is about 'the redemptive power of writing'.[37] Ultimately, there is no question in its dramatic composition about whom the reader is meant to sympathise with. The relationship between Sheldon and his nemesis, Annie Wilkes, is complex, but it is finally unambiguous. Wilkes represents a demonised, arguably overheated, composite of the Victorian 'Constant Reader', an 'Angel of Death' and – in a sign of the author simultaneously deploying whilst seeking to critique several generic tropes at once – 'graven images worshipped by superstitious African tribes in the novels of H. Rider Haggard, and stories, and doom'.[38] A mass murderer whose victims include babies, it is imperative that the 'dangerously crazy' Wilkes dies, not just for Sheldon's survival, but for the satisfaction of King's anticipated reader.[39] Despite a false coda involving a cat and a sofa, she is duly eliminated, as are George Stark, the antagonist in *The Dark Half*, or the finally murderous Morton Rainey in *Secret Window*. The appearance of resolution and closure is all-important in these Gothic narratives. By comparison, there are more victims than villains, and no easy 'answers', in Campbell's imaginative universe. S.T. Joshi, with King's fictions in mind, rightly praises Campbell for rarely taking recourse to such simple 'moral fantasy' in his own fictions, on the grounds that he 'is far too aware of the triumph of evil in the real world, or rather that good and evil are merely fronts of perspective' found in any individual or society.[40] Vitally, Campbell's works seek not to 'redeem', but, in contrast to King, to discomfort. Campbell has admitted to hoping 'that they will disturb the reader and make them look again at things they may have taken for granted', and 'engage with reality in some way'.[41]

Pre-eminent amongst the victims in Campbell's vision is the figure of the bibliophile: his fictions are populated by characters who write or who depend upon books for their survival. Campbell has described writing as 'a compulsion' and has even likened the activity to substance abuse.[42] In a typically confessional 1995 essay, he ventures the theory

> that creativity is or can be a form of addiction, to the emotional highs and imaginative pleasures it brings. The perhaps inevitable obverse or side effects are depression of comparable intensity ... Depression is apparently the price I pay for having developed a gift to the point that it gives me my greatest pleasure. Sometimes that compensation can seem only just enough.[43]

The allusion to a form of mental illness reinforces the impression of a sour tone, demarcated by paranoia and obsession, as seen previously with *The Face That Must Die* and other texts. It is a tonality that is largely absent in King's 'plain', deliberately accessible writing but which is pervasive in Campbell's. Another of King's author-protagonists, Thad Beaumont in *The Dark Half*, conscious that he has materialised a monstrous alter ego in the form of the murderous Stark, defends himself on the grounds that he 'had only wanted to find a way to write another good story, because doing that made him happy'.[44] By contrast, contentment of any kind is in short supply in Campbell's fictions, in which characters more often than not act under duress or 'compulsion'. Moreover, the validity and morality of their actions are open to question. Transposed explicitly to the bibliophile protagonist, the creative manifestation of this 'compulsion' in Campbell's vision are obsessive, haunted and paranoid figures – unreliable narrators seemingly traversing across or entrapped within a bleak and threatening landscape. None embody these qualities more vividly than the protagonists of Campbell's novellas, *Needing Ghosts* and *The Booking*. The next section outlines the theoretical and comparative status of both in the context of Campbell's other fictions and analyses his approach to the novella. Campbell's use of this medium, a form of intermediate length between the short story and the novel, is itself highly deliberate. Like Campbell's relationship with King, it deserves a degree of attention which it has not, until now, received.[45]

Campbell's Oneiric Texts and the Novella Form

Needing Ghosts and *The Booking* cover some familiar urban Gothic terrain. As already discussed, Campbell's metropolitan settings are distinctively bleak. Typically, they recount the physical and psychological experience of an individual consciousness. It is an experience that has the quality of a dystopian nightmare. For example, like the ill-fated Gregor Samsa in Franz Kafka's novella *The Metamorphosis* (1915), *Needing Ghosts* opens with its protagonist waking alone and vulnerable in the dark. Simon Mottershead lacks 'sense of his body', is surrounded by 'hints of shapes', and fancies that he hears voices whispering (p. 9). Both *Needing Ghosts* and *The Booking* appear to equate commercial development with the encroachment upon and decay of pre-existing civic structures and values. The library in *Needing Ghosts* is encased in a shopping mall 'through an arch of massive concrete blocks reminiscent of the entrance to an ancient tomb' (p. 28). On a similarly elegiac note, the bookshop setting of Campbell's later text is located on 'the nearest street the precinct hadn't encompassed or destroyed yet', one seemingly 'abandoned by the new development and by humanity itself'.[46] As James Goho argues in relation to Campbell's short stories, the author 'animates the city as a modern Gothic space'.[47] The reference to entombment in *Needing Ghosts* echoes Baudrillard's description of the 'cemetery' function of postmodern urban spaces, settlements that are now 'ghost towns, cities of death'.[48]

This affinity demonstrates how Campbell's Gothic fictions appear to adhere to the invidious vision of human autonomy that characterise a certain trend in postmodernist thought. Indeed, such Baudrillardian concepts as the simulacra and the hyperreal themselves suggest human immersion and 'entombment'. As with Kirk Morris in the earlier narrative 'Concussion', the protagonists of *Needing Ghosts* and *The Booking* encounter challenges both to their sense of self and to any sense of social bearing that would enable them to maintain control over the reality they inhabit. To some theorists, the consequences for the subject of lack of any authority over its experienced spatial and temporal spheres are acutely invidious. For example, Jameson's argument on the lack of free will of the postmodern self, if applied to the author as protagonist, would inhibit their creative potentiality. His reasoning implies creative incoherence, if not impotence:

> If indeed the subject has lost its capacity actively to extend its pro-tensions and re-tensions across the temporal manifold, to organise its past and future into coherent experience, it becomes difficult enough to see how the cultural productions of such a subject could result in anything but 'heaps of fragments' and in practice of the randomly heterogeneous and fragmentary and the aleatory.[49]

Such 'cultural productions' would also, according to this deeply pessimistic paradigm, be necessarily non-polemical and ambivalent, because 'the indignant moral denunciation of the other [also] becomes unavailable'.[50]

It is apparent in applying such concepts to Campbell that his work dramatises the threat to the humanist perception of a coherent, autonomous and controlling self. This is particularly the case with Campbell's oneiric or dream Gothic fictions, a significant subgrouping within his corpus, to which both *Needing Ghosts* and *The Booking* belong. Dreams and their relationship with the reality of the conscious, 'real' world are a topic to which Campbell has returned repeatedly throughout his career. For instance, the ensemble novel *Incarnate* from 1983 proposes and elucidates the predatory nature of dreams. This 'dream world', one character insists, is 'alive', a sentient force of malevolence which 'wants to feed on what we call reality, feed on it so it can take its place'.[51] *Incarnate*, one of Campbell's longest fictions, is, like *The Nameless*, a fascinating if occasionally artistically and intellectually opaque melange of ideas, not all of them, as Joshi notes, fully formed.[52] By contrast, in referring to Campbell's short stories in *Demons by Daylight*, for example, Joshi singles out for praise the writer's representation, via 'an intense almost stream of consciousness' technique, of a given protagonist's 'mental state as he or she becomes insidiously enmeshed in the bizarre'.[53] There is a comparability of scale between the short story's focus upon the individual and the description of the novella, given in *The Oxford Dictionary of Literary Terms*, as a work 'usually concentrating on a single event or chain of events, with a surprising turning point': both tend to economy.[54] Joe Fassler describes the latter form as 'a narrative of middle length, that can be read at a single sitting'.[55] The evocation of an image of domestic comfort here, akin to a long M. R. James ghost story, does not, admittedly, suggest an immediate affinity between the novella, which emerged in Europe as a predominantly realist mode of narrative in the late eighteenth century, and the disorientation and challenges posed by postmodernism. Nevertheless, it is worth engaging with Ian McEwan's similar claim that the brevity of the novella appeals to readers because 'you can hold the whole thing structurally in your mind at once'.[56] With respect to Campbell's oneiric works, the novella form, by virtue of its aforementioned inherent focus on a single character and condensed time frame, allows for expansion beyond the constraints of the short story. Yet at the same time it also affords a tighter and more coherent forum for analysis of portrayal of the subject and its relationship with extratextual reality. Further, the kind of representation lauded by Joshi in Campbell's short stories, which is of the isolated and paranoid psyche amidst condensed temporal and spatial terms of reference, is even more effectively developed aesthetically in Campbell's use of the longer form. It is the challenge to notions of structure and control, to the idea of being able to 'hold the whole thing in your mind at once', that confer upon these narratives their peculiar power and philosophical richness.

Needing Ghosts was Campbell's first substantial novella. It remained his only such text for over two decades, before being followed over thirty years later by three others in relatively quick succession: *The Last Revelation of Gla'aki* (2013) and *The Pretence* (2016), as well as the same year's *The Booking*. In one respect, Campbell's use of the form accords with established generic tradition set by texts like Henry James's *The Turn of the Screw* (1898) or H. P. Lovecraft's *At the Mountains of Madness* (1936). As indicated, Campbell's entries in the field, at least in the case of *The Booking* or *Needing Ghosts*, appear to exemplify the urban Gothic, replete with urban Gothic's presentation of paranoia and decay. Yet Campbell's readiness to use the novella format also constitutes another important contrast to King, whose own *magnum opus* contains several works like *IT* (1986), running to over a thousand pages, epics which dwarf even *Incarnate* in length. King, to 2020, had produced only three stand-alone novellas in his career: *Cycle of the Werewolf* (1983), *Gwendy's Button Box* (co-written with Richard Chizmar, 2017), and *Elevation* (2018); but ten collections of fictions of varying sub-novel length.[57] He has memorably described the novella as 'a really terrible place, an anomaly-ridden literary banana republic'.[58] King's tone here is typically hyperbolic and humorous, but the approach to the form shown is soberly utilitarian, driven by concern about 'genre markets'.[59] For example, in his Foreword to *Four Past Midnight* (1990), King states baldly that one *raison d'être* for his previous anthology *Different Seasons* (1982) was that it contained stories 'which were too long to be published as short stories and just a little too short to be books on their own'.[60] In contrast to this largely pragmatic, even prosaic approach to the production of novellas, Campbell has more specific aesthetic intentions in utilising this format. In an interview given in 2016, he states that a publisher

> approached me to contribute to his ongoing series of novellas of psychological horror, and *The Booking* was the result ... developing a couple of ideas that had been waiting for the impetus. The crucial point about novellas for me [is that] I'll only write one if I feel that the form is best suited to the idea. That is to say, it mustn't be an extended short story, nor yet a condensed novel.[61]

In the case of both *Needing Ghosts* and *The Booking*, this deliberation is borne out by the notable and highly stylised illustrations, by Jamil Akib and Santiago Caruso respectively, accompanying the first editions of both texts. Akib's cartoonish and grotesque caricatures of human figures for *Needing Ghosts*, complete with long legs and bug eyes, viewed from below, serve to intensify the text's Kafkaesque atmosphere of distortion, nightmare and persecution. The presence of his and of Caruso's contrastingly more ethereal cobweb- and spiral-themed artwork for *The Booking*, reflecting the seeming 'enmeshment' of that novella's protagonist in a 'bizarre', woven netherworld, contributes to the impression of these texts as being carefully produced for and marketed at a niche base of readers.[62]

However, beyond the packaging of his work, the recurrence of 'intense' as an adjective in relation to Campbell is striking, both in what little scholarship has been thus far undertaken on his fictions to date and in the writer's paratextual material. Expressing strong opposition to what he sees as a tendency towards evocation of the historical past in supernatural tales by writers like Susan Hill, Campbell has declared that

> For me at least, nostalgia muffles the effect of any good ghost story: I don't want to feel comfortably distant from the supernatural experience he [the writer] seeks to communicate, I want the experience to be communicated as intensely as possible.... The same is true for the horror story, a genre recurrently overtaken by nostalgia.[63]

In contrast to the formally and politically conservative Hill, Campbell thus usually displays a propensity for contemporary settings for his fictions. Simultaneously, Campbell's admission to being an intuitive and instinctive writer who is striving to achieve certain 'intense' psychological effects in this way has led commentators like Goho and Joel Lane to describe his work as being consequently somewhat *a*political. Writing of Campbell's novels in the early 1990s, Lane notes that their 'essential concerns become personal responsibility and the integrity of the self in different times', and that a political focus is 'less visible'.[64] According to Goho, Campbell 'does not or tries not to write about society'.[65] Whether one defines Campbell's work as postmodernist or not, and Hutcheon, for one, views such fictions as being on the contrary 'resolutely historical and inescapably political', even cursory analysis of a socially aware text like *The One Safe Place* makes obvious that these readings of Campbell's vision are, or were to become very quickly with hindsight (Lane's article dates from 1993), incomplete and therefore unsatisfactory.[66] It is undeniable that artistic and philosophical concerns, having in fact been present from the beginning of Campbell's career, progressively attain more prominence in his fictions. Nevertheless, this book has already demonstrated that Campbell's work is, consistently if often obliquely, engaged in sociopolitical critique. Despite a focus upon psychological interiority, and in spite of their presenting an obvious formal contrast to the social realism and naturalism of novels like *One Safe Place* or *Obsession*, both *Needing Ghosts* and *The Booking* also feature protagonists who seek to extract meaning and exert autonomy over their own lives, but who are, or who feel intensely dependent upon, and at the mercy of, external forces which deprive them of such controls. Further, they are highly significant works. Separated by a quarter-century, they highlight a responsiveness to sociopolitical change and associated advances in technology that demarcates a major development within Campbell's Gothic vision. The next section examines the complex and prescient mediation of the 'paranoid author' figure in the first of these texts, *Needing Ghosts*, arguably Campbell's ultimate *tour de force* as a Gothic writer.

The Author Who Haunts Himself: Needing Ghosts

Appearing mid-way through Campbell's extensive career, this 1990 novella is a central text in understanding Campbell's highly personal interpretation of the Gothic. It is also a hybrid one. *Needing Ghosts* combines seemingly contradictory elements of the personal and humanist perspective with literary postmodernism, a tendency denoted by thematic resistance to notions of egocentrism, ascription of cultural meaning and historical placement. 'The reader must decide how autobiographical *Needing Ghosts* may be', Campbell claims regarding his novella in a later essay, 'in particular, the image of a writer wandering the streets of an unfamiliar town and not finding his books in the shops.'[67] Campbell's noncommittal statement notwithstanding, *Needing Ghosts* certainly functions from one perspective as thinly veiled autobiography. It is his most sustained and concentrated portrait of the travails of a professional writer of Gothic horror and the tensions encountered in an author's relationships with other writers and their audiences. In the course of events, the novella's protagonist, Mottershead, named after a bookshop employee acquaintance of Campbell's (and, like his creator, a married father of two) does indeed embark on a quest in which 'the compulsion to find himself on the shelves' grows and the prospect of failing to do so prolongs the 'black depression' described as a terrifying experience 'seep[ing] through him like poison' (pp. 47, 52). As with so many of Campbell's lead characters, Mottershead is passionate about literature. His ultimate ambition is to run a bookshop containing works by obscure and forgotten authors. This is envisaged as a sanctuary, where Mottershead 'can choose to resurrect whatever they achieved as the fancy guides him', and the sensation makes the character 'feel as if he has found within himself a power he wasn't aware of possessing' (p. 22). The parallels with Campbell's own varied and substantial paratextual activity beyond his own writing, specifically the revival of works by neglected writers like Adrian Ross, are unmistakable. Mottershead thus clearly serves as an instance of what Waugh describes as 'surfiction', in which, without resorting to extradiegesis, the author, or a surrogate for the author, is deliberately incorporated into a narrative.[68]

Concurrently, whilst it displays authorial self-consciousness *Needing Ghosts* is also, by Campbell's admission, the most subconsciously driven and, in form, 'close to surrealism' of his longer Gothic fictions.[69] If his most successful short stories, according to Goho, are 'a grim updating' of James Joyce's *Dubliners*, then *Needing Ghosts* is surely Campbell's emulation of the same author's *Ulysses*.[70] In a refrain of the fractured and elliptical narrative structure of 'Concussion', the novella's plot is a hallucinogenic odyssey. It purports to relate a day's experience in the life, or the dream life, of an amnesiac writer. The narrative follows Mottershead from the moment he awakes, through his travels across an unnamed city, the vicissitudes and repeated sense of *déjà vu* that he experiences along the way, and, eventually, his attempts to return home to reunite with his family – whom he finally finds apparently murdered by his own hand. The ambivalence around the reality or non-reality of their deaths is crucial. Again, this invites comparison with *American Psycho*

(1991), Ellis's almost exactly contemporary study of a real or imagined would-be murderer, an affinity returned to shortly.

During Mottershead's darkly picaresque journey to this point, as he delivers an ill-received address to a group of fellow writers and tries to track down copies of his work in retail outlets, the protagonist encounters a series of bizarre, unsympathetic, insinuating and even menacing figures. In support of the view that there is some degree of similitude between surrealism and postmodernism as well as modernism, the presence of these beings and their largely unexplained hostility exemplify what Jerry Aline Flieger describes as a 'paranoid modality' characterising much postmodern writing.[71] With *Needing Ghosts*, Campbell, like Thomas Pynchon or Paul Auster, presents a protagonist who is, as Flieger describes, 'haunted by cryptic characters, at once ubiquitous and maddeningly elusive, sinister shadows which the hero can't quite figure, or finger'.[72] Such unreliability of perspective is, of course, symptomatic of the larger-scale disparagement of all authoritative discourse under the various postmodernist critiques proposed by Jameson, Baudrillard and Lyotard. To appropriate the latter's terminology, the certitude of waking reality, like religious dogma or political ideology, can be interpreted as another illusory metanarrative, perched on the precarious and vulnerable foundations of convention.

The protagonist's situation in *Needing Ghosts* seems to exemplify the 'struggle for self-knowledge, definition and access to the real' which Maria Beville describes as the 'engine' propelling Gothic-postmodern narratives.[73] As an amnesiac, Mottershead is an inherently unstable subject. He is subject to extreme anxiety about his own sanity against the increasing *in*sanity of his predicament. Mottershead is also the victim of depression, a sensation likened, as he struggles to remember past events, to 'a black pit into which he is falling with increasing speed' (p. 66). The comparison of psychological anguish to a dark 'pit' of despair is entirely conventional, but the protagonist's vulnerability also throws the veracity and authority of his perspective into doubt. It renders him, like Patrick Bateman in Ellis's *American Psycho*, an acutely unreliable narrator. As with Mottershead's recollection that 'in one of his stories a man who's obsessed with the impossibility of knowing if he's died in his sleep convinces himself that he has, and is dreaming' (p. 73), the division between dream and reality, or of the memory of reality, is elided. This state of ambiguity is articulated repeatedly through interrogative narrative. Thus, for example, Mottershead muses that a remembrance of walking in the park with his family could alternatively be just something that he wrote or intended to write, and the final hope that they will return is undercut by the uneasy, questioning recollection: 'hasn't he tried this before, more than once, many times?' (p. 80).

Naturally, the sense of precognitive psychological experience or *déjà vu* evokes Sigmund Freud's famous description of the uncanny, as 'that species of the frightening that goes back to what was once well known and had long been familiar'.[74] *Needing Ghosts* can be interpreted as perhaps Campbell's most sustained fictional exposition on the theme of the uncanny. The narrative focuses upon the perspective of one 'anchor' character. It is a perspective from which events external to that character, marked by ambiguity between and the constant threat posed by or eruption of proximate surrealistic 'fantasy' into a besieged 'reality', can be perceived as the projections of a damaged psyche. In Mottershead's quest, the text additionally has affinities with what Hutcheon describes as historiographic metafiction's tendency to 'use memory to try to make sense of the past'.[75] It is testament to the complexity of Campbell's fiction – the novella's rich allusiveness, mixed tonal register and, in the mode of Alain Resnais, its ambiguity – that such varied readings as, for example, the psychoanalytical, are possible. *Needing Ghosts* affords multiple interpretations of and ascription as to its final textual 'meaning'. For Joshi, the novella's writer protagonist has '*fallen into his own fictional universe*'.[76] However, a more purely metaphysical interpretation is also as valid. As Steven J. Mariconda argues, the text may also be read as the reverie, life review and exploration of alternate realities of a dying man seeking 'the endless sunlit forest' (p. 80).[77] Here, as ever with Campbell, an acute awareness of both literary and cinematic precedents is evident. Thematically and structurally, *Needing Ghosts* recalls texts as varied as Ambrose Bierce's 'An Occurrence at Owl Creek Bridge' (1890), William Golding's novel

Pincher Martin (1956) and Adrian Lynne's film *Jacob's Ladder* (1990). All these works are marked by disrupted temporality and by the protagonist's stream of consciousness, and conclude with their deaths. With similar implications, the bus driver's ominous reply to Mottershead, that 'you'll end up where you need to go' (p. .64) echoes E. F. Benson's short story 'The Bus-Conductor' (1906) and its adaptation in the portmanteau film *Dead of Night* (Basil Dearden and others, 1945) as the 'The Hearse Driver' segment. The framing story of *Dead of Night* also features a character like Mottershead that experiences *déjà vu* and appears to commit murder, and who, in a surrealist climax, realises that he is trapped in a recurring nightmare.[78]

Campbell's learned literary and cinematic sensibilities and fertile imagination are reflected in the transmutation of many familiar tropes drawn from Western cultural tradition. These include the figure of Charon the ferryman from classical Greek mythology. This psychopomp is updated in the forms of both the bus driver and, especially, the unlit ferry with its silent and largely unseen crew which finally takes Mottershead over water to his island home. However, for the most part Campbell adopts familiar Gothic trappings, right until the moment Mottershead finally enters 'the locked room' (p. 78) with its dreadful secret. Familial concerns are conventionally understood to be central to the Gothic tradition from foundational texts like *The Castle of Otranto* (1764). Accordingly, threats to the family unit have been a preoccupation of Campbell's since the advent of his own paternity in the 1970s – whether that threat is averted, as in *The Claw* (1984), or pursued to a tragic conclusion, as it is in *The Long Lost* (1993) and *The House on Nazareth Hill* (1996). Mottershead's wife and daughter in *Needing Ghosts*, even when he perceives them as alive, are portrayed as animate and sentient corpses, their hair 'grey with dust' (p. 65). As such, they are the last in a gauntlet of sinister but familiar generic presences, from the men wearing dark suits who silently watch Mottershead at the bus stop to the human-animal hybrid nurse at the 'Wild Rest Home'. The latter's 'face like a hound's skull, pallid flapping belly, limbs white and thin as bones' (p. 62) suggests a fusion of carnivalesque grotesquerie and death-symbolism. Campbell evokes several cultural phobic pressure points here; amongst others, fear of chimeric inter-species degeneration. Some derive directly even from the period of medieval historical Gothic, as when the upper storeys of shops appear to Mottershead to be populated by 'gargoyle'-like figures (p. 43). The half-seen presence which threatens him on the bus, with its 'hint of a face in the air, a glimmering of eyes and teeth' and 'thin white fingers' (pp. 66–7) clearly mimics the reticence of M. R. James's ghost stories, along with that writer's taste for emaciated but malevolent spectres. Elsewhere, as in the references to red-eyed beckoning mannequins, a taxi driver's 'curly red wig' and 'dollish eyes' (pp. 25–6) and a two-foot-high doll the head of which the hero stamps on in a climactic fit of revulsion, the text draws variously upon a rich vein of autonomatophia, coulrophobia and pedophobia.[79]

However, most significantly in this macabre procession, the protagonist is stalked by his own *doppelgänger*. This takes the form of a black-gummed entity with a loose skull cap. Malevolent doubles and impostors also feature in two of Campbell's preceding longer fictions, *Incarnate* and *The Influence* (1988), although in both these instances the victim and villain had been a child. *Needing Ghosts* marks the first substantive deployment of this entity in relation to an adult subject. This trope was to attain great prominence in several of Campbell's twenty-first-century fictions, as discussed in the next chapter, but the peculiarly antagonistic and unsettling nature of social interactions which distinguish his fictions is manifested to an extreme degree here. Mottershead displays an immediate and intense dislike for this persistent interloper. Disproportionately hostile to the stranger at every encounter, he refuses the man's insistence that they have 'lots in common' and need to 'talk about ourselves' (p. 42), and eventually even removes his teeth to silence him. It is only at the end of the narrative, when Mottershead sees a videotape of himself gripping his own scalp that the extremity of their encounters, insinuating and overfamiliar on the stranger's side, antagonistic and finally violent on the writer's, and their significance, are retrospectively explained.

It is with the writer's confrontation with a being that is in fact himself that the centre of the 'labyrinth' of *Needing Ghosts* is reached. In Campbell's vision of authorship, the haunter is himself haunted, and becomes his own 'other'. Mottershead's tormentor's eyes are described as 'looking as if being compelled to see too much has swollen them almost too large for their sockets' (p. 42). At one level, *Needing Ghosts* can be interpreted as Campbell's updating of Lovecraft's short story 'The Outsider' (1921), with writers as denizens of the windowless, asylum-like 'soundproof room' (p. 31) and the author-protagonist, like the unnamed narrator of Lovecraft's tale, as much the source of fear as its victim. Campbell satirises, almost embraces, the socially marginalised, even pariah, status popularly associated with the horror author. Mottershead, on leaving his house, strikes an ironic and defiant note. He reflects that

> he isn't surprised to find himself alone on the road; presumably nobody else rises at this hour. He can't recall ever having met his neighbours, but if they want to avoid him, that suits him. 'He's out again,' he announces at the top of his voice. 'Lock your doors, hide behind the furniture, pull the blankets over your heads or he'll know you're there.' (p. 12)

Mottershead's fellow writers at the library are portrayed as similarly eccentric. They are vaguely menacing, a motley collection of the earnest and the querulous who are obviously drawn from, if caricaturing, Campbell's real-life observations of such assemblies. There is no doubt that Campbell himself views the entire narrative as being at least partly 'comic' (Acknowledgements in *Needing Ghosts*, p. 5), as demonstrated when Mottershead finds only pederast pornography of borderline legality bearing his name in one bookshop, and, in an episode neatly spoofing Lovecraft's classic anti-miscegenation tale, 'The Shadow over Innsmouth' (1936), is berated by its staff, who are all dressed as bridal frogs to promote a children's book.

The overall register of Campbell's text, though, is intensely *serious*. The core scene is Mottershead's ill-fated address to the writers' group. It is nakedly autobiographical, to the extent that any pretence of division between fictional text and factual paratext largely disappears. In an otherwise stilted and uncompleted performance, Mottershead, in a moment and passage of lucidity, articulates his creator's view on the isolation of the writer, and the centrality of and 'compulsion' involved in the act of writing:

> Nobody except a writer knows how it feels to be a writer ... I'll tell you how it felt to me ... Every day I'd be wakened by a story aching to be told. Writing's a compulsion. By the time you're any good at it you no longer have the choice of giving it up. It won't leave you alone even when you're with people, even when you're desperate to sleep ... it's like seeing everything with new eyes. It's like dreaming while you're awake. (p. 34)

The text's continuous representation of a single consciousness confers upon Mottershead's pronouncements at this point a sense of urgency and of authority. He goes on to liken the writer's mind to a spider seeking to 'catch reality and spin it into patterns' (p. 34). This underlines the novella's representation of the creative urge, akin to dream, as being both sentient and predatory. Reality is 'raw material to be shaped', woven, cobweb-like, by the hapless writer, and the narrative reveals that the impulse 'continuing to make demands on him after he had lost the power to write' (p. 74) is responsible for Mottershead's insanity. In a strikingly vivid image, conveying tenacious malignancy, it is compared to 'teeth buried in his brain, growing rat-like at its substance' (p. 70). This is a fiercely paranoiac interpretation of creativity. Its association with the predatory stands in stark contrast to King's concept of telling stories to attain personal 'happiness'.

The implications of this self-inflective, anti-narrative stance are profound, for both the author as surrogate for the subject and, by implication, the reader. For *Needing Ghosts*, like *American Psycho*, seeks to 'disturb' and disorientate the latter. The deployment of a present-tense narrative mode, as in Ellis's novel, is implicitly anti-nostalgic. It removes the sense of comfort for the reader afforded by retrospective reportage, conferring instead a documentary immediacy and unpredictability upon Mottershead's experiences and their outcome. Further, use of the present grammatical tense intensifies an impression of the subject's entrapment in an eternal, nightmarish cycle: Mottershead is caught in an environment which has substituted a temporal circularity for the certainties of linearity and progression. 'As a child', the narrator relates, 'he hoped life would never end; when he grew up he was afraid it might not' (p. 77). Recounted in a perpetual present, this narrative is thus far from adhering to the traditional form of the *Künstlerroman*. There is no sense of 'growth' of experience in *Needing Ghosts* towards maturity. Rather, as in *American Psycho*, the impression is one of the subject's stasis and entrapment. The repeated evocation of existential crisis, as Mottershead's surroundings seem to lose three-dimensional coherence and his own reflection 'shimmers like disturbed water', and darkness seems about to consume him (p. 52), echoes the protagonist's condition in Ellis's novel. Bateman describes himself similarly as being perpetually in 'some kind of existential chasm', in which he is 'simply imitating reality', or 'simply was not there'.[80]

As in King's novel *Misery*, Campbell's work includes within itself a commentary upon its own narrative. This is expressed in the form of the fictional text within the text, *Cadenza*. Described by Mottershead as his best work and the quarry of his fevered search throughout the narrative, its opening sentence, 'He knows this dark' (pp. 9, 27) – a quintessentially existentialist statement – is also the opening sentence of the novella itself. The text is thus in a sense caught in its own 'web', self-contained and self-reflective. Its name evoking a masterpiece, the virtuoso performance of the artist, *Cadenza* represents not so much the 'found manuscript' in Campbell's version of the Gothic, as it does the lost text. *Cadenza* affirms the centrality of writing as a theme, serving as a symbol of the loss of ownership and control wielded by the author over their work. Yet moreover, taking Campbell's avatar Mottershead himself as representative of the subject, it also has an ontological resonance, for it symbolises the subject's simultaneous desire for and the loss of control over meaning. The attainment of such security is a common goal for characters in Campbell's fictional universe. Whether they are protagonists, antagonists or minor figures, like the disaffected and discontented attendees of the 'Undying Light' meetings in *The Nameless*, they all seek 'faith' or 'anything that would explain their lives'. Unlike 'Misery Returns' or the 'Memory Lane' scrapbook, which function in *Misery* respectively as Sheldon's means of survival or a record of Wilkes's warped psychosis ('like a novel so disgusting you just had to finish it'), the function of *Cadenza* is presented as being, through its self-consumption and circularity, fundamentally meaningless, and finally amoral.[81] As Ellis's Bateman states of his own narrative, the entire preceding text of *American Psycho*, 'this confession has meant nothing.'[82]

In a powerful metaphor for the disorientation and struggle of the subject, the writer literally loses control of his work. Campbell's avatar Mottershead finds that his own acquired and cherished copy of *Cadenza* physically slips from his grasp. He loses his identity as author when his name disappears and then, in an image of surrealistic body horror which recalls John Carpenter's film version of *The Thing* (1982), witnesses what had been his photograph develop multiple legs, fall to the floor and scuttle through a crack beneath a skirting board. This representation of the literary artefact itself as monstrous alterity is explicable in the context that such a response is symptomatic and one form of articulation of what Savu describes as 'crises of author, subject [and] representation' that have been wrought by postmodernism.[83] These perceived 'crises', or transformations, could only intensify with rapid sociopolitical change and profound growth in communications. Campbell's later poioumenomic novella of psychological horror, *The Booking*, featuring not one but an entire bookshop of sentient tomes, was able not only to address these transitions more explicitly, but to engage with some key dystopian assumptions underlying postmodernist paradigms.

Defending Against 'The Dreadful Dark': The Booking

'In the computer age', Lyotard asserted at the close of the 1970s, 'the question of knowledge is more than ever the question of government.'[84] With hindsight, by alluding to the growth of technology and in its rich inferences regarding the availability, form, ownership and control of information and even surveillance by the executive over those seeking it, Lyotard's statement appears prescient, even poignantly understated. The ensuing decades were obviously marked by seismic sociopolitical changes with the ascent of neoliberalism, and by rapid developments in mass communications. The 'computer age', in the form of personal computer, laptop or mobile phone, now permeates every professional and domestic sphere.[85] An awareness of the exact nature of these transformations and the sheer scale of their pervasiveness in contemporary life experiences could not have been available to either the theorist or the novelist during the pre-millennial period, when Campbell wrote *Needing Ghosts*.

Campbell's 2016 novella, *The Booking*, deftly combines consciousness of the contemporary with fidelity to both antecedence within the literary Gothic and the author's own created fictional universe. Its concept and setting evoke earlier texts such as M. R. James's 'The Tractate Middoth' (1911) or Algernon Blackwood's 'The Whisperers' (1912), in which the intellectual content of volumes from a former library haunt a protagonist in the present day, and Campbell's own short story, 'Cold Print' (1969), in its seedy, menacing and ultimately monstrous bookseller. Campbell also set an earlier full-length novel in a bookshop, the semi-comic supernatural thriller *The Overnight* (2004). However, that text, in featuring a large ensemble of characters trapped in a modern commercial outlet, is necessarily episodic. Despite articulating a critique of corporate capitalism, represented by a store manager who fails to recognise the supernatural menace at work and persists in subordinating himself to his employers to the very end, the novel's effect is diluted by Campbell's perceived need to stage mini-climaxes at the end of each chapter – in this case, through use of the 'cliff-hanger' plot device and the somewhat repetitious depiction of elaborate deaths for his sizeable cast.[86] The later novella is a tighter and much richer hybrid. Within what appears as a highly traditional milieu, *The Booking* presents a concentrated microcosm of Campbell's individual and iconoclastic distillation of the subject's experience under postmodernity.

The dramatic action of *The Booking* is straightforward. In an unnamed urban community, a seemingly young, unemployed librarian, Kiefer Abloose, applies for and takes a job as a technician at 'Books Are Life', a cobweb-strewn antiquarian and second-hand bookshop. The narrative recounts Kiefer's relationship with its proprietor, Alfred 'Alf' Brookes, an apparently fusty, eccentric and cantankerous older man. Brookes seems to be a living and decrepit relic from an earlier, pre-technological era. His ill-fitting suit has 'frayed cuffs', while the man himself has a 'stringy neck' and – with dark connotations of generic alterity recalling 'Cold Print' – 'long fingernails' (pp. 14, 16). The bookseller also has pronounced technophobic and especially cyberphobic views, and an oddly possessive attitude to his stock. Despite his antipathy, Brookes wants Kiefer to create a website to advertise the store's wares, to catalogue them, and, seemingly, to record electronically Brookes's own proud *magnus opus* creation, a vast ledger of the shop's contents: 'a real book. One man's vision' (p. 40). Brookes, like Mottershead in *Needing Ghosts*, thus partly functions as an author surrogate, although the avatar is much less obviously autobiographical here, as the character is not a professional writer. Brookes's vocation is proximate, more compensatory: as Kiefer reflects sardonically on his employer, he 'wanted to be a writer, after all' (p. 58). Rich in dialogue exchanges and unfolding almost entirely in a single setting, the text possesses a theatrical quality. Its human interaction enacted largely between Kiefer and Brookes, the narrative effectively becomes a 'three-hander', with the shop itself, its books 'fidgeting on the shelves' (p. 30), becoming another living, collective presence. The place functions as an intensifier or silent chorus as the uneasy relationship between the 'two' men becomes more fractious and reaches a final crisis. Recalling the spirit of a Blackwood or M. R. James narrative, *The Booking* thus has a highly familiar Gothic locale, one which could seem, in the contemporary context, quaintly insular and anachronistic. Nonetheless, the text successfully reflects and mediates both external political and technological developments. Compared to *Needing Ghosts*, the later novella represents a widening of focus to consider the form, function and status of 'information' – in the form of the written word, literature itself – in what has become an electronic era. It does so while also continuing, and developing, Campbell's vision of the survival of literary creativity, the author and the subject.

In terms of establishing its scenario and its tonality, *The Booking*, like *Needing Ghosts*, aligns overtly with the postmodern. Indeed, in contrast to its predecessor, Campbell makes explicit reference to external sociopolitical and economic contexts, conferring a topical relevance upon the familiar Gothic trope of urban malaise. Kiefer is an instantly recognisable analogue for the displaced victim of the austerity policies pursued by British governments in the wake of the 2008 'Great Recession'. Kiefer, indeed, represents an economic 'everyman', in that he has previously experienced a long-term and unsuccessful quest for employment, including submissions to supermarkets and fast-food outlets as an overqualified applicant. In an overtly topical reference, Kiefer discloses to Brookes that he had worked in public libraries 'until half of them were shut down' (p. 16).[87] The central character thus joins John Horridge and other Campbell protagonists in that he incarnates the plight of the subject under the 'present-day, multinational capitalism' described by Jameson.[88] At the same time, Kiefer, similarly to Mottershead in *Needing Ghosts*, undergoes an acute existential crisis. He loses both his sense of memory of an existence prior to entering the bookshop and of the security afforded by the external, 'real' world. Even Kiefer's most valued relationship to another person, his supposed 'girlfriend' Cynthia, becomes occluded. In what may be viewed as an enactment of Jameson's vision of the failure of 'our faulty representations of some immense communication and computer network' and of Baudrillard's 'disappearance of the subject and its identity', even Cynthia's image, mediated by Kiefer's laptop, begins to disintegrate.[89] Moreover, in Kiefer's early sense that he is being observed by security cameras and store guards, a sense of acute paranoia is immediately established. This depiction and evocation of vexed psychological disorientation is sustained throughout the ensuing narrative, crucially in the passive-aggressive relationship between Kiefer and his apparent employer. It is an arrangement in which the former appears never to know quite where he stands. Brookes's utterances, from the first, interrogative responses, 'Who's asking?' and 'Looking at it, were you?' (p. 10) to Kiefer's initial enquiry about the job, are consistently evasive, sardonic, sarcastic, and insinuating. Creating as much tension as mystery, both Brookes's language, recalling the deliberate minimalism of Samuel Beckett or Harold Pinter, and his behaviour are acutely disconcerting, not merely for the recipient, but for the reader. Campbell's ambiguous characterisation here again contrasts with the approach adopted by King, in which dialogue generally has a more straightforward and less opaque, 'plain' expository function which drives the narrative or all-important 'story' forward.[90] As in most of Campbell's texts, there are no unambivalent 'villains' in *The Booking*. Much more overtly than the conflict between Mottershead and his loose-scalped revenant pursuer in *Needing Ghosts*, the later novella's denouement reveals that both characters, Kiefer and Brookes, are in fact the same man, and that Cynthia, although real, is not Kiefer Alfred Brookes's partner but his daughter. This, of course, demonstrates the intra-psychic anatomisation and fragmentation of the subject (here, the male psyche) characterising many earlier Gothic works like James Hogg's *Memoirs and Confessions of a Justified Sinner* (1824) and more familiar postmodernist fictions, exemplified by Chuck Palahniuk's novel, *Fight Club* (1996).[91]

Analogous to the deployment of *Cadenza* in *Needing Ghosts*, *The Booking* immediately presents a postmodernist self-reflexivity in terms of form, in this case with the almost incantatory and intensifying use of the refrain 'this text was all' (p. 9 *passim*). However, if *Needing Ghosts* presents the author-subject's ordeal in terms of an unending nightmarish circular journey, in which an empty and nihilistic meaningless is the feared 'meaning', *The Booking* enacts, in the most concentrated and claustrophobic form, Campbell's version of a heterotopia. Its near-single setting is akin to the poststructuralist idea of the museum or library described by Michel Foucault, a space in which an 'absolute breach' with traditional notions of temporality and a 'perpetual and indefinite accumulation of time' are experienced.[92] Like Caruso, the novella's illustrator, Campbell's text is itself surrealist and symbolic. The non-realist and allegorical quality is established early, via the protagonist Kiefer's confusion as to whether the bookstore is in 'Fable' or 'Faber' Close (p. 12). Campbell's deliberate word play here teasingly presents alternation between fictions and publisher of fictions. This elision symbolises and foretells the shading between reality and fantasy, the material of insidious dream, which takes place in the ensuing drama. Once reached, the shop 'Books Are Life' itself seems akin, in retrospect, to what Foucault describes as 'a heterotopia of deviation', an environment in which an individual nonconformist consciousness has been placed.[93] As Brookes, the 'jailer' side of Kiefer's personality puts it, 'you're already in my text. You're quite a character' (p. 76). In this case, the 'deviancy' appears to be the continuation of bibliophilia in an electronic era. This is not only on the part of Brookes, whose possessiveness – 'I should have felt them go' (p. 34), he laments at one point – suggests the neo-parental, but Kiefer. The employee concomitantly 'relish[es]' (p. 34) the familiar sensation and physical weight of a book in his hands, and does not want to leave the sanctuary of the shop. Its very name, 'Books Are Life', an imperative, conflates the survival of the text as physical artefact with the survival of the subject. The bewildering dimensions of the shop's premises present an uncanny realm of simultaneous desiccation and expansion, the labyrinth becoming a metaphorical externalisation of the tortuous mental geography of the text's protagonist. Its narrative almost entirely confined to this setting, *The Booking* has the artificial, staged quality of a symbolist enterprise. To develop an analogy of deliberation, the text presents a symposium or workshop. It functions as a space in which competing views of the nature and future of literature, the conduit of information, and by extension the resilience and future of the data-generating and receiving subject, are voiced, and even interrogated – but without the unambivalent certitude of a final resolution.

From one perspective, *The Booking* articulates a familiar range of anxieties concerning the subject's control over itself and the reality it inhabits associated with postmodernism. These concerns are led by and mainly channelled through the medium of Brookes. The bookseller appears to be a representation of paranoia towards the technological trappings of the contemporary world. Brookes's adherence to preserving the written word, symbolised in the form of the ledger which he describes, ironically, as 'as solid as we are' (p. 41), represents a desperate attempt to preserve the integrity of the subject. Demonstrating a fear of a mass surveillance society familiar from George Orwell's *Nineteen Eighty-Four* (1948) and many other texts, Brookes views, and literally dissects, even the humble house fly (full of 'wires' and 'oil in the works') as an instrument of espionage, and insists that the camera on Kiefer's laptop is switched off so that he 'won't be watched by electronics' (pp. 53, 28). He distrusts computers, ascribing to them deleterious effects, at once monotonising, infantilising and hallucinogenic: 'they thin your brain and take you where you never chose to go' (p. 17). Brookes attributes to cyberspace an arrogant sentience, believing that it 'thinks it's bigger than the whole of creation' (p. 47). The Internet is also described as an actively malevolent consciousness, 'using' the subject for the purposes of consumption, with the aim of assimilating all information and ultimately turning everything 'into itself' (p. 37). Indeed, Brookes later compares the Internet to an incapacitating agent: 'That net of yours, if you ask me it's more like a drug. It gets hold of your mind and weakens it, and then who knows what it can make you imagine, especially if you're in some kind of vulnerable state' (p. 68). The language here directly echoes, and updates, Campbell's paratextual comment made two decades previously, in which he likens the creative urge to an 'addiction'. The potency afforded by modern technology, the infinite vastness of the web, is likened to a narcotic and presented as potentially being as harmful as it is creatively enhancing.

Brookes's paranoid worldview is validated by other aspects within the text which ascribe a disturbingly Gothicised quality to technology. Kiefer's struggle to find 'Books Are Life', an eventuality during which the icon on his phone seems 'more real than the identifiable streets' and where he expresses that 'he could easily have felt like an element in a computer game' (p. 12), suggest reality and the subject being reduced to virtual, even ludic representation. Like Brookes, Kiefer also maintains a wariness of the power of the

Internet. In an echo of Mottershead's sensation of being preyed upon by predatory forces in *Needing Ghosts*, he feels, remembering the online advertisement, 'as though the net had fastened on a hollow in his brain' (p. 17). Later, there is seamless continuity between what Kiefer is told by the symbolically named 'browser' and the content of the conspiracy website, 'Wot They Dont Wancher Ter Know' (*sic*, p. 37), which he shortly thereafter discovers – by 'browsing'. This mutual reinforcement foregrounds a fear that because a microchip can store and convey vast amounts of information, and do so instantly, the possibility of individual authorship, the reality of the book as physical artefact and the pleasures of research, discovery and book ownership will all be invalidated. Even worse, the 'chip' can be used as an instrument of personal violation. It simulates experience, and thus potentially becomes a weapon for the programming, manipulation and control of the subject by another. As the 'browser' insists, 'there's plenty they get up to without telling the likes of us' (p. 31). Such anxieties of paranoia are of course also familiar recurring themes in postmodernist theoretical and critical discourse. For example, Baudrillard argues that the possibility of independent thought is under attack from and nullified by 'a gigantic technical and neural simulation' in favour of 'the authority of the virtual'.[94] Flieger notes the rise of a popular perception of a surveillance culture amidst the widespread and now routine incorporation of personal information onto databases like credit rating systems. 'In the postmodern age', Flieger argues, the subject is susceptible to 'becoming programmable, given over by bits and pieces to communication which is circulatory and regulatory rather than progressive and circulatory'.[95] Campbell's text, with its references to 'electronics watching', and the ingenious or conspiratorial 'chip' (pp. 28, 83–4), which may or may not be in its protagonist's head, clearly internalise the contemporary *zeitgeist*.

Conversely, however, *The Booking* also articulates a complex critique of this very paranoid perspective. Kiefer, wary as he is, maintains a critical distance about being absorbed into the browser's microchip 'fantasy', a path which seems to him like 'yielding to the notion of being tied to the online web' (p. 13). The obviousness of and crudely colloquial misspelling of the website's name suggests a satirical distance on the part of the author from the notion of conspiracy theories. Kiefer regards its espionage-related content sceptically, almost dismissively, as 'just another wild idea generated by the uncontrolled consciousness, too often close to deranged, that was the web' (p. 37). Rather, repeating a pragmatic perspective that has been consistent throughout Campbell's career, the protagonist advocates the continued viability of print by arguing to Brookes that 'I honestly don't think that the net will ever do away with books' (p. 39). This is a principled position explicit in and familiar from 'The Franklyn Paragraphs' and in the bibliographic settings of and passions frequently expressed by Campbell, both in his fiction and elsewhere. Yet the computer itself is also presented here as retaining a positive, life-affirming value. 'The lit screen' of his laptop, it is narrated

> put Kiefer in mind of a refuge – today's version of the light the first humans were said to have kindled against the dreadful dark. He could almost have fancied that the onscreen image of a book was a talisman to fend it off. Surely the only darkness that could bother him was ignorance, and the computer was its opposite. (p. 36)

Stylistically, Campbell is again here marrying traditional, indeed ancient, motifs of folklore and literature (the talisman as a ward against evil) with the contemporary trappings of modern technology (the computer). Moreover, the text at this point recalls Diana Kramer's recourse to song, or 'a cry for healing', during the climax of *The Hungry Moon* (1985), Campbell's much earlier Gothic novel on combating the power of 'darkness' posed by fundamentalism. In Campbell's vision, the computer and the access to information which it provides has now supplanted music as a weapon against another controlling 'grand narrative', the dogma of 'ignorance'.

The ambivalent ending of *The Booking* foregrounds the tension between the text's representation of anxieties typifying postmodernism and its own profound iconoclasticism. According to Baudrillard, the era of mass communication is characterised by oversaturation, resulting in an overwhelming disempowerment of the human subject. It is an outcome that, in his pessimistic view, tends to 'evil', whereby 'our culture of meaning is collapsing beneath the excess of meaning, the culture of reading collapsing beneath the excess of reading, the information culture collapsing beneath the excess of information, and the signs and reality sharing a simple shroud.'[96] Campbell's text, with its hero struggling to hold on to 'the real world' (p. 71), appears to literalise Baudrillard's pessimistic, funereal vision. There is an 'excess' of sentient volumes impinging upon the subject, and throughout the narrative Kiefer fears being subsumed and 'buried' beneath them. At the novella's climax, he is described as feeling

> hemmed in on every side by a confusion of knowledge so hungry for assimilation that it wouldn't be satisfied until every scrap was stored in his head. Books had begun dropping to the floor like insects swarming out of a nest, and the familiar dull thuds revived his vision of a general collapse, of being buried under a multitude of books. (p. 79)

However, the text concludes not on a note of fatalism but one of defiance, as the protagonist refuses to obey the forces of law and order, the police, and instead withdraws further into the shop towards another classically Gothic space, the mysterious hidden or 'furthest room' (p. 83). Crucially, the level of 'danger' entailed by doing this is, Kiefer insists to an unknown observer, 'exactly what I make it' (p. 83).

This enigmatic non-closure invites two competing interpretations. According to one, Kiefer's utterance and the final scene signify the disintegration and withdrawal of the paranoid schizophrenic into psychosis, in which the subject is mentally overwhelmed, consumed by, and becoming synonymous with, the text. Such an interpretation retrospectively confers upon the novella's opening sentence, '[w]hen they found him, this text was all he had' (p. 9), the quality of posthumous elegy or obituary. Yet according to an alternative reading, by refusing to comply with conventional authority, represented by the police, the subject has been able to strike out, to positively assert its will against the invalidating vicissitudes of contemporary life. It is possible in turn to derive two tentative conclusions from this more positive interpretation. One, what may be termed a 'pro-bibliophile' judgement, would ascribe an intrinsic value to the plethora of unregulated information, seeing it as inherently positive and personally enriching. Campbell, with *The Booking*, seems to align with what Savu suggests is an ability of 'the second generation' of postmodernist writers, to 'afford and celebrate the centrality of literature both as an aesthetic object and as a cultural artefact in a world increasingly sceptical of its value'.[97] A second conclusion would be that *The Booking* displays fidelity to what Savu notes as a tendency in some later postmodernist author fiction, 'its antihumanist bias notwithstanding', to *not* discount 'the human', that is the life experience, actions and values of the subject.[98] According to Savu, such new writers and fictions have affirmed the possibility of 'an individual subjectivity – for readers, characters *and* authors – that is constantly enacted or expressed in a myriad of representations'.[99] With respect to Campbell's novella, such a 'myriad' complexity is suggested in this enigmatic and ambiguous ending, and the alternate perspectives upon it which are offered by the text.

Indeed, such an offering can be further interpreted as a challenge to the containment or 'holding' of content and meaning by the reader as receiving subject cited by McEwan as being a distinguishing feature of the novella. For, through the intense prism of the depiction of the experience of an individual consciousness which the novella offers, Campbell, certainly with both these hybrid and symbolic Gothic texts, dramatises the desire and struggle for control of meaning in a 'reality' that seems as disorientating, precarious and potentially overwhelming as the restless contents and constantly expanding shelves in Brookes's bookshop. The depiction of the subject's almost literal subjugation in *The Booking* itself not only enacts Baudrillard's vision of the overwhelming dominance of simulacra within and over contemporary consumer culture. To apply Hutcheon's argument, through both such literalisation and the divided protagonist's scepticism, it offers a parodic perspective, an alternative viewpoint that she describes as a distinguishing feature of postmodernism. This is a propensity to critique the 'simulacrisation' of the present by 'problematising the entire notion of the representation of reality' and by therefore suggesting 'the potentially reductive quality of the new upon which Baudrillard's laments are based'.[100] Campbell's own vision is an iconoclastic as well as a parodic one, because in his imaginative universe a liberal humanist perspective and values ostensibly antithetical to postmodernism are both articulated and, as Brookes's arguable success in exerting a final state of independence suggests, not entirely lost.

As the reference in *The Booking* to the Internet being a predatory 'mind looking for somewhere to live' (p. 39) indicates, the primary ontological challenge and potential threat to the integrity and future of the subject has been increasingly perceived to come from technological sources. In particular, such confrontation has come from the computer. In Campbell's vision as a writer of Gothic horror, the computer serves the same function as an *ouija* or spirit board by virtue of both its potency and its potential danger. It is a recurrent presence in his longer fictions of the twenty-first century. It is to Campbell's metaleptic narratives, corporeal metafictions in which fictional beings intrude into and serve to interrogate what has been delineated as the 'real' world via the portal of the computer, that I wish to turn in the last chapter. Paying due attention to the role of digital technology in Campbell's late fictions allows Gothic scholarship to move beyond his critique of the postmodern subject, with its necessarily atomised and paranoid psyche, and into an examination of the ways in which such a subjectivity is being specifically transformed by digital communication technologies, or, in other words, to explore how the postmodern becomes *posthuman*. This shift involves switching the focus from the subject to the medium and the spectres and terrors that a disembodied and instant form of communication – and in the case of the writer, the act of creation – engender.

4

'Ghosts' from the Machine: Campbell's Gothic Techno-Fictions

ಬಂಡ

Campbell, Postmodernism and Posthumanism

The paranoia exhibited towards computers, digital communication and the Internet by 'Alfred Brookes' in *The Booking* demonstrates Campbell's concern with both broadening the genre and retaining topicality as a writer of contemporary Gothic horror. This self-consciousness has not gone unnoticed by the critics who have accorded Campbell any attention. S. T. Joshi, for example, taking account of Campbell's long-term parallel careers as a film, DVD and music critic, has observed the writer's ongoing use of 'all forms of art' beyond the written word at his disposal, and, latterly, to 'absorb new developments in technology to augment the horrors of his scenarios'.[1] This is the case even given the oscillation throughout Campbell's career, noted in my Introduction, between psychological horror and more overtly supernatural subject matter. Such heterogeneity attests to Campbell's versatility and continuing tendency to experimentation. Foremost among the 'new developments in technology' which Campbell has absorbed, the Internet is now ubiquitous to the point of being all-pervasive. This computer network has been aptly described by Stefan Herbechter as 'by far the most significant and socially transformative medium of western capitalist information societies within a few decades'.[2]

Herbrechter, as his own substantial study *Posthumanism: A Critical Analysis* (2013) attests, is a scholar operating within an important and emergent cross-disciplinary theoretical trend.[3] Like postmodernism, posthumanism reconceptualises the human subject in its relation to both technology and the natural world. A posthumanist approach radically reconfigures the subject's own nature and its relational and even hierarchical status. The 'decentring of the human' through its imbrication in technological, medical and other networks, argues Cary Wolfe, 'is increasingly impossible to ignore.'[4] Also increasingly, according to N. Katherine Hayles, pioneering theorist in the field, the computer is actually 'taken as the measure of all things, including humans'.[5] For academics such as Hayles and Pramod K. Nayar, although the consequences of such hierarchical deprivileging need not be disempowering and negative (or, as Campbell's Brookes would phrase it, 'brain-thinning'), the subject is now 'an amalgam' or 'an assemblage'.[6] Indeed, as far as Nayar is concerned, the human explicitly amounts to 'an instantiation of a network of connections, exchanges, bondages and crossings with all forms of life'.[7] Similarly to postmodernism, posthumanism thus constitutes a challenge to the subject's autopoietic autonomy, that is, to the master or 'grand' narrative of Enlightenment liberal humanism. At stake, and under implicit threat, are humanism's associated notions of possession of secure identity and uniqueness, and its senses of identifiable origin, teleological continuity and temporal closure.

Campbell's Gothic fictions, particularly in the twenty-first century, articulate an acute awareness and present a distinctive mediation of these theoretical currents. The previous chapters of this book have analysed Campbell's treatment of metanarratives pertaining to religious belief systems, to late capitalist societal and political orthodoxies and to authorial practices and creativity, together with the fraying and disintegrating influences upon the subject that these can encourage – influences which generate and portray anxiety and terror. In widening analysis beyond Campbell's meta-horror analyses of the professional or aspiring writer, this chapter focuses specifically upon the presentation of variant and emergent technologies. Campbell's representation, it is proposed, signify variations of a transformation or morphology of the subject more than its dissolution. After establishing the validity of applying posthumanist theory through tracing points of affinity with postmodernism, I will examine aspects of what is elucidated as the posthuman presence as it manifests in three of the author's key longer Gothic fictions. These are a linked if autonomous triptych of major works written in the decade preceding *The Booking*. Campbell's novels *The Grin of the Dark* (2007), *The Seven Days of Cain* (2010) and *Think Yourself Lucky* (2014) are all texts, or 'techno-fictions', which feature various, then new, forms of social media and digital technology.[8] They are important works in tracing the evolution of Campbell's vision of the contemporary world and of the complex status of the human subject within it. The highly networked and digital 'reality' depicted explicitly in each of them serves to amplify his concerns about society and autopoiesis. These novels extend Campbell's already evident preoccupation with the capacity of the human to retain its integrity and its intelligibility to others and to itself. Moreover, their appearance coincides with what Bruce Clarke and Manuela Rossini have observed as a burgeoning 'growth in the posthuman academy' of theory and critical analysis since 2007.[9] In the course of exploring the posthuman content of these particular novels, my analysis sets out Campbell's unique exposition of the challenges to and transformations of subjectivity presented by this diverse, and still developing, set of paradigms.

Posthumanism as artistic phenomena, as opposed to an organised field of theoretical enquiry, is, of course, not new within the Gothic. Representation of the enhancement or even supersedence of the human has a significant literary history prior to Campbell, as Mary Shelley's *Frankenstein* (1818) or H. P. Lovecraft's portrayal of a non-anthropocentric future and explicit reference to a 'post-human' race of super-intelligent beetles in his short story 'The Shadow Out of Time' (1936) famously exemplify.[10] In cross-disciplinary scholarship, seminal discourses on cybernetics by Norbert Wiener (1948), Ihab Hassan, whose article 'Prometheus as Performer' (1977) pioneered an application of posthumanist thinking to wider culture beyond the sciences, and Donna Haraway's influential concept of the cyborg (1984), all helped establish the breadth, legitimacy and vigour of posthumanism within intellectual enquiry long before Hayles's work and the twenty-first century expansion of scholarship noted by Clarke and Rossini.[11] In an essay for the latter pair's *Cambridge Companion to Literature and the Posthuman* (2017), Herbrechter himself notes an affinity between emergent posthumanist positioning and the challenge to notions of a stable and unified self in postmodernist literature. Postmodernist texts, he rightly maintains, already implicitly destabilise notions of anthropocentric value systems and embodiment through their presentations of ontological pluralities and of reality as an artificial inter- and metatextual construct, and their occlusion of division between high and low cultural forms.

Amidst this tendency to destabilise, Herbrechter elevates Jean-François Lyotard as 'the thinker of the postmodern *par excellence*'.[12] He cites the latter's collection of essays, *The Inhuman: Reflections on Time* (1991), as being a seminal influence on posthuman theory. Lyotard's earlier volume, *The Postmodern Condition*, had already warned of the propensity of the growth of science, the 'technological megalopolis', to signify 'cultural imperialism' and 'produce not the known but the unknown', although the philosopher's recommendation for 'free access to memory and databases' seemed to present an optimistic, and perhaps arguably retrospectively naïve, gloss upon such technological expansion.[13] *The Inhuman*, by contrast, promotes fully the alienating, 'other'-ing aspect of technology. In 'a blow to human narcissism', technology is perceived as having invented the human, rather than vice versa.[14] According to this non-Cartesian idiom, developments in fields such as Artificial Intelligence see the subject 'becoming' and 'inhabited' by the non-human, developments which generate and foster sensations of 'threats and terror'.[15] Moreover, consciousness is divided from corporeal materiality: '[t]he separation of Thought from the Body', Lyotard argues, 'leaves behind a poor binarised ghost of what it [that is, the whole human] was before.'[16] It is the poignant as well as divided figure of this 'poor binarised ghost' which is central to discussion here. The notion of an encroachment upon or presence within a vulnerable and itself divided subject by the non- or inhuman is a significant point of continuity between postmodernism and posthumanism. This is demonstrated in Clarke and Rossini's own similar argument that posthumanism 'observes the inhuman or non-human other inhabiting the ostensibly human, and so deconstructing the humanist concept of the human'.[17]

The keen internal sense, or, as Michael Sean Bolton describes it, 'dread', that alterity 'already inhabits' the subject also, and crucially for an analysis of Campbell's fictions, manifests itself in an emergent sub-branch of enquiry within posthumanism: the posthuman Gothic.[18] According to Bolton, the fear of the subject's distintegration which characterises literary postmodernism is replaced in posthuman Gothic by anxiety as to the self's integration or supersedence, a fear of 'what we will become and what will be left of us', that is, of a 'continued existence [but] reconstituted' as something else, something 'other'.[19] As Bolton's own work on the encroaching 'technological other' attests, and as Anya Heise-von der Lippe also argues, this new tendency within posthumanist cultural and especially literary studies serves to counter an extant bias in the field towards the analysis of science fiction.[20] Science fiction had been singled out by Marshall McLuhan in his seminal *The Medium is the Massage* (1967) as the optimum literary mode for 'enabl[ing] us to perceive the potential of new technologies', and is described by Herbrechter as 'the most posthuman of all genres'.[21] To a degree, texts like *Frankenstein* or, especially, 'Shadow Out of Time', display a fidelity to science fiction, while the work of authors like J. G. Ballard and Philip K. Dick have conventionally been, in part or totality, associated with that genre. As far as posthumanism is concerned, posthuman Gothic studies represent an attempt to incorporate a seemingly incongruous mode, the apparently archaic, historically delineated and preoccupied Gothic, under the same intellectual firmament of posthumanism as the more obviously compatible futurological and speculative concerns of science fiction. Yet, taking further Fred Botting's argument that Gothic 'engenders a new relationship between technology and the supernatural', Heise-von der Lippe points out that the Gothic mode, in contrast to science fiction, pre-emptively contemplates the negative 'horrors of technology' by virtue of its being a literature which is *already* explicitly defined by anxiety and liminality.[22] Neatly tying Gothic, posthumanism and postmodernism together, she observes that

> [t]he posthuman's decidedly uncanny connations are rooted in the subject's incapability to [*sic*] abject its monstrous/posthuman features in the process of trying to establish a coherent identity narrative – a discursive feat that is, moreover, highly problematic after postmodernism.[23]

Such a linkage of monstrous alterity, a central tenet of horror, with posthuman paradigms serves to validate a consideration of Gothic horror in conjunction with the latter. It is, I argue, particularly relevant for discussion of Campbell, whose desire to probe generic boundaries and admiration for Ballard and Dick are a matter of record.[24]

In their introduction to *Digital Horror: Haunted Technologies, Network Panic and the Found Footage Phenomenon* (2016), Linnie Blake and Xavier Aldana Reyes outline three sources of fear engendered by a computer-based, technologically advanced society. These are the online experience of surveillance, exposure to the predation of strangers 'from beyond', and digital haunting's 'impact on human identity'.[25] Although his own medium is obviously literary rather than cinematic, Campbell's fictions mediate and engage with all three varieties of persecution, or 'haunting'. In contrast to the depiction of psychic fragmentation in *The Booking* and *Needing Ghosts*, and the ambivalence of the apparitions in the latter (which may or may not be manifestations of Mottershead's psyche), all three novels present more explicitly supernatural narratives of alterity. It is important, however, to define what these narratives and the metaleptic entities contained within them are *not*. Campbell's fictions have not been, to date, concerned with futurology, Artificial Intelligence, the depiction of cyborgs or robotic characters or transhuman or speciesist themes – the latter a preoccupation for example for Nayar, one of the few posthumanist theorists or critics, thus far, to engage with literary genres and to do so beyond science fiction. Nor, crucially, are Campbell's 'ghosts' strictly defined as simply deceased human figures from the past, even, as may be seen, the figure of 'Tubby Thackeray' or the force which he represents in *Grin*. Whether they are entities metaphysically outside normal human comprehension of parameters of life and death, projections of aspects of personality, or fictional characters created within the text's own diegesis, the 'strangers' and disembodied virtual lives in Campbell's version of hauntology are more ontologically and philosophically challenging. In comparison with the conventional 'ghost', with its connotations of incorporation within the somewhat formal and formulaic structure of the ghost story, the definition of spectrality offered by Julian Wolfreys, that is as a presence, 'neither living nor dead', seems more apposite to the presentation of the metaleptic entities or 'poor binarised ghosts' in Campbell's vision of the Gothic, and especially to the unsettling effects wielded by their manifestation in experiential reality.[26] In defining the spectral, Wolfreys argues that

> there is, there *takes place*, an arrival from somewhere else, made manifest as a figure of otherness disrupting orders and systems of representation, logic, and so forth, and which, in arriving, returning, or coming to pass, traverses and blurs any neat analytic distinction.[27]

The imminence, advent or presence of the entity thus in itself attains centrality. Each 'arrival' or interloper in Campbell's techno-fictions articulates themes of monstrosity, or at least instability, disruption and transformation, and, ultimately, can be shown to reflect and contribute to philosophical debates informing posthumanism. Campbell's trilogy of novels each employ, and reinterpret for a technologically advanced era, familiar Gothic antecedents and leitmotifs. *Grin* draws on a tradition of coulrophobia and the ambiguous, sinister quality latent in dark comedy, especially the carnivalesque, to explore fear of subsumption into alterity and of what the transformed subject may become. Campbell's 2014 novel *Think Yourself Lucky* revisits the *doppelgänger* and dual personality traditions familiar from Hogg's *Private Memoirs and Confessions of a Justified Sinner* (1824) and, most obviously, Robert Louis Stevenson's novella *Strange Case of Dr Jekyll and Mr Hyde* (1886) in addressing embodiment. In also returning explicitly to the social concerns of earlier novels explored in Chapter 2, the text re-examines the subject's socially inflected potentiality for violence in the context of more recent technological developments. Finally, the intermediate novel, *Cain*, among Campbell's most cross-generic long fictions and perhaps, alongside *Needing Ghosts*, his most thoroughly exploratory artistic and philosophical statement, updates Shelley's *Frankenstein* to articulate the posthuman created being's fear of isolation, loneliness and abandonment.

Campbell himself, characteristically, has eschewed any such posthumanist theoretical perspectives, or (in contrast to Thomas Ligotti, for example) ambitions to make a philosophical treatise or statement. Consistently, he has intended, as his own website declares, to 'write horror' and thus create narratives of fear – in these cases, nightmares of autopoiesis. As noted in the first chapter, at an early stage in his career Campbell had concocted a working formula by which an ordinary, that is working- or middle-class, protagonist, is threatened by 'something out there that is out to get them for whatever reason'.[28] *Grin*, the first of the novels, in which the protagonist-victim's very access to a plethora of media and technologies exposes them to an ancient and malevolent force which is using these new forms of communication as a conduit, appears to conform most fully to the classical, Lovecraftian notion of an external threat from 'out there'. The reality is, however, more complex than it appears.

'Some Older and More Savage God': Technology as 'New Religion' in The Grin of the Dark

Campbell has described his 2007 Gothic novel as a dark comedy 'of derangement and chaos'.[29] Prior to the *Three Births of Daoloth* trilogy (2016–18), *Grin* presents the author's most sustained attempt to unify the Lovecraftian cosmic vistas seen in *The Hungry Moon* with the portrayal of a besieged individual psyche, as portrayed in

Needing Ghosts. This is crystallised in a first-person and present-tense narrative, conveying sensory immediacy to the experiences and growing paranoia of Simon Lester, the novel's protagonist. Despite his initial assertion that 'I'm going to take charge of my life', Lester is another of Campbell's unreliable narrators.[30] Like Kiefer in *The Booking*, indeed like most other lead characters in Campbell's *oeuvre* of the embittered, Simon is both economically compromised and socially marginalised. The narrative's setting is a familiar, urban one, replete with keenly depicted mundaneness, frustration and drudgery. A media studies graduate, whose career in film journalism has been truncated by a libel scandal that closed a magazine to which he contributed, Lester scrapes a living working in video and petrol station shops. He also struggles in his relationships with his partner, Natalie, whose young son, Mark, is his only real ally, and with Natalie's parents, who disapprove of him and also happen to be his landlords. In an apparent positive turn of fortune, Simon accepts a lucrative commission from Rufus Wall, his former university tutor, to turn his undergraduate dissertation on early silent film comedy into a monograph. Specifically, Lester is encouraged by Wall to expand his research on Tubby Thackeray, a once controversially anarchic but now largely forgotten stage and silent film comedian. 'Tubby Thackeray', it emerges, is the innocuous-sounding pseudonym of an early twentieth-century medievalist and occultist, Thackeray Lane, who has dedicated himself to propagating the 'joy of infantilism' (p. 255). In the course of an increasingly surreal narrative, Lester, among other bizarre events, witnesses a violent and sexually charged performance by a troupe of itinerant, silent clowns, is drawn into fractitious correspondence with a malevolent Internet chatroom poster operating by the log-in name 'Smilemime', and experiences hallucinogenic and debilitating episodes in Los Angeles and Amsterdam. Thackeray Lane is dead, and neither he nor Tubby appear to the hero in corporeal form. However, to deploy a circus analogy, Simon's endeavours to balance his life on a tightrope against the insidious attack of an apparently supernatural antagonist, and without a safety net, seem to end in failure. In the novel's climax, the protagonist plunges into, and is apparently subsumed in, an abyss of the eponymous 'dark'. Far from asserting 'control', he appears to lose his own identity and to assume a virtual, non-physical existence as his own previous nemesis, 'Smilemime'. Simon has finally become, like Tubby, or the force which Tubby incarnates, 'part of the Internet' (p. 317).

The plot of Campbell's earlier Gothic novel *Ancient Images* (1989) had also concerned the search for a 'lost' film. To an even greater degree than that text, though, *Grin* showcases Campbell's meticulous research and experience as a film critic.[31] Allusions to real individuals like Mack Sennett or Stan Laurel, and to events, notably the Roscoe 'Fatty' Arbuckle scandal (1921–2), are woven seamlessly into a fictional narrative. This narrative itself draws upon a range of film texts for its construction of both Tubby, whose perpetual grin evokes the antagonist in *Mr Sardonicus* (William Castle, 1961), and his pictures, from the asylum-set climax of *The Cabinet of Dr. Caligari* (Robert Wiene, 1920) to the appearance of multiples of the titular actor in the surreal comedy, *Being John Malkovitch* (Spike Jonze, 1999).[32] However, *Ancient Images*, in that its denouement concerns 'cursed land', takes final recourse to pre-cinematic 'folk horror' conventions. With some justification, Joshi criticises the earlier work for thus 'failing to probe the many interesting philosophical issues it raises', such as the diversification and social roles of media or the relationship between film and reality.[33] In contrast, as Richard Bleiler notes, *Grin*, with its protean, multi-media antagonist, reflects and mediates 'a recognizably data-driven and mutable twenty-first-century world'.[34]

This story outline barely conveys the complexity of this text, which is both seemingly technophobic and playful. To a degree greater even than his earlier tragicomic serial killer narrative, *The Count of Eleven* (1991), *Grin* represents Campbell's most overt and sustained combination of comedy and horror. The novel, with its ill-fated protagonist on a quest for 'lost' artefacts, displays formal fidelity to horror tradition. Campbell's uncharacterised, infantile 'greedy chaos' (p. 340) obviously recalls Azathoth, blind, idiot god from Lovecraft's Cthulhu Mythos, a being first alluded to in the novella *The Dream-Quest of Unknown Kadath* (1926). The likening of Tubby himself to a long-legged 'grasshopper with a man's face' (p. 121) inciting anarchy amongst his audience again recalls the Martian insects and their combination of ancient, alien intelligence and dominion over primal humanity in Nigel Kneale's teleplay, *Quatermass and The Pit* (1958–9). *Grin* itself may be interpreted as a conscious cross-media updating by Campbell of the then fashionable 'found footage' subgenre, a trend popularised by *The Blair Witch Project* (Daniel Myrick and Eduardo Sánchez, 1999) and described as 'highly Gothic' by Blake and Aldana Reyes.[35] Simon pursues Lane's elusive films, and the text of the novel itself finally becomes Lester's own testament or 'found footage'.

In particular however, from the protagonist's first glimpse of a grinning moon-faced man eyeing him from a barge, *Grin* draws upon another familiar cultural as well as Gothic trope: the 'evil clown' figure. Coulrophobia had had a high profile in the Anglo-American *zeitgeist* in the two decades preceding the novel's appearance. It was published in the wake of the crimes and execution of the media-labelled 'Killer Clown', John Wayne Gacy (1942–94), the release of films like *Killer Klowns From Outer Space* (Stephen Chiodo, 1988) and literary works by Alan Ryan, (*Dead White*, 1983), Stephen King (the aforementioned *IT*, first adapted, for television, in 1990) and Ligotti ('The Last Feast of Harlequin', 1991). An allusive and metatextual novel, *Grin* at one point presents a partial, pseudo-historical account of the origins of clowning, from the medieval Feast of Fools splintering into the Troupe of Fools and the Black Mass, to the near present. Campbell even acknowledges Ligotti's story directly in the passing reference to the Troupe being 'heard of in the town of Mirocaw' (p. 255). However, the significance of the text's deployment of the clown trope lies not especially with its originality, referentiality or the historical accuracy, or otherwise, of associating the Troupe with Satanism, but its purpose and cumulative effect. For example, in comparison with Ligotti or King's carnivorous, people-eating entities, Campbell's Thackeray presents an alterity of the insidious. Only half-glimpsed, overheard or dreamed about by the protagonist almost until the end, Thackeray's encroachment upon Lester's quotidian existence emulates the approaching threat in an M. R. James narrative. The professor's trepidation regarding the approaching figure in his dream in James's "'Oh Whistle, And I'll Come To You My Lad'" (1904), that 'there was something about its motion that made Parkins very reluctant to see it at close quarters', is echoed explicitly in one of Simon's own nightmares.[36] In Campbell's reboot for the twenty-first century, the beach is replaced by the monitor. Defamiliarised, the personal computer becomes a portal for 'other'-ness:

> The yellow keys rattle like boxes . . . The screen is no longer featureless. Its sides extend backwards to form the floor and walls and ceiling of a corridor. Though it appears to stretch almost to infinity I can just distinguish a figure that is waiting at the end. It's approaching, or am I? I would very much prefer it to keep its distance. (p. 109)

As in a typical James story, the entity itself is described as repellently inhuman: compared to a jellyfish, limbless, cold, pale, glistening and displaying an unwelcome penchant for slithering under the protagonist's bed. Like James's hapless Professor Parkins, Lester dreads his tormentor's proximity and touch. In the novel's climax of physical horror, Simon finally watches helplessly as 'it clambers limblessly up my body and closes over my face' (p. 338). *Grin* in one sense thus presents a classic 'possession' narrative in succession to earlier Campbell novels like *The Parasite* (1980), which the author had described as 'a study of the derangement of a personality' by another, invasive one.[37]

What confers upon Campbell's later novel greater ideological complexity is that the clown, by virtue of its inherent anarchy, symbolises iconoclasticism. It is the perfect, irreverent inhabitant of the kind of contemporary world described by Jean Baudrillard in *The Ecstasy of Communication* (1987). This is a landscape denoted by 'obscenity', saturated with information, in which 'everything eludes itself, everything scoffs at its own truth', and attainment of such 'truth', that is, reality, is *'quite simply impossible'*.[38] The online ticket booking system for the troupe, 'Clwons [*sic*] Unlimited' (p. 29) – 'clwons' itself being a play on 'clones' – later mysteriously disappears without trace. In the manner of Luis Buñuel's surrealist comedy *L'Age d'Or* (1930), Lane's comedy films, as when Tubby's face is variously substituted for those of a queen, mayor, monk, mitred bishop and a long-haired saint with a halo, satirise figures of secular and religious authority. In another short, Tubby's head is described as smashing through the back of a nativity tableau and appearing 'above the occupants of the stable like a manifestation of an older and more savage god' (p. 272). *Grin* thus continues the subversion of the 'grand narrative' of organised religion, especially Christian worship, seen in Campbell's earlier novel *The Hungry Moon*. Summarised in its protagonist's exasperated temptation 'to wonder aloud if faith in technology is the new religion' (p. 267), the burgeoning 'technology' perceived as the new incarnation of belief has become the main focus.

Campbell's most hard- and software-dominated long fiction to date, *Grin* presents a contemporary world in which Marshall McLuhan's vision of an 'electric technology' which pervades and reshapes all aspects of both social relations and personal life has been realised.[39] The novel actualises the theorist's notion of media reflecting and even simulating human consciousness, but also, in reciprocation, leaving no part 'untouched, unaffected, unaltered'.[40] 'We're all part of the Internet', Lester declares, 'exactly as we've made it part of us. We've added it to human consciousness' (p. 340). Expanding information technology, new forms of social media and, above all, the greater connectivity afforded by the Internet may be interpreted as proffering greater freedoms, enhanced communication and instant gratification. However, as Blake and Aldana Reyes point out in their study of digital horror films, nothing is really 'free': such enhanced technology has 'itself become widely monitored in the interests of maintaining the global hegemony of corporate capitalism'.[41] In Campbell's imaginative universe, the 'Frugo' organisation fulfils this role and represents faceless commerce. This corporation serves as a leitmotif or backdrop in many of Campbell's late works. Almost Lester's first action in *Grin* is to register a 'Frugonet' email address, thus signalling immediately his own enmeshment in the 'system'. A wryly humorous scene in which Simon's party have to use a mouse just to communicate orders to a restaurant kitchen suggests the absurd drawbacks of overdependence on technology. Simon's subsequent financial misfortune, in which he becomes overdrawn and encounters the bureaucratic claim that his declined credit card 'needs your number', because 'everyone needs a number now' (p. 189), dramatises McLuhan's claim that information retrieval and data banks 'form one big gossip column that is unforgiving, unforgetful and from which there is no redemption, no erasure of easy '"mistakes"'.[42] In posthumanist terms, the protagonist is diminished by the seemingly autonomous and sentient machine, a new, altered reality which appears to belie a bank official's sarcastic assurance that 'computers don't make payments on their own' (p. 267). The hapless Lester seems to meet, indeed literalise with his card, Herbrechter's observation that 'global virtual capitalism needs an equally plastic and flexible individual subject'.[43]

From one perspective then, the novel is a satirical portrait of technophilic cultural trends, carried almost to the point of obsessive fetishising. This obsession is conveyed overtly through a narrator-protagonist who largely works and lives by screen monitor. Simon has access to and uses a range of media in addition to videotape, such as mobile phones and DVDs, and online tools like eBay, email and the Internet Movie Database with its chatroom – resources which either did not exist or were in relatively limited and unsophisticated form when *Ancient Images* was written. Conversely, however, much of the narrative focuses upon the potential of this greatly enhanced digital world to generate fear, and the compromised subject's increasing *lack* of control, both against predation by strangers and of their own ontological integrity. Campbell's text presents a comprehensive Gothic interpretation of old and emergent technologies. There are constant insinuations of an undefined malevolent supernaturalism acting against the protagonist, such as a videotape from which a Thackeray film excerpt myseriously disappears except for a hissing, malevolent-sounding static, or Simon's feeling that 'someone or something has gone to ground' inside his computer (p. 110). Aesthetically, such details, alongside the continuous half-glimpses of sinister, grinning figures and overheard laughter, may seem repetitive and overdone. Nevertheless, they convey a powerful sense of the accretion of evil.

In its treatment of two negative phenomena experienced online, trolling and malicious software or computer 'viruses', *Grin* suggests that this evil is actively empowered by an increasingly digital world. The network confers a persona or mask of anonymity, demonstrated by the presentation of the malign troll Smilemime.[44] The practice of trolling – that is, online attack upon one consciousness by another, an assailant who may or may not be known to the victim but who uses the disguise of an assumed identity – is returned to in representation of social media in the later two novels, especially *Cain*, but it is given its first representation in *Grin*.[45] Smilemime is an arrogant, vicious and cynical presence which undermines Lester constantly, denying the expertise and even identity of the protagonist in tirades of deliberately misspelt, consonant-laden postings. Trolls are explicitly dehumanised in the text, likened to 'monsters' that the Internet has somehow dredged up 'from the depths', 'let loose', or even 'created' (pp. 158, 301). Confirming the intention to confer an aura of supernatural mystery, it is left unresolved whether Smilemime is in fact an alias for Lane, his alter ego Tubby, or the force which both represent.[46] Psychologically, Smilemime always seems to be one step ahead of Lester. His derisive and hectoring tone resembles a 'maniacal and mechanical laughter' (p. 301), a phrase neatly combining Gothic madness and new technology. Yet, like the source of the sound, the troll remains intangible, invisible.

In reality, only some such malicious posters have the inclination, let alone technical ability, to create and distribute malicious software. However, Campbell's novel explicitly associates the invisible troll with another 'unseen' menace, the computer 'virus'. Deploying a metaphor of infection, the text implies that the network has enabled its dissemination. Lester describes Smilemime's messages as 'multiplying like a virus in his dreams' and feeling as if the entity's 'monomania has invaded his skull' (pp. 135, 156). He later suffers the indignity of seeing his work misattributed to another writer, and, finally, corrupted completely by 'some kind of virus' into incoherent 'rubbish' (p. 301). Even Lester's social interactions gradually become contaminated and debilitated, as when he and Mark are described 'infect[ing] each other with painfully silent mirth' (p. 288). Although a literary text, *Grin* therefore chimes with what Steffen Hantke identifies as a 'digital anxiety' trend in cinema, in which technology serves as 'a conduit for malignant forces travelling along the network's arteries'.[47] A still more useful analogy, to a point, is with Neal Kirk's concept of 'networked spectrality', denoted by polymorphous, shape-shifting and 'omnipresent' ghosts that, rather than a singular identity and location of 'haunting', have taken on 'the unbounded, multiple, distributive and participatory qualities of our digital networks'.[48] The novel's climax, in which the Internet is revealed as a portal which can never be closed, aligns with Kirk's description of an 'apocalyptic digital contagion' acting through portals and websites in films like *Pulse* (Jim Sonzero, 2006).[49] Rufus Wall's exposition indicts the Internet for spreading this 'contagion', and Simon for unleashing it:

> It's his [Lane/Tubby's] ideal medium, the one he's been waiting for, or whatever he represents has ... Everything's true on the net, and it lets anyone use a mask who wants to. It's the medium he kept talking about ... he'll be everywhere, or what's used him for a mask will. You've seen to that. (p. 335)

Combining the analogy of viral transmission with survivalist instincts, Wall insists that 'you have to pass him on to other people' (p. 335). The long-standing Gothic staple of the 'curse' had already been updated to assimilate modern technology in texts like *Ringu* (both Kōji Suzuki's 1991 novel and Hideo Nakata's subsequent 1998 film adaptation), in which unwarily watching a video precedes dabbling in the Internet as a means of summoning a malevolent and malignant spectre. However, Campbell's text, whilst ostensibly being a conservative, cautionary tale like *Ringu*, is arguably more ontologically challenging than the earlier revenant narrative. Also, unlike *Pulse*, which finally portrays its infection by ghosts of the dead in terms of global catastrophe, *Grin*, despite Dr Wall's pronouncements regarding the force's universality, presents an 'apocalypse' which is far more *personal* in scope.

Campbell's novel foregrounds concerns around communication, isolation and victimisation, especially subsumption by and becoming 'other'. The protagonist's experience within the narrative is a journey of increasing sensory disorientation, where boundaries between what is real and unreal become opaque. In contrast to, for example, King's *IT*, which finally becomes a Manichaean narrative of collective good against evil, clowning in *Grin* signifies an escalating and unsettling 'comedy' of humiliation. Lester variously falls flat on his face before an audience, feels as if he is being repeatedly trapped in a comedy routine, and has the embarrassing perception of acquiring 'a jester's cap complete with a silent bell' (p. 266). Campbell again uses epidemiological terminology in an episode in which Simon is viewing a deteriorating microfilm. He feels 'as if nonsense is spreading through the text – as if the silent clamour of Lane's misshapen language in my skull is infecting the historical record' (p. 257). In his analysis of the ontological implications of posthumanism, Herbrechter maintains that language 'cannot be trusted' as a guarantor of identity.[50] *Grin* appears to anticipate and dramatise Herbrechter's argument. It is one of Campbell's most self-consciously lexicographic narratives, as attested to by its word play, deliberate misspellings, anagrammatic chapter names and, above all, a protagonist whose control over speech deteriorates to the point where 'struggle for coherence simply produces worse gibberish until my babbling gags on itself' (p. 338). Lester's verbal disenfranchisement precedes the psychological invasion of the subject by malign technology. As he explains, 'once the net captures you it can reprogram your mind, reconfigure you in its image' (p. 341), an idea refrained with Brookes's cyberphobia in *The Booking*. This 'reprogramming' accords with Bleiler's observation on Campbell's narratives that 'the very essences of identity are fluid and malleable, for the underlying data that gave them meaning can be restructured'.[51] Its significance can actually be taken even further. The novel's ending suggests a literalisation of Baudrillard's vision of human bodies themselves becoming 'superfluous', existing only 'as terminals of multiple networks'.[52] Simon's fate is to be removed from Natalie and others 'on the far side of the screen', and relocated with the click of a mouse (p. 336). In following Lane's invocation that 'he who opens the portal is the portal' (p. 317), the protagonist has himself become a disembodied consciousness and part of virtual reality. Lester seems to represent, *in extremis*, the 'deep-seated virtualization of human beings' which Baudrillard envisages as symptomatic of a culture 'in a state of socio-photo-and video synthesis'.[53] However, as noted by Andy Sawyer regarding another of Campbell's long fictions, *Creatures of the Pool* (2009), there is also a 'final, Ballardian embracing of the monstrous' in this novel.[54] The troll Smilemime's boast, 'that's me in the middle of the web, and I've got tricks I haven't even thought of yet', is echoed in Simon's final undertaking (or threat) to 'keep posting my knowledge' (pp. 225, 341).

As a hybrid of Gothic horror and comedy, *Grin*, to return to circus imagery, performs its own delicate balancing act. On the one hand, as cosmic horror fiction it represents an update, or upgrade, from texts like *The Hungry Moon* in its depiction of an ancient and malevolent force using all the accoutrements of modern technology. As demonstrated by the fractured identity of the antagonist – Lane, Tubby, Smilemime, and finally Lester himself – what exactly this force *is* remains undefined. Campbell has declared that 'some tales try to hold the darkness back, while others illuminate it and its contents in an uncanny light, or demonstrate that much of the dark is inside us'.[55] On the other hand, the novel's mock-triumphant ending, which anticipates Kiefer's defiant statement in *The Booking* that 'it's exactly what I make it' (p. 83), suggests both internal desire and even anarchic joy at the possibilities open to the transformed subject. This, plus the ambiguous corporeal status of its protagonist at the novel's conclusion and the possibility, as with *The Booking* and *Needing Ghosts*, that the entire preceding narrative may have been the outpourings of a consciousness experiencing mental illness, suggests an iconoclasticism on the part of the author. From one perspective, Campbell's dark comedy portrays recognisable aspects of the imbricated postmodern and posthuman subject. The historical verisimilitude denoted by blending of many referents to the real, such as Mack Sennet, with the entirely fictitious, for example the film director Orville Hart, mirrors the sensory disorientation of the protagonist in his quest, in which the boundary between reality and unreality is opaque. This accords with Baudrillard's argument regarding hyperreality, that 'the more one nears truth the more it retreats towards the omega point and the greater the rage to get at it', a 'rage' which it proves 'impossib[le]' to master.[56] Further, whether *Grin* is interpreted as a portrait of creeping paranoid psychosis or as a supernatural narrative, digital media are portrayed as pervasive, affective and realising McLuhan's argument that 'all media are extensions of some human faculty – psychic or physical'.[57] Yet the ambiguity of the novel's conclusion, with its protagonist's 'psychic' and 'physical' status uncertain, suggests that Campbell is presenting such concepts without passing moral or value judgements. As I have previously remarked, his concerns have been primarily aesthetic, for 'broadening the genre' and for 'exploration of numerous different modes of horror fiction in search of the perfect form'.[58] In this light, *Grin* may be interpreted not as a critique of postmodern subjectivity or the impact of globalisation upon it, but as a presentation of the subject in its atomised seclusion, an intimate apocalypse. In this comedy blending clowning traditions and ATMs, the reader is thus being presented, as it were, with a last laugh on the author's part.

At one point, Simon, after realising that he may have imagined a visit to the circus and struggling to assert 'some sort of control', insists that 'writing is one way to make sense of the world' (p. 279). While this 2007 novel is a text focused upon the impact of technology in all its variety of forms upon the subject, Campbell's later Gothic narrative *Think Yourself Lucky* turns more explicitly to both the exact nature of this transformed subjectivity and the status and responsibilities of authorship in the digital age. As a serial killer story, in which the only humour is contained in the excoriating and cruel ruminations of its antagonist, *Think Yourself Lucky* presents immediate contrasts of subject matter and approach to its predecessor. An apparently non-Lovecraftian text, *Think Yourself Lucky* is nevertheless a work of supernaturalism strongly within the Gothic tradition, and one which develops the theme of disembodiment. This time the ethereal alter ego depicted is clearly terrestrial, generated within and by a subject explicated as a writer in denial, rather than extraterrestrial in origin. In positing a being whose nature and behaviour is produced by the environment in which the subject is imbricated, the text also readdresses the sociopolitical concerns of Campbell's earlier works.

'A New Species of Monster': Posthuman Sociopathy in Think Yourself Lucky

In contrast to its semi-comedic predecessor, *Think Yourself Lucky* reflects the culture of austerity characterising British life at macro- and microlevels after the financial crisis of 2008. 'We're Still Left', the name of a bookshop which plays a background role in the narrative, suggests both a defiance and a melancholy concession of isolated obsolescence against the dominant ideology of neoliberalism. The novel's protagonist, David Botham, is another cowed and economically compromised graduate. The son of two social workers working with vulnerable people, Botham is employed at a Liverpool travel agency, 'Frugogo'. Not only is the name a signposting manifestation of the author's default corporate entity, but the outlet's viability itself is threatened due to its creeping anachronism in an age of online travel services. As Andrea, David's former partner and now overbearing line manager says, 'we're competing with the Internet as well.'[59] With her warnings about possible redundancies and the compulsory need to 'feel we're all part of the firm' (p. 34), Andrea is a cipher for the brute impersonality of multinational companies. This working environment is Campbell returning to what Joshi memorably described as the white collar 'slow-burning hell' of petty office politics depicted in *Secret Story*. Unlike that novel's Dudley Smith though, Botham insists that he is never going to be a writer and does not like horror films either. Despite repeated disclaimers regarding any desire for authorship, the reader learns that David has casually attended a local writers' group. On hearing one of his verbal tirades, the bookseller hosting it insists that David has the unique ability to articulate people's repressed, negative feelings. The Internet, Kinnear maintains, is 'democratising' (p. 6) the ability and opportunity to write. Feeling under peer pressure at the time, Botham has suggested a title.

The novel's main narrative, presented conventionally in the third person and past tense, recounts the protagonist's increasing horror as he realises that his choice, 'Better Out Than In', has been adopted by a murderous web blogger using the moniker 'Lucky Newless'. The name was a private childhood invention of Botham's for an imaginary companion. Worse, Newless's victims, who each seem objectively to be the subjects of unfortunate accidents, are all known or connected to Botham in some way. The entity Newless has the ability to conceal or reveal its appearance at will. Though rarely seen except by these casualties, third parties like a security guard comment on an uncanny resemblance which the stranger, 'the other feller' (p. 140), bears to Botham. In contrast with *Grin*, where the force of supernatural alterity is an insidious but emergent presence, Campbell interpolates this main narrative with a second, parallel one from the outset, told in the first person and present tense from the perspective of the antagonist. Reproducing its web log postings, these chapters express Newless's highly misanthropic worldview and its perpetually 'unfinished business' (p. 10) – that is, its homicidal activities – as they happen.

Think Yourself Lucky signals, then, Campbell as novelist returning to the theme of serial murder inaugurated by *The Face That Must Die*. Here the theme is updated for a digital era, and, unlike the 1983 novel and the other 'killer' narratives, *The One Safe Place* and *Secret Story*, tenets of the paranormal are deployed.[60] As with *Grin*, the text appears, at one level, to adopt a conservative critique of perceived dangers posed by the Internet's sheer ubiquity. Trolling is, again, not the least of these negative collaterals. As Botham observes resignedly, 'vicious comments were often posted online after people died, not infrequently by total strangers lent courage by disguise or anonymity' (p. 83). Yet, in the shift away from abuse by unseen others to web blogging, this text achieves a subtle switch of analytical focus to the subject and to creativity and, tentatively, the responsibilities it entails. Browsing the Internet, as it does in *Grin*, exposes the protagonist to predation through the network's potentially addictive, narcotic power. The network is described as 'taking hold' of David's brain:

one site leading him to another that tempted him to several more, besides which he found himself following random notions that seemed to belong less to his mind but to the electronic medium. No wonder they called it the net or the web; he could have imagined that thoughts he hardly knew he had were being trawled for, if not drawn in by an insubstantial trap. (pp. 45–6)

Botham then immediately looks at the 'Better Out Than In' web log, which expresses 'thoughts' in writing. With the murderous blog in mind, Botham explicitly blames the Internet for awarding licence to unleash these proscribed aspects of the psyche, unacknowledged thoughts, incognito. He muses that 'if he were a writer perhaps he might have said that the dark matter that had been released was forming a new species of monster' (p. 46). Technology is thus attributed a seductive power of inducing psychosis, in which the subject's sense of 'reality' is lost, and understood as an outright breeding ground for antisocial disorder or sociopathy. Both psychiatric conditions are supernaturalised through their being couched in terms of leading astray, entrapment, darkness and monstrosity.

Botham's understanding is shown to be only partial: in Campbell's vision, individual psychology, aberrant or otherwise, is linked inextricably to socioeconomic environment. The text deftly refrains the acerbic cultural commentary present in the author's earlier socially conscious but non-supernatural Gothic novels like *Face That Must Die* and *One Safe Place* which examine the incidence of sociopathy within a pathologised culture. Despite the instant connectivity brought by digitalisation, societal relations are, again, defined by disconnection: aggression, suspicion and atomisation. As in *Grin*, the vicious online troll is an element of this bleak landscape. Unlike the persistent Smilemime though, the troll in *Think Yourself Lucky* is an almost ephemeral background hazard in comparison with the hostilities the protagonist encounters in his quotidian experience. This is encapsulated in the observation from an unfriendly neighbour that 'there's a sight too much familarity these days' (p. 121). In a development in Campbell's treatment of moral relativism which proves to be key, even characters that should engender sympathy according to contemporary political strictures, such as a mobility scooter user who asserts the right to live, are depicted as singularly rude, unsympathetic and uningratiating. Simultaneously, the novel updates ruminations, explored in *Secret Story* and *Needing Ghosts* respectively, on the artistic anxieties and financial status of authorship. As the writers' group leader speculates concerning the future of literary agents: 'do you really want to give away a percentage of yourself? Maybe the electronic age will do away with that and publishers as well' (p. 27). The subject is thus inevitably imbricated in a matrix by external forces on all sides. *Think Yourself Lucky* explores what happens when digital representation attains primacy, challenging the notion of unified selfhood through a dissolution of boundaries and restraints – including that of the material body.

In acknowledging the 'electronic age', Campbell's novel adheres to recognisable Gothic tradition, relating this awareness to the subject. In an acutely metatextual passage, Botham is described leaving the bookshop:

> As he stepped out of We're Still Left he saw the roofless church across the road, the walls left standing as a monument to the blitz, and it put him in mind of a hollow prayer. He suspected that was how a writer might think, and he expelled the fancy from his mind as he tramped downhill to the station. (p. 31)

The leitmotif of the abandoned building, such as the dilapidated theatre in *Obsession*, is a recurrent one in Campbell's fictions. Here, the 'roofless church' together with its connotations of 'hollow prayer', a ruin which reappears throughout the narrative, seems both a self-conscious acknowledgement of the text's Gothic inheritance and a symbol of postmodernity's rootless spiritual *ennui*, within which the subject is enmeshed, and with which the subject, as reluctant 'writer', must struggle. Moreover, the novel itself is Campbell's most substantial reimagining of the criminal double or *doppelgänger* trope, a belated competitor to King's *The Dark Half*.[61] Campbell's choice of language, as observed, is always self-conscious and deliberate. His intentions in *Think Yourself Lucky* are signalled immediately, as Gary Fry points out, in the protagonist's apt surname, *both-am*.[62] The ensuing narrative, in which Newless's web log becomes a source of fear and a compulsion for the protagonist, lends itself to interpretation according to both postmodern and posthuman paradigms. For Baudrillard, the unacknowledged double is a 'spectre that haunts the subject as its "other"': it causes 'him [*sic*] to be himself while at the same time never seeming like himself'.[63] In Campbell's novel, Botham, on first reading Lucky's blogposts, feels similarly, 'as if the contents of his skull were drifting loose' (p. 19). Herbrechter, focusing on the complexity of the subject's response to alterity, maintains that fear of such monstrous alterity is combined with 'desire to live out forbidden practices in a "secure" fashion', in the form of 'exotic, escapist and exorcising phantoms'.[64] The confident and assertive Newless, declaring 'I'm no idiot of any kind ... the watcher you couldn't be bothered to notice ... Mr Lucky on another mission' (p. 41), bears the same relationship to the callow Botham as, for example, Gil-Martin does to Wringham in *Private Memoirs and Confessions of a Justified Sinner*, a brash entity which 'never go[es] but where I have some great purpose to serve' in self-advancement 'or in thwarting of my enemies'.[65] In its concern with a divided subject, *Think Yourself Lucky* even replicates the epistolary structure of Hogg and Stevenson's seminal works.

Fry's shrewd but incomplete analysis interprets Campbell's novel specifically as a successor to *Strange Case of Dr Jekyll and Mr Hyde*. With the authority of a psychologist, Fry correctly distinguishes between the threat posed by Stevenson's repressed 'monster' to the entire social order of its time, and the more subtle challenge *within* its society posed by Campbell's antagonist.[66] Newless indeed draws its energy from what Fry calls the protagonist's 'conflict avoidance in the micro routines which constitute twenty-first century life', that is, the codes and strictures of political correctness which, paradoxically, engender aggression in the form of irritation and annoyance in response.[67] In the novel's pivotal epiphany, Botham realises that 'it isn't what I wish that makes these things happen, it's what I can't admit I wish' (p. 222). Although Fry does not elaborate on this point, these protocols relating to disability, obesity, the rights of pregnant women and other facets denoting issue-based politics are also themselves obviously contradictory, in the context of a societal culture which is *itself* pervaded by incipient mutual antagonisms. More significantly, Botham's vexed self-repression demonstrates a subject's aforementioned inability to abject its 'monstrous' features, a weakness which Heise-von der Lippe associates with Gothic posthumanism. The entity Newless is, as Fry notes, a '*disembodied*' descendant of Hyde.[68] It is, he goes on to argue, 'a monster which could only have been created by the Internet', an immaterial presence freed from social strictures on the human body and '*re-embodied* as a supernatural force capable of causing certain people to die'.[69]

Crediting the Internet itself with actually originating a malevolent ethereal alterity is, it is immediately apparent, contentious. Gil-Martin in Hogg's novel, for example, is variously described as having a 'cameleon [sic] art' and 'flitt[ing] about . . . like a shadow, or rather like a spirit'.[70] Fritz Leiber's short story 'Smoke Ghost' (1941), an urban narrative greatly admired by Campbell, also features disembodied spectrality: 'no longer a world of material atoms and empty spaces', but one 'in which the bodiless existed and moved according to its own obscure laws and and unpredictable impulses'.[71] Of greater import is that the liminality on display in Campbell's text, between material and immaterial experiential realms, is consistent with what Herbrechter describes as an exploration of 'the increasing extent of the body into virtual spaces', an undertaking symptomatic of posthumanism.[72] Although deliberately likened to forebears like Gil-Martin as a demon which has been 'called up' or 'invoked' (pp. 51, 195), Newless is, as Fry notes, an archetypal entity for a new electronic or e-culture.[73] 'We're past those', Lucky declares, regarding books, and 'I've never needed one [a telephone]', it later boasts to a victim, as 'I'm electronic enough' (pp. 65, 157). Like *Grin*, the text derives inspiration from M. R. James's evocation of fear induced by the half-seen but keenly sensed proximity of 'other'-ness. This time though, emphasis is placed on the indefinability of the entity's appearance and movement, as when Botham watches Newless following Kinnear, 'dodg[ing] into view' and appearing to borrow its own visibility 'from gaps in the crowd' (p. 195). Campbell's portrayal of Newless and of the anxiety of surveillance – that is, of being watched and stalked by something elusive, intangible and protean – has an affinity with Eric Knudsen's 'Slender Man' Internet meme (2009), another amorphous, wraith-like entity. The commonality is the ability not only to induce fear and terror but to cause actual harm. Botham protests that Newless's victims 'killed themselves' and dismisses the entity as 'just words in the air' (pp. 237–8). This reductionist argument is accepted by Fry, who compares Newless to the 'blag of Internet trolls' – unpleasant, invidious and petty, but fundamentally powerless to cause actual violence or injury because its weaponry is confined to the purely verbal.[74] David's argument is, though, logically contradicted by a value system in which language in the form of thought clearly *is* power, manifested in a being which can physically pull one victim off a ladder or wrest a steering wheel from another. In its exploratory nature, Newless is a truly liminal entity: a virtual being, but one also capable of physical materialisation into, and impacting upon the 'real' world at will.

This materialisation, however, is unfinished. *Think Yourself Lucky* repeats the attribution of what Joshi notes as, with respect to an earlier Campbell novel, a 'curiously *incomplete* appearance' to representation of spectrality.[75] Newless is described in the final encounter with Botham as being only a faceless 'suggestion of a presence', reminding the protagonist of 'a childish sketch of bones' or 'elongated foetus' (pp. 226, 230). These pediatric and prenatal allusions underline a sense of extreme dependence, conveyed in an earlier chapter when Newless sees David at the travel agency and admits, atypically, to doubt and insecurity. As opposed to its normal confident bravado, the entity speculates:

> What would happen if I wait for him to come out of the staff room – if I try to speak to him? The prospect seems to paralyze me, and I feel in danger of growing no more perceptible to myself than I am to the hypocrites lined up behind the counter like targets in a fairground. (p. 154)

The climactic confrontation between protagonist and antagonist on the bridge, an obviously symbolic setting representing a contrast between life and death, the real world and Newless's one, and the choice which Botham must make, confirms the vulnerability of the entity. Experiencing 'a dank chill', Botham has a momentary 'threat of glimpsing somewhere so barren of light and warmth that it consisted purely of a yearning for sensation, for any token of existence' (p. 234). It is a subliminal vision of Newless's private hell, completing a portrait of isolation and loneliness as much as malevolence.

The novel's epilogue, set close to a year after Botham plunges into the lake, taking Newless with him, thus presents a level of *permitted* monstrousness, a tenderness within evil. It is also an accommodation and acceptance on the part of the protagonist. To prevent further deaths, protect others and 'contain' Newless, Botham has performed a *volte-face* regarding being a writer: 'I had to be honest', he admits to Kinnear with heavy verbal irony; 'it's the only way to live' (p. 244). David's reversal signifies far more than having found 'a writing job that pays' (p. 244), as a disapproving Kinnear observes, acidly. This denouement correlates with Nayar's argument on an essential compromise within posthumanism, wherein 'only when the human recognises that the Other [*sic*] is within, that the Other shares life with itself, can the human be more responsive to life itself'.[76] The protagonist's conscious decision to become a writer appears to enact this process of the accommodation of alterity, recognition and coexistence. 'There's nothing easier than being myself', Botham asserts, 'now I know who I am' (p. 242). There is, however, a price. In becoming 'Mr Nasty from the north', a polemicist producing a column entitled 'Bad Thoughts' for a weekly publication, Botham has deliberately isolated himself by ending his romantic relationship and alienating all former contacts. In Campbell's previous narrative on serial murder, *Secret Story*, Dudley Smith becomes 'a cultural icon' after his death (*Secret Story*, p. 377). *Think Yourself Lucky* develops this theme of media celebrity: through ethical necessity, its protagonist identifies in public with his media creation and therefore *becomes* his own 'new species of monster'. The title hosting Botham's inflammatory columns is, pointedly, non-electronic. Defiantly entitled *Print*, this attests to Campbell's career-long adherence to the medium, evident since 'The Franklyn Paragraphs', and his scepticism regarding its supersedence by new (electronic) forms of communication. Rather, his novel presents an interplay between modes of media, and, especially, their potentially detrimental societal role, as when David is surprised by 'the amount of support he'd attracted in the paper and online', and 'the tone, some of which makes Newless seem restrained' (p. 247). The protagonist as monster may therefore be seen to have 'spawned' its own viral contagion, in the form of trolling, in its wake.

A writer's potential to affect their social environment, positively or adversely, has also been a continuing preoccupation of Campbell's. His aforementioned short story of precognition from the 1970s, 'The Depths', for example, is a thematic predecessor of *Think Yourself Lucky*. It also features a protagonist, Jonathan Miles, who is forced to express negative experiences in writing, in this case the nightmares of what is revealed as the collective unconscious, to prevent their actualisation as real-life murders. 'I think the public is outgrowing fantasy', Miles's publisher remarks breezily, provocatively and ironically in the course of that narrative, 'now we're well and truly in the scientific age'.[77] Campbell's later text fully reflects post-1970s technological developments characterising the 'scientific age', but *Think Yourself Lucky* is more intimate in scope than 'The Depths'. It employs parenthood as emotive and explicit metaphor for a writer's obligation to assume responsibility for their work and for what may result as consequence. Regarding her own son, the protagonist's neighbour remarks sourly that 'you're responsible for what you create whether you like it not', and David's father later implores him to 'never create a life unless you're sure you want it to live' (pp. 120, 181). Like 'Slender Man' and that entity's video logs, Lucky Newless, whether it is Botham's aborted brother or product of his own imagination, exemplifies what Joseph Crawford describes as the propensity of any new form of media technology to generate a new narrative or 'monstrous birth' which threatens to disrupt the cultural landscape hosting it.[78] However, Campbell's vision of Gothic posthuman forms of life extends beyond the depiction of monstrosity. The themes of creative responsibility and artificial and vulnerable created lives which are dependent upon their creator are explored most comprehensively in Campbell's earlier meditation on natalism, the cross-generic novel, *The Seven Days of Cain*.

The Lives of Others: The Seven Days of Cain as Posthuman Tragedy

While *Think Yourself Lucky* may be seen as a successor to Hogg and Stevenson's texts updated for an electronic era, Campbell's 2010 novel serves as a contemporary version of *Frankenstein*, the quintessential Gothic disquisition on the 'overreacher' who dares to assume prerogatives reserved for the divine. Atmospherically set mostly in the coastal town of Crosby, Merseyside, the narrative's protagonist is, again, one of Campbell's compromised artists whose past dabblings in authorship exact macabre consequences. In this case, catastrophe is precipitated by the use of an occult website as 'a magical way to create life'.[79] Creative responsibility, along with time and the preservation and loss of memory are all key concerns. The central character, Andy Bentley, is a married photographer and heir to his parents' studio. Bentley's father, a self-denigrating portrait seller is, it is implied through repeated reference to his amnesia, in the early stages of dementia. Like Botham in *Think Yourself Lucky*, the protagonist gradually discovers his own connection to a series of deaths. In this case the killings are sadistic murders, and are not, it transpires, of real people but of fictional characters. Their names are avatars derived from facets of Botham's own personality which he had, much earlier, invented for a website, 'YourSelves'. Andy had found that 'once you set them up they kept writing themselves' (p. 144). However, as he is to learn, they exist not only as web blogs but autonomous beings. In a neat elaboration and satirisation of this metatextuality, Campbell even portrays one victim, Penny Scrivener, as a dramatist, whose last work features a protagonist creating Internet personalities which also attain sentience. Scrivener's play is a musical farce, featuring a climax in which the heroine herself disappears, thus revealing her own fictional status to the audience.

Anticipating Lucky Newless, the killer in *Cain* is another dexterous shapeshifter drawn from the Internet.[80] It appears for most of the narrative as 'Max Beyer', a writer and wealthy client of Andy's, and is, explicitly, the protagonist's abjection. Originally named Septimus Battle, Beyer is described by Bentley as the worst part of himself, 'the one I tried not to make up' (p, 145). Like the other novels discussed in this chapter, manifestation of monstrous alterity accords with an apparently technophobic and cyberphobic position. As the entity itself asks, ironically, 'is there anything that can't be done on a computer?' (p. 49). Again, the Internet is presented as a 'trap' that can lure the unwary 'to ramble to site after site' (p. 37). Similarly to Smilemime's victimisation of Lesser in *Grin*, the antagonist commences its attack on the protagonist through trolling emails. Sent anonymously from 'Frugomail' accounts, these read 'like a product of the sort of immaturely talented mind that the Internet gave scope to play havoc with other people's computers, creating viruses or hacking into sites or stealing identities' (p. 63). Bentley finally exorcises Beyer by confronting the entity with its own unreality, as 'just words and too many of them' and, thus, its inability to harm 'real people' (pp. 294, 297). However, this is not before it has succeeded in inveigling itself into the life of Claire, Andy's wife, by posing as an old schoolfriend. As Tim Battle, an actor, Beyer ultimately causes Claire to discover that she too is a fictional creation of Andy's from the website, and that her past life is a complete fabrication assembled from the memories of others.

Cain is a richly intertextual as much as metatextual work. In the linkage of the 'YourSelves' website's origins to Roland Franklyn, described in turn as having been a student of Thackeray Lane's, Campbell refers back to his own created Gothic mythos. The title, *Cain*, itself invokes the Book of Genesis, and the novel's diegesis echoes Luigi Pirandello's absurdist play *Six Characters in Search of an Author* (1921).[81] Yet Campbell's naming of Beyer's unseen and fictitious publisher as 'Teddy Ballard' also foregrounds a conscious engagement with the science fiction genre, an affinity which remains largely salient in *Grin* or *Think Yourself Lucky*. Like Ballard's *Crash* (1973) and that novelist's other dystopias, *Cain* explores the effect of technology on external and internal, psychological landscapes, and how a reality mediated by that technology is entwined with the production of identity. Moreover, the novel's portrayal of the endeavours of normal as opposed to socially-elevated beings, both real and artificial, as they seek to comprehend and assert their own lives, recalls the fictions of Philip K. Dick. Campbell himself has acknowledged the American writer's influence on this novel's 'ordinariness of characters' and its concern with the 'nature of reality and identity'.[82] Dick's narratives have been described accurately by Jason P. Vest as reconciling the concerns of humanism with postmodern scepticism about the possibility of progress in an age where 'grand narratives and institutions' enabling human advancement no longer function.[83] Campbell's fictions, as I have demonstrated in previous chapters, display a similar engagement with such postmodern concerns. Like Dick's, they do so largely without the elite stylisation of high postmodernism.[84] Dying in 1982, Dick did not experience the full advent of the Internet and its web-generated 'ghosts'. Nevertheless, his concern with sentient android lives is replicated in Campbell's portrayal of autonomous virtual ones. Campbell, in describing his own field as 'capable of development' and welcoming generic broadening, has described *Cain* as 'a tragedy'.[85] In also engaging with the destructive *and* constructive potency of the digital world, Campbell creates a generic hybrid that is also his most circumspect and probing engagement with Gothic posthumanism. Despite preceding *Think Yourself Lucky*, the novel represents the culmination of his experimentation.

Echoing the original subtitle of *Frankenstein*, *Cain* can be interpreted as a postmillennial adaptation of the Prometheus myth. Indeed, both artistically and philosophically, Anthony J. Fonseca notes the likeness of this work to that of Robert Aickman, in that it depicts and evokes the 'mythic rather than horrific'.[86] As with Aickman's ghost stories, the narrative seems to strive, in the author's own words, 'to glimpse the eternal'.[87] There are allusions to Beyer's acts of torture, mutilation and murder, as in the entity's gloating reference to Penny – 'as it was, she was gutted' (p. 62) – but these tend to the indirect, veiled by implication or sardonic word play. The acidic social critique as backdrop that denotes texts like *The Face That Must Die*, *Secret Story* or *Think Yourself Lucky*, which confer upon each of those works a highly specific contemporeality, is also largely absent here. Unlike Lucky Newless, for example, the digital entity Beyer seems to derive its energising 'excellent nastiness' (p. 118) from the protagonist's psyche rather than social causality or prevailing mores. Instead, the text utilises powerful symbols drawn from other, non-literary media – sculpture and photography – to elucidate the malleability of time and human subjectivity. Most obviously, the real-life 'Another Place' sculptures by Anthony Gormley on Crosby's beach, erected in 2005, are a consistent presence. The sea itself is accorded a primal power: 'too much rearing up of water, too much spray and dark uncontaminated violence' (p. 224). Lent an almost spectral status, Gormley's beach figures act as both sentinels and, as in ancient Greek drama, a silent chorus within the narrative. Repeatedly likened to clones, their uniformity becomes uncanny and disturbing for Bentley:

> Usually he found the watchers on the beach – their impregnable serenity and the suggestion that they were intent on some distant vision – as calming as she [Claire] did, but now the sense of so many bodies with a single personality, if even that, unnerved him. (pp. 33–4)

It crystallises the relationship between artistic creator and artificial creation, and the potential threat posed by an anonymous, blank-faced and unsympathetic crowd to an isolated individual. More profoundly, the figures' 'single personality, if even that' becomes an obsession of other artificial but digital creations seeking to assert their own individuality and reality. The figures become the target of mockery and vandalism by Beyer, a similarly void being. Like Ellis's Patrick Bateman and Campbell's own Dudley Smith in *Secret Story*, Beyer seeks to deny its own superficiality and assert full selfhood by desecrating and exposing the interior, material bodies of others. In contrast, Claire observes that the statues' hollowness makes her 'feel hollow inside. Not real' (p. 34). Although different reactions, Beyer's attack and Claires's anxiety both literalise what Baudrillard describes as the subject's 'fear of being just a clone', submerged in a plethora of signs, simulacra and data.[88] The uniformity of these pitiless, undifferentiated and empty structures seems to embody his argument that 'we manufacture a profusion of images in which there is nothing to see' and where the image 'has taken over, imposed its own ephermeral logic'.[89]

Further, Bentley's profession and his father's amnesia herald a narrative in which photography is presented as pivotal in the capture or construction of memory and self-definition. Posing as a client, Beyer constantly seeks 'more life' (p. 21) from Bentley's services, but the importance of the photographic record really governs the central relationship between Andy and Claire. As Fonseca notes, photography '(re)creates the physical world as the psychological landscape, where memories invariably evoke ghosts, literal and metaphorical'.[90] As she is herself, like Beyer, a poor, 'ghostly' and digital construct, Claire cannot perceive her fellow entity's face on photographic likenesses. Andy's wife can see only 'a black hole' which insidiously 'lodg[es] inside her' and contributes to insecurity about her own reality (pp. 190, 193). Equally, Claire enacts what Baudrillard describes as 'the fetishization of the lost object' with respect to the desperate preservation of artificial, borrowed memories. After photographs of her deceased 'parents', whose faces she is dismayed that she cannot recall, disappear, Claire pleads to her husband that 'they're part of me. You understand that surely' (p. 257).[91] Ultimately, for Andy, his wife's own physiognomy on photographs becomes blurred, 'an absence' at their core that leaves 'an aching hole in his consciousness' (p. 313), as he realises that he is unable to remember her face. I return to the specific significance of Claire herself later; here, it is the medium of interpretation that the couple rely upon for verification and self-validation which is the focus. In literary form, the text enacts Linda Hutcheon's argument regarding postmodern photography, that such 'representations' are, like film, one of the only available 'means of access' to or 'traces' of history, by which that past can be (re)constructed and known.[92] This is in opposition to Fredric

Jameson's more pessimistic conclusion that the 'waning of affect' wrought by late capitalism terminates the possibility of such expressions of the 'unique and the personal ... the individual brush stoke'.[93] In contrast to Jameson's vision, with *Cain* there remains a comprehending consciousness, 'a self present to do the feeling'.[94] That 'self' is in fact multiple, and it is both human and posthuman.

Central to the reinterpretation of the Prometheus myth posited by *Frankenstein* and its literary heirs is, naturally, its horrific potential: the generation of life which evades its creator's control and is potentially monstrous. In its portrayal of the website's founder as a paranoid schizophrenic who uses the lexicographically loaded pseudonym 'Adam Caboodle', *Cain* revises the anxiety about the act of creative writing expressed in *Needing Ghosts*.[95] In the earlier text, the compulsion to write stories 'won't leave you alone even when you're with people, even where you're desperate to sleep' (p. 34). In the later novel, Internet characters are now the proliferating narratives and described in similar persecutory terms. Caboodle complains to Andy:

> You'd understand if you had any of your selves in you. You don't know what it's like. Try waking up every morning for a week and finding another's come in while you're asleep. And then try getting any of them to leave you alone for a second. It's like being shut in a room for the rest of your life with them and there's no door where they came in and they'll never shut up, not even when you want to sleep or when you manage. (p. 176)

This state of flux, representing what Rosi Braidotti would deem an 'ontologically polyvocal subject', is the antithesis of the 'stable human essence' championed by other, more conservative theorists of posthumanism like Francis Fukuyama.[96] Through their independence, Bentley's self-writing characters, or narratives, are similar to Ellis's 'book' in *Lunar Park*, the American author's overtly postmodernist and metatextual sequel to *American Psycho*: that is, an enterprise which 'wrote itself', oblivious to its author's misgivings.[97] While *Grin* addresses the potential of the Internet to accommodate and distribute a lurking and transmuted alterity, *Cain* focuses on the generation, multiplicity and empowerment of this 'other'-ness. Akin to Ellis's psychopath Patrick Bateman, Beyer is a 'monster' which has 'escaped' from a fictional 'novel', in this case its creator's imagination.[98] The final confession of the antagonist and unreliable narrator of *American Psycho*, that Bateman 'simply was not there', is repeated in Beyer's ultimate defeat and banishment through its emasculating exposure as unreal.[99] Described at the beginning as 'just an absence where a person ought to be', the entity is vanquished, far from the 'real man, coming closer' (pp. 19, 247) that it vaunts itself as being. Like Bateman, Beyer's obsessive but ultimately empty quest literalises 'the struggle for self-knowledge, definition and access to the real' which Maria Beville describes as 'essentially the engine propelling postmodern narratives'.[100] However, Andy's prevailing argument in this confrontation asserts a more liberal and humanist credo than Ellis's nihilistic fiction: 'show some humanity for once. That's how to be human. That's how you can be real' (p. 298).

This positioning is central to explicating the novel's meaning and contribution to Campbell's overall Gothic vision, for *Cain* is more complex in its analysis of the 'human' than its obvious reproduction of generic motifs would suggest. Whilst Beyer, unlike Frankenstein's monster, is presented as wholly destructive from the outset, it is a single entity amongst the many which the protagonist creates. The text both expands upon Shelley's novel, in that there is now a plethora of artificial 'humans' rather than just one, and emulates it, in its treatment of the themes of responsibility, abandonment, guilt and selfhood as well as innocence. The complaint of Frankenstein's creature against its creator for rejecting it, 'how dare you sport thus with life?', and its call for Victor to 'do your duty towards me', are refrained in Beyer's criticism of an absent 'guardian' that 'thought he was responsible for me till I turned into somebody he didn't like', and who 'gave up by the seventh day' (pp. 52, 118).[101] Bentley's titular association, not only with the role of God but with Cain, the first murderer, implicates him in primal sin. More directly, the protagonist is also admonished by his other creations whose existence he has denied, such as Louisa Carmichael, who sardonically remarks, 'don't say you've started caring about us now …' (p. 113).

Both married and a step-parent since Bentley created her as 'Louisa Ruse', Louisa has forged an independent existence. Her self-determination and desire for life are shared by Andy's other characters. 'Regis King', the surname a homage to Campbell's most well-known contemporary as Gothic horror writer, acts as spokesperson for these new lives. King asserts that 'we're individuals, the whole lot of us', and that he and Bentley's other digital beings 'can do without a past' (p. 153), on the grounds that their belief in their present reality is sufficient. The pursuit of 'reality' and 'more life' thus animates *all* Bentley's created characters. Beyer and his other new 'humans' incarnate what Hayles defines as 'embodied virtualities'.[102] The world depicted in *Cain* is one in which the boundary between the real and these fictional 'virtualities' has been occluded at quotidian level. For the theorist, these born-digital beings' relationships with each other, and their interactions with Bentley and other 'real' people, would demonstrate the process of independent thought being undertaken 'by both human and non-human actors', an occurrence denoting posthumanism.[103] Further, with respect to all except perhaps the explicitly *anti*social Beyer, the physicality and assertiveness which they show have affinity with a process described by Nayar as a 'de- and re-terrorialisation of the body within conduits of information exchange and datasets'.[104] For Nayar, it is a positive development that defines 'the rise of a new biological citizenship that is [also] posthuman'.[105]

With its cast of artificial beings clinging to their individuality and life, *Cain* interrogates such notions of 'citizenship'. It does so, above all, in the presentation of Claire Bentley. Claire represents the 'poor binarised ghost' at its most poignant. Employed, significantly, by 'Home from Home', an assisted charity for the homeless, and thus displaced and marginalised, she is also haunted by her own infertility. The narrative traces her personal odyssey, from self-assertiveness over Andy opening her letters to her sensory dissipation, final withdrawal and literal disappearance through a sense of shame at 'not being real' (p. 303). Throughout, Claire increasingly senses her involvement in an artificial performance, as if she were 'enacting a domestic tableau that she hoped would become more real' (p. 192). Hayles cautions that, despite the phenomenon of posthuman independent thought, 'we can no longer assume that consciousness guarantees existence of the self'.[106] Claire's (re)discovery of her own fictionality, that her history is a construct from another narrative, the autobiographical *Clare's Tale* by one Michaela Pocus, typifies not only the novel's acute metatextuality but its deconstruction of subjectivity.[107] As with, for example, the lives of the clones in Kazuo Ishiguro's science fiction novel, *Never Let Me Go* (2005), there may be, as Nayar maintains, 'inclusivity' of posthuman lives alongside human ones, but there are still implicit 'power relations', or more accurately power hierarchies: this new life's existence is owed to, and has its parameters defined by, the lives of others.[108] Bentley creates, covets and eventually mourns Claire as his intended Eve, 'the best part of me' or, as Beyer mockingly observes, '[e]verything you wanted in a single package' (pp. 314, 89). Comparison with the biblical character is made explicit in Claire finally gazing into a pool and perceiving only 'an abyss' of 'utter emptiness . . . the void that was herself' (p. 306). The scene evokes and parodies two famous precedents: Eve seeing her reflection in John Milton's *Paradise Lost* (1667/1674) and the creature's repulsion upon beholding its own visage in *Frankenstein*, itself Shelley's revisitation of Milton's text.[109] Appropriately, Beyer, the murderous dissector, is the primary agent of Claire's deconstruction. By asking 'Tim' to 'imagine' something for her, Claire unwittingly invites her own anatomisation and exposure as artificial. In an acute instance of the text's multilayered self-inflection, Beyer, disguised as an actor and adopting a persona created by the actor to impersonate their mutual creator, tells her, theatrically:

> I'm the voice you're not sure if you're hearing . . . I'm the man who tells you what to think and you believe you're thinking it yourself. Anything you do, I've already thought of it. You can't even dream unless I give you dreams. Perhaps you only see what I put into your head. I'm what you have for a soul. (p. 108)

Malicious and devastating as this diatribe and Beyer's acting as 'whistleblowing' informant regarding *Clare's Tale* prove to be, the reference to 'soul' refrains an earlier pledge, itself repeating an imagined childhood vow, which Claire makes to Andy: 'I'll always be there if you need me. I promise with my soul' (p. 33). Such referencing serves to foreground a metaphysical dimension to the novel, already established by Campbell's use of Gormley's eerie sculptures and the photograph motif. The theme of spiritual connection between human and posthuman is represented in Andy and Claire's marriage, in which her husband tells Claire that he senses 'as if I'd been looking for you all my life', and she had felt similarly that 'we're part of each other' (pp. 41, 314). The possibility of the promised renewed union being fulfilled is refrained in the novel's ambiguous ending on the beach. As the setting for King and Claire's terminated lives, this sinister, preternatural location has previously been associated with omen and death. With the tentative question 'Is it you?' (p. 315), Andy instead half hopes for and half senses the latter's returned presence. Through this finale, *Cain* may conclude, however obliquely, an overall accord with a positive interpretation of posthumanism, as 'affording new opportunities for social bonding and empowerment', proposed by theorists like Hayles, Nayar and Braidotti.[110] If the novel's final scene seems to support Lyotard's statement that 'the union of soul and body remains an intractable enigma', the text as a whole certainly enacts his argument that the subject, acting as a 'transformer', ensures, through 'techno-science' and other cultural developments, and the 'new memorization they involve', the introduction of 'a supplement of complexity' to the universe.[111] *Cain* remains Campbell's most thorough examination, to date, of the complex implications, for both good and ill, of digital technology.

What emerges in Campbell's evocation and updating of familiar Gothic tropes of clowns, doubles and Frankenstein monsters in these three techno-fictions is an iconoclastic treatment of subject, authorship and even, as examined, assumptions about the linearity and immutability of history itself. As Lester speculates resignedly in *Grin*, 'the past has finally caught up with me, or is it the future, or both?' (p. 338). In a manner not available to him when writing, say, *The Nameless* or *Needing Ghosts*, Campbell uses postmillennial advances in technology in the form of new, interactive media to probe the contested nature of reality and what Heise-von der Lippe describes, regarding the posthuman Gothic, as 'our treacherously safe human subject positions'.[112] Central to this new medium are the computer and the Internet as extensions of human consciousness and tools in the establishment of selfhood. In Campbell's vision of the Gothic, they serve as further mediators for creativity, and thus as a constitutive element of the postmodern and posthuman digital subject. Consciousness is, it is speculated, physically metamorphosised and absorbed into virtual reality in *Grin*. This journey is reversed with the physical realisation of virtual beings into material reality: in part in *Lucky*, and completely in *Cain*. However, for Campbell, such creativity and subjectivity take on a fragmented, schizoid hue, symbolised in Internet chatroom allusions to Franklyn and Lane's belief in 'lots of selves . . . not all of them on earth' and serving as 'masks of chaos', and, of course, the indelible image of a broken, paranoid schizophrenic website manager (*Cain*, p. 115). Far from a means of self-completion, the plethora of 'selves' or others unleashed threatens to overwhelm the original subject. It is also, therefore, a paranoid subject, paranoia being the defensive default and the sole means for Campbell's variously baffled, isolated or struggling characters – real or unreal – to comprehend the contemporary world and their place within it.

Conclusion: 'Something to Believe in': Repositioning Campbell in the Gothic – and Beyond

ಜಲಚ

Ramsey Campbell's contribution to the Gothic is unique. In his seminal treatise, 'Supernatural Horror in Literature' (1927, revised 1934), H. P. Lovecraft, Campbell's great forebear and influence, nominates and praises twentieth-century 'modern masters' for, amongst other qualities, their 'artistic smoothness', advanced 'technique' and 'craftmanship'.[1] In attempting to assess Campbell's place within Gothic studies, both in terms of canonicity and scholarly appraisal, and the writer's status beyond it, Lovecraft's aesthetic criteria seem apposite as a starting point. Therefore, I return in the first instance to Campbell's distinctive style. This combines a subtle, highly personal fusion of precisely observed accumulation of detail and an imputation of a disturbing, ominous and uncanny quality to the incongruously mundane, the quotidian and even inanimate.

An almost throwaway passage from Campbell's late novel, *The Seven Days of Cain*, the final text discussed in the last chapter, comes to mind. On his way to meet the doomed Louisa Carmichael in London, Andy Bentley encounters the statue of the film comedian Charlie Chaplin in Leicester Square. It is described thus:

> The blank eyes without pupils reminded him of the figures on the beach at home. The eyes were as unrelievedly black as the rest of the effigy – the bowler hat and baggy trousers, the stick bent into a curve

like an initial letter. The shiny surface reminded Andy of the carapace of a beetle, so that he could have fancied that a giant insect was looming beside him on its stone plinth, keeping still so that its prey would wander within reach. (p. 115)

This vignette, utterly irrelevant to the plot, echoes the image of rubble-strewn desolation in the early short story 'Concussion', covered in the Introduction. Importantly, it encapsulates the individual quality of Campbell's prose. It is a prime example of Campbell's evocation of the urban sublime, born from his desire 'to produce awe and terror' in an audience.[2] On Campbell's twentieth-century Gothic fictions, Steffen Hantke rightly notes that the author is 'a keen and devoted chronicler of the urban blight afflicting his native Liverpool and the industrial north'.[3] However, an obviously wider geographic setting aside (Bentley is away from Merseyside), it is clear at such moments that Campbell has also developed into something more. The writer himself has always espoused 'precise selection of language', and his facility with diverse art forms, noted by S. T. Joshi, is on full display with the deployment of highly contrasting sculptures and photography in *Cain*.[4] Although completely tangential to the novel's diegesis, the Chaplin scene encapsulates Campbell's knowledge of media and especially film history, and, in its connotations of paranoia and suggestion of the sinister in representation of the iconic figure of the little tramp, the generic fluidity of his work. Campbell has described horror as being 'an enormously capacious field'.[5] Here, as in *The Grin of the Dark* and the earlier tragicomic novel *The Count of Eleven*, he is blending and exploring the liminal boundary between horror and comedy.

Yet the Chaplin episode also symbolises Campbell's highly idiosyncratic sensibility and terms of reference. As such, the passage is indicative of the peculiar dichotomy of the author's own position. Subtle, literate, widely read and highly allusive, Campbell acknowledges the influence of Graham Greene and Vladimir Nabokov as well as and as much as that of Lovecraft, Robert Aickman and M. R. James.[6] Conversely, with few exceptions, the author's vast output has remained consistently British in setting, arguably, from the point of view of detractors, to the point of parochialism.[7] Despite recognition from no less than Stephen King and the plethora of awards conferred upon him, this book has suggested that this has had the effect of marginalising him internationally, both commercially and in terms of scholarship. Further, in so 'proud[ly]' identifying himself as a horror writer and as 'a great believer' in the field's 'tradition', Campbell, conscientious historian and student of the genre, has also implicated himself in that genre's traditional critical disparagement.[8] King's National Book Award for Distinguished Contribution to American Letters (2003) was, after all, a decision famously criticised by Harold Bloom as 'another low in the shocking process of dumbing down' of that country's cultural life.[9] For his part, 'horror fiction', writes Campbell in an excoriation of the mainstream critic Leslie Fiedler, 'is beset with ignorance masquerading as informed criticism'.[10] This monograph germinated from an intention to accord overdue attention to a prolific writer's work, but it is also from such an exasperated predicament that *Ramsey Campbell* has attempted a rehabilitation.

In contrast to Campbell's short stories, which have received the majority of critical notice and praise from Joshi and others, I have deliberately focused on Campbell's neglected longer fictions. It is with his novels and novellas that the writer's fertile imagination is awarded more breadth to explore in depth issues around the position of the subject in the contemporary world. A wider aim of this book was to elucidate the contribution that more serious academic scrutiny of Campbell can make to Gothic studies. It argues that both the literary canon and its scholarship can gain much from the admission of what is a unique voice, ambassadorial but ceaselessly interrogative. What Joshi accurately describes as the blend of 'flamboyant cosmicism and social realism' in Campbell's varied corpus, inspired by Lovecraft and Aickman but transformed by the author's unique history and imagination into something entirely original, can deepen understanding of the parameters and possible expansion of the genre.[11] Simultaneously, a recuperation of Campbell affords various possibilities for sociopolitical, aesthetic and wider philosophical critique. It is impossible not to be struck by a note of self-projection in Campbell's defence of his fellow British writer James Herbert – another, thus far, understudied author. He describes Herbert as something of a scourge to the Establishment, 'challeng[ing] the class bias of English horror fiction', and, more tellingly, as 'an unmistakably English and unmistakably contemporary writer who refuses to conform to what's expected of him or to stop questioning what he sees and feels'.[12]

Campbell's own sociopsychological concerns have arguably been wider in scope than Herbert's, but they are surely no less passionate or consistent. As an interview given in 2018 attests, Campbell's preoccupations remain 'the vulnerability of children, the willingness of people to espouse a belief system that denies them the right to question, the growing tendency to create scapegoats for the ills of the world'.[13] This sceptical, anti-totalitarian stance naturally suggests affinity with Jean-François Lyotard's critique of 'grand narratives', those various religious, political and other totalising belief systems which had collapsed under postmodernism.[14] Campbell's work is sophisticated enough to bear such comparisons. Alongside close textual analysis, this enterprise has accordingly deployed an appropriately eclectic theoretical approach, for the most part informed by, but at the same time critically distant from, postmodern paradigms. It has clearly demonstrated Campbell's evolution as a writer. Campbell, in his development and thematic shifts, illustrates the potential of both his fiction and his chosen 'field' for affording sociopolitical critique and philosophical investigation into the value, place and transformations of subject, writer and writer-as-subject in contemporary, increasingly technologically driven societies. Although his work aligns with postmodernism's critique of master narratives, and variously displays the hallmarks of intertextuality, metatextuality, paradox, unreliable narration, authorial angst, paranoia and final irresolution associated with postmodernist fictions, it is also suffused with a strain of paradoxical, but consistent, liberal humanism. The various struggles depicted and the fates of the haunted characters populating Campbell's landscapes may represent an enactment of distinctly Baudrillardian concepts of a 'murder[ed]' reality being replaced by an endless 'procession of simulacra', and of a hyperreal 'nebula' where 'truth is indecipherable', but his fictions never abandon this stance of ethical commitment.[15] Campbell assumes a dissident, sceptical position with respect to the continuing viability of metanarratives. Yet his work does not concur with Jean Baudrillard and Fredric Jameson's implicitly apolitical, disempowering and nihilistic vision of the 'waning of effect' and absent universal truths or 'self'.[16]

According to Baudrillard's somewhat self-consumptive cosmology of eternal and circular irony, 'God himself has only ever been his own simulacrum'.[17] On matters of religious belief, Campbell's hostility to the metanarrative of dogmatism is well documented. The largest of metaphysical questions, as well as an obvious point of comparison between the agnostic Campbell and the atheist Lovecraft, seemed a fitting point of entry for this monograph. Therefore, its first chapter explored Campbell's multifaceted deconstruction of religious dogma in the fevered and polarised sociopolitical climate of the 1980s. The urban and female Gothic occult thriller *The Nameless* anatomises the abnegation of free will and self which is entailed in submission to the (oc)cult. I suggested that the anti-natalist cult of the Nameless represents, in Campbell's vision, a neo-Baudrillardian 'seductive chaos'.[18] However, despite the author's admitted 'timid' agnosticism, it argued that the text tentatively posits that such 'chaos' can be resisted via a liberal and humane alternative, an embrace of the maternal.[19] The later ensemble work, *The Hungry Moon*, was shown to expand the critique further, to address shortfalls of established pagan and both orthodox and fundamentalist Christian belief systems. A climactic triumph over destructive evil is finally secured by what is suggested as primeval humanist instinct. However, here alterity is not destroyed, only banished. This, the narrowness of averted catastrophe, and the implication of circularity, all suggest the dormancy of, and continuing threat implied by, resurgent fundamentalism. Lastly, the transitional novel *Obsession* foregrounds the author's hybrid fusion of realism and naturalism with individual psychology. This ostensibly non-supernatural narrative is infused by what was suggested as being an equally characteristic flirtatious note of transcendence and inference of the sublime. Further, the deliberately named character of 'Peter Priest' articulates insecurities about perception and experience, doubt, notions of selfhood and the subject's place, both in a secular, pathologised society and in the universe, which was to distinguish and be developed in Campbell's later work.

Campbell's Gothic is concerned with ethical questions about how we live now. My second chapter addressed his representation of the invidious effect of secular metanarratives within contemporary culture, principally orthodox belief systems around neoliberalism, monetarism, consumerism and social class, refracted through mass media. In Campbell's vision these discourses are transformed into generators of psychological horror. The agent of threat is the familiar Gothic serial killer trope, a figure to which Campbell returns repeatedly. Explicitly sociopathic in Campbell's non-supernatural works, that is, impacted by experiences of abuse, inequality, deprivation and celebrity culture rather than innate or metaphysically originated depravity, the repeat murderer appears to incarnate the Baudrillardian notion of symbiosis between individual depression and cultural neurosis which is readily convertible to violence.[20] However, in Campbell's hands the archetype is more complex than the familiar symbol of 'alienation' and symptomatic 'bitter comment' on the breakdown of social cohesion described by David Punter.[21] *The Face That Must Die*, which first appeared in 1979 before its expansion in 1983, was not only prescient for its anti-homophobia.[22] With this novel and its non-supernatural successors, Campbell demythologises the 'bogeyman', first deconstructing the conservative crime-detection narratives within which they are often framed: after all, Horridge, the arch-conservative and counter-countercultural antagonist of *Face*, imagines himself as a detective. Campbell's murderers are not socially elevated and do not represent demonised criminality. Nor, unlike Thomas Harris's Hannibal Lecter or Jeff Lindsay's Dexter Morgan, do they display any particular insight, charm or charisma. In contrast, I demonstrated that Campbell articulates a decidedly anti-romantic and deglamourised tonality. His serial killers are deliberately drab figures, drawn from the working and lower middle classes. Being that these are also texts denoted by misrecognition, cognitive dissonance, passive-aggression and ambivalent endings, in contrast to the accessible Manichaean narratives of more popular writers, for whom King may be regarded as template, the net effect is disturbing. In agreeing with Peter Connelly's stricture against aesthetising and therefore euphemising the brutal realities of the act of murder and murderers, it would be easy also to concur that a 'pessimistic culture' which emphasises 'negative' portraiture of society and its members will, inevitably, 'tend to produce misanthropic or life-devaluating narratives'.[23] However, in contrast to texts like *American Psycho*, which can be interpreted as affirming that view, Campbell's early subversion of the detective genre presaged ongoing ambition and inventiveness. His narrative from the next decade on the formation of a killer, *The One Safe Place*, combines urban Gothic settings and social realism. The novel anatomises the causes and 'contagion' of violence in Anglo-American culture, an undertaking which in scale, and of itself, refutes accusations of parochialism or lack of ambition. By doing so, *The One Safe Place* develops a sympathetic, minutely observed critique of class, gender and cross-generational conflict. In interrogating media commodification of violence, the text also exposes the contradictions within censorship, a conservative mantra which, signifying the suppression of free speech, Campbell has consistently opposed. Lastly, the metatextual *Secret Story*, whilst refraining portraiture of oppressive societal mores through its astute depiction of petty office politics, both deconstructs and then reconstructs the serial killer as author. Campbell, it was suggested, does this to satirise both the perceived excesses of his own Gothic horror fiction industry, which has thrived on the 'serial killer' phenomenon, with all its associated lurid visceral detail and excesses, and the complex relationship of the authorial persona to its readership. He begins to induce the Gothic and its audience to behold itself in a mirror. As the novel's heroine-survivor declares, 'this is our story now' (p. 382).

Campbell possesses the aesthetic dexterity to explore the roles of authors, texts and audiences. The third chapter of *Ramsey Campbell*, on his use of the novella form, illustrated the writer's willingness to experiment. In doing so, it demonstrated the astuteness of Campbell's choice, both in terms of his own artistic achievement and for his contribution to the Gothic. The novella in his hands proves to be an ideal vehicle, between short story and novel, for the concentrated mediation of the experience and journey of a haunted single consciousness over time. Simultaneously, I proposed that the author's employment of the novella demonstrates an investigative approach to aesthetic and broader philosophical questions. It is an interrogation undertaken in the full knowledge that answers and a conclusion may not be possible, or even desirable. The oneiric *Needing Ghosts*, a central text in Campbell's *oeuvre*, is his most explicitly autobiographical representation of authorship. However, it is also his most postmodern stylistically and thematically, its protagonist/unreliable narrator and circular present-tense narrative challenging notions of a teleological interpretation of history. I demonstrated that in comparison with King, who has also utilised the novella form, Campbell takes a markedly less populist and more paranoiac stance on creativity in which writing is, consistently, 'a compulsion'.[24] The trapped author-figure also appears to function as an avatar for the subject, and, by implication, the reader, who must reinterpret the nature and 'meaning' of Mottershead's journey and its ambivalent end with every reading. This multiplicity of representation is explored in Campbell's late novella twenty-six years later, *The Booking*. This text, virtually framed as a claustrophobic two-hand single-set stage drama, portrays the complex response of a fractured consciousness to both debilitating sociopolitical changes and the advent of technology in the much-touted 'information era'. Campbell's ingenious narrative overtly channels paranoia concerning the potential for surveillance and control occasioned by the phenomenon of the Internet and the World Wide Web. Yet simultaneously, the protagonist's use of a computer and the ambiguous climax, which seems to strike a note of freedom and independence, can also be read as demonstrating scepticism towards such anxieties, and, by implication, the debilitating simulacrisation underpinning the postmodernist paradigm. The multiplicity of interpretation afforded by both texts suggests enactment of what Linda Hutcheon describes as 'a challenging and exploiting of the commodification of art by our own consumer culture', in which the text is 'an open process' which 'changes with each receiver'.[25] Campbell thus uses ideas from postmodernism, including overt narrative experimentation, *without* commitment to its profoundly apolitical or atheistic conclusions.

As the fourth chapter demonstrates, this iconoclastic nonconformity comes to the fore in Campbell's metaleptic narratives of the early twenty-first century, which borrow from and display as much fidelity to then emergent posthumanist concepts as they do to postmodern ones. In three key postmillennial novels, Campbell shifts focus from anatomisation of the splintered, paranoid subject to an exploration, firstly, of the incursion of 'others' conferred with sentience by digital technology upon the subject and the 'reality' it inhabits, and, secondly, the ontological status of these new, posthuman lives. *The Grin of the Dark* hedonistically combines a Lovecraftian cosmic vision, coulrophobia from the Gothic tradition, vaudevillian comedy and a plethora of forms of old and new communication, presented in fetishised terms to almost narcotic effect – on the reader as much as upon the novel's hapless and finally overwhelmed protagonist. The presentation of online trolling and metaphors of virus and infection may imply an anti-technological positioning. However, as with Campbell's novellas, the hero-victim's final ambiguous physical and psychic status, simultaneously subsumed but also transformed and independent, suggests final abstinence from any definitive moral judgement. Similarly, *Think Yourself Lucky*, which reworks the Gothic *doppelgänger* motif and revisits both the societal exploration of Campbell's earlier serial killer narratives and concern with authorship, functions, on one level, as another cautionary narrative on the 'dangers' posed by the Internet. However, other ontological and ethical vistas are in fact opened in the process: exploration of the body in virtual space, the subject's isolation, loneliness, and vulnerability, and – in a return to Campbell's familial concerns – the parental responsibility of author as creator. The classic Gothic template for the latter is, of course, Shelley's *Frankenstein*, which it was shown is partly rewritten in *The Seven Days of Cain*, a novel that expands Campbell's earlier meditation on natalism, this time in a posthuman context. Bentley, the text's update of 'Victor Frankenstein', is seen to have completed self-realisation to excess, creating a multiplicity of 'selves', new posthuman citizens, whose physical and metaphysical dimensions and 'rights' are explored. The mutability of history and the 'reality' which the protagonist and his creations inhabit suggest that paranoia is Campbell's default for comprehending the world and one's place in it. These texts align with the developing subfield of the posthuman Gothic in their portrayal of anxiety and liminality. They also provide more evidence of Campbell's propensity for generic hybridity, here with science fiction. Further, as with, for example, Philip K. Dick's narratives, they reflect some complex theoretical concepts, here both postmodern and posthuman paradigms, without the elite stylisation of what Jameson deems the 'high literary novel'.[26]

Campbell observes that Lovecraft was engaged on a continuous quest 'for the perfect form'.[27] Emulating the restlessness of the American writer, Campbell has declared of his chosen genre that 'I don't think I've exhausted its boundaries by any means' and that the 'field' is broad enough 'to allow me to deal fully with any theme I want to deal with'.[28] This sheer breadth, reflected in the protean heterogeneity of his output, also demonstrates an adaptability to other modes of interpretation – for instance psychoanalytic, feminist or queer – which the present book has had space to allude to only briefly. For example, Campbell has admitted that the intensity of Horridge's paranoid schizophrenia in *Face* draws upon his own mother's mental illness.[29] Conversant with knowledge of Campbell's copious paratexts, it is equally impossible to ignore a splintered autobiographical, indeed confessional, element in the portrayals of Robyn Laurel and Priest in *Obsession*. Both characters experience and suffer guilt at the hands of elderly relatives transformed into, respectively, living and undead 'revenant' figures. Similarly, *The Nameless* and a range of other texts, such as *The Parasite* (1980), *The Influence* (1988) and *Pact of the Fathers* (2004), with their female protagonists and haunted and haun*ting* child figures, address themes of maternity, domesticity, familial power structures and the vulnerabilities and terrors of childhood. Meanwhile, Horridge's homophobic fear of emasculation in *Face* could be analysed alongside

Lester's terror of the proximity and contact with, implicitly penetration by, the other in the later novel, *Grin*. Simon, for instance, dreams of Tubby's 'pale luminous face swelling close to mine', and of it 'widen[ing] its eyes and its grin at me before slithering under the bed' (pp. 197–8). The representation of a repulsive alien alterity and the response it evokes recalls the entities of M. R. James's narratives, but with an intensification of leering insidiousness and arguably even, in the subject's passivity, desire.[30] Any of these theoretical approaches, and they are by no means the only ones available (*Grin*, for example, equally lends itself to Bakhtinian analysis), could afford studies of equivalent length and substance to what has been offered in this book using postmodern and posthuman paradigms.

This observation on the diversity of interpretation that can be made relating to Campbell's work leads to two summarising propositions. The first follows on naturally. It is, of course, that Campbell's vast and varied corpus, and particularly his longer fictional output, deserves further attention for what it brings to Gothic studies, both to the canon of Gothic literature and to its scholarship. It is not just that Campbell is a prominent, conscientious and industrious figure and an assiduous networker – although in the breadth of his acknowledged influences and espousal of his peers' work, from Thomas Ligotti to Steve Mosby, José Carlos Somoza Ortega and many others, Campbell not only 'writes horror' but is arguably a living encyclopedia of the genre.[31] He contributes a unique, finely honed prose style. It is literate, highly personal and evocative of an intense paranoia, a voice far removed from and thus far more unsettling than King's Manichaean narratives. Campbell's interpretation of literary horror is inclusive and amorphous: in one essay Campbell has remarked that 'many tales of horror don't involve the supernatural, but they surely convey terror, and I maintain that horror is the term that best contains all three fields'.[32] His fictions also mount a distinctive critique of the religious and sociopolitical metanarratives permeating contemporary culture. In a market where writers like Shaun Hutson have dominated commercially, Campbell's works afford an incisive and satirical perspective on the status of authors, their works and relationships with their audiences.

Fundamentally, the majority of Campbell's career coincides with the rise and trajectory of literary postmodernism. Campbell is a challenging, polymorphic and hybrid presence. His fiction utilises attributes associated with the postmodern but is not exclusively *of* it. As Maria Beville notes, there is a natural sympathy between the Gothic's transgression of the liminal 'borders' between reality and fiction and the postmodern movement's interrogation and denunciation of 'grand narratives.'[33] In this vein, and in his work, Campbell has clearly critiqued what he perceives as repressive metadiscourses. His fictions are also self-conscious, self-reflexive, experimental and imbued with cultural references. However, Campbell is more complex and chameleonic than the descriptor of 'postmodernist writer' or even 'Gothic-postmodernist writer' would allow for. Justifiably, the writer has been praised by Joshi and other critics for his portrayal of paranoia. Yet Campbell's fictions reflect broader concerns and are more varied structurally than the psychiatrically informed works of, say, Patrick McGrath, whom Catherine Spooner credits with creating 'a calculatedly Gothic aesthetic with a pronounced interest in extreme mental illness'.[34] It is difficult, for example, to envisage works more different in form, scale, style and subject matter than Campbell's *Needing Ghosts* and *The One Safe Place*. Far from its failing to offer the aesthetic and wider philosophical 'complexity' of authors such as J. G. Ballard, as Punter claims, Campbell's work draws from and reflects contemporary postmodernist and emergent posthumanist paradigms.[35] It does so, though, without total alignment to any one theoretical school. Campbell's simultaneous adherence to a consciousness of historical tradition and espousal of genre finds a ready corollary in postmodernism's elision of the barrier between high literary and popular culture. Nonetheless, his vision is agnostic and, whilst it is sceptical, it is also morally and socially engaged. This contrasts with the atheism, amorality, insularity or apoliticism often identified with the postmodernist theory of figures such as Baudrillard. Campbell's voice, as with his ethical priorities – that is, his interests in the vulnerability of children, freedom of expression against the forces of dogmatism, and 'the right to question'– remain consistent and distinctive.[36]

As Campbell's alternation between supernatural and non-supernatural themes attests, it has an iconoclastic timbre: playful and sometimes comic, experimental, sceptical towards shibboleths, and always restlessly interrogative. For audiences and academics working within Gothic studies, the entirety of Campbell's work is worth – in fact, is overdue – both revisiting and re-evaluation.

A second proposition arises from Campbell's obvious exclusion from the canon of 'high' literary culture insofar, denoted by the descriptor 'contemporary literature', as it applies to late twentieth-century- and early twenty-first-century writers. With the possible exceptions of Brett Easton Ellis and Mark Danielewski (and the latter for one text, *House of Leaves*, published in 2000), it is obvious that few authors associated primarily or significantly with the Gothic found admission to the academy alongside the likes of Ian McEwan or Kazuo Ishiguro and their peers. The hostile reception given to King's 2003 National Book Award by Harold Bloom illustrates how far even the genre's indisputably most prominent and successful writer has been from acceptance and respectability. It is arguable that at least one of Campbell's novels, *The One Safe Place*, his hugely ambitious and near-mainstream epic tragedy of social realism engaging with two national cultures, may have been included in Colin Hutchinson's study of the social novel, and indeed more widely reviewed in British and other national media, if it had not been perceived and marketed as the work of a 'horror writer'.[37] However, the concurrent elision of postmodernist theories, an essentially atheistic movement denoted by what Terry Eagleton described as 'grave doubts about truth and reality', by *post*-postmodernist trends can offer a more sympathetic critical environment for reappraising Campbell.[38] Joshi summarises Campbell perceptively, describing him as being 'a humanist who knows how difficult it is to be a fully moral human being, and what courage it takes to be so' against hostile and destructive forces.[39] A sense of haunted agnosticism, and, especially, the assertion of liberal humanist values and a belief in the subject's independence, no matter how vexed or besieged, are consistent features of Campbell's writing, and perhaps above all in his endings. It is there, for example, in Diana's 'cry for healing' in *Hungry Moon* (p. 416); Patricia's insistence that this is 'our story now' (*Secret Story*, p. 382); Brookes's defiant conclusion that 'It's exactly what I make it' (*The Booking*, p. 83), and most explicitly vocalised in Andy's final challenge to Beyer, in *Cain*, to 'show some humanity' as a means of becoming 'human', and therefore demonstrating 'how you can be real' (p. 298). Rather than what Eagleton scathingly describes as the 'post-tragic realm of postmodernism,' in which there is a 'nihilistic absence of salvation', because 'there is 'nothing to be saved', Campbell's fictions can be interpreted as being more fully aligned with emergent paradigms which confer greater status upon value systems and meaning.[40]

For example, it is possible to see an affinity with the struggles of the subject, the representation of which is so prevalent in Campbell's writing, in Irmtraud Huber's concept of 'reconstructive fantasy.' Huber perceives an attempted reassertion of the pragmatics of fiction 'as a form of communication that actually manages to convey meaning, however unstable and compromised it may be', and 'a renewed humanist subtext' in texts like *House of Leaves*.[41] With the partial exception of Danielewski, her supporting case studies are drawn from what has been considered contemporary literary fiction – Jonathan Safran Foer, Michael Chabon and David Mitchell – rather than from the Gothic. Huber's chosen combination-model of mimesis and an embedded fantasy or 'marvellous' text within the text, an embedded narrative 'which never entirely revokes its mimetic grounding' may also be more applicable to some of Campbell's works, such as *Cain* and *Think Yourself Lucky*, than to others.[42] Nevertheless, Huber's espousal of a post-ironic and more pragmatic hermeneutical system, one which places a premium on the 'effect' of texts, the author as 'guarantor for the sincerity of the act of communication' and the 'communicative bond between author and reader', suggest a new, more ethical and empathic arena in theory, in which Campbell's liberal and humane poetics and politics may be more favourably appraised.[43] For, like the metafictions which Huber draws upon for her exemplar, Campbell's Gothic meta horror texts focus on methods by and trials through which we, as subjects, 'draw upon fictions to make sense of ourselves, our past, our present and our future'.[44] Huber is, it must be acknowledged, by no means the only theorist working in this emergent school of enquiry.[45] In the spirit of Lyotard, I have merely intended here to start a debate, not conclude it: to encourage and foster a consensus that Campbell is worth the attention of scholars, within *and* outside Gothic studies, as 'a particular state of discussion, not its end'.[46]

It is a state of perpetual dynamism with which Campbell, it is hoped, would find favour. The writer has expressed the hope that he 'never find[s]' the limits of his chosen 'enormously capacious' field.[47] Since *The Booking*, Campbell has continued to be highly productive, but his work revisits and reworks the key earlier themes examined in this monograph. The *Three Births of Daoloth* or 'Brichester Mythos' trilogy (2016–18), for example, returns to the writer's early imaginative landscape, and in particular the Lovecraftian cosmic horror of *The Hungry Moon* and the later 'black magic' narrative, *The Darkest Part of the Woods* (2002).[48] Certain preoccupations, notably the vulnerability of the family unit, the dangerous seductiveness of cults, and a besieged but resilient scepticism which must counter the latter to protect the former, are refrained in an epic supernatural narrative, told in the first person, which spans three generations. In one scene in the last novel of the triptych, *The Way of the Worm* (2018), Dominic Sheldrake, the protagonist, testifies in court against the antagonists, the villainous Noble family triad. He is asked:

> 'Mr Sheldrake, how would you describe your view of religion?'
> 'Undecided.' This hardly helped, and I fumbled for the truth.
>   'As I grow older,' I said,
> 'I'm more anxious to find something to believe in.'
> 'Does that mean you believe in nothing at the moment?'
> 'No, it means I'm searching. It means I hope there's something to believe.' (p. 135)

Like Sheldrake, his avatar here, Campbell is engaged on a continuous quest, 'for the perfect form.' Yet, more widely, in an age where new but jadedly familiar 'seductions', the totalitarian grand narratives of neoliberalism and illiberal populism, hold disturbing sway, Campbell's continuously interrogative narratives illustrate how the flames of healthy iconoclasticism and a subtle emancipatory politics may still flicker and endure.

Notes

ഌരു

Introduction: A Neglected 'Poet': Campbell and Gothic Tradition

1. Ramsey Campbell, website available online at *www.ramseycampbell.com* (accessed 1 December 2021). See also, for example, Campbell, 'Why I Write Horror Fiction', *Necrofile*, 2 (Fall 1991), reprinted in S.T. Joshi (ed.), *Ramsey Campbell, Probably: On Horror and Sundry Fantasies* (Harrogate: PS Publishing, 2002), pp. 301–5, in which the author states that 'I write horror stories, and I make it public that I do' (p. 301).
2. Anonymous, 'Horror Fiction', in Dinah Birch (ed.), *Oxford Companion to English Literature*, 7th edition (Oxford: Oxford University Press, 2009), p. 499.
3. Ramsey Campbell, *The Inhabitant of the Lake and Less Welcome Tenants* (Sauk City, WI: Arkham Press, 1964). Campbell subsequently dropped the 'J.' (for John) after this first volume.
4. Campbell has also authored several novelisations of 1930s and 1940s Universal horror films using a pseudonym 'Carl Dreadstone' in 1977, and, under his own name, a novelisation of the screenplay for M. J. Bassett's film, *Solomon Kane* (2009) in 2010.
5. Stephen King, *Danse Macabre* (London: Hodder & Stoughton, 2012 [1981]), pp. 405, 402.
6. See *Meddling with Ghosts: Stories in the Tradition of M. R. James*, selected and introduced by Campbell (Boston Spa and London: British Library, 2001); Campbell's introduction to Thomas Ligotti, *Songs of a Dead Dreamer* (Albuquerque, NM: Silver Scarab Press, 1986), reprinted in

Joshi, *Ramsey Campbell, Probably*, pp. 266–7, and Campbell (ed.), *Uncanny Banquet: Great Tales of the Supernatural* (New York: Little, Brown, 1992).

7 Sales of King's books, for example, have been cited as being in the region of 350 million copies. See Karen Heller, 'Meet the elite group of authors who sell 100 million books – or 350 million', *Independent*, 28 December 2016, available online at h*ttps://www.independent.co.uk/arts-entertainment/books/meet-the-elite-group-of-authors-who-sell-100-million-books-or-350-million-paolo-coelho-stephen-king-a7499096.html* (accessed 9 June 2018).

8 Three of Campbell's novels have been filmed to date, all in Spain: the 1981 text *The Nameless* (as *Los sin nombre*, 2005), 1988's *The Influence* (as *La influencia*, 2019) and 2001's *Pact of the Fathers* (as *Second Name*, or *El segundo nombre*, 2002). However, these will not be widely known to an Anglophone audience.

9 On King, see for example, John Sears, *Stephen King's Gothic* (Cardiff: University of Wales Press, 2011) and Clotilde Landais, *Stephen King as a Postmodern Author* (New York: Peter Lang, 2013). For Barker (b. 1952), Sorcha Ní Fhlainn (ed.), *Clive Barker: Dark Imaginer* (Manchester: Manchester University Press, 2017), offers a recent collection of essays.

10 Amongst many examples of reviews, the social website *Goodreads* available online at <*www.goodreads.com*> yields over 530 'hits' using the search term 'Ramsey Campbell', and the specialist website *Vault of Evil! Brit Horror Pulp Plus* has nearly 40 threads dedicated to the author at *http://vaultofevil.proboards.com/board/46/ramsey-campbell* (both accessed 9 June 2017).

11 Campbell, Stefan Dziemianowicz and S. T. Joshi, *The Core of Ramsey Campbell: A Bibliography and Reader's Guide* (West Warwick, RI: Necronomicon Press, 1995).

12 Michael Ashley, *Fantasy Reader's Guide to Ramsey Campbell* (Wallsend: Cosmos, 1980); Gary William Crawford, *Ramsey Campbell* (Mercer Island, WA: Starmont House Inc., 1988). The appearance of S. T. Joshi's later, revised and expanded introductory monograph, *Ramsey Campbell: Master of Weird Fiction* (Hornsea: PS Publishing, 2022), unfortunately came too late in the editorial process for acknowledgement or discussion in this book. However, Joshi's welcome contribution does not affect my overall evaluation or the general ethos of this study.

Notes

[13] S. T. Joshi, *The Modern Weird Tale* (Jefferson, NC and London: McFarland & Company, 2001), p. 13.

[14] See, for example, Giles Menegaldo, 'Gothic Convention and Modernity in John Ramsey Campbell's Short Fiction', in Victor Sage and Allan Lloyd Smith (eds), *Modern Gothic: A Reader* (Manchester: Manchester University Press, 1996), pp. 188–97, or Adam L. G. Nevil, 'Wonder and Awe: Mysticism, Poetry and Perception in Ramsey Campbell's *The Darkest Part of the Woods*', in Daniel Olson (ed.), *21st Century Gothic* (London: Scarecrow Press, 2011), pp. 149–57.

[15] See S. T. Joshi (ed.), *The Count of Thirty: A Tribute to Ramsey Campbell* (West Warwick, RI: Necronomicon Press, 1993) and Gary Crawford (ed.), *Ramsey Campbell: Critical Essays on the Modern Master of Horror* (Lanham, MD: Scarecrow Press, 2014).

[16] David Punter, *The Literature of Terror: A History of Gothic Fictions from 1765 to the Present Day*, 2nd edition (Harlow: Longman, 1996), 2 vols, II: *The Modern Gothic*, pp. 182, 183.

[17] Punter, *Literature of Terror*, p. 163.

[18] Punter, *Literature of Terror*, p. 163, emphasis in original. Joshi, interestingly, offers a diametrically opposed and positive reading of this text in *Ramsey Campbell and Modern Horror Fiction*, praising what he describes as the novel's 'deft' fusion of supernaturalism and the psychological, p. 121.

[19] Joshi repeatedly describes Campbell as such, for instance in *Modern Weird Tale*, p. 148, and *Ramsey Campbell and Modern Horror Fiction*, p. 97.

[20] Campbell, 'Concussion', in *Demons by Daylight* (London: Star, 1980 [1973]), pp. 134–61 (p. 152). All subsequent references for 'Concussion' and 'The Franklyn Paragraphs' (pp. 39–61) are to this edition, and page numbers hereafter in the text.

[21] S. T. Joshi, *Unutterable Horror: A History of Supernatural Fiction* (New York: Hippocampus Press, 2014), 2 vols. II, p. 662; Xavier Aldana Reyes, 'Post-Millennial Horror, 2000–16', in Aldana Reyes (ed.), *Horror: A Literary History* (London: British Library, 2016), pp. 189–214 (p. 196).

[22] From an interview with Campbell by Mark James Kermode, July 1990, in Kermode's 'The radical, ethical and political implications of modern British and American horror fiction' (unpublished PhD thesis, University of Manchester, 1991), 35.

[23] S. T. Joshi, 'Ramsey Campbell: Alone with a Master', in S. T. Joshi, *Classics*

and Contemporaries: Some Notes on Horror Fiction (New York: Hippocampus Press, 2009), pp. 109–31 (p. 110).

24. David McWilliam, 'Ramsey Campbell Interviewed' (24 September 2012), available online at *http://www.gothic.stir.ac.uk/interviews/ramsey-campbell-interviewed-by-david-mcwilliam/* (accessed 9 June 2017).

25. The term is appropriated from Humberto R. Maturana and Francisco J. Varela, *Autopoiesis and Cognition: The Realization of the Living*, 2nd edition (Dordrecht: D. Reidel, 1980), p. 16.

26. Campbell, 'Dig Us No Grave', *Fantasy Review*, 9/3 (March 1986), reprinted in Joshi, *Ramsey Campbell, Probably*, pp. 29–34 (p. 33); Campbell, 'My Roots Exhumed', prefatory essay in Joshi, *Ramsey Campbell and Modern Horror Fiction*, pp. 1–5 (p. 4).

27. Campbell, quoted in interview with Kermode, 'Radical, ethical and political implications', p. 32; 'Shaun Hutson', *Necrofile*, 3 (Winter 1992), reprinted in Joshi, *Ramsey Campbell, Probably*, pp. 171–7 (p. 177). This reticence and distance are despite Campbell's own experimentation with more sexually explicit themes in some short stories during the 1970s, collected as *Scared Stiff: Stories of Sex and Death* (Los Angeles: Scream Press, 1987). Driven by commercial impulse, these works may also exemplify, like Campbell's early novel *The Parasite* (1980), what the author describes as 'pretty well exactly the opposite of the kind of fiction I'd been writing since I began to sound like myself', Afterword to *The Parasite* (London: Headline, 1993 [1980]), reprinted in Joshi, *Ramsey Campbell, Probably*, pp. 370–3 (p. 370).

28. Xavier Aldana Reyes, *Body Gothic: Corporeal Transgression in Contemporary Literature and Horror Film* (Cardiff: Cardiff University Press, 2014), p. 27.

29. Campbell, *Ancient Images* (London: Arrow Books, 1990 [1989]), p. 75.

30. Stefan Dziemianowicz, 'Interview with Ramsey Campbell', in Joshi, *Count of Thirty*, pp. 7–26 (p. 26).

31. Campbell, 'My Roots Exhumed', p. 2.

32. M. R. James, 'Ghosts – Treat Them Gently', *Evening News*, 17 April 1931, republished in *M. R. James: Collected Ghost Stories* (Adelaide: University of Adelaide Library, 2016) as section (vii) of Appendix, available online at *https://ebooks.adelaide.edu.au/j/james/mr/collect/appendix.html* eBook (accessed 9 June 2017).

33. Campbell, 'To the Next Generation', in *L. Ron Hubbard Presents Writers*

of the Future, IV, ed. Algis Budrys (East Grinstead: New Era, 1988), reprinted in Joshi, *Ramsey Campbell, Probably*, pp. 49–54 (p. 49).

[34] Edmund Burke, *A Philosophical Enquiry into the Sublime and the Beautiful*, ed. David Womersley (London: Penguin, 1998 [1757]), p. 86.

[35] Ann Radcliffe, 'On the Supernatural in Poetry', *New Monthly Magazine*, 16/1 (January 1826), reprinted in E. J. Clery and David Miles (eds), *Gothic Documents: A Sourcebook, 1700–1820* (Manchester: Manchester University Press, 2000), pp. 163–72 (p. 168).

[36] Campbell, 'My Roots Exhumed', p. 4.

[37] Stacey McDowell, 'Folklore', in William Hughes, David Punter and Andrew Smith (eds), *The Encyclopedia of the Gothic* (Chichester: Wiley-Blackwell, 2013), 2 vols, I, pp. 252–4 (p. 252). The associated subgenre of 'folk horror' and Campbell's relationship with it is discussed further in Chapter 1.

[38] See also Hurley's *The Loney* (2014).

[39] Campbell, 'Terry Lamsley', combination of 'Introduction' to Lamsley's *Conference for the Dead* (Ashcroft, BC: Ash-Tree Press, 1996) and entry in *St. James Guide to Horror, Ghost & Gothic Writers*, ed. David Pringle (Detroit, MI: St. James Press, 1998), reprinted in Joshi, *Ramsey Campbell, Probably*, pp. 154–9 (p. 159); 'R. R. Ryan', *Necrofile*, 27 (Winter 1998), also reprinted in Joshi, *Ramsey Campbell, Probably*, pp. 228–33 (p. 233).

[40] As, for example, Campbell states explicitly, relating to his own development as a writer in the Afterword to *The Parasite* (1980), reprinted in Joshi, *Ramsey Campbell, Probably*, pp. 370–3 (p. 370), or to his striving after prose effects in the essay, 'Horror Fiction and the Mainstream', *Necrofile*, 12 (Spring 1994), also reprinted in Joshi, *Ramsey Campbell, Probably*, pp. 39–43 (p. 43).

[41] Catherine Spooner, *Contemporary Gothic* (London: Reaktion Books, 2006), p. 23.

[42] Joshi, *Modern Weird Tale*, p. 9.

[43] Joshi, *Modern Weird Tale*, p. 136.

[44] Dziemianowicz, 'Interview', p. 16.

[45] Dziemianowicz, 'Interview', p. 22.

[46] Simon Best, 'Interview: Ramsey Campbell', 19 October 2016, *This is Horror*, available online at *http://www.thisishorror.co.uk/interview-ramsey-campbell/* (accessed 9 June 2017).

[47] Best, 'Interview'.
[48] Dziemianowicz, 'Interview', p. 18.
[49] Campbell, 'My Roots Exhumed', p. 5.
[50] Robert Aickman, Introduction, in Aickman (ed.), *The Second Fontana Book of Great British Ghost Stories* (London: Fontana, 1966), pp. 7–10 (p. 7).
[51] Aickman, Introduction, in Aickman (ed.), *The Third Fontana Book of Great British Ghost Stories* (London: Fontana, 1966), pp. 7–11 (p. 7).
[52] Campbell, 'My Roots Exhumed', p. 5.
[53] Alan Lloyd Smith, 'Postmodernism/Gothic', in *Modern Gothic: A Reader*, pp. 6–19. Lloyd Smith lists common affinities between the two throughout this essay.
[54] Patricia Waugh, *Metafiction: The Theory and Practice of Self-Conscious Fiction* (Florence, KY: Routledge, 1984), p. 9.
[55] Brian McHale, *Postmodernist Fiction* (London: Routledge, 2003 [1987]), p. 10.
[56] David Punter, 'Theory', in *Encyclopedia of the Gothic*, II, pp. 686–93 (p. 688).
[57] Fredric Jameson, *Postmodernism: or, The Cultural Logic of Late Capitalism* (London: Verso, 1991), pp. 289, 290.
[58] Alex Link, 'The Mysteries of *Postmodernism*, or Fredric Jameson's Gothic Plots', *Gothic Studies*, 11/1 (May 2009), 70–85 (p. 70). Link argues that this sense is inescapable and pervades Jameson's *Postmodernism* as a text itself.
[59] Maria Beville, *Gothic-postmodernism: Voicing the Terrors of Postmodernity* (Amsterdam: Rodopi, 2009), p. 42.
[60] Beville, *Gothic-postmodernism*, p. 7.
[61] Beville, *Gothic-postmodernism*, p. 10.
[62] Jean-François Lyotard, *The Postmodern Condition: A Report on Knowledge*, trans. Geoff Bennington and Brian Massumi (Manchester: Manchester University Press, 1984 [1979]), p. 37.
[63] Lyotard, *Postmodern Condition*, p. 17.
[64] Jean Baudrillard, *The Perfect Crime*, trans. Chris Turner (London and New York: Verso, 1996 [1995]), p. 27.
[65] The term used by King in *Danse Macabre*, p. 296 *passim*.

Notes

Chapter 1: Impractical Magic: Campbell's 'Agnostic' Gothic

[1] Lesley Hazleton, *Agnostic: A Spirited Manifesto* (New York: Riverhead Books, 2016), p. 103.
[2] Campbell, 'Horror Fiction and the Mainstream', p. 39.
[3] Dziemianowicz, 'Interview', p. 18.
[4] Jeffery Klaehn, 'Reaching for the Awesome and Numinous: An Interview with Horror Author Ramsey Campbell', *New Writing*, 13/2 (2016), 308–14 (p. 314). See also Matt Cardin, 'An Interview with Ramsey Campbell', October 2016, in Cardin (ed.), *Horror Literature Through History: An Encyclopedia of the Stories That Speak to Our Deepest Fears* (Westport, CT: Greenwood Publishing Inc. 2017), 2 vols, I, pp. 269–72, in which Campbell again decries a 'willingness to espouse belief systems that deny the right to question' (p. 270).
[5] Hazleton, *Agnostic*, p. 79.
[6] See, for example, the definition of the term given at *Oxford Living Dictionaries Online*, available online at *https://en.oxforddictionaries.com/definition/occult* (accessed 28 February 2018).
[7] See, for example, the principles of Law of Similarity and Law of Contagion, outlined in James Gordon Frazer, *The Golden Bough: A Study in Magic in Religion*, abr. edition (London: Macmillan, 1922 [1890]), p. 11. Frazer's text was an influence for Lovecraft and many other writers.
[8] There are, of course, numerous definitions of 'black magic', as given, for example, in Merriam-Webster Dictionaries, as 'magic that is associated with the devil or with evil spirits', available online at *www.merriam-webster.com/dictionary/black%20magic* (accessed 12 October 2020).
[9] Lyotard, *Postmodern Condition*, p. 37.
[10] Douglas E. Cowan and David G. Bromley, in *Cults and New Religions* (Hoboken, NJ: John Wiley & Sons, 2015), for example, note 'a profound crisis of meaning and identity' (p. 7) that developed from the mid-1960s onwards in response to such varied events as political assassinations and the 'Watergate' crisis (1972–4) in the United States.
[11] Lyotard, *Postmodern Condition*, p. 43, emphasis added.
[12] Hugh McLeod, *The Religious Crisis of the 1960s* (Oxford: Oxford University Press, 2007), p. 15.

[13] The term used by Steven J. Sutcliffe, 'The Dynamics of Alternative Spirituality', in James R. Lewis (ed.), *The Oxford Handbook of New Religious Movements* (Oxford: Oxford University Press, 2004), pp. 460–90 (p. 467).

[14] Christopher Partridge, 'Alternative Spiritualities, New Religions and the Re-enchantment of the West', in *Oxford Handbook of New Religious Movements*, pp. 39–67 (p. 46).

[15] Farah Mendleson and Edward Jones, *A Short History of Fantasy* (London: Middlesex University Press, 2009), p. 114.

[16] Mendleson and Jones, *Short History of Fantasy*, p. 14.

[17] Hayden White, 'The Fiction of Factual Representation', in White, *Topics of Discourse: Essays in Cultural Criticism* (Baltimore, MD: Johns Hopkins University Press, 1978), pp. 122–34 (pp. 122, 134).

[18] Philip Jenkins provides a succinct, if highly critical, summary of these various discourses in his essay, 'Satanism and Ritual Abuse', in *Oxford Handbook of New Religious Movements*, pp. 221–42 (see, especially, pp. 232–40). The discredited far-right 'QAnon' conspiracy theory of Satanic abuse (2017–present) constitutes an interesting contemporary refrain and mutation.

[19] Letter in H. P. Lovecraft, *Selected Letters, 1911–1937*, ed. August Derleth, Donald Wandrei and James Turner (Sauk City, WI: Arkham Press, 1965–76), 5 vols, IV: 1932–1934, p. 57, quoted in S. T. Joshi, *A Subtler Magick: The Writings and Philosophy of H. P. Lovecraft* (Berkeley Heights, NJ: Wildside Press, 1999), p. 33.

[20] S. T. Joshi, *A Dreamer and a Visionary: H. P. Lovecraft in His Time* (Liverpool: Liverpool University Press, 2001), p. 131; Joshi, *A Subtler Magick*, p. 29.

[21] Lovecraft, *Selected Letters*, IV, pp. 417–18, quoted in Joshi, *A Subtler Magick*, p. 48.

[22] Robin Le Poidevin, *Agnosticism: A Very Short Introduction* (Oxford: Oxford University Press, 2009), p. 118.

[23] Jenkins, 'Satanism and Ritual Abuse', p. 228.

[24] Wheatley's *The Devil Rides Out* was followed by seven more 'black magic' novels: *Strange Conflict* (1941), *The Haunting of Toby Jugg* (1948), *To the Devil a Daughter* (1953), *The Ka of Gifford Hillary* (1956), *The Satanist* (1960), *They Used Dark Forces* (1964) and *Gateway to Hell* (1970). Campbell would continue to acknowledge the author in texts as late as

The Searching Dead (Hornsea: PS Publishing, 2016); Wheatley even has a minor 'walk-on' role in that novel in being quoted by doomed journalist Eric Wharton (p. 243).

[25] Stephen Jones, '*Weird Tales* talks with Ramsey Campbell', *Weird Tales*, 301 (Summer 1991), quoted in *Ramsey Campbell and Modern Horror Fiction*, p. 66, emphasis in original.

[26] Cowan and Bromley, *Cults and New Religions*, p. 1.

[27] Dziemianowicz, 'Interview', p. 18.

[28] Campbell, 'To the Next Generation', p. 51.

[29] Joshi, *A Subtler Magick*, p. 102.

[30] Campbell, 'Introduction: So Far', in *Alone with the Horrors: The Great Short Fiction of Ramsey Campbell, 1961–1991* (New York: Tor, 2005), pp. 11–20 (p. 16).

[31] Campbell, 'Introduction: So Far', p. 16.

[32] It is of note that the three cinematic adaptations of Campbell's works to date have all been of texts centring on the child in peril – this novel, *The Influence* and *Pact of the Fathers* – suggesting its enduring saliency as a transcultural phobic pressure point.

[33] Campbell, Afterword to *The Nameless* (London: Little, Brown and Company, 1992 [1981]), pp. 273–8 (p. 275). Page numbers hereafter in the text.

[34] H. P. Lovecraft, 'The Call of Cthulhu', in *The H. P. Lovecraft Omnibus 3: The Haunter of the Dark and Other Tales* (London: Grafton Books, 1985), pp. 61–98 (pp. 80–1).

[35] Lovecraft, letter quoted in Gerry Carlin and Nicola Allen, 'Slime and Western Man: H. P. Lovecraft in the Time of Modernism', in David Simmons (ed.), *New Critical Essays on H. P. Lovecraft* (New York: Palgrave Macmillan, 2013), pp. 73–90 (p. 86).

[36] The references are, obviously, to Polidori's *The Vampyre* (1819) and Stoker's *Dracula* (1897).

[37] Campbell's earlier novel *The Parasite* had featured a psychiatrist who transpires, like the doctor in Ira Levin's *Rosemary's Baby*, to have been part of the cultist conspiracy. Such negative portraiture of health professionals may originate in Campbell's own experiences during his mother's mental decline, documented in an essay, 'Near Madness'. This memoir first appeared as the foreword to the revised edition of his second novel,

The Face That Must Die (1983), reprinted in Joshi, *Ramsey Campbell, Probably*, pp. 273–85.

[38] Punter, *Literature of Terror*, II, pp. 146, 158.

[39] Emily Alder, 'Urban Gothic', in *Encyclopedia of the Gothic*, II, pp. 703–6 (pp. 704–5).

[40] Hazleton, *Agnostic*, p. 52.

[41] Joshi, *Ramsey Campbell and Modern Horror Fiction*, p. 131.

[42] Aleister Crowley, *Magick in Theory and Practice* (New York: Castle, 1960 [1913]), p. 57.

[43] Simon MacCulloch, 'Glimpses of Absolute Power: Ramsey Campbell's Concept of Evil', in Joshi, *The Count of Thirty*, pp. 32–8 (pp. 36, 35).

[44] Carlin and Allen, 'Slime and Western Man', p. 83.

[45] Jean Baudrillard, *Simulacra and Simulation*, trans. Paul Foss, Paul Patton and Phillip Beichmann, excerpt in Baudrillard, *Selected Writings*, 2nd edition, ed. Mark Poster (Cambridge: Polity Press, 2001 [1981]), pp. 169–87 (p. 171).

[46] Baudrillard, *Perfect Crime*, p. 2.

[47] Jean Baudrillard, *Fatal Strategies* [1983], trans. Philip Beichmann and W. G. J. Niesluchowski, excerpt in Baudrillard, *Selected Writings*, pp. 188–209 (p. 202).

[48] Diana Wallace, 'Female Gothic', in *Encyclopedia of the Gothic*, I, pp. 231–6 (p. 234).

[49] Campbell, Afterword to *Obsession* (London: Futura, 1990 [1985]), pp. 281–3 (p. 281). Page numbers to this novel hereafter in the text.

[50] Julia Kristeva, *Powers of Horror: An Essay in Abjection*, trans. Leon Roudiez (New York: Columbia University Press, 1982), p. 4. There is also, perhaps, an echo of 'indefinability' being a source of horror noted by Joshi in relation to Lovecraft in narratives like 'The Colour Out of Space' (1927). See Joshi, *Dreamer and a Visionary*, p. 256.

[51] Both female victims suffer their grisly fates, moreover, in traditional, enclosed, urban 'Gothic' spaces.

[52] The Gothic lineage of child as victim *and* villain extends even further back, of course, as the ambiguous Miles and Flora in James's *Turn of the Screw* exemplify. However, Campbell is, consciously or unconsciously, following the trend for psychically gifted children popularised by King with this novel, *The Shining* (1977) and *Firestarter* (1980).

[53] Joshi, *Ramsey Campbell and Modern Horror Fiction*, p. 130. One thinks, for example, of the monstrous spiders in M. R. James's tale, 'The Ash-tree' (1904).
[54] See David Mathew, 'An Interview with Ramsey Campbell', available online at *http://www.infinityplus.co.uk/nonfiction/intcam.htm* (accessed 1 June 2020).
[55] Joshi, *Ramsey Campbell and Modern Horror Fiction*, p. 130.
[56] Campbell, 'A Small Dose of Reality', *Fantasy Review*, 8/11 (November 1985), reprinted in *Ramsey Campbell, Probably*, pp. 294–300 (p. 296).
[57] Lyotard, *Postmodern Condition*, p. 65.
[58] The film adaptation, *Los sin nombre*, offers a bleaker conclusion, in which the daughter engineers the death of her father, who has been a cult member all along, and then kills herself, to ensure that her mother 'will suffer more'.
[59] Lyotard, *Postmodern Condition*, pp. 18–19.
[60] Lyotard, *Postmodern Condition*, p. 60.
[61] Baudrillard, *Fatal Strategies*, p. 188.
[62] Campbell has described the book in one interview as a 'failed attempt' to emulate the 'kind of multiple character small town novel' that Stephen King had been producing. Anonymous, 'Ramsey Campbell Talks to the Horror Zine', available online at *http://www.thehorrorzine.com/Special/RamseyCampbell/RamseyCampbell.html* (accessed 1 June 2020).
[63] Joel Lane, 'Beyond the Light: The Recent Novels of Ramsey Campbell', in Joshi, *Count of Thirty*, pp. 46–51 (p. 46).
[64] Campbell, Afterword to 1994 edition of *The Hungry Moon*, reprinted in *Ramsey Campbell, Probably*, pp. 402–7 (p. 402).
[65] Joshi, *Ramsey Campbell and Modern Horror Fiction*, p. 37.
[66] These affinities with Greek myth are noted by Joshi in *Ramsey Campbell and Modern Horror Fiction*, p. 37.
[67] The success of *The Blair Witch Project* (Daniel Myrick and Eduardo Sánchez, 1999) and more recent releases such as *The Witch* (Robert Eggers, 2016) and *Midsommar* (Ari Aster, 2019) indicate a cinematic revival and broadening of geographical reference, New England and Swedish settings in these instances. This has run in parallel with a literary renaissance, exemplified by Andrew Michael Hurley's *The Loney* (2016) and Lucie McKnight Hardy's *Water Shall Refuse Them* (2019). 'Folk

horror' is also an emergent field of scholarly enquiry. The website *http://www.folklore.com/* (accessed 10 October 2017) defines it as 'a subgenre of horror fiction . . . characterised by reference to European, pagan traditions'.

[68] Adam Scovell, *Folk Horror: Hours Dreadful and Things Strange* (Leighton Buzzard: Auteur, 2017), p. 183.

[69] Scovell, *Folk Horror,* pp. 17–18.

[70] Campbell, *The Hungry Moon* (London: Arrow Books, 1987 [1986]), p. 22. Page numbers hereafter in the text.

[71] For example, *The Sun* and the Daily Mail, British national newspapers owned, respectively, by Rupert Murdoch and the Harmsworth family, were amongst publications responsible for vituperative coverage of anti-nuclear campaigners in the period, particularly the Greenham Common Women's Peace Camp (1981–2000). Media treatment of these campaigners is considered by Nick Couldry, 'Disrupting the media frame at Greenham Common: a new chapter in the history of mediations?', *Media, Culture & Society*, 21/3 (2013): 337–58.

[72] Joshi, *Ramsey Campbell and Modern Horror Fiction*, p. 37; Lovecraft, 'The Colour Out of Space', in *The H. P. Lovecraft Omnibus 3: The Haunter of the Dark and Other Tales* (London: Grafton Books, 1985), pp. 237–71. Mrs Gardner undergoes a similar metamorphosis, growing 'slightly luminous in the dark' (p. 250).

[73] See, for example Gina Wisker, '"Spawn of the Pit": Lavinia, Marceline, Medusa, and All Things Foul: H. P. Lovecraft's Liminal Women', in David Simmons (ed.), *New Critical Essays on H. P. Lovecraft* (New York: Palgrave Macmillan, 2013), pp. 31–54.

[74] Kristeva, *Powers of Horror*, p. 4.

[75] MacCulloch, 'Glimpses of Absolute Power', p. 38.

[76] Lane, 'Beyond the Light', p. 46. There has been continuity and indeed resurgence of anti-democratic and authoritarian populism since Lane's 1993 essay.

[77] See, in particular, Stephen D. Arata, 'The Occidental Tourist: Dracula and the Anxiety of Reverse Colonisation', *Victorian Studies*, 33/4 (1990), 621–45. In that Mann is both American and Californian, in this instance 'reverse colonisation' heralds from the opposite direction, from the New World of the American West, rather than from Eastern Europe.

[78] This trait is evident from early short stories such as 'The Interloper' in the *Demons by Daylight* collection and recurs in other later novels such as *Midnight Sun* (1990), and, as discussed later in this chapter, *Obsession*. Again, this foregrounds an autobiographical tendency in Campbell's work.
[79] Scovell, *Folk Horror*, p. 22.
[80] Dziemianowicz, 'Interview', p. 20.
[81] Joshi, *Ramsey Campbell and Modern Horror Fiction*, p. 37.
[82] See, for example, Lovecraft's description in 'Call of Cthulhu', regarding the Old Ones: 'their dead bodies had told their secrets in dreams to the first men, who formed a cult that had never died', p. 78.
[83] Lovecraft, *Selected Letters, II: 1925–1929*, p. 310, quoted in Joshi, *A Subtler Magick*, p. 35.
[84] Joshi, *Ramsey Campbell and Modern Horror Fiction*, p. 37.
[85] Campbell, Afterword to 1994 edition of *Hungry Moon*, p. 404.
[86] MacCulloch, 'Glimpses of Absolute Power', p. 38.
[87] Lovecraft, 'Call of Cthulhu', p. 61.
[88] Beville, *Gothic-postmodernism*, p. 54.
[89] Beville, *Gothic-postmodernism*, p. 55.
[90] Joshi, *Ramsey Campbell and Modern Horror Fiction*, p. 70.
[91] Jean Baudrillard, *The Transparency of Evil*, trans. James Benedict (London: Verso, 1993 [1990]), p. 83.
[92] Baudrillard, *Simulacra and Simulations*, pp. 182, 185.
[93] Lane, 'Beyond the Light', p. 47.
[94] For diverse contemporary perspectives, see, for example, Joel Kriger, *Reagan, Thatcher and the Politics of Decline* (New York: Oxford University Press, 1986), and Peter Riddell, *The Thatcher Decade: How Britain Has Changed During the 1980s* (New York: Basil Blackwell, 1989), while Andy McSmith, *No Such Thing as Society: A History of Britain in the 1980s* (London: Constable, 2011) offers a retrospective. Colin Hutchinson, *Reaganism, Thatcherism and the Social Novel* (Basingstoke: Palgrave Macmillan, 2008) assesses the response of contemporary novelists, specifically those on the liberal left, to the ascendant conservative hegemony during the period.
[95] Again, as with health professionals, there is an unavoidable autobiographical element, Campbell's estranged father having been a policeman. Negative representation of the British police as either sinister agents of oppression or as buffoons is a recurrent feature in his fictions.

Notes

[96] Campbell's vivid essay-memoir, 'Near Madness' describes his mother's decline and death. For example, Robin being 'shaken by the sudden utter hatred she felt for her mother' (*Obsession*, p. 175), echoes Campbell's recollection of a relationship that had deteriorated to one of 'mutual loathing' in which '[s]ometimes I considered killing her' (*Ramsey Campbell, Probably*, p. 284).

[97] Beville, *Gothic-postmodernism*, p. 30. See also Slavoj Žižek, *The Sublime Object of Ideology* (London: Verso, 1998), p. 203.

[98] Lane, 'Beyond the Light', p. 46.

[99] The sardonic reference is to the so-called 'Tinker Bell effect', after J. M. Barrie's play *Peter Pan* (1904), in which death is conquered by the audience's applause.

[100] Lane, 'Beyond the Light', p. 46.

[101] Gary Crawford, 'A Religion of His Own Making: Peter in *Obsession*', in Gary Crawford (ed.), *Ramsey Campbell: Critical Essays on the Modern Master of Horror*, pp. 171–7 (p. 176).

[102] Crawford, 'Religion of His Own Making', p. 173.

[103] M. R. James, '"Oh Whistle, And I'll Come To You, My Lad"', in *The Penguin Complete Ghost Stories of M. R. James* (London: Penguin Books, 1984), pp. 75–91 (p. 81).

[104] James, '"Oh Whistle"', p. 76.

[105] Joshi, *Ramsey Campbell and Modern Horror Fiction*, p. 72.

[106] Crawford's reference is to Revelation 15:2: 'And I saw as it were a sea of glass mingled with fire: and them that had gotten the victory over the beast, and over his image, and over his mark, and over the number of his name, stand on the sea of glass, having the harps of God.' Passage in King James Version of the Bible, available online at *https://www.biblegateway.com/passage/?search=Revelation+15:2-4&version=KJV* (accessed 10 October 2017).

[107] Charles Maturin, *Melmoth the Wanderer*, ed. Douglas Grant (Oxford: Oxford University Press, 1989), p. 541.

[108] Beville, *Gothic-postmodernism*, p. 30.

[109] Rudolf Otto, *The Idea of the Holy: An Inquiry into the Non-Rational Factor in the Idea of the Divine and Its Relation to the Rational*, 2nd edition, trans. John W. Harvey (London: Oxford University Press, 1958 [1923]), pp. 13, 10.

Notes

[110] Otto, *Idea of the Holy*, p. 16.
[111] Otto, *Idea of the Holy*, p. 67.
[112] Hazleton, *Agnostic*, p. 19.
[113] S. L. Varnado, *Haunted Presence: The Numinous in Gothic Fiction* (Tuscaloosa, AL: University of Alabama Press, 1987), p. 129.

Chapter 2: Of Bonds and Beings: Campbell's Gothic Sociopaths

[1] Philip L. Simpson, *Psycho Paths: Tracking the Serial Killer through Contemporary American Film and Fiction* (Carbondale and Edwardsville, IL: Southern Illinois University Press, 2000), p. 11.
[2] Lyotard, *Postmodern Condition*, p. 18.
[3] Julia Kristeva, *Black Sun: Depression and Melancholia*, trans. Leon S. Roudiez (New York: Columbia University Press, 1989), p. 4.
[4] Kristeva, *Black Sun*, p. 4.
[5] Kristeva, *Black Sun*, p. 5, the reference being to Jean-Paul Sartre's philosophy of existentialism, as expounded in *Being and Nothingness: An Essay on Phenomenological Ontology* (1943).
[6] Lyotard, *Postmodern Condition*, p. 15; Kenneth J. Gergen, 'Identity Through the Ages', *US News and World Report*, 1 July 1991, p. 59, quoted in Robert M. Collins, *Transforming America: Politics and Culture During the Reagan Years* (New York: Cornell University Press, 2007), p. 49.
[7] Collins, *Transforming America*, p. 150.
[8] Jean Baudrillard, *The Consumer Society: Myths and Structures*, trans. George Ritzer (London: Sage, 1998 [1970]), p. 293.
[9] See *https://en.oxforddictionaries.com/definition/violence* (accessed 1 August 2018).
[10] Joshi, *Ramsey Campbell and Modern Horror Fiction*, p. 12.
[11] Campbell, 'Contemporary Horror: A Mixed Bag', *Fantasy Review*, 8/6 (June 1985), reprinted as 'The Crime of Horror' in *Ramsey Campbell, Probably*, pp. 24–8 (p. 24).
[12] Campbell, 'Contemporary Horror', pp. 25, 28.
[13] Robert K. Ressler, Ann W. Burgess and John E. Douglas, *Sexual Homicides: Patterns and Motives* (New York: Free Press, 1996), quoted in Sarah Hodgkinson, Hershel Prins and Joshua Stuart-Bennett, 'Monsters,

Madmen ... and Myths: A Critical Review of the Serial Killing Literature', *Aggression and Violent Behavior*, 34 (2017), 282–9 (p. 283).

[14] Anthony King, 'Serial Killing and the Postmodern Self', *History of the Human Sciences*, 19/3 (2006), 109–25 (p. 113).

[15] Colin Wilson and David Seaman, *The Serial Killers: A Study in the Psychology of Violence* (London: BCA, 1991), p. 2.

[16] Wilson and Seaman, *Serial Killers*, p. 76.

[17] Wilson and Seaman, *Serial Killers*, pp. 109, 32.

[18] See, for example, the array of artistic products advertised at *http://www.serialkillercalendar.com* (accessed 1 August 2018). These include *Serial Killer Magazine*, the blurb for which claims, somewhat contradictorily, that the publication takes its subject 'very seriously' while also providing 'a unique collection of rare treats'.

[19] David Schmid, *Natural Born Celebrities: Serial Killers in American Culture* (Chicago, IL: University of Chicago Press, 2006), p. 4.

[20] Joyce Carol Oates, 'Three American Gothics', in *Where I've Been and Where I'm Going: Essays, Reviews and Prose* (New York: Plume, 1999), pp. 232–43 (p. 233).

[21] Fred Botting, *Gothic* (London and New York: Routledge, 1996), p. 3.

[22] Definition given in Merriam-Webster Dictionaries, available online at *https://www.merriam-webster.com/dictionary/psychopath* (accessed 1 August 2018). Although superseded by antisocial personality disorder in medical literature and described by Hodgkinson et al. as 'now a somewhat outdated and discredited psychiatric label' (p. 286), undifferentiated 'psychopathy' has featured prominently in critical discourses concerning literary and cinematic works.

[23] In Harris's novel, Chilton describes Lecter slightly less dramatically, as 'a pure sociopath' (London: Mandarin, 1991 [1988]), p. 10.

[24] Schmid, *Natural Born Celebrities*, p. 6.

[25] Catherine Spooner, 'Gothic 1950 to the Present', in *Encyclopedia of the Gothic*, I, pp. 294–304 (p. 299).

[26] Schmid, *Natural Born Celebrities*, p. 25; Mark Seltzer, *Serial Killers: Death and Life in America's Wound Culture* (New York: Routledge, 1998); Richard Tithecott, *Of Men and Monsters: Jeffrey Dahmer and the Construction of the Serial Killer* (Madison, WI: University of Wisconsin Press, 1997), p. 178.

[27] Harris, *Silence of the Lambs*, p. 6.

Notes

[28] Hodgkinson et al., 'Monsters', p. 283.
[29] Peter J. M. Connelly, 'The representation of serial killers' (unpublished PhD thesis, University of Stirling, 2010), 2.
[30] Connelly, 'Representation of serial killers', p. 121.
[31] Hodgkinson et al., 'Monsters', pp. 286, 283.
[32] Hodgkinson et al., 'Monsters', p. 288.
[33] Douglas Keay, Interview with Margaret Thatcher for *Woman's Own*, 23 September, 1987, Thatcher Archive (THCR 5/2/262): COI transcript, p. 30, *https://www.margaretthatcher.org/document/106689* (accessed 1 August 2018).
[34] Colin Hutchinson, *Reaganism, Thatcherism and the Social Novel* (Basingstoke and New York: Palgrave Macmillan, 2008), p. 99.
[35] Campbell, *The Face That Must Die* (London: Macdonald & Co., 1991 [1983]), p. 30. Page numbers hereafter in the text.
[36] Jameson, *Postmodernism*, pp. 387, 405.
[37] Simpson, *Psycho Paths*, p. 70.
[38] Joshi, *Ramsey Campbell and Modern Horror Fiction*, p. 110.
[39] Joshi, *Ramsey Campbell and Modern Horror Fiction*, p. 110; Joshi, *Unutterable Horror*, II, p. 665.
[40] Polanski's 'Trilogy' consists of *Repulsion* (1965), *Rosemary's Baby* (1968, based on the novel by Ira Levin, published the previous year) and *The Tenant* (1976, based on the 1964 novel *Le Locataire chimérique* by Roland Topor).
[41] R. D. Laing, *The Divided Self: An Existentialist Study in Sanity and Madness* (London: Pelican Books, 1965), p. 56.
[42] Laing, *Divided Self*, p. 76.
[43] Linda Hutcheon, *The Politics of Postmodernism*, 2nd edition (London: Routledge, 2002), p. 105.
[44] Punter, *Literature of Terror*, II, p. 167.
[45] Simpson, *Psycho Paths*, p. 19.
[46] 'Fanny Adams' refers both to the notorious murder of an eight-year-old English girl (1867), and a bowdlerised colloquialism for knowing nothing – a perfect example of Campbell's *double entendre* and word play.
[47] Harris, *Silence of the Lambs*, p. 155.
[48] Harris, *Silence of the Lambs*, p. 20.

Notes

[49] Alan Morton, *On Evil* (New York: Routledge, 2004), p. 4.
[50] Wilson and Seaman, *Serial Killers*, p. 34; Connelly, 'Representation of Serial Killers', p. 6, in discussion of Wilson's own novel, *The Killer* (1970).
[51] Jameson, *Postmodernism*, p. 387.
[52] Hutchinson, *Reaganism, Thatcherism and the Social Novel*, p. 40. On the twenty-first-century resurgence of right-wing populism, see also Arthur Goldwag, *The New Hate: A History of Fear and Loathing on the Populist Right* (New York: Pantheon Books, 2012) and numerous other works.
[53] Hutchinson, *Reaganism, Thatcherism and the Social Novel*, p. 39.
[54] See, for example, the media-fixated behaviour of the real-life serial killer Dennis Rader or 'BTK' (b. 1945), and the character of Francis Dolarhyde in Harris's novel *Red Dragon* (1981).
[55] Amongst the many fictional and critical treatments of aspects of British pub culture, see, for instance, Alan Sillitoe's novel, *Saturday Night and Sunday Morning* (1958), or Stephen Tomsen, 'A Top Night: Social Protest, Masculinity and the Culture of Drinking Violence', *British Journal of Criminology*, 37/1 (Winter 1997), 90–102.
[56] Connelly, 'Representation of Serial Killers', p. 158.
[57] A. E. van Vogt, *A Report on the Violent Male* (London: Pauper's Press, 1992 [1956]), section 11.
[58] Schmid, *Natural Born Celebrities*, p. 7.
[59] Campbell, *The One Safe Place* (London: Headline Feature Publishing, 1995), p. 63. Page numbers hereafter in the text.
[60] By Joshi, in *Ramsey Campbell and Modern Horror Fiction*, p. 108.
[61] Dominic Head, *The Cambridge Introduction to Modern British Fiction, 1950–2000* (Cambridge: Cambridge University Press, 2002), p. 2. Head regrettably, but in the context of Campbell's association with a specific genre unsurprisingly, omits *The One Safe Place* and its author from his own survey.
[62] Joshi, *Unutterable Horror*, II, p. 705.
[63] Joshi, *Ramsey Campbell and Modern Horror Fiction*, p. 106.
[64] Campbell, 'Horror Fiction in the Mainstream', *Necrofile*, 12 (Spring 1994), reprinted in *Ramsey Campbell, Probably*, pp. 39–43 (p. 43).
[65] Joshi, *Ramsey Campbell and Modern Horror Fiction*, p. 107, emphasis in original.

[66] This is a clear reference to the 'killer's point of view' camera technique, familiar from horror films like *Halloween* (John Carpenter, 1978) from the 1970s onwards.

[67] See, for example, BBC news: 'England riots: broken society is top priority – Cameron', 15 August 2011, available online at *https://www.bbc.co.uk/news/uk-politics-14524834* (accessed 10 July 2018). The last line of dialogue in Watkins's film is 'We look after our own down here' – a sentiment which could have been lifted from Campbell's text.

[68] See, in particular, Owen Jones, *Chavs: The Demonization of the Working Class*, updated edition (London: Verso, 2012), pp. 130–1.

[69] Van Vogt, *Report on the Violent Male*, section 10.

[70] Baudrillard, *Consumer Society*, p. 53.

[71] Jean Baudrillard, 'Mass Media Culture' [1970], in *Revenge of the Crystal: Selected Writings on the Modern Object and its Destiny, 1968–83*, ed. and trans. Paul Foss and Julian Pefanis (London: Pluto Press, 1990), pp. 63–97 (p. 89).

[72] Hutchinson, *Reaganism, Thatcherism and the Social Novel*, p. 5.

[73] Hutchinson, *Reaganism, Thatcherism and the Social Novel*, pp. 4, 33.

[74] Schmid, *Natural Born Celebrities*, p. 14. Campbell's novel is also prescient in anticipating the excesses of the British *Jeremy Kyle Show* (2005–19).

[75] See, for example, 'Video Link to Bulger Murder Disputed', *Independent*, 29 November 1993, available online at *www.independent.co.uk/news/video-link-to-bulger-murder-disputed-1506766.html* (accessed 1 August 2018).

[76] R. D. Laing, *The Politics of the Family and Other Essays* (London: Tavistock Publications, 1971), p. 24.

[77] Joshi, *Ramsey Campbell and Modern Horror Fiction*, p. 110.

[78] Campbell, 'Beyond the Pale', *Fantasy Review* (August 1985), reprinted in *Ramsey Campbell, Probably*, pp. 57–62 (p. 57); 'In My Opinion: Psycho by Design', *Fear* (31 July 1991), reprinted in *Ramsey Campbell, Probably*, pp. 160–4 (p. 163).

[79] Campbell, 'Horror Fiction in the Mainstream', p. 43.

[80] Baudrillard, *Transparency of Evil*, p. 104.

[81] Jeremy Dyson, 'Introduction', in Campbell, *Secret Story* (London: Drugstore Indian Press/PS Publishing, 2012 [2005]), pp. v–vii (p. vii). The novel originally appeared as *Secret Stories* in 2005. Page numbers hereafter in the text.

[82] Harris, *Silence of the Lambs*, p. 196.
[83] Brett Easton Ellis, *American Psycho* (London: Picador Press, 1991), p. 246.
[84] Joshi, 'Ramsey Campbell: Alone with a Master', p. 126.
[85] Wilson and Seaman, *Serial Killers*, p. 158.
[86] Wilson and Seaman, *Serial Killers*, p. 58.
[87] Hodgkinson et al., 'Monsters', p. 288.
[88] Simpson, *Psycho Paths*, p. 22.
[89] Harris, *Silence of the Lambs*, p. 165.
[90] Ellis, *American Psycho*, p. 238, emphasis in original.
[91] Ellis, *American Psycho*, p. 11.
[92] Slavoj Žižek, 'Neighbors and Other Monsters: A Plea for Ethical Violence', in Eric Santner, Kenneth Reinhard and Slavoj Žižek, *The Neighbor: Three Inquiries in Political Theory* (Chicago, IL: University of Chicago Press, 2005), pp. 134–90 (p. 180). Žižek's use of upper case for 'Other' is preserved here as he consistently refers specifically to the Lacanian Other.
[93] Baudrillard, *Transparency of Evil*, p. 75.
[94] Campbell, 'To the Next Generation', p. 53.
[95] That is, as: 'I'm Ramsey Campbell. I write horror . . .' on the author's website, available online at *http://www.ramseycampbell.com/*.
[96] Mark Currie, Editor's Introduction, in Currie (ed.), *Metafiction* (London: Longman, 1995), pp. 1–18 (pp. 17–18).
[97] Jean-Paul Sartre, *Being and Nothingness: An Essay on Phenomenology*, trans. Hazel E. Barnes (London: Routledge, 1995 [1943]), p. 32.
[98] The sobriquet accorded by the British tabloid press to serial killer Peter Sutcliffe (1946–2020).
[99] Connelly, 'Representation of serial killers', 192.

Chapter 3: Writing with Intensity: Campbell's Gothic Novellas

[1] Aleid Fokkema, 'The Author: Postmodernism's Stock Character', in Paul Fransen and Tons Hoensselaars (eds), *The Author as Character: Representing Historical Characters in Western Literature* (Cranbury, NJ: Associated University Presses, 1999), pp. 39–51 (p. 41).
[2] Lyotard, *Postmodern Condition*, p. 17.

Notes

[3] Patricia Waugh, *Metafiction: The Theory and Practice of a Self-Conscious Genre* (Florence, KY: Routledge, 1984), p. 3.
[4] Baudrillard, *Consumer Society*, p. 191.
[5] Jameson, *Postmodernism*, p. 14.
[6] Waugh, *Metafiction*, pp. 3, 18.
[7] Linda Hutcheon, *A Poetics of Postmodernism* (London: Routledge, 1988), p. 175.
[8] Hutcheon, *Poetics of Postmodernism*, p. 223.
[9] Laura E. Savu, *Postmortem Postmodernists: The Afterlife of the Narrator in Recent Narrative* (Madison, WI: Fairleigh Dickinson University Press, 2009), p. 16.
[10] Jesse Nash, 'Postmodern Gothic: Stephen King's Pet Sematary', *Journal of Popular Culture* (Spring 1997), 30/4, 151–60.
[11] Landais, *Stephen King*, p. 93. Studies like Maroš Buday's 'Demystification of Stephen King's Fiction in the Context of Postmodernism' (Presov: Vydavatelstvo Presovskej Univerzity, 2016), continue the trend.
[12] Examination of this theme is central to Sears's study, *Stephen King's Gothic*. See also Amy J. Palko, 'Charting habitus: Stephen King, the author protagonist and the field of literary production' (unpublished PhD thesis, University of Stirling, 2009).
[13] Stephen King, *On Writing: A Memoir of the Craft* (London: Hodder, 2012), p. 119 passim.
[14] Sears, *Stephen King's Gothic*, p. 8.
[15] To illustrate, by 2020 King had produced some sixty-three long fictions, ten collections and five books of non-fiction, as well as being involved in various other enterprises, including the libretto for a musical (*Ghost Brothers of Darkland County*, 2013).
[16] Punter, *Literature of Terror*, II, p. 164.
[17] Jameson, *Postmodernism*, p. 307.
[18] King, *On Writing*, p. 188.
[19] Stephen King, *Misery* (London: Hodder, 2011 [1987]), p. 306, emphasis in original.
[20] Dziemianowicz, 'Interview', p. 18.
[21] Campbell, 'Introduction: So Far', *Alone with the Horrors*, p. 14; Dziemianowicz, 'Interview', p. 16.
[22] Dziemianowicz, 'Interview', p. 21.

23 Keith M. C. O'Sullivan,, email correspondence with author, 12 April 2019.
24 King, *On Writing*, p. 219.
25 Campbell, 'Horror Fiction and the Mainstream', p. 39.
26 King, *Misery*, p. 272.
27 King was to be the recipient of a National Book Award for Distinguished Contribution to American Letters in 2003.
28 King, *Misery*, p. 314.
29 Palko, 'Charting Habitus', p. 6.
30 Campbell, *Needing Ghosts* (London: Century, 1990), p. 29. Page numbers hereafter in the text.
31 Campbell, 'Dig Us No Grave', p. 32.
32 King, *Danse Macabre*, p. 346, emphasis in original.
33 King, *On Writing*, p. 247.
34 King, *Misery*, p. 26; *On Writing*, p. 269. The notion of Wilkes as surrogate for the reader is one I return to immediately. As noted by Palko and others, the character also functions as both critic and editor.
35 Campbell, 'Horror Fiction and the Mainstream', p. 43. On the influence of Resnais, see also Campbell, 'My Roots Exhumed', p. 5.
36 King, Afterword to *Different Seasons* (London: Hodder, 2012 [1982]), pp. 669–79 (p. 676).
37 King, *On Writing*, p. 195.
38 King, *Misery*, pp. 71, 19, 8.
39 King, *Misery*, p. 10.
40 Joshi, *Ramsey Campbell and Modern Horror Fiction*, p. 69.
41 Interview in Kermode, 'Radical, political and ethical implications', pp. 33, 34.
42 Best, 'Interview'.
43 Campbell, 'Writing and Depression', *Necrofile*, 15 (Winter 1995), reprinted in *Ramsey Campbell, Probably*, pp. 336–40 (p. 337).
44 Stephen King, *The Dark Half* (London: Hodder, 1989), p. 394.
45 There is a surprising dearth of general criticism on the novella compared to the short story and the novel forms, but see, for example, George Fetherling, 'Briefly: The Case for the Novella', *Seven Oaks: A Magazine of Politics, Culture & Resistance*, 22 January 2006, available online at *https://archive.li/20120912031610/http://www.evenoaksmag.com/commentary/94_comm1.html* (accessed 1 June 2019).

Notes

46. Campbell, *The Booking* (Portland, OR: Dark Regions Press, 2016), p. 12. Page numbers hereafter in the text.
47. James Goho, 'An Archaeology of Urban Dread: The Short Fiction of Ramsey Campbell', in *Ramsey Campbell: Critical Essays on the Modern Master of Horror*, pp. 55–89 (p. 60).
48. Jean Baudrillard, *Symbolic Exchange and Death*, trans. Iain Hamilton Grant (London: Thousand Oaks, 1993 [1976]), p. 127.
49. Jameson, *Postmodernism*, p. 25.
50. Jameson, *Postmodernism*, p. 46.
51. Campbell, *Incarnate* (London: Macdonald & Co., 1990 [1983]), p. 427. The theme is developed rather more succinctly in a later novel, *The Grin of the Dark* (2007), discussed in Chapter 4.
52. Joshi, *Ramsey Campbell and Modern Horror Fiction*, p. 84.
53. Joshi, *Ramsey Campbell and Modern Horror Fiction*, p. 109.
54. Chris Baldick, *The Oxford Dictionary of Literary Terms*, 4th edition (Oxford: Oxford University Press, 2015), p. 254.
55. Joe Fassler, 'The Return of the Novella, the Original #Longread', *The Atlantic*, 24 April, 2012, available at *https://www.theatlantic.com/entertainment/archive/2012/04/the-return-of-the-novella-the-original-longread/256290/* (accessed 1 June 2019).
56. Anonymous, 'Ian McEwan Claims the Novella is Better Than the Novel', *Daily Telegraph*, 15 October, 2012, available at *https://www.telegraph.co.uk/culture/books/booknews/9608935/Ian-McEwan-claims-the-novella-is-better-than-the-novel.htm* (accessed 1 June 2019).
57. Certain works by King, for example *The Body*, which first appeared in *Different Seasons*, have, of course, been published individually since, often as a 'tie-in' to cinematic adaptations of which *Stand by Me* (Rob Reiner, 1986) is an example.
58. King, *Afterword to Different Seasons*, p. 673.
59. King, *Afterword to Different Seasons*, p. 674.
60. King, *Foreword to Four Past Midnight* (London: Hodder, 1990), pp. 1–7 (p. 5).
61. Best, 'Interview'.
62. For example, *The Booking* was the third in a series of psychological horror long fictions for Dark Regions Press's Black Labyrinth Imprint series, all intended to be illustrated by Caruso. Fassler (in 'The Return of the

Novella') also notes a revival outside the horror genre in Melville House Publishing's *Art of the Novella* (founded 2002) and *Contemporary Art of the Novella* (2006) series. King's works have also, although infrequently, featured illustrations, for instance Bernie Wrightson's for *Cycle of the Werewolf*.

63 Campbell, 'Dig Us No Grave', p. 34.
64 Lane, 'Beyond the Light', p. 50.
65 Goho, 'Archaeology of Urban Dread', p. 60.
66 Hutcheon, *Poetics of Postmodernism*, p. 4. It must be qualified that key concepts such as commodification, simulacra and hyperreality proposed by Jameson and Baudrillard, and associated with postmodernism, arguably *do* tend towards a disengaged sociopolitical stance, in that they suggest the subject's powerlessness and favour nihilism. It is this dystopian or 'pessimistic' sense of disempowerment which theorists like Hutcheon seek to address in advocating the possibility of critique.
67 Campbell, 'Writing and Depression', p. 339.
68 Waugh, *Metafiction*, p. 3.
69 Campbell, email correspondence with the present author, 12 April 2019. Campbell is using the descriptor 'surrealism' in a loose, ahistorical sense as opposed to alluding specifically to the historical Surrealist movement identified with the 1920s and 1930s.
70 Goho, 'Archaeology of Urban Dread', p. 76.
71 Jerry Aline Flieger, 'Postmodern Perspective: The Paranoid Eye', *New Literary History*, 28/1 (Winter 1997), 87–108 (p. 90). In magic realist or oneiric fictions, of which Campbell's texts under discussion here are examples, fantastic elements are present within a realist narrative. These attest to the continuing influence of surrealism beyond its identification with the specific cultural and historically delineated Surrealist movement.
72 Flieger, 'Postmodern Perspective', p. 90.
73 Beville, *Gothic-postmodernism*, p. 54.
74 Sigmund Freud, 'The Uncanny' (1919), in *The Uncanny*, trans. David McLintock (London: Penguin, 2003), pp. 121–62 (p. 124).
75 Hutcheon, *Poetics of Postmodernism*, p. 118. However, it must be qualified that none of Campbell's fictions would strictly qualify for inclusion in Hutcheon's key categorisation as historiographic metafiction, as, unlike

novels by Peter Ackroyd (with, for example, *The Last Testament of Oscar Wilde*, 1983) and others that she selects, they do not centre upon 'real historical events and personages' (*Poetics of Postmodernism*, p. 5).

[76] Joshi, *Ramsey Campbell and Modern Horror Fiction*, p. 86, emphasis in original.

[77] Steven J. Mariconda, Review of *Needing Ghosts* and *Midnight Sun*, *Studies in Weird Fiction*, 9 (Spring 1991), cited in Joshi, *Ramsey Campbell and Modern Horror Fiction*, p. 86.

[78] The French science fiction short film *La Jetée* (Chris Marker, 1962) and Martin Scorsese's dystopian satire on American 'yuppie' culture, *After Hours* (1984), employ a similar self-reflexive and circular structure.

[79] The first and last of these are also alluded to, famously, in Freud's 'The Uncanny', p. 141. For interesting if frustratingly brief surveys of the role of dolls in the genre, see Leigh Blackmore, '"A Puppet's Parody of Joy": Dolls, Puppets and Mannikins as Diabolical Other in Ramsey Campbell', in *Ramsey Campbell: Critical Essays on the Modern Master of Horror* (pp. 23–46), and Sandra Mills, 'Discussing Dolls: Horror and the Human Double', in Kevin Corstorphine and Laura R. Kremmel (eds), *The Palgrave Handbook to Horror Literature* (Cham, Switzerland: Springer International Publishing, c.2018), pp. 249–5, which focuses on Campbell's first novel, *The Doll Who Ate His Mother* (1976). My own analysis in Chapter 4 of his coulrophobic long fiction, *The Grin of the Dark* (2007), is intended to add to scholarship in this still overlooked field.

[80] Ellis, *American Psycho*, pp. 179, 282, 376.

[81] King, *Misery*, p. 213.

[82] Ellis, *American Psycho*, p. 377.

[83] Savu, *Postmortem Postmodernists*, p. 13.

[84] Lyotard, *Postmodern Condition*, p. 9.

[85] Amongst voluminous discourses, see, for example, John L. Campbell and Ove. K. Pedersen (eds), *The Rise of Neoliberalism and Institutional Analysis* (Princeton, NJ: Princeton University Press, 2001), and Reuters, 'Computers in Use Pass 1 Billion Mark', 23 June 2008, available online at *http://www.reuters.com/article/us-computers-statistics/computers-in-use-pass-1-billion-mark-garter-idUSL2324525420080623* (accessed 1 July 2019).

[86] Campbell's earlier tragicomic serial killer novel *The Count of Eleven* (1991) manages such a critique more successfully through its character study of a protagonist/antagonist deconstructed by capitalism.

[87] See, for example. Deborah Summers, 'David Cameron Warns of "New Age of Austerity"', *The Guardian*, 29 April 2009, available online at *https://www.theguardian.com/politics/2009/apr/26/david-cameron-conservative-economic-policy1*, and Daniel Wainwright et al., 'Libraries Lose a Quarter of Staff as Hundreds Close', *BBC News* online version, 29 March 2016, available online at *https://www.bbc.co.uk/news/uk-england-35707956* (both accessed 1 July 2019).

[88] Jameson, *Postmodernism*, p. 37.

[89] Jameson, *Postmodernism*, p. 37; Baudrillard, *Perfect Crime*, p. 94.

[90] One thinks, for example, of the opening sentence of King's *Secret Window*, in which 'John Shooter' warns the protagonist that '[y]ou stole my story and something's got to be done about it' – a statement that effectively summarises and propels the novella's entire plot. See King, *Four Past Midnight*, pp. 324–420 (p. 324).

[91] Again, in marked contrast to Campbell's work, Palahniuk's novel (and its cinematic adaptation by David Fincher, 1999), has generated sizeable scholarship. See, for example, Jason J. Dodge, 'Spaces of Resistance: Heterotopia and Transgression in Chuck Palahniuk's *Fight Club*', *Literature Interpretation Theory*, 26 (2015), 318–33 for a more detailed application of Foucault's concept that I have referenced briefly here.

[92] Michel Foucault, 'Of Other Spaces', trans. Jay Miskowiec, *Diacritics*, 16/1 (1986), 22–7 (p. 26). Ostensibly a retail outlet, the 'shop' in *The Booking* has the preservative logic of a library or museum, in that none of its contents are really for sale or are ever absent for long.

[93] Foucault, 'Of Other Spaces', p. 25.

[94] Baudrillard, *Perfect Crime*, p. 79.

[95] Flieger, 'Postmodern Perspective', pp. 87, 100.

[96] Baudrillard, *Perfect Crime*, p. 17.

[97] Savu, *Postmortem Postmodernists*, p. 18. Most of the authors in her study – Ackroyd, Peter Carey, Colm Tóibín and Michael Cunningham – are near-contemporaries of Campbell. Unlike Campbell, however, all of them have been adjudged as writers of contemporary rather than popular or genre fiction. Nevertheless, Savu's resurrection of 'the human' is important

in highlighting and harbingering a tendency in recent 'post-postmodernist' thought, a trend considered in this book's conclusion.

[98] Savu, *Postmortem Postmodernists*, p. 14.
[99] Savu, *Postmortem Postmodernists*, p. 244, emphasis in original.
[100] Hutcheon, *Poetics of Postmodernism*, p. 223.

Chapter 4: 'Ghosts' from the Machine: Campbell's Gothic Techno-Fictions

[1] Joshi, *Ramsey Campbell and Modern Horror Fiction*, p. 88; *Unutterable Horror*, p. 705.
[2] Stefan Herbrechter, *Posthumanism: A Critical Analysis* (London: Bloomsbury, 2013), p. 19.
[3] The field of posthumanist theory and criticism, embracing growth and innovations in nano-technology, neuroscience, biogenetic enhancement and much else, is a substantial one. Even an outline of its parameters and citation of all its leading specialists is beyond the scope of the present project. I have cited scholars whose work, in my view, is most relevant to evaluation of literature and to Campbell in particular.
[4] Cary Wolfe, *What is Posthumanism?* (Minneapolis, MN: University of Minnesota Press, 2011), p. 121.
[5] Hayles, cited in Arjen Mulder, 'How Does It Feel to Be Posthuman?' Interview with Katherine Hayles', in Joke Brouwer et al., *The Art of the Accident: Art + Architecture + Media Technology* (Rotterdam, NL: Nederlands Architectuurinstuut :V2 Organisatie, 1998), available online at *https://v2.nl/archive/articles/how-does-it-feel-to-be-posthuman* (accessed 1 February 2020).
[6] N. Katherine Hayles, *How We Became Posthuman: Virtual Bodies in Cybernetics, Literature and Informatics* (Chicago, IL: University of Chicago Press, 1999), p. 3; Pramod K. Nayar, *Posthumanism* (Cambridge: Polity Press, 2014), p. 4. By contrast, Francis Fukuyama, in *Our Posthuman Future: Consequences of the Biotechnology Revolution* (London: Profile, 2002) takes a more alarmist, conservative view of the threat of biotechnology to 'alter human nature' and urges strict state regulation of activities such as cloning (pp. 7, 17).

Notes

[7] Nayar, *Posthumanism*, p. 5.

[8] They form a distinct grouping in contrast to other Campbell long fictions from the same period, notably *Thieving Fear* (2008), *Creatures from the Pool* (2009) and *The Kind Folk* (2012), in, as I demonstrate, the high profile accorded to technology.

[9] Bruce Clarke and Manuela Rossini, Preface, in Clarke and Rossini (eds), *Cambridge Companion to Literature and the Posthuman* (Cambridge: Cambridge University Press, 2017), pp. xi–xxi (p. xiii).

[10] H. P. Lovecraft, 'The Shadow Out of Time', in *H. P. Lovecraft Omnibus 3*, pp. 464–544 (p. 498). Clarke and Rossini, in a prefatory chronology, push the timeline of literary posthumanism back even – and much – further, to Ratramnus of Corbie's 'Letter on the Cynocephali' (AD 865). *Cambridge Companion to Literature and the Posthuman*, pp. xx–xxix (p. xxv).

[11] Norbert Wiener, *Cybernetics: Or Control and Communication in the Animal and the Machine* (Paris: Hermann & Co., 1948); Ihab Hassan, 'Prometheus as Performer: Toward a Posthumanist Culture?', *Georgia Review*, 31/4 (Winter 1977), 830–50, and Donna Haraway, 'A Cyborg Manifesto: Science, Technology and Socialist-Feminism in the Late Twentieth Century' (1984), reprinted in *International Handbook of Virtual Learning Environments*, pp 117–58, available online at *https://link.springer.com/chapter/10.1007/978-1-4020-3803-7_4* (accessed 20 February 2020).

[12] Herbrechter, 'Postmodern', in *Cambridge Companion to Literature and the Posthuman*, p. 55, emphasis in original.

[13] Lyotard, *Postmodern Condition*, pp. 60, 27, 60 and 69. Lyotard, in his democratic ruminations, could not have anticipated organisations like News Corp and the growth in subscription 'pay-per-view' services.

[14] Jean-François Lyotard, *The Inhuman: Reflections on Time*, trans. Geoffrey Bennington and Rachel Bowlby (Cambridge: Polity Press, 1991 [1988]), p. 45.

[15] Lyotard, *Inhuman*, p. 67.

[16] Lyotard, *Inhuman*, p. 17.

[17] Clarke and Rossini, Preface, *Cambridge Companion to Literature and the Posthuman*, p. xiv.

[18] Michael Sean Bolton: 'Monstrous Machinery: Defining Posthuman Gothic', *Aeternum: The Journal of Contemporary Gothic Studies*, 1/1 (June 2014), 1–15 (p. 5).

19 Bolton, 'Monstrous Machinery', pp. 3, 2.
20 Bolton, 'Monstrous Machinery', p. 4.
21 Marshall McLuhan, Quentin Fiore, *The Medium is the Massage*, co-ord. by Jerome Agel (London: Penguin Books, 1967), p. 124; Herbrechter, *Posthumanism*, p. 116.
22 Fred Botting, *Limits of Horror: Technologies, Bodies, Gothic* (Manchester: Manchester University Press, 2008), p. 86; Anya Heise-von der Lippe, 'Introduction: Post/human/Gothic', in Heise-von der Lippe (ed.) *Posthuman Gothic* (Cardiff: University of Wales Press, 2017), pp. 1–16 (p. 5), emphasis added.
23 Heise-von der Lippe, 'Introduction: Post/human/Gothic', p. 6.
24 See, for example, McWilliam, 'Ramsey Campbell Interviewed', in which Campbell acknowledges Dick as being 'a favourite', and the naming of a character after Ballard in *The Seven Days of Cain*, discussed later in this chapter.
25 Linnie Blake and Xavier Aldana Reyes, 'Introduction: Horror in the Digital Age', in Blake and Aldana Reyes (eds), *Digital Horror: Haunted Technologies, Network Panic and the Found Footage Phenomenon* (London: I. B. Tauris, 2016), pp. 1–13 (p. 3).
26 Julian Wolfreys, 'Spectrality', in *Encyclopedia of the Gothic*, II, pp. 638–44 (p. 639).
27 Wolfreys, 'Spectrality', p. 638, emphasis in original.
28 Jones, 'Weird Tales talks with Ramsey Campbell', p. 66.
29 McWilliam, 'Ramsey Campbell interviewed'.
30 Campbell, *The Grin of the Dark* (London: Virgin Books, 2008 [2007]), p. 7. Page numbers hereafter in the text.
31 The 2009 novel, *Creatures from the Pool*, in its blend of real-life secondary sources and the purely fictional, similarly conveys the author's conscientiousness as a local (Merseyside) historian.
32 In addition to *Mr Sardonicus*, Tubby's permanent grin also recalls *The Man Who Laughs* (Paul Leni, 1928), an adaptation of Victor Hugo's novel, *L'homme qui rit* (1869), although foregrounding the grotesque rather than the historic or tragic.
33 Joshi, *Ramsey Campbell and Modern Horror Fiction*, p. 92; *Modern Weird Tale*, p. 146.

[34] Richard Bleiler, 'Ramsey Campbell and the Twenty-First-Century Weird Tale', in *Ramsey Campbell: Critical Essays on the Modern Master of Horror*, pp. 47–54 (p. 50). Bleiler, disappointingly, does not explore in detail the philosophical ramifications beyond superficial comparison of technology in the two novels.

[35] Blake and Aldana Reyes, 'Introduction: Horror in the Digital Age', p. 4.

[36] M. R. James, '"Oh Whistle"', p. 83.

[37] Campbell, 'A Small Dose of Reality', *Fantasy Review*, 8/11 (November 1985), reprinted in *Ramsey Campbell, Probably*, pp. 294–300 (p. 295). The victim in *The Parasite* is female, and Campbell specifies that the 'invasion' is that 'of a female personality by a (dormant) [because dead] male' (p. 295), with 'rape' acting as 'central metaphor' (p. 296). Like several of Campbell's short stories, notably 'Cold Print' (1966), 'The Staircase' (1968) and 'The Telephones' (1976), *Grin* lends itself profitably to Queer studies analysis. However, it is the ontological significance of, rather than sexual threat posed by, the novel's antagonist which concerns me here.

[38] Jean Baudrillard, *The Ecstasy of Communication*, trans. Bernard Schütze and Caroline Schütze (South Pasadena, CA: Semiotext(e), 2012 [1987]), pp. 26, 62, emphasis in original.

[39] McLuhan and Fiore, *Medium is the Massage*, p. 4.

[40] McLuhan and Fiore, *Medium is the Massage*, p. 26; Marshall McLuhan, *Understanding Media: The Extensions of Man* (London and New York: Routledge, 2001 [1964]), pp. 3–6.

[41] Blake and Aldana Reyes, 'Introduction: Horror in the Digital Age', p. 5.

[42] McLuhan and Fiore, *Medium is the Massage*, p. 12.

[43] Herbrechter, *Posthumanism*, p. 28.

[44] The literature on behaviours in relation to the Internet is substantial. See, for example, Yair Amichair-Hamburger, 'Personality, Individual Differences and Internet Use', in Adam Joinson et al. (eds), *The Oxford Handbook of Internet Psychology* (Oxford: Oxford University Press, 2007), pp. 187–204. Amongst differences to face-to-face interaction, Amichair-Hamburger identifies greater anonymity, control over time and pace of interaction, and 'ease of finding others' (pp. 187–8).

[45] Amongst many definitions of the Internet slang term 'troll', see, for example, that given by Claire Hardaker, as a computer user whose

'intention(s)is/are to cause disruption and/or to trigger or exacerbate conflict for the purposes of their own amusement'. 'Trolling in Asynchronous Computer-mediated Communication: From User Discussions to Academic Definitions', *Journal of Politeness Research*, 6/2 (2010), 215–42 (p. 237).

46   Or indeed all of these and Lester himself, a point which is returned to shortly.
47   Steffen Hantke, 'Network Anxieties: Prefiguring Digital Anxieties in the American Horror Film', in *Digital Horror*, pp. 17–28 (p. 18).
48   Neal Kirk, 'Networked Spirituality: *In Memorium* [sic], *Pulse* and Beyond', in *Digital Horror*, pp. 54–65 (pp. 59, 57).
49   Kirk, 'Networked Spirituality', p. 60.
50   Herbrechter, *Posthumanism*, p. 88.
51   Bleiler, 'Ramsey Campbell and the Twenty-First-Century Weird Tale', p. 52.
52   Baudrillard, *Ecstasy of Communication*, pp. 24, 23.
53   Baudrillard, *Perfect Crime*, pp. 27–8.
54   Andy Sawyer, '"That Ill-Rumoured and Evilly-Shadowed Seaport": Ramsey Campbell's Lovecraftian Secret History of Liverpool', in *Ramsey Campbell: Critical Essays on the Modern Master of Horror*, pp. 1–22 (p. 21).
55   Klaehn, 'Reaching for the Awesome and Numinous', p. 314.
56   Baudrillard, *Ecstasy of Communication*, p. 62.
57   McLuhan, Fiore, *Medium is the Massage*, p. 26.
58   Campbell, 'Dig Us No Grave', p. 32; 'My Roots Exhumed', p. 4.
59   Campbell, *Think Yourself Lucky* (Hornsea: PS Publishing, 2014), p. 6. Page numbers hereafter in the text.
60   It is pre-dated in this respect by *The Seven Days of Cain* (2010). However, owing to what I demonstrate as that earlier novel's wider philosophical significance for author and subject and what it communicates about Campbell's vision, *Cain* is discussed last.
61   With respect to its 'divided' protagonist, Campbell's novel may also of course be compared to Chuck Palahniuk's earlier work, *Fight Club* (1996). Like Newless, Tyler Durden, the unnamed narrator's 'dark half', can similarly 'run off and do something wild, something crazy, something completely out of my mind' (London: Vintage Books, 2006, p. 163).

However, Palahniuk's novel, unlike the others discussed here, has not usually been interpreted as a *supernatural* narrative within the parameters of the Gothic.

62 Gary Fry, 'A New Place to Hyde: Self and Society in Ramsey Campbell's *Think Yourself Lucky*', in *Thinking Horror: A Journal of Horror Philosophy*, I (2015), 25–35 (p. 30), emphasis in original. Prior to the present project, Fry's essay appeared to be unique in according this novel scholarly attention, so is worth engagement with at some length.

63 Baudrillard, *Transparency of Evil*, pp. 122, 113.

64 Herbrechter, *Posthumanism*, p. 86.

65 James Hogg, *The Private Memoirs and Confessions of a Justified Sinner*, ed. John Carey (Oxford: Oxford University Press, 1990 [1824]), p. 144.

66 Fry has a doctorate in psychology. 'New Place to Hyde', p. 25.

67 Fry, 'New Place to Hyde', p. 31.

68 Fry, 'New Place to Hyde', p. 30, emphasis in original.

69 Fry, 'New Place to Hyde', p. 30, emphasis in original.

70 Hogg, *Private Memoirs*, pp. 124, 170.

71 Fritz Leiber, 'Smoke Ghost', repr. in *Meddling with Ghosts: Ghost Stories in the Tradition of M. R. James*, pp. 142–56 (p. 152).

72 Herbrechter, *Posthumanism*, p. 97.

73 Fry, New Place to Hyde', p. 30. Lucky is *not* however, as Fry implies, the 'first' (p. 32) such, given the creations of social media in Campbell's earlier novel, *The Seven Days of Cain*.

74 Fry, 'New Place to Hyde', p. 33.

75 Joshi, 'Ramsey Campbell: Alone with a Master', p. 121, regarding *The House on Nazareth Hill* (1996), emphasis in original.

76 Nayar, *Posthumanism*, p. 32. Nayar's choice of capitalisation is stylistic, not a reference to the Lacanian Big Other.

77 Campbell, 'The Depths', in *Alone with the Horrors*, pp. 287–304 (p. 293).

78 Joseph Crawford, 'Gothic Fiction and the Evolution of Modern Technology', in Edwards (ed.), *Technology of the Gothic in Literature and Culture: Technogothics* (New York: Routledge, 2015), pp. 35–47 (p. 36).

79 Campbell, *The Seven Days of Cain* (Cincinnati, OH: Samhain Publishing, 2010), p. 158. Page numbers hereafter in the text.

80 I have used the pronoun 'it' in reference to Max Beyer/Tim Battle/Septimus Battle throughout deliberately, in recognition of this entity's

monstrosity and protean nature. Bentley's other creations, like Claire Bentley or Regis King, are accorded the pronouns 's/he'.

[81] There are also, as John Llewellyn Robert points out, cinematic references in Campbell's naming of the Hotel Balaguero and Plaza Paco in Barcelona after the respective directors of the first two film adaptations of his work. See 'Grinning in the Dark: The Humour of Ramsey Campbell', in *Ramsey Campbell: Critical Essays on the Modern Master of Horror*, pp. 147–54 (p. 149). Moreover, the attention to the order of deaths in *Seven Days of Cain* recalls that accorded in the *Final Destination* film franchise (James Wong et al, pp. 2000ff.).

[82] McWilliam, "Ramsey Campbell interviewed'.

[83] Jason P. Vest, *The Postmodern Humanism of Philip K. Dick* (Lanham, MD: Scarecrow Press, 2009), p. xii.

[84] See, for example, Christopher Palmer's earlier study, *Philp K. Dick: Exhilaration and Terror of the Postmodern* (Liverpool: Liverpool University Press, 2003) for discussion of Dick's accessible, and thus non-'postmodern' style, p. 8. Campbell's *Needing Ghosts* is, as argued, a partial departure from his normal 'realist' approach.

[85] Campbell, 'Dig Us No Grave', p. 32; Nik Glover, 'Ramsey Campbell' [interview], *Bido Lito!*, 9 (March 2011), available online at *https://www.bidolito.co.uk/ramsey-campbell/* (accessed 3 May 2020).

[86] Anthony J. Fonseca, 'What Develops in the Darkest Room of the Mind: The Photographic Technique in *Nazareth Hill* and *The Seven Days of Cain*', in *Ramsey Campbell: Critical Essays on the Modern Master of Horror*, pp. 159–69 (p. 168).

[87] Campbell, 'Dig Us No Grave', p. 33.

[88] Baudrillard, *Transparency of Evil*, p. 24.

[89] Baudrillard, *Transparency of Evil*, p. 17.

[90] Fonseca, 'What Develops in the Darkest Room of the Mind', p. 166.

[91] Baudrillard, *Symbolic Exchange and Death*, p. 140.

[92] Hutcheon, *Politics of Postmodernism*, p. 109.

[93] Jameson, *Postmodernism*, p. 15.

[94] Jameson, *Postmodernism*, p. 15.

[95] That is, the name is laden with meaning in having both biblical and collectivist connotations. It is another instance of Campbell's highly deliberate use of language.

[96] Rosi Braidotti, *The Posthuman* (Cambridge: Polity Press, 2013), p. 93; Fukuyama, *Our Posthuman Future*, p. 9.

[97] Brett Easton Ellis, *Lunar Park* (London: Picador, 2005), p. 19. Indeed, as Maria Beville notes, the novel 'takes on a life of its own beyond the control of its professed author' (*Gothic-postmodernism*, p. 175).

[98] Ellis, *Lunar Park*, p. 219.

[99] Ellis, *American Psycho*, p. 376.

[100] Beville, *Gothic-postmodernism*, p. 54,

[101] Mary Shelley, *Frankenstein: or, The Modern Prometheus*, in *Three Gothic Novels*, ed. Peter Fairclough (London: Penguin Books, 1986 [1818, rev. edn, 1831]), pp. 257–497 (p. 363).

[102] Hayles, *How We Became Posthuman*, p. 48.

[103] Hayles, *How We Became Posthuman*, p. 290. This has affinity with Lyotard's earlier, but anti-humanist, argument that the subject, in a blow to its human 'narcissism', in fact 'does not have the monopoly of mind' (*Inhuman*, p. 45).

[104] Nayar, *Posthumanism*, p. 72.

[105] Nayar, *Posthumanism*, p. 72.

[106] Hayles, *How We Became Posthuman*, p. 280.

[107] The author's name is another example of Campbell's humorous but deliberate word play, in this case the evocation of magicians and 'hocus pocus'.

[108] Nayar, *Posthumanism*, p. 34. The point about dependence in Ishiguro's novel is also made in Mads Rosenthal Thomsen's *The New Human in Literature: Posthuman Visions of Change in Body, Mind and Society after 1900* (London: Bloomsbury, 2013), p. 209.

[109] The iconic passages are from *Paradise Lost*, Book IV, lines 461 –5: 'A Shape within the watry gleam appear'd / Bending to look at me, I started back / It started back, but pleas'd I soon return'd / Pleas'd it return'd as soon with answering looks / Of sympathie and love . . .', in, for example, John Milton, *The Complete Poems*, ed. B. A. Wright (London: J. M. Dent & Sons, 1980 [1667/1674]), p. 226; Shelley, *Frankenstein*: '[H]ow was I terrified when I viewed myself in a transparent pool! . . . and when I became fully convinced that I was in reality the monster that I am, I was filled with the bitterest sensations of despondence and mortification' (p. 379).

[110] Braidotti, *Posthuman*, p. 2.
[111] Lyotard, *Inhuman*, pp. 38, 45.
[112] Heise-von der Lippe, 'Introduction: Post/human/Gothic', p. 13.

Conclusion: 'Ghosts' from the Machine: Campbell's Gothic Techno-Fictions

[1] H. P. Lovecraft, 'Supernatural Horror in Literature' (1927, revised 1933–5), in *The H. P. Lovecraft Omnibus 2: Dagon and Other Macabre Tales* (London: Grafton Books, 1985), pp. 423–512 (p. 493).
[2] Campbell, 'To the Next Generation', p. 49.
[3] Steffen Hantke, 'The Rise of Popular Horror, 1971–2000', in *Horror: A Literary History*, pp. 159–88 (p. 174). Hantke is referring particularly to the 1980s.
[4] Luke Walker, 'Meet Ramsey Campbell: "Britain's Most Respected Living Horror Writer"' (interview, 14 August 2018), available online at *https://www.lounge-books.com/award-winners-we-lov/ramsey-campbell-horror-author-interview* (accessed 1 June 2020); Joshi, *Ramsey Campbell and Modern Horror Fiction*, p. 88.
[5] Klaehn, 'Reaching for the Awesome and Numinous', p. 313.
[6] Campbell, 'Ramsey Campbell Talks to the Horror Zine'.
[7] The aforementioned *The Claw* (1983), partly set in Nigeria, and *Thirteen Days at Sunset Beach* (2015, a Greek island) are notable exceptions.
[8] Campbell, 'Dig Us No Grave', p. 50; Walker, 'Meet Ramsey Campbell'.
[9] Harold Bloom, 'Dumbing Down American Readers', *Boston Globe*, 24 September 2003, available online at *http://www.public.asu.edu/~atsjd/bloom.html* (accessed 9 June 2017).
[10] Campbell, 'Fiedler on the Roof', *Fantasy Review*, 7/8 (September 1984), reprinted in *Ramsey Campbell, Probably*, pp. 19–23 (p. 19).
[11] Joshi, *Unutterable Horror*, II, p. 561.
[12] Campbell, 'James Herbert: Notes Towards a Reappraisal', reprinted in *Ramsey Campbell, Probably*, pp. 256–65 (pp. 256, 264–5).
[13] Walker, 'Meet Ramsey Campbell'.
[14] Lyotard, *Postmodern Condition*, p. 37.
[15] Baudrillard, *Perfect Crime*, p. 2; *Transparency of Evil*, p. 83.

Notes

[16] Jameson, *Postmodernism*, pp. 10, 15.
[17] Baudrillard, *Simulacra and Simulation*, p. 172.
[18] Baudrillard, *Fatal Strategies*, p. 202.
[19] Best, 'Interview'.
[20] Baudrillard, *Consumer Society*, p. 293.
[21] Punter, *Literature of Terror*, II, p. 205.
[22] Campbell states that he believes *The Face That Must Die* to be 'the first anti-homophobic horror novel' in his interview with Simon Best.
[23] Connelly, 'Representation of Serial Killers', p. 192.
[24] Best, 'Interview'.
[25] Hutcheon, *Poetics of Postmodernism*, pp. 207, 220.
[26] Jameson, *Postmodernism*, p. 298.
[27] Campbell, 'My Roots Exhumed', p. 4.
[28] Campbell, 'Why I Write Horror Fiction', p. 304; Walker, 'Meet Ramsey Campbell'.
[29] Klaehn, 'Reaching for the Awesome and Numinous', p. 312.
[30] Numerous examples in James's homosocial narratives can be deployed to support a Queer studies reading, the animated bedsheet in '"Oh Whistle, And I'll Come To You, My Lad"' (1904) perhaps being the most obvious.
[31] See, for example, McWilliam, 'Ramsey Campbell Interviewed' for copious lists of authors whom Campbell has admired. Campbell's respective praise for Mosby and the Cuban Spaniard Somoza indicates his interests in both generic boundaries (Mosby writes suspense thrillers; Somoza, historical mysteries) and non-Anglophone literature.
[32] Ramsey Campbell, 'The H-Word: H for Honesty', *Nightmare*, 17 (February 2014), available online at *https://www.nightmare-magazine.com/nonfiction/the-h-word-h-for-honesty* (accessed 31 October 2020).
[33] Beville, *Gothic-postmodernism*, p. 15.
[34] Spooner, 'Gothic 1950 to the Present', p. 299. This is not to disparage McGrath's own creative evolution, from early parody of Gothic tropes to consideration of 'issues of historicity, national and personal identity and the figure of the artist', as described by Sue Zlosnik in *Patrick McGrath* (Cardiff: University of Wales Press, 2011), p. 12.
[35] Punter, *Literature of Terror*, II, p. 183.
[36] Dziemianowicz, 'Interview', p. 18.

[37] The same publishing house, Headline Book Publishing, issued Campbell's next, overtly supernatural, novel, *The House on Nazareth Hill*, his major contribution to the 'haunted house' subgenre, the following year (1996), with a strikingly similar cover illustration of a child's face in profile. Campbell, of course, is unapologetic and indeed proud of his recognition and classification as a writer of 'horror'.

[38] Terry Eagleton, *After Theory* (London: Penguin Books, 2004 [2003]), p. 73. For Eagleton, postmodernism had itself been no more than a late phase of modernism.

[39] Joshi, *Ramsey Campbell and Modern Horror Fiction*, p. 159.

[40] Eagleton, *After Theory*, p. 58. Eagleton is pithily summarising the pessimistic implications of arguments by theorists like Jameson and Baudrillard.

[41] Irmtraud Huber, *Literature after Postmodernism: Reconstructive Fantasies* (New York: Palgrave Macmillan, 2014), pp. 15, 75.

[42] Huber, *Literature after Postmodernism*, p. 51.

[43] Huber, *Literature after Postmodernism*, pp. 12, 27, 40.

[44] Huber, *Literature after Postmodernism*, p. 221.

[45] See, for example, the essays collected in Robin van der Akker, Alison Gibbons and Timotheus Vermeulen (eds), *Metamodernism: Historicity, Affect and Depth After Postmodernism* (London: Rowman & Littlefield, 2017). In discussion of the works of Nobel laureate Toni Morrison and David Foster Wallace, whose final novel *The Pale King* (2011) was a Pulitzer Prize finalist, there remains a focus on contemporary literature rather than the genre fictions with which Campbell is identified.

[46] Lyotard, *Postmodern Condition*, p. 65.

[47] Klaehn, 'Reaching for the Awesome and Numinous', p. 313.

[48] Campbell returns to folk horror themes yet again in the novel *The Wise Friend* (London: Flame Tree Press, 2020).

Select Bibliography

Literary Works by Ramsey Campbell

Ancient Images (London: Arrow Books, 1990 [1989])
The Booking (Portland, OR: Dark Regions Press, 2016)
'Concussion', in *Demons by Daylight* (London: Star, 1980 [1973]), pp. 134–61
'The Depths' (1978), in *Alone with the Horrors: The Great Short Fiction of Ramsey Campbell, 1961–1991* (New York: Tor, 2005), pp. 287–304
The Face That Must Die (London: Macdonald & Co., 1991 [1983])
'The Franklyn Paragraphs', in *Demons by Daylight* (London: Star, 1980 [1973]), pp. 39–61
The Grin of the Dark (London: Virgin Books, 2008 [2007])
The Hungry Moon (London: Arrow Books, 1987 [1986])
Incarnate (London: Macdonald & Co., 1990 [1983])
The Inhabitant of the Lake & Other Unwelcome Tenants (London: Drugstore Indian Press/PS Publishing, 2013 [1964])
The Nameless (London: Little, Brown & Company, 1985 [1981])
Needing Ghosts (London: Century, 1990)
Obsession (London: Futura, 1990 [1985])
The One Safe Place (London: Headline Feature Publishing, 1995)
The Searching Dead (Hornsea: PS Publishing, 2016)
Secret Story (London: Drugstore Indian Press/PS Publishing, 2012 [2005])
The Seven Days of Cain (Cincinnati, OH: Samhain Publishing, 2010)
The Way of the Worm (Hornsea: PS Publishing, 2018)
Think Yourself Lucky (London: PS Publishing, 2014)

Select Bibliography

Articles and Essays by Ramsey Campbell

Afterword to 1994 edition of *The Hungry Moon*, reprinted in S. T. Joshi (ed.), *Ramsey Campbell, Probably: On Horror and Sundry Fantasies* (Harrogate: PS Publishing, 2002), pp. 402–7

Afterword to 1993 edition of *The Parasite*, reprinted in S. T. Joshi (ed.), *Ramsey Campbell, Probably: On Horror and Sundry Fantasies* (Harrogate: PS Publishing, 2002), pp. 370–3

'Beyond the Pale', *Fantasy Review*, 8/8 (August 1985), reprinted in S. T. Joshi (ed.), *Ramsey Campbell, Probably: On Horror and Sundry Fantasies* (Harrogate: PS Publishing, 2002), pp. 57–62

'Contemporary Horror: A Mixed Bag', *Fantasy Review*, 8/6 (June 1985), reprinted as 'The Crime of Horror', in S. T. Joshi (ed.), *Ramsey Campbell, Probably: On Horror and Sundry Fantasies* (Harrogate: PS Publishing, 2002), pp. 24–8

with Stefan Dziemianowicz and S. T. Joshi, *The Core of Ramsey Campbell: A Bibliography & Reader's Guide* (Warwick, RI: Necronomicon Press, 1995)

'Dig Us No Grave', *Fantasy Review*, 9/3 (March 1986), reprinted in S. T. Joshi (ed.), *Ramsey Campbell, Probably: On Horror and Sundry Fantasies* (Harrogate: PS Publishing, 2002), pp. 29–34

'Fiedler on the Roof', *Fantasy Review*, 7/8 (September 1984), reprinted in S. T. Joshi (ed.), *Ramsey Campbell, Probably: On Horror and Sundry Fantasies* (Harrogate: PS Publishing, 2002), pp. 19–23

'Horror Fiction and the Mainstream', *Necrofile*, 12 (Spring 1994), reprinted in S. T. Joshi (ed.), *Ramsey Campbell, Probably: On Horror and Sundry Fantasies* (Harrogate: PS Publishing, 2002), pp. 39–43

'The H-Word: H for Honesty', *Nightmare*, 17 (February 2014), available online at *https://www.nightmare-magazine.com/nonfiction/the-h-word-h-for-honesty/* (accessed 31 October 2020)

'In My Opinion: Psycho by Design', *Fear* (31 July 1991), reprinted in S. T. Joshi (ed.), *Ramsey Campbell, Probably: On Horror and Sundry Fantasies* (Harrogate: PS Publishing, 2002), pp. 160–4

Introduction to *Alone with the Horrors: The Great Short Fiction of Ramsey Campbell, 1961–1991* (New York: Tor, 2005), pp. 11–20

'James Herbert: Notes Towards a Reappraisal', *Fantasy Review*, 8/2 (February 1984), reprinted in S. T. Joshi (ed.), *Ramsey Campbell,*

Select Bibliography

Probably: On Horror and Sundry Fantasies (Harrogate: PS Publishing, 2002), pp. 256–65

'My Roots Exhumed', prefatory essay in S. T. Joshi, *Ramsey Campbell and Modern Horror Fiction* (Liverpool: Liverpool University Press), pp. 1–5

'Near Madness' (1983), reprinted in S. T. Joshi (ed.), *Ramsey Campbell, Probably: On Horror and Sundry Fantasies* (Harrogate: PS Publishing, 2002), pp. 273–85

'Nightmares', *Necrofile*, 8 (Spring 1993), reprinted in S.T. Joshi (ed.), Ramsey Campbell, *Probably: On Horror and Sundry Fantasies* (Harrogate: PS Publishing, 2002), pp. 312–17

'On Reading My Stories', *Necrofile*, 7 (Winter 1993), reprinted in S.T. Joshi (ed.), *Ramsey Campbell, Probably: On Horror and Sundry Fantasies* (Harrogate: PS Publishing, 2002), pp. 306–11

'R. R. Ryan', *Necrofile*, 27 (Winter 1998), reprinted. in S. T. Joshi (ed.), *Ramsey Campbell, Probably: On Horror and Sundry Fantasies* (Harrogate: PS Publishing, 2002), pp. 228–33

'Shaun Hutson', *Necrofile*, 3 (Winter 1992), reprinted in S. T. Joshi (ed.), *Ramsey Campbell, Probably: On Horror and Sundry Fantasies* (Harrogate: PS Publishing, 2002), pp. 171–7

'Terry Lamsley', combination of 'Introduction' to Lamsley's *Conference for the Dead* (Ashcroft, BC: Ash-Tree Press, 1996) and entry on Lamsley in David Pringle (ed.), *St. James Guide to Horror, Ghost & Gothic Writers* (St. James Press, 1998), reprinted in S.T. Joshi (ed.), *Ramsey Campbell Probably: On Horror and Sundry Fantasies* (Harrogate: PS Publishing, 2002), pp. 155–9

'To the Next Generation', in *L. Ron Hubbard Presents Writers of the Future, IV*, ed. Algis Budrys (East Grinstead: New Era, 1988), reprinted in S. T. Joshi (ed.), *Ramsey Campbell, Probably: On Horror and Sundry Fantasies* (Harrogate: PS Publishing, 2002), pp. 49–54

'Why I Write Horror Fiction', *Necrofile*, 2 (Fall 1991), reprinted in S. T. Joshi (ed.), *Ramsey Campbell, Probably: On Horror and Sundry Fantasies* (Harrogate: PS Publishing, 2002), pp. 301–5

'Writing and Depression', Necrofile, 15 (Winter 1995), reprinted in S.T. Joshi (ed.), Ramsey Campbell, Probably: On Horror and Sundry Fantasies (Harrogate: PS Publishing, 2002), pp. 336–40

Select Bibliography

Interviews with Ramsey Campbell

Anonymous, 'Ramsey Campbell Talks to the *Horror Zine*', available online at *http://www.thehorrorzine.com/Special/RamseyCampbell/Ramsey Campbell.html* (accessed 1 June 2020)

Best, Simon, Interview with Ramsey Campbell, Web blog post. *This is Horror*, 19 October 2016, available online at *www.thisishorror.co.uk/interview-ramsey-campbell/* (accessed 13 January 2017)

Cardin, Matt, 'An Interview with Ramsey Campbell', October 2016, in Cardin (ed.), *Horror Literature Through History: An Encyclopedia of the Stories That Speak to Our Deepest Fears* (Westport, CT: Greenwood Publishing Inc. 2017), 2 vols, I, pp. 269–72

Dziemianowicz, Stefan, 'Interview with Ramsey Campbell', in S. T. Joshi (ed.), *The Count of Thirty: A Tribute to Ramsey Campbell* (West Warwick, RI: Necronomicon Press, 1993), pp. 7–26

Glover, Nik, 'Ramsey Campbell', [interview], *Bido Lito!*, 9 (March 2011), available online at *https://www.bidolito.co.uk/ramsey-campbell/* (accessed 3 May 2020)

Klaehn, Jeffery, 'Reaching for the Awesome and Numinous: An Interview with Horror Author Ramsey Campbell', *New Writing*, 13/2 (2016), 308–14

Mathew, David, 'An Interview with Ramsey Campbell', available online at *http://www.infinityplus.co.uk/nonfiction/intcam.htm* (accessed 1 June 2020)

McWilliam, David, 'Ramsey Campbell interviewed by David McWilliam', posted 24 September 2012, available online at *http://www.gothic.stir.ac.uk/interviews/ramsey-campbell-interviewed-by-david-mcwilliam/* (accessed 12 February 2017)

Walker, Luke, 'Meet Ramsey Campbell "Britain's Most Respected Living Horror Writer"' (interview, 14 August 2018), available online at *https://www.lounge-books.com/award-winners-we-lov/ramsey-campbell-horror-author-interview* (accessed 1 June 2020)

Select Bibliography

Critical Works on Ramsey Campbell

Bleiler, Richard, 'Ramsey Campbell and the 21st Century Weird Tale', in Gary Crawford (ed.), *Ramsey Campbell: Critical Essays on the Modern Master of Horror* (Lanham, MD: Scarecrow Press, 2014), pp. 47–54

Crawford, Gary, 'A Religion of His Own Making: Peter in *Obsession*', in Gary Crawford (ed.), *Ramsey Campbell: Critical Essays on the Modern Master of Horror* (Lanham, MD: Scarecrow Press, 2014), pp. 171–7

Crawford, Gary William, *Ramsey Campbell* (Mercer Island, WA: Starmont House, 1988)

Dyson, Jeremy, 'Introduction', in Ramsey Campbell, *Secret Story* (London: Drugstore Indian Press/PS Publishing Ltd., 2012 [2005]), pp. v–vii

Fonseca, Anthony J., 'What Develops in the Darkest Rooms of the Mind: The Photographic Technique in *Nazareth Hill* and *The Seven Days of Cain*', in Gary Crawford (ed.), *Ramsey Campbell: Critical Essays on the Modern Master of Horror* (Lanham, MD: Press, 2014), pp. 159–69

Fry, Gary, 'A New Place to Hyde: Self and Society in Ramsey Campbell's *Think Yourself Lucky*', *Thinking Horror: A Journal of Horror Philosophy*, I (2015), 25–35

Goho, James, 'An Archaeology of Urban Dread: The Short Fiction of Ramsey Campbell', in Gary Crawford (ed.), *Ramsey Campbell: Critical Essays on the Modern Master of Horror* (Lanham, MD: Scarecrow Press, 2014), pp. 55–89

Joshi, S. T., 'Alone with a Master', in *Classics and Contemporaries: Some Notes on Horror Fiction* (New York: Hippocampus Press, 2009), pp. 109–31

—, *Ramsey Campbell and Modern Horror Fiction* (Liverpool: Liverpool University Press, 2001)

—, *Ramsey Campbell: Master of Weird Fiction* (Hornsea: PS Publishing, 2022)

Lane, Joel, 'Beyond the Light: The Recent Novels of Ramsey Campbell', in S. T. Joshi (ed.), *The Count of Thirty: A Tribute to Ramsey Campbell* (West Warwick, RI: Necronomicon Press, 1993), pp. 46–51

MacCulloch, Simon, 'Glimpses of Absolute Power: Ramsey Campbell's Concept of Evil', in S.T. Joshi (ed.), *The Count of Thirty: A Tribute to Ramsey Campbell* (West Warwick, RI: Necronomicon Press, 1993), pp. 32–8

Royle, Nicholas, 'Ramsey Campbell', in William Hughes, David Punter and Andrew Smith (eds), *The Encyclopedia of the Gothic* (Oxford: Wiley-Blackwell, 2013), 2 vols, I, pp. 105–6

Select Bibliography

Sawyer, Andy, '"That Ill-Rumoured and Evilly-Shadowed Seaport": Ramsey Campbell's Lovecraftian Secret Histories of Liverpool', in Gary Crawford (ed.), *Ramsey Campbell: Critical Essays on the Modern Master of Horror* (Lanham, MD: Scarecrow Press, 2014), pp. 1–22

Other Secondary Literary and Theoretical Works

Aickman, Robert, 'Introduction', in Aickman (ed.), *The Second Fontana Book of Great British Ghost Stories* (London: Fontana, 1966), pp. 7–10
—, 'Introduction', in Aickman (ed.), *The Third Fontana Book of Great British Ghost Stories* (London: Fontana, 1966), pp. 7–11
Aldana Reyes, Xavier, *Body Gothic: Corporeal Transgression in Contemporary Literature and Horror Film* (Cardiff: University of Wales Press, 2014)
—, 'Post-Millennial Horror, 2000–16', in Aldana Reyes (ed.), *Horror: A Literary History* (London: British Library, 2016), pp. 189–214
Alder, Emily, 'Urban Gothic', in William Hughes, David Punter and Andrew Smith (eds), *The Encyclopedia of the Gothic* (Oxford: Wiley-Blackwell, 2013), 2 vols, II, pp. 703–6
Amichai-Hamburger, Yair, 'Personality, Individual Differences and Internet Use', in Adam Joinsen et al. (eds), *The Oxford Handbook of Internet Psychology* (Oxford: Oxford University Press, 2007), pp. 187–204
Anonymous, 'Horror Fiction', in Dinah Birch (ed.), *Oxford Companion to English Literature*, 7th edition (Oxford: Oxford University Press, 2009), p. 499
—, 'Ian McEwan Claims the Novella is Better Than the Novel', *Daily Telegraph*, 15 October 2012, available online at https://www.telegraph.co.uk/culture/books/booknews/9608935/Ian-McEwan-claims-the-novella-is-better-than-the-novel.htm (accessed 1 June 2019)
Baldick, Chris, *The Oxford Dictionary of Literary Terms*, 4th edition (Oxford: Oxford University Press, 2015)
Baudrillard, Jean, *The Consumer Society: Myths and Structures*, trans. George Ritzer (London: Sage Publications, 1998 [1970])
—, *The Ecstasy of Communication*, trans. Bernard Schütze and Caroline Schütze (South Pasadena, CA: Semiotext(e), 2012 [1987])

Select Bibliography

—, *Fatal Strategies*, trans. Philip Beichmann and W. G. J. Niesluchowski, excerpt in Mark Poster (ed.), *Selected Writings*, 2nd edition (Cambridge: Polity Press, 2001 [1983]), pp. 188–209

—, 'Mass Media Culture' [1970], in *Revenge of the Crystal: Selected Writings on the Modern Object and its Destiny, 1968–83*, ed. and trans. Paul Foss and Julian Pefanis (London: Pluto Press, 1990), pp. 63–97

—, *The Perfect Crime*, trans. Chris Turner (London and New York: Verso, 1996 [1995])

—, *Simulacra and Simulation*, trans. Paul Foss, Paul Patton and Phillip Beichmann, excerpt in Mark Poster (ed.), *Selected Writings, 2nd edition* (Cambridge: Polity Press, 2001 [1983]), pp. 169–87

—, *Symbolic Exchange and Death*, trans. Iain Hamilton Grant (London: Thousand Oaks, 1993 [1976])

—, *The Transparency of Evil*, trans. James Benedict (London: Verso, 1993 [1990])

Beville, Maria, *Gothic-postmodernism: Voicing the Terrors of Postmodernity* (Amsterdam: Rodopi, 2009)

Blake, Linnie, Xavier Aldana Reyes, 'Introduction: Horror in the Digital Age', in Blake and Aldana Reyes (eds), *Digital Horror: Haunted Technologies, Network Panic and the Found Footage Phenomenon* (London: I. B. Tauris, 2016), pp. 1–13

Bloom, Harold, 'Dumbing Down American Readers', *Boston Globe*, 24 September 2003, available online at *http://www.public.asu.edu/~atsjd/bloom.html* (accessed 9 June 2017)

Bolton, Michael Sean, 'Monstrous Machinery: Defining Posthuman Gothic', *Aeternum: The Journal of Contemporary Gothic Studies*, 1/1 (June 2014), 1–15

Botting, Fred, *Gothic* (London and New York: Routledge, 1996)

—, *Limits of Horror: Technology, Bodies, Gothic* (Manchester: Manchester University Press, 2008)

Braidotti, Rosi, *The Posthuman* (London: Polity Press, 2013)

Burke, Edmund, *A Philosophical Enquiry into the Sublime and the Beautiful*, ed. David Womersley (London: Penguin, 1998 [1757])

Carlin, Gerry and Nicola Allen, 'Slime and Western Man: H. P. Lovecraft in the Time of Modernism', in David Simmons (ed.), *New Critical Essays on H. P. Lovecraft* (New York: Palgrave Macmillan, 2013), pp. 73–90

Clarke, Bruce, and Manuela Rossini, editors' preface, in Clarke and Rossini (eds), *Cambridge Companion to the Posthuman* (Cambridge: Cambridge University Press, 2007), pp. xi–xii

Collins, Robert M., *Transforming America: Politics and Culture During the Reagan Years* (New York: Cornell University Press, 2007)

Connelly, Peter J. M., 'The Representation of Serial Killers' (unpublished PhD thesis, University of Stirling, 2011)

Cowan, Douglas E. and David G. Bromley, *Cults and New Religions* (Hoboken, NJ: John Wiley & Sons, 2015)

Crawford, Joseph, 'Gothic Fiction and the Evolution of Media Technology', in Justin D. Edwards (ed.), *Technology of the Gothic in Literature and the Gothic: Technogothics* (New York: Routledge, 2005), pp. 35–47

Crowley, Aleister, *Magick in Theory and Practice* (New York: Castle, 1960 [1913])

Currie, Mark, Introduction, in Currie (ed.), *Metafiction* (London: Longman, 1995), pp. 1–18

De Man, Paul, 'Autobiography as De-facement', *MLN*, 94/5 (1979), 919–30

Eagleton, Terry, *After Theory* (London: Penguin Books, 2004 [2003])

Edwards, Justin D., 'Introduction: Technogothics', in Edwards (ed.), *Technology of the Gothic in Literature and the Gothic: Technogothics* (New York: Routledge, 2005), pp. 1–16

Ellis, Brett Easton, *American Psycho* (London: Picador Press, 1991)

—, *Lunar Park* (London: Picador, 2011)

Fassler, Joe, 'The Return of the Novella, the Original #Longread', *The Atlantic*, 24 April 2012, available online at https://www.theatlantic.com/entertainment/archive/2012/04/the-return-of-the-novella-the-original-longread/256290/ (accessed 1 June 2019)

Felluga, Dino Franco, *Critical Theory: The Key Concepts* (London: Routledge, 2015)

Flieger, Jerry Aline, 'Postmodern Perspective: The Paranoid Eye', *New Literary History*, 28/1 (Winter 1997), 87–108

Fokkema, Aleid, 'The Author: Postmodernism's Stock Character', in Paul Fransen and Tons Hoensselaars (eds), *The Author as Character: Representing Historical Characters in Western Literature* (Cransbury, NJ: Associated University Presses, 1999), pp. 39–51

Foucault, Michel, 'Of Other Spaces', trans. Jay Miskowiec, *Diacritics*, 16/1 (1986), 22–7

Frazer, James Gordon, *The Golden Bough: A Study in Magic and Religion*, abr. edition (London: Macmillan, 1922 [1890])

Freud, Sigmund, 'The Uncanny' (1919), in *The Uncanny*, trans. David McLintock (London, Penguin, 2003), pp. 123–62

Fukuyama, Francis, *Our Posthuman Future: Consequences of the Biotechnology Revolution* (London: Profile, 2002)

Hantke, Steffen, 'Network Anxieties: Prefiguring Digital Anxieties in the American Horror Film', in Linnie Blake and Xavier Aldana Reyes (eds), *Digital Horror: Haunted Technologies, Network Panic and the Found Footage Phenomenon* (London: I. B. Tauris, 2016), pp. 17–28

—, 'The Rise of Popular Horror, 1971–2000', in Xavier Aldana Reyes (ed.), *Horror: A Literary History* (London: British Library, 2016), pp. 159–88

Hardaker, Claire, 'Trolling in Asynchronous Computer-mediated Communication: From User Discussions to Academic Definitions', *Journal of Politeness Research*, 6/2 (2010), 215–42

Harris, Thomas, *The Silence of the Lambs* (London: Mandarin, 1991 [1988])

Hayles, N. Katherine, *How We Became Posthuman: Virtual Bodies in Cybernetics, Literature, and Informatics* (Chicago, IL: University of Chicago Press, 1999)

Hazleton, Lesley, *Agnostic: A Spirited Manifesto* (New York: Riverhead Books, 2016)

Head, Dominic, *The Cambridge Introduction to Modern British Fiction, 1950–2000* (Cambridge: Cambridge University Press, 2002)

Heise-von der Lippe, Anya, 'Introduction: Post/human/Gothic', in Heise-von der Lippe (ed.), *Posthuman Gothic* (Cardiff: University of Wales Press, 2017), pp. 1–16

Herbrechter, Stefan, *Posthumanism: A Critical Analysis* (London: Bloomsbury, 2013)

—, 'Postmodern', in Bruce Clarke and Manuela Rossini (eds), *The Cambridge Companion to Literature and the Posthuman* (Cambridge: Cambridge University Press, 2017), pp. 54–68

Hodgkinson, Sarah, Hershel Prins and Joshua Stuart-Bennett, 'Monsters, Madmen . . . and Myths: A Critical Review of the Serial Killing Literature', *Aggression and Violent Behavior*, 34 (2017), 282–9

Select Bibliography

Hogg, James, *The Private Memoirs and Confessions of a Justified Sinner*, ed. John Carey (Oxford: Oxford University Press, 1990 [1824])

Horner, Avril and Sue Zlosnik, *Gothic and the Comic Turn* (Houndmills: Palgrave Macmillan, 2005)

Huber, Irmtraud, *Literature After Postmodernism: Reconstructive Fantasies* (New York: Palgrave Macmillan, 2014)

Hutcheon, Linda, *A Poetics of Postmodernism* (London: Routledge, 1988)

—, *The Politics of Postmodernism*, 2nd edition (London: Routledge, 2002)

Hutchinson, Colin, *Reaganism, Thatcherism and the Social Novel* (Basingstoke: Palgrave Macmillan, 2008)

James, M. R., 'Ghosts – Treat Them Gently', *Evening News*, 17 April 1931, republished in *M. R. James: Collected Ghost Stories* (Adelaide: University of Adelaide Library, 2016) as section (vii) of Appendix, available online at *https://ebooks.adelaide.edu.au/j/james/mr/collect/appendix.html* (accessed 12 February 2017)

—, '"Oh Whistle, And I'll Come To You, My Lad"' (1904), in *The Penguin Complete Ghost Stories of M. R. James* (London: Penguin Books, 1984), pp. 75–91

Jameson, Fredric, *Postmodernism, or, The Cultural Logic of Late Capitalism* (London: Verso, 1991)

Jenkins, Philip, 'Satanism and Ritual Abuse', in James R. Lewis (ed.), *The Oxford Handbook of New Religious Movements* (Oxford: Oxford University Press, 2004), pp. 221–42

Jones, Darryl, *Horror: A Thematic History in Fiction and Film* (London: Arnold/Hodder Headline, 2002)

Jones, Owen, *Chavs: The Demonization of the Working Class*, updated edition (London: Verso, 2012)

Joshi, S. T., *A Dreamer and a Visionary: H. P. Lovecraft in His Time* (Liverpool: Liverpool University Press, 2001)

—, *The Modern Weird Tale* (Jefferson, NC, and London: McFarland & Company, 2001)

—, *A Subtler Magick: The Writings and Philosophy of H. P. Lovecraft* (Berkeley Heights, NJ: Wildside Press, 1999)

—, *Unutterable Horror: A History of Supernatural Fiction*, 2 vols, II (New York: Hippocampus Press, 2014)

—, *The Weird Tale: Arthur Machen/Lord Dunsany/Algernon Blackwood/M.R. James/Ambrose Bierce/H.P. Lovecraft* (Austin, TX: University of Texas Press, 1990)

Keay, Douglas, Interview with Margaret Thatcher for *Woman's Own*, 23 September, 1987, Thatcher Archive (THCR 5/2/262): COI transcript, p. 30, available online at *https://www.margaretthatcher.org/document/106689* (accessed 1 August 2018)

Kermode, Mark. J., 'The Radical, Ethical and Political Implications of Modern British and American Horror Fiction' (unpublished PhD thesis, University of Manchester, 1991)

King, Anthony, 'Serial Killing and the Postmodern Self', *History of the Human Sciences*, 19/3 (2006), 109–25

King, Stephen, Afterword to *Different Seasons* (London: Hodder, 2012 [1982]), pp. 669–79

—, *Danse Macabre* (London: Hodder & Stoughton, 2012 [1981])

—, *The Dark Half* (London: Hodder, 2002 [1989])

—, Foreword to *Four Past Midnight* (London: Hodder, 1990), pp. 1–7

—, *Misery* (London: Hodder, 2011 [1987])

—, *On Writing: A Memoir of the Craft* (London: Hodder, 2012 [2000])

—, 'Secret Window, Secret Garden', in *Four Past Midnight* (London: Hodder, 1990), pp. 324–420

Kirk, Neal, 'Networked Spirituality: In Memorium [sic], Pulse and Beyond', in Linnie Blake and Xavier Aldana Reyes (eds), *Digital Horror: Haunted Technologies, Network Panic and the Found Footage Phenomenon* (London: I. B. Tauris, 2016), pp. 54–65

Kristeva, Julia, *Black Sun: Depression and Melancholia*, trans. Leon S. Roudiez (New York: Columbia University Press, 1989)

—, *Powers of Horror: An Essay in Abjection*, trans. Leon Roudiez (New York: Columbia University Press, 1982)

Laing, R. D., *The Divided Self: An Existentialist Study in Sanity and Madness* (London: Pelican Books, 1965)

—, *The Politics of the Family and Other Essays* (London: Tavistock, 1971)

Landais, Clotilde, *Stephen King as a Postmodern Author* (New York: Peter Lang, 2013)

Leiber, Fritz, 'Smoke Ghost' (1941), in *Meddling with Ghosts: Stories in the Tradition of M. R. James*, selected and introduced by Ramsey Campbell (Boston Spa: British Library, 2001), pp. 142–56

Select Bibliography

Le Poidevin, Robin, *Agnosticism: A Very Short Introduction* (Oxford: Oxford University Press, 2009)

Link, Alex, 'The Mysteries of Postmodernism, or Fredric Jameson's Gothic Plots', *Gothic Studies*, 11/1 (May 2009), 70–85

Lloyd Smith, Allan, 'Postmodernism/Gothic', in Victor Sage and Allan Lloyd Smith (eds), *Modern Gothic: A Reader* (Manchester: Manchester University Press, 1996), pp. 6–19

Lovecraft, H. P., 'The Call of Cthulhu' (1928), in *The H. P. Lovecraft Omnibus 3: The Haunter of the Dark and Other Tales* (London: Grafton Books, 1985), pp. 61–98

—, 'The Colour Out of Space' (1927), in *The H. P. Lovecraft Omnibus 3: The Haunter of the Dark and Other Tales* (London: Grafton Books, 1985), pp. 237–71

—, 'The Shadow Out of Time' (1936), in *The H. P. Lovecraft Omnibus 3: The Haunter of the Dark and Other Tales* (London: Grafton Books, 1985), pp. 464–544

—, 'The Shadow Over Innsmouth' (1936), in *The H. P. Lovecraft Omnibus 3: The Haunter of the Dark and Other Tales* (London: Grafton Books, 1985), pp. 382–463

—, 'Supernatural Horror in Literature' (1927, rev. 1933–5), in *The H. P. Lovecraft Omnibus 2: Dagon and Other Macabre Tales* (London: Grafton Books, 1985), pp. 423–512

Lyotard, Jean-François, *The Inhuman: Reflections on Time*, new edition, trans. Geoff Bennington and Rachel Bowlby (Cambridge: Polity Press, 1991 [1988])

—, *The Postmodern Condition: A Report on Knowledge*, trans. Geoff Bennington and Brian Massumi (Manchester: Manchester University Press, 1984 [1979])

Maturin, Charles, *Melmoth the Wanderer*, ed. Douglas Grant (Oxford: Oxford University Press, 1989 [1820])

Maturana, Humberto R., Francisco J. Varela, *Autopoiesis and Cognition: The Realization of the Living*, 2nd edition (Dordrecht: D. Reidel, 1980)

McLuhan, Marshall, *Understanding Media: The Extensions of Man* (London: Routledge, 2001 [1964])

McLuhan, Marshall and Quentin Fiore, co-ord. by Jerome Agel, *The Medium is the Massage* (London: Penguin Books, 1967)

McHale, Brian, *Postmodernist Fictions* (London: Routledge, 2003 [1987])

Select Bibliography

McLeod, Hugh, *The Religious Crisis of the 1960s* (Oxford: Oxford University Press, 2007)

Mendleson, Farah and Edward Jones, *A Short History of Fantasy* (London: Middlesex University Press, 2009)

Milton, John, *Paradise Lost* (1667/1674), in *The Complete Poems*, ed. B. A. Wright (London: J. M. Dent & Sons, 1980), pp. [149] –388

Morton, Adam, *On Evil* (New York: Routledge, 2004)

Mulder, Arjen, Interview with Katherine Hayles, in Joke Brouwer et al. (eds), *The Art of the Accident: Art + Architecture + Media Technology* (Rotterdam, NL: Nederlands Architectuurinstuut: V2 Organisatie, 1998), available online at *https://v2.nl/archive/articles/how-does-it-feel-to-be-posthuman* (accessed 1 February 2020)

Nayar, Pramod K., *Posthumanism* (Cambridge: Polity, 2014)

Oates, Joyce Carol, 'Three American Gothics', in Oates, *Where I've Been and Where I'm Going: Essays, Reviews and Prose* (New York: Plume, 1999), pp. 232–43

Otto, Rudolf, *The Idea of the Holy: An Inquiry into the Non-Rational Factor in the Idea of the Divine and Its Relation to the Rational*, 2nd edition, trans. John W. Harvey (London: Oxford University Press, 1958 [1923])

Palahniuk, Chuck, *Fight Club* (London: Vintage Books, 2006 [1996])

Palko, Amy J., 'Charting Habitus: Stephen King, the Author Protagonist and the Field of Literary Production' (unpublished PhD thesis, University of Stirling, 2009)

Partridge, Christopher, 'Alternative Spiritualities, New Religions and the Re-enchantment of the West', in James R. Lewis (ed.), *The Oxford Handbook of New Religious Movements* (Oxford: Oxford University Press, 2004), pp. 39–67

Punter, David, *The Literature of Terror: A History of Gothic Fictions from 1765 to the Present Day*, 2nd edition, 2 vols, II: The Modern Gothic (Harlow: Longman, 1996)

—, 'Theory', in William Hughes, David Punter and Andrew Smith (eds), *The Encyclopedia of the Gothic* (Oxford: Wiley-Blackwell, 2013), 2 vols, II, pp. 686–93

Radcliffe, Ann, 'On the Supernatural in Poetry', *New Monthly Magazine*, 16/1 (January 1826), reprinted in E. J. Clery and Robert Miles (eds),

Gothic Documents: A Sourcebook, 1700–1820 (Manchester: Manchester University Press, 2000), pp. 163–72

Sartre, Jean-Paul, *Being and Nothingness: An Essay on Phenomenological Ontology*, trans. Hazel E. Barnes (London: Routledge, 1995 [1943])

Savu, Laura E., *Postmortem Postmodernists: The Afterlife of the Narrator in Recent Narrative* (Madison, WI: Fairleigh Dickinson University Press, 2009)

Schmid, David, *Natural Born Celebrities: Serial Killers in American Culture* (Chicago, IL: University of Chicago Press, 2006)

Scovell, Adam, *Folk Horror: Hours Dreadful and Things Strange* (Leighton Buzzard: Auteur, 2017)

Sears, John, *Stephen King's Gothic* (Cardiff; University of Wales Press, 2011)

Shelley, Mary, *Frankenstein: or, The Modern Prometheus*, in Peter Fairclough (ed.), *Three Gothic Novels* (London: Penguin Books, 1986 [1818, rev. edn, 1831]), pp. 257–497

Simpson, Philip L., *Psycho Paths: Tracing the Serial Killer through Contemporary American Film and Fiction* (Carbondale and Edwardsville, IL: Southern Illinois University Press, 2000)

Spooner, Catherine, *Contemporary Gothic* (London: Reaktion Books, 2006)

—, 'Gothic 1950 to the Present', in William Hughes, David Punter and Andrew Smith (eds), *The Encyclopedia of the Gothic* (Oxford: Wiley-Blackwell, 2013), 2 vols, I, pp. 294–304

Sutcliffe, Steven J., 'The Dynamics of Alternative Spirituality', in James R. Lewis (ed.), *The Oxford Handbook of New Religious Movements* (Oxford: Oxford University Press, 2004), pp. 460–90

Thomsen, Mads Rosendahl, *The New Human in Literature: Posthuman Vision of Changes in Mind, Body and Society After 1900* (London: Bloomsbury, 2013)

Tithecott, Richard, *Of Men and Monsters: Jeffrey Dahmer and the Construction of the Serial Killer* (Madison, WI: University of Wisconsin Press, 1997)

Van Vogt, A. E., *A Report on the Violent Male* (London: Pauper's Press, 1992 [1956])

Varnado, S. L., *Haunted Presence: The Numinous in Gothic Fiction* (Tuscaloosa, AL: University of Alabama Press, 1987)

Vest, Jason P., *The Posthuman Humanism of Philip K. Dick* (Lanham, MD: Scarecrow Press, 2009)

Select Bibliography

Wallace, Diana, 'Female Gothic', in William Hughes, David Punter and Andrew Smith (eds), The Encyclopedia of the Gothic (Oxford: Wiley-Blackwell, 2013), 2 vols, I, pp. 231–6

Waugh, Patricia, *Metafiction: The Theory and Practice of a Self-Conscious Genre* (Florence, KY: Routledge, 1984)

White, Hayden, 'The Fiction of Factual Representation', in White, *Topics of Discourse: Essays in Cultural Criticism* (Baltimore, MD: Johns Hopkins University Press, 1978), pp. 122–34

Wilson, Colin and David Seaman, *The Serial Killers: A Study in the Psychology of Violence* (London: BCA, 1991)

Wisker, Gina, 'Horror Fiction', in William Hughes, David Punter and Andrew Smith (eds), *The Encyclopedia of the Gothic* (Oxford: Wiley-Blackwell, 2013), 2 vols, I, pp. 328–33

Wolfe, Cary, *What is Posthumanism?* (Minneapolis, MN: University of Minneapolis Press, 2012)

Wolfreys, Julian, 'Spectrality', in William Hughes, David Punter and Andrew Smith (eds), *The Encyclopedia of the Gothic* (Oxford: Wiley-Blackwell, 2013), 2 vols, II, pp. 638–44

Žižek, Slavoj, 'Neighbors and Other Monsters: A Plea for Ethical Violence', in Eric Santner, Kenneth Reinhard and Slavoj Žižek, *The Neighbor: Three Inquiries in Political Theory* (Chicago, IL: University of Chicago Press, 2005), pp. 134–90

—, *The Sublime Object of Ideology* (London: Verso, 1998)

Zlosnik, Sue, *Patrick McGrath* (Cardiff: University of Wales Press, 2011)

Index

A

abjection 24, 27, 31, 33, 35, 39–40, 52, 136, 155, 160
  see also Kristeva, Judith
agnosticism 13, 16, 17, 20, 21, 22, 23, 25, 42, 44, 55, 175, 182–3
Aickman, Robert 13, 161, 172, 173
Aldana Reyes, Xavier 5, 6, 136, 141, 143
Alder, Emily 30
Allen, Nicola 32
alteriority 20, 26, 28, 36, 39, 40, 70, 78, 119, 121, 135, 136, 137, 141, 151, 154, 155, 157, 160, 164–5, 175, 181
  see also otherness
American Psycho (novel by Brett Easton Ellis) 61, 64, 67, 86, 90, 94, 111, 117–18, 119, 165, 177
'Another Place' (sculpture by Antony Gormley) 162
Ashley, Michael 3

B

Ballard, J. G. 4, 135–6, 148, 160–1, 182
Barker, Clive 2
Baudrillard, Jean 16, 19, 32, 36, 46–7, 54, 59, 79, 80, 90, 97, 105, 112, 122, 126, 127–8, 129, 130, 142, 147–8, 149, 154, 163, 174–5, 176, 182
Beville, Maria 15, 45, 46, 49, 52, 112, 165, 182
Blackwood, Algernon 4, 120, 121
Blake, Linnie 136, 141, 143
Bleiler, Richard 140, 147
Bloom, Harold 173, 183
Bolton, Michael Sean 135
Botting, Fred 61, 135
Braidotti, Rosi 164
Brite, Poppy Z. 8
Bromley, David G. 27
Burke, Edmund 7, 15

Index

C

Campbell, Ramsey, works:
- *Ancient Images* 7, 54–5, 140, 144
- *Booking, The* 19, 96, 104–10, 119–30, 131, 133, 136, 147, 148, 184, 185
- *Claw, The* 28, 114
- 'Cold Print' 120–1
- 'Concussion' 5, 7, 9–10, 11, 23, 66, 99, 105, 111, 172
- *Count of Eleven, The* 84, 140, 172
- *Creatures from the Pool* 148
- *Demons by Daylight* (collection) 8, 10, 106
- 'Depths, The' 27, 158
- *Doll Who Ate His Mother, The* 1, 9, 29, 59
- *Face That Must Die, The* 2–3, 18, 46, 57, 64, 65–74, 75, 76, 77, 79, 84, 85, 88, 90, 104, 151, 162, 176, 180
- 'Franklyn Paragraphs, The' 10–11, 23, 95, 100, 127, 158
- *Grin of the Dark, The* 19, 133, 137, 138–50, 151, 152, 155, 160, 161, 164, 168, 169, 172, 179, 181
- *House on Nazareth Hill, The* 3, 114
- *Hungry Moon, The* 17, 23, 36–46, 52, 127, 138, 148, 183–4, 185
- *Incarnate* 12, 106, 108, 115
- *Influence, The* 28, 44, 115
- *Inhabitant of the Lake & Other Unwelcome Tenants, The* (collection) 1
- *Kind Folk, The* 23
- *Last Revelation of Gla'aki, The* 107
- *Long Lost, The* 4–5, 50, 114
- *Nameless, The* 17, 23, 27–36, 37, 40, 44, 45, 46, 47, 52, 54, 70, 106, 175
- *Needing Ghosts* 19, 96, 101, 104, 105–8, 110-19, 123, 124, 178, 182
- *Obsession* 17, 23, 45–54, 57, 66, 69, 75, 110, 153, 175–6, 180
- *One Safe Place, The* 3, 18, 57, 64, 73–84, 86, 87, 90, 91, 92, 93, 98, 110, 151, 152, 177, 182, 183
- *Overnight, The* 120
- *Pact of the Fathers* 180
- *Parasite, The* 23, 29, 44, 142, 180
- *Pretence, The* 107
- *Secret Story* 18, 57, 64, 73, 84–94, 95, 150, 153, 157, 162, 177, 184
- *Seven Days of Cain, The* 19, 20, 133, 138, 145, 159–69, 171–2, 179–80, 184
- *Thieving Fear* 23
- *Think Yourself Lucky* 19, 20, 59, 133, 137–8, 149–58, 159, 161, 162, 169, 179, 184

Way of the Worm, The 185
Wise Friend, The 8
cannibalism 42
Carlin, Gerry 32
Clarke, Bruce 133, 134, 135
Collins, Robert M. 58
comedy 4, 20, 84, 91, 92, 116, 120, 137, 138, 139, 140, 143–4, 147–8, 149, 172, 183
see also parody
Connelly, Peter J. M. 63, 71, 73, 94, 177
Cowan, Douglas E. 26–7
Crawford, Gary 3, 50
Crawford, Joseph 158
Crowley, Aleister 31
Currie, Mark 92

D

Danielewski, Mark 183, 184
Derleth, August 1, 8, 11
Dick, Philip K. 135, 136, 161, 180
doppelgänger 20, 78, 115, 137–8, 153–4, 179
Dyson, Jeremy 84
Dziemianowicz, Stefan 3, 21

E

Eagleton, Terry 183, 184

F

Fassler, Joe 107
Fight Club (novel by Chuck Palahniuk) 123
Flieger, Jerry Aline 112, 126
Fokkema, Aleid 96

folk horror 8, 37–8, 140
Fonseca, Anthony J. 161, 163
Foucault, Michel 17, 47, 123, 124
Frankenstein: or, The Modern Prometheus (novel by Mary Shelley) 20, 63, 133, 135, 138, 159, 161, 164, 165, 167, 168, 179
Freud, Sigmund 23, 39, 113
Fry, Gary 154–6

G

Gergen, Kenneth J. 58
ghost 9, 13, 35, 51–2, 107, 109, 115, 134, 137, 146, 155–6, 161, 163, 166
Goho, James 105, 109, 111

H

Hantke, Steffen 146, 172
Hayles, N. Katherine 16, 132, 134, 166–7, 168
Hazleton, Lesley 21, 22, 30, 54
Head, Dominic 75
health professions 29, 48
Heise-von der Lippe, Anya 16, 19, 135–6, 155, 169
Herbert, James 37, 174
Herbrechter, Stefan 16, 19, 131, 132, 134, 135, 144, 147, 154, 155
Hill, Susan 109
Hodgkinson, Sarah 63, 88
Huber, Irmtraud 184–5
Hutcheon, Linda 68, 97, 109, 113, 129–30, 163

Index

Hutchinson, Colin 65, 71, 80, 183
Hutson, Shaun 6, 181

I
Ishiguro, Kasuo 167, 183

J
Jackson, Shirley 4
James, Henry 27, 107
James, M. R. 2, 7, 12, 51, 59, 107, 115, 120, 121, 142, 155, 172, 181
Jameson, Fredric 14, 16, 18, 67, 71, 97, 99, 106, 112, 122, 164, 175, 180
Jenkins, Philip 26
Jones, Edward 24
Joshi, S.T. 3, 4, 5, 6, 11, 12, 16, 20, 25, 27, 31, 34, 35, 37, 39, 43, 44, 46, 51, 59, 67, 75, 76, 77, 81, 87, 103, 106, 107, 113, 131, 140, 150, 156, 172, 173, 182, 183

K
King, Anthony 60
King, Stephen 1, 2, 3, 8, 17, 18, 24, 26, 34, 70, 77, 95–104, 108, 117, 118, 123, 141, 147, 153, 166, 173, 177, 178, 181, 183
Kirk, Neal 146
Klein, T. E. D. 5
Kneale, Nigel 37, 141
Kristeva, Julia 33, 39, 58
  see also abjection

L
Laing, R. D. 16, 68, 81
Lamsley, Terry 8
Landais, Clotilde 98
Lane, Joel 37, 40, 47, 49, 50, 109
Leiber, Fritz 155
Le Poidevin, Robin 25
Ligotti, Thomas 2, 5, 8, 13, 98, 138, 141, 181
liminality 8, 9–10, 20, 53, 58, 67, 136, 155–6, 172, 180, 181
Lindsay, Jeff 62, 176
Link, Alex 14–15
Lloyd Smith, Allan 14
Lovecraft, H. P. 3, 4, 6, 8, 10, 11, 12, 13, 17, 20, 23, 25, 26, 27, 28, 29, 32, 36, 37, 39, 43–4, 45, 54, 59, 83, 107, 116, 133, 138, 140, 149, 171, 172, 173, 175, 179, 180, 185
Lunar Park (novel by Brett Easton Ellis) 11, 15, 164
Lyotard, Jean-François 16, 17, 19, 23, 35, 36, 57, 58, 96, 112, 119–20, 134, 168, 174, 185

M
MacCulloch, Simon 31, 39, 45
Machen, Arthur 4, 30
McEwan, Ian 107, 129, 183
McGrath, Patrick 182
McHale, Brian 14
McLeod, Hugh 24
McLuhan, Marshall 17, 135, 143, 144, 149

Melmoth the Wanderer (novel by Charles Maturin) 52
Mendleson, Farah 24
'Monkey's Paw, The' (short story by W. W. Jacobs) 46
Morton, Adam 71

N
Nayar, Pramod K. 16, 132, 136–7, 157, 166, 167, 168

O
Oates, Joyce Carol 61
'On the Supernatural in Poetry' (essay by Ann Radcliffe) 7
otherness 40, 45, 52, 60, 61, 68, 78, 90, 93, 106, 116, 126, 134, 135, 137, 142, 145, 147, 151, 154, 155, 157, 164–5, 179, 180–1
see also alterity
Otto, Rudolf 16, 53–4

P
Palko, Amy J. 101
Paradise Lost (poem by John Milton) 167
paranoia 4, 6, 14, 15, 18, 19, 20, 24, 25, 41, 48, 61, 65, 66, 67, 68, 70, 94, 97, 104, 107, 108, 110, 112, 117, 122, 124–6, 128, 130, 131, 139, 149, 164, 169, 172, 174, 178, 179, 180, 181, 182
parody 7, 15, 39, 40, 42, 43, 64, 69, 80–1, 91–2, 129–30, 167
see also comedy

Partridge, Christopher 24
photography 91, 119, 159, 162, 163–4, 168, 172
Poe, Edgar Allan 98
police 6, 47–8, 62, 68, 69, 71, 74, 75, 80, 81, 83, 128–9
Polidori, John 29
Prins, Hershel 63, 88
Private Memoirs and Confessions of a Justified Sinner, The (novel by James Hogg) 13, 123, 137, 154, 155
Punter, David 4–5, 14, 29, 68, 99, 176, 182

R
Resnais, Alain 13, 102, 113
Ross, Adrian 2, 111
Rossini, Manuela 133, 134, 135
Ryan, R. R. 8

S
Sartre, Jean-Paul 58, 92
Savu, Laura E. 97, 119, 129
Sawyer, Andy 148
Schmid, David 61, 62, 74, 81
Scovell, Adam 37, 41
Seaman, David 60–1, 71, 87, 88
Sears, John 98
Silence of the Lambs, The (novel by Thomas Harris) 18, 61, 63, 64, 70, 86
Simpson, Philip L. 57, 62, 67, 68, 86, 88
Spooner, Catherine 4, 9, 62, 182
Stoker, Bram 29, 40

Strange Case of Dr Jekyll and Mr Hyde (novella by R. L. Stevenson) 138, 154, 155
Stuart-Bennett, Joshua 63, 88

T
teachers 41, 50, 81, 91
Thatcher, Margaret 40, 65, 72

V
Van Vogt, A. E. 17, 73, 79
Varnado, S. L. 54
Vest, Jason P. 161

W
Wallace, Diana 33
Waugh, Patricia 14, 97, 111
Wheatley, Denis 26, 35
White, Hayden 24–5
Wilson, Colin 60–1, 71, 87, 88
Wolfe, Cary 132
Wolfreys, Julian 137

Z
Žižek, Slavoj 90